THE
MURDER
NOTEBOOK

Jonathan Santlofer

WM WILLIAM MORROW

An Imprint of HarperCollins*Publishers*

THE MURDER NOTEBOOK. Copyright © 2008 by Jonathan Santlofer. All rights reserved. Printed in the United States of America. No part of this book may be used or reproduced in any manner whatsoever without written permission except in the case of brief quotations embodied in critical articles and reviews. For information address HarperCollins Publishers, 10 East 53rd Street, New York, NY 10022.

HarperCollins books may be purchased for educational, business, or sales promotional use. For information please write: Special Markets Department, HarperCollins Publishers, 10 East 53rd Street, New York, NY 10022.

FIRST EDITION

Designed by Betty Lew

Library of Congress Cataloging-in-Publication Data

Santlofer, Jonathan, 1946–
    The murder notebook : a novel of suspense / Jonathan Santlofer.
—1st ed.
      p. cm.
    ISBN 978-0-06-088204-4
      1. Police artists—Fiction. 2. Serial murders—Fiction. I. Title.
PS3619 .A58M87 2008
813' .6—dc22   2007046609

08 09 10 11 12 DT/RRD 10 9 8 7 6 5 4 3 2 1

For my sister, Roberta

*"Whenever science makes a discovery
the devil grabs it while the angels are debating
the best way to use it."*

—ALAN VALENTINE

*"How does one kill fear, I wonder?
How do you shoot a spectre through the heart,
slash off its spectral head,
take it by the spectral throat?"*

—JOSEPH CONRAD

*D*ust *flecked with blood, shards of debris and bone, smoke so thick he can't breathe or see or maybe he's gone blind; the noise, horrific a moment ago, leveling out to a dull thump, thump, thump in his eardrums, until it dissolves into an absence of sound as if the world had exploded and he is the lone survivor.*

The smoke clears.

He looks around at cars and buses and taxicabs; at passersby walking talking laughing frowning, some smoking cigarettes, others sipping coffee, no one alarmed, no one dodging for cover, no one crying or screaming.

He leans back against a wall to catch his breath.

"Hey, buddy, you all right?"

The man's face zooms into focus, soft blurry features suddenly sharp and all too real only inches away, touching something at the back of his mind: other faces in close-up, studying him like a bug under glass.

"Me? All right? Oh, sure. Sure."

The man stares at him a minute before turning away and he thinks that perhaps it was a trick, the enemy in disguise. But he has out-smarted him, given the right answer to the test. He knew it was a test; it's always a test.

He sets his shoulders and taps his backpack to make sure it is still there. He has a job to do, a mission.

The city street stretches out in front of him like something in a mir-rored fun house, but this is no fun, and the heat, the heat is unreal.

And then he is cold. Body shuddering, shaking, everything cool and white and the smell of something chemical in his nose.

". . . bandwidth . . . propranolol . . . peptide . . ."

The words make no sense and fade so fast he isn't even sure he heard them.

A pinprick, a bug bite? Then a shot of buzzing electricity—in the air or in his brain?—warmth spreading under the skin, leaching into arterial paths, bringing a flood of surreal Technicolor imagery; one gritty reality exchanged for another, bodies scrambling and sand gone muddy with blood.

He has to get there, has to save his best buddy, Ron.

But Ron is dead. Didn't I see that happen?

He turns one way, then the other; the scene shifting, sand exchanged for city streets, dunes that morph into funnels of smoke.

Come on. You can do this. Complete the mission. Because every-thing—Ron, the other guys—everything depends on you, and this is it: your last chance to make it right.

Hang on, buddy, I'm coming.

The music starts up, electric guitar strummed loud and hard, that

Zevon song that Ron liked and would play over and over, "Lawyers, Guns and Money."

The landscape flip-flops, a video game of shifting worlds: First a concrete jungle, then a cold white room, now it's all thick gray clouds and red-hot flames, explosions, and more blood and bone and ash, and from somewhere deep within this chaos there are piercing screams and muffled plaintive cries, but he is outside it, watching, watching himself walk right into it, and though he feels the fire on his skin and the smoke in his lungs, he is absolutely unafraid—the very notion of fear a mystery.

He has got to get there. He has got to tell his story. That is the mission; what he has to do to make it right again.

1

Lieutenant Bill Guthrie spread the crime scene photos across his desk. "Maybe these will help."

I didn't see how. The vic looked like a piece of charcoal.

I glanced up at the Bronx lieutenant's round face, thin hair over a high forehead dotted with sunspots that begged for a dermatologist's opinion.

"And there's this." Guthrie held the skull out in front of him, contemplated it like he was about to recite Hamlet's soliloquy, which I didn't think a Bronx homicide lieutenant could do, but I'd known cops who read Proust, and ones who knew the words to every Broadway musical, so it was possible.

There were two holes in the frontal eminence, the forehead. Guthrie poked a finger into one, then the other.

"The bullets are what killed him. Being burned up was just a cover." Guthrie rotated the skull for inspection.

"Looks pretty clean. Acid bath?" I asked.

"I guess," he said. "That's part two, right? I hear that in part one they give it over to bugs who gnaw away whatever flesh is left on the bone. I didn't know about that, did you?"

I did, but didn't like to think about it.

"So, you think you can do it, Rodriguez?"

I hadn't made a sculptural reconstruction in a long time, but had studied forensic anthropology along with forensic art as part of my course work at Quantico almost eight years ago. Recently, I had taken a brush-up course in osteological profiling—identifying victims from their bones, teeth, and whatever else is left of them—at Fordham University, here in the city. Plus, I'd been making my own study of forensic anthropology over the past five years, particularly the skull, and how it shapes the face. I got interested after a visit to the body farm, in Knoxville, Tennessee. I can't say I enjoyed seeing—or smelling—the decomposing corpses spread around "Death's Acre," as the founder, Bill Bass, referred to it, but it taught me a hell of a lot about the body, from the inside out.

I took the skull from Guthrie and looked it over, half the teeth knocked out or broken, which would add to the challenge. I think a part of me had been waiting for this opportunity.

I started making a mental list of the supplies I'd need: oil-based modeling clay, sculpture tools, Duco cement, cotton balls, swabs, sandpaper, mesh, eyeballs—prosthetic ones if the PD was going to reimburse me because they were expensive—doll's eyes, if they were not.

I looked at the eye sockets and for a moment saw a flash of blue. Maybe my mind was playing tricks on me, but I decided to go with the color.

Guthrie flipped through some pages in the case file. "Like I said, there was no way to ID our John Doe. Apartment where he was turned into a crispy critter was strictly month-to-month rental, cash sent to a real estate PO box, and his fingerprints were charred right off."

"Poor guy. I wonder what he did?"

"You mean for a living—or to get himself killed?" Guthrie shrugged. "Who knows, but Rauder wants full reports."

Mickey Rauder was chief of operations, a lifer who had worked with my dad in Narcotics, way back when. He'd asked me to help Guthrie with this case and I'd agreed because whenever I was with Rauder he would bring up my father and I'd get so damn flustered I'd agree to anything.

"If Rauder wants some John Doe to be priority, he's priority," said Guthrie. "And I appreciate your help, Rodriguez."

"What about the other people in the building, anyone who might have known who the guy was?"

"Only one other resident, old lady on the second floor, but she didn't make it through the fire."

"So your arsonist has two murders on his hands."

Guthrie nodded. "The building was slated for demo, some real estate developer had bought the land, planned to build a new high-rise on it."

"Fire's a good way to get tenants out of a building," I said.

"Yeah, but the realtor checked out. Seems to be a reputable guy," said Guthrie. "So, Rauder tells me he worked with your old man."

"Uh, yeah. That's right."

A picture of my father, dead in the street, unfolded in my brain.

"The coroner is waiting for me," I said. "He's got more stats on the John Doe that might help." I used the excuse to get going. I didn't want to hang around and talk about my father.

Guthrie slid the skull into a brown paper bag and handed it to me like he was giving me my lunch.

The medical examiner was in his forties, with sad eyes and skin the color of newsprint. His name tag, BAUMGARTEN, ADAM, was smeared with blood. He was eating a tuna on rye and offered me half, but the stench of formaldehyde and dead bodies only a few feet away made it easy to decline.

He exchanged the tuna for a report. "You know the basics, right? White male, mid-to-early-fifties, just under six feet tall."

"You measured the femur, the thighbone, to get his height?"

The M.E. looked up, assessing me. "I see you've been studying your forensic anthropology. Not every sketch artist knows that." He flipped a page in the autopsy file. "Weight has to be adjusted, too. Autopsy reports it as approximately a hundred and eighty, but you have to remember that's with a lot of flesh and muscle burned off. I'd add another twenty to thirty pounds, at least, which puts him on the heavy side."

I made a note: His face would show the weight in the masseter muscles of the jaw into the platysma of the neck.

"I didn't do the autopsy," said Baumgarten, "or I would've noted that. It was Dr. Abbott's case, but she retired, moved to Vegas with her husband. I'm not saying anything negative about Dr. Abbott. Megan is an excellent physician, but the case was a John Doe, not much police attention at the time, so . . ." He flipped a page. "Basically, I'd say you've got an overweight fiftysomething man, with some serious arterial buildup. Not exactly a picture of health."

"Not after someone set fire to him," I said. "No."

"Good point," said Baumgarten. "There were traces of lighter fluid on a couple of surviving scraps of clothing." He closed the report and checked out the skull I'd brought with me. "Too bad about the teeth."

"Would it do any good to show it to a forensic dentist, an odontologist?" I asked.

"Already did," he said. "Too much of a mess for an ID."

I noted again the prominent brow ridge and blunt borders of the upper eye sockets that confirmed it was a man's skull.

"High-velocity trauma," said Baumgarten, tapping the bullet holes.

"From ventral to dorsal, right?"

"That's right. Shot from the front, exited through the back."

He handed it back to me and I reached for the autopsy report.

"Sorry," he said. "I can't let you have that unless you've got written permission."

"But Guthrie sent me over; isn't that enough?"

"Nope. I need it in writing. Sorry, but I always follow procedure."

A couple of EMT guys brought in a body bag and Baumgarten told them to put it on a vacant steel slab. Then he went back to his tuna on rye.

I hopped a train down to Canal Street and spent an hour and a week's salary at Pearl Paint, the biggest art supply store in the world.

When I got back to my Hell's Kitchen apartment I went directly into my work area, two long tables tucked against a wall, twelve running feet of desktop; above it a rogues' gallery of recent sketches, studies of faces I'd made to keep my hand and eye in shape, necessary in my line of work.

I unpacked the supplies: armature, clay, wire, wooden and metal sculpture tools, plastic brayer, a Boley-style gauge for measurement, sandpaper, and a set of doll's eyes, blue. Then I got out some of the books I'd amassed over the years: William Bass's *Human Osteology*, which he'd personally autographed at the body farm; another by a Smithsonian curator of anthropology; two more on the study of bones; one on identifying skeletal remains; another by a bio-archaeologist; and a two-part illustrated volume on facial anatomy. I'd read them all, a few more than once.

Under the entire length of my worktable were stacks of old books, my sketch pads from the past seven years, newspaper articles that related to criminology, forensics, and violence, along with every notebook from the forensic classes I had taken at Quantico, many of them dusty and dog-eared. It made me think I could end up living like those crazy Collyer Brothers found dead in their New York tenement surrounded by a hundred tons of rubbish. But every time I vowed to throw the stuff away I realized there was something in the mess I needed.

Like right now, when I unearthed my old Quantico notebook on facial reconstruction and was happy I had saved it. It explained the process and listed the steps, but it was the notes I'd jotted down while I'd made it that brought it all back to me.

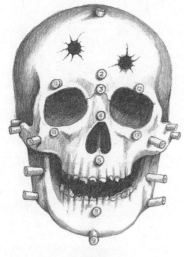

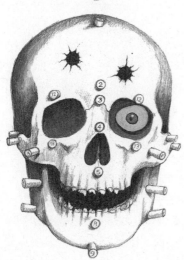

I started with step one, cutting up eraser cylinders and gluing them down to mark the depth of the facial tissue. I worked slowly and carefully. I thought about thickness of muscle and flesh, and of my John Doe's excess weight.

After that, I measured the distance from the cornea to the lateral margin, squirted on some Duco cement, glued the eyeballs into the skull sockets, and made sure they were securely fastened to the lacrimal bone and eye cavity.

They weren't real eyes but they did the trick, adding a dimension of life that hadn't been there before.

Then I rolled out some clay with the brayer, cut it into uniform strips, and laid the first ones onto the John Doe's skull.

I was getting into it, using the strips of clay like flesh.

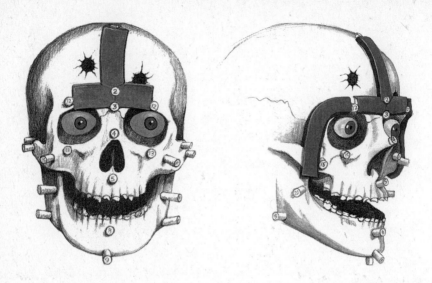

I started thinking about him, the John Doe, mundane questions going through my mind: Where was he born, where did he grow up? It was like the beginning of a relationship.

I smoothed clay around the eyes first with a tool, then my fingertips, and felt a chill. There was no face yet, nothing identifiable, yet I sensed a presence, something outside of myself directing my hands.

2

Chief of Department Perry Denton's office smelled of cigar and lemony aftershave, an odor Terri Russo remembered and wished she did not.

They were both detectives back then, only a few years ago, she in Vice, Denton in Narcotics. How was she supposed to know he'd end up being her boss?

"I hear your boyfriend is working with Guthrie up at Fort Apache."

"Is that why you wanted to see me, to talk about Rodriguez?"

Denton grinned and Terri realized she'd fallen into his trap, confirming the fact that she *was* seeing Rodriguez.

Denton sat back with a self-satisfied grin and Terri tried not to sigh as she folded herself into a chair opposite.

He slid the *Post* across the table and stabbed a finger at the headline: COPS GET *F* ON HONOR ROLL.

Terri did not have to read the story; the *F* referred to the PD's failure to turn up anything on the student who'd been murdered in Times Square. "I saw it," she said.

"That's not the question."

"I didn't know there was a question."

"Don't get smart, Russo. This has been on the front page for a week. A city university student—a kid who the papers had just profiled as the top student in his class, a former ghetto kid on full scholarship—getting killed upsets New Yorkers, and that upsets me! You'd think the war in Iraq or the conditions at the fucking Walter Reed Hospital would have knocked it into Metro, but—"

"We've interviewed over a hundred people and so far no one saw anything. I don't know how someone can get stabbed to death in a crowd and not be seen, but I guess—"

"You *guess*? What is this, the academy, Russo?"

Terri swallowed her words. Denton was right. Her task force hadn't uncovered anything and it was embarrassing. "We've gone through the vic's life, past and present. He was a straight arrow, no enemies, no drugs, no shady secret life." She sighed loudly. "The murder appears to be unprovoked. The way I see it, the unsub sidles up to the vic, stabs him twice, and disappears into the crowd before the kid even falls over."

"I've read the report. Let me know when you're going to tell me something I don't know."

"Look, I—"

"No, *you* look." Denton leaned across his desk and aimed his finger like a gun. "I just got another call from the mayor—and I don't like getting calls from the mayor."

Bullshit, Terri thought. Denton *loved* getting calls from the mayor.

"If your task force can't handle this, I'll give the case to someone else."

"My task force is exactly three men right now, and this is not our only case."

"Well, now it is. You and your men are on this twenty-four/ seven."

"Fine, but I need more staff."

"I can't spare anyone from RHD, but I'll give your other cases to Morelli. And how about your boyfriend, Rodriguez, the psychic?"

Boyfriend? Just what she did *not* want circulating around the station house.

"Rodriguez isn't a psychic" was all she could think to say.

"Whatever." Denton sat forward. "But I'm serious; why not use him?"

Terri didn't know why Denton wanted to throw her together with Rodriguez. Did he think the togetherness would break them up?

"Because he's busy."

"Up in the Bronx, so I've heard."

"I don't control where Rodriguez works," she said, and would have added neither do you, but didn't want to push her luck. She knew it irked the hell out of Denton that Rodriguez was freelance and therefore not his to get rid of. Rodriguez was the best sketch artist in the city, possibly in the U.S., and it wouldn't look good to lose him, particularly after Rodriguez had made a name for himself helping to crack the so-called Sketch Artist case.

"You asked for more help and that's who I'm offering." Denton dragged a hand across his forehead. "Look, the mayor wants a solution. *I* want a solution. It's that simple. We can't have honor-roll students stabbed to death in midtown. It's murder on tourism. Plus, the vic's parents have been on TV. Christ, have you seen them? Two decent blue-collar work-a-day stiffs. Father's like a plumber or something and the mother's a fucking nurse and this was like their only kid. Jesus. The media loves them and we'd better get an answer or we are going to be crucified!"

Denton plucked a cigar stub out of a cut-glass ashtray, lit it, and puffed a gray cloud toward the ceiling. "I'm serious. You should ask Rodriguez to work with your team. He already knows them and did a great job last time out."

"Last time I had to beg you to get Rodriguez on my team."

"Last time was different. I didn't know how talented Rodriguez was."

Terri still wasn't sure it was a good idea. She didn't want to fuck up what seemed like a good thing, the first good thing in her adult life when it came to men.

"It's up to Rodriguez."

"I'm sure you can persuade him," said Denton, a slight sneer on his lips. "And the Bronx thing isn't important. Just some derelict burned to death, a waste of Rodriguez's talent. You need him more than Guthrie."

"I'm sure Guthrie will be happy to hear that."

"Leave Guthrie to me."

The room is so fucking hot, his old military jacket soaked with sweat, but he doesn't think to take it off. He rubs his bruised thumb over the name tag stitched onto the jacket, o'reilly, j, and tries to remember: *Is that my name?*

The TV screen rolls.

He lumbers across the room, one bad ankle aching and swollen, entire body sluggish from too much medication, and whacks the side of the set. A man speaking in Spanish to a woman in so much makeup he thinks her face is made of plastic, and he's right: It melts like a multicolored candle, red lips oozing out the bottom of the TV set right onto the floor. He stares at the puddle until it disappears and knows it isn't real because there she is, the woman with all the makeup, back on the screen.

He sags into bed, looks up at a naked lightbulb, snippets of his life playing like the Spanish soap opera: wife, daughter, outbursts, arguments, full-scale war, sad scared moments that no longer belong to him, and he sees himself falling, over and over.

He drags a hand across his face, presses his eyes closed and tries to remember what his little girl looks like—blond curly hair, big smile, but can't hold on to it.

"Fuck!"

A pinging sensation—like a bell going off in the distance—builds to a dull thudding knock, as if someone is tapping on his skull.

His eyes burn; images smolder red-hot, then fade to black.

Light cuts around the beat-up shades, so he knows it's daytime but can't remember if it's today, tomorrow or yesterday that he said he'd meet that guy in the park again.

He punches his thighs, feels the pain; yes, he is awake, alive, still here in this hot, stinking room, and his life not worth shit. He looks around at the stained walls, filthy rug, and says, "I am in a lovely tea garden."

It makes no sense, but there it is, imprinted on his brain like the bar code on a box of cereal.

The guy in the park . . .

He recognized him, remembers exactly what he did.

And for that, he will make him pay.

3

I sat up, shivering, the sweat on my chest going cold from the air conditioner turned up to high. It was the dream I'd been having for years, but it had morphed. I was no longer killing my father; he was killing himself.

I glanced over at Terri asleep beside me, chest rising and falling beneath a thin cotton tank top, full lips slightly parted. I wanted to kiss her, but didn't think she'd appreciate it at 4:00 A.M. I hadn't heard her come in last night, but I was glad she was here.

I pulled myself out of bed, careful not to wake her, padded barefoot across the apartment to my work area, flipped on a high-intensity desk lamp, opened my sketch pad to a clean page and stared at the white paper. I didn't know where the falling man was coming from, but needed to get it down.

I sketched it out quickly, the figure from my dream, then sat back, chewed the end of my pencil, remembered what that bad habit had almost cost me six months ago, and stopped.

A shadow fell across my paper and I flinched.

"Easy there, tiger."

It was Terri, face pillow-smudged, thick hair tangled.

"It's five in the morning, Rodriguez. What are you doing?"

"I was drawing—or trying to." I closed my pad.

For a moment I felt annoyed. I still wasn't used to having someone around.

We weren't exactly living together—Terri kept her own apartment, a studio over in Murray Hill, not ready to give up her little piece of real estate freedom—but she stayed over every few nights, kept a toothbrush and makeup in the medicine cabinet, and her stuff was starting to crowd the little clothing I had out of my closet.

I hoped my face wasn't showing the question going through my mind: *Is it better to be alone and get my work right, or have someone in my life and always be interrupted?* I tried on a smile.

"That's a phony smile if I ever saw one."

"You reading faces now?"

"You think you're the only one who can?" Terri smiled, the orbicularis oculi and pars orbitalis muscles around her eyes contracting to prove it was genuine.

I learned how to read faces when I studied forensic art at Quantico. I'd apprenticed with the master, Paul Ekman, memorized his Facial Action Coding System, which documents thousands of facial expressions. So far I've gotten the basic forty-three down, but I'm working on the others.

Terri ran her fingers through my hair and kissed my cheek and I got the answer: *I liked living together better than living alone.*

"What's so important that you have to draw it before dawn?" she asked.

"Just something I was thinking about."

"Like?"

Terri was a pit bull when she wanted to know something, which was what made her a good cop.

She tapped the sketch pad, and I showed her.

"Jesus, is the guy diving or flying?"

"I'm not sure. I think there's more to it, but it's still in my head."

Terri's eyes narrowed.

"Don't look at me like I'm some gypsy with a crystal ball."

"Aren't you?"

I firmly believed that ninety-nine percent of what I did was training and talent. But there was another one percent that was hard to explain.

I glanced at the candle above my worktable, the decal of the god Chango half peeled off, just one of the many Santerian artifacts—candles, beads, shell-encrusted crosses—my *abuela* was constantly giving to me.

"When did you start that?" she asked, looking over at the sculptural reconstruction.

"Today."

"Weird," she said. "Is it for Guthrie?"

"Yeah, why?"

"Just that I saw Denton today."

"Lucky you."

"Let's not start, okay? The sun's not even up."

"I'm not starting anything." I put my hands up in peace. Denton was a sore spot between us.

"Denton wants you to work with me on the Hunter College murder."

"You're kidding?"

"Not at all. In fact, he was pretty insistent that I use you."

"Now there's a first," I said. "But I thought we decided it was best if we didn't work together."

"Well, you're all I've got, Rodriguez. Denton won't give me anyone else."

"So, I'm like what—the consolation prize?"

"Don't get your shorts in a knot, Rodriguez. I didn't mean it like that." She patted my cheek and yawned. "I'm going to take a shower."

I watched her walk away, my eyes lingering on the soft curves beneath the silky boxers she'd bought for me, and had immediately made her own. I had to admit they looked better on her.

It was odd, Denton forcing me on Terri, and I wasn't sure it was such a good idea.

A couple of months ago we had made the decision that we would avoid working together because Terri didn't want her colleagues to find out we were involved. She said it was hard enough being a woman heading up a task force with all men under her and didn't need anything that might undermine her authority. But if she needed my help I couldn't say no. Fact is, it had worked out just fine the last time, which, incidentally, was how we'd met, on a case.

I pushed away from my worktable, stripped, and joined her in the shower. I slid my arm around her waist and moved my hand to her breasts. After a couple of minutes, biology took over, convex meeting concave, and when I finally slid inside her my heart wanted to tell her that I loved her, but the words got stuck in my throat.

I'd had a series of girlfriends, the record holder before Terri was about three months, and I'd never said the *L* word out loud, except once, to my father when he was laid out in a box, a mortician's pancake makeup disguising his features but unable to mask the fact that the man I was whispering to—*I'm sorry, Papi, I love you*—was no longer the man I knew, just a shell, and it was too late.

"Hey, Rodriguez, you with me?"

I came back to the moment.

"You know, having a guy disappear in the middle of sex doesn't do much for a girl's ego."

"Sorry, but we were finished, weren't we?"

"That's for sure." She turned off the shower and grabbed a towel. "You can talk to me, Rodriguez, you know, words strung together to form sentences? You should try it sometime."

"Funny," I said.

I'd known Terri less than a year, but she could read me better than anyone.

I tried to say it again, that I loved her, but it didn't happen. I put on a pair of boxers, sat on the bed, and watched her get dressed, T-shirt, jeans, holster, and a light jacket to hide her 9-mm Glock, which didn't hide it at all.

"I can't wait to meet your mother," she said. "I take that back. I'm really nervous about meeting her."

I'd made the mistake of telling her that my mom was coming to town and Terri decided we should all go out. "It was your idea," I said, "not mine."

"You don't want us to meet?"

"No, it's fine."

"*Fine?* Now that's an endorsement if I ever heard one. I just thought, since she's coming, and you and I are—fuck, I don't know what we are—but I thought it would be nice if we all got together."

"And it will be nice. Let's not make it into a big deal."

"You're the one making it into a big deal."

"Sorry, it's just that my mother coming makes me nervous, too."

She sighed, flipped the TV on and tuned to *New York 1*, where an overly cheery guy was saying that the city was in for a heat wave. She shrugged off the jacket and exchanged the Glock for a Kel-Tec "mouse" gun, which is what the small handguns were called. Not exactly standard issue for a cop, but Terri liked them because they were easy to carry and easy to conceal, the same virtues that made the guns so popular with street hoods.

"Is that a new one?" I asked. Terri had a collection of light-weight guns.

She displayed the chrome-finished pistol proudly. "I couldn't resist. Here, try it." She handed it over.

It felt like a toy but I knew it wasn't. My father used to say that holding a gun made men feel like gods and he didn't mean that as a good thing.

"It's the lightest and flattest nine-millimeter single-stack pistol ever made," she said.

"Should be a big hit with the teens," I said. "They can wear it on chains around their necks, just another piece of bling."

Terri made a face. But she knew it was true. The guns were easy to get. There was even an Internet site, Mouseguns.com, where you could order up any one of a dozen mouse guns, which were forever getting smaller and easier to hide. Personally, I didn't think the guns made sense, as it took four shots to take out a two-hundred-pound perp, and I said so. "Sort of like hurling a pebble from a slingshot."

"Oh, yeah? Tell that to David and Goliath," she said. "There are plenty of delicate areas a nice light Cor-Bon bullet can poke a hole and do damage. You just need to think creatively, Rodriguez." Terri slipped the gun into her pocket. "Oh, I've got the Hunter vic's girlfriend coming in to see you at ten."

"Thanks for telling me."

"I just did. I want you to do a sketch with her."

"Did she see anyone?"

"She says no."

"So what do you expect me to do?"

"Your usual magic, that's all."

It's what brought us together in the first place, my ability to draw a face that no one thought they had seen.

Terri kissed me, then stroked the scar on my chin, and it brought me back to when I'd gotten it—in a fight for my life six months ago.

I tried to tug her closer, but she pushed me away.

"Sorry, Rodriguez, but homicide waits for no man—or woman."

I got dressed and went back to my work space, cutting across the living room. I ran my hands over the new furniture Terri had made me buy—a Crate & Barrel sofa to replace the cracked leather one I'd found on the street and kept for seven years, matching club chair, a sleek midcentury-modern coffee table instead of milk crates.

I settled in at my worktable, looked at my sketch, and it flipped from positive to negative.

I blinked, and it was normal again, though the afterimage hovered on my retina. I rolled a pencil between my fingers and waited for more to come, but nothing did. The falling man was all mixed up with the dream of my father and I couldn't shake it. But there was something else. I didn't know what it was, but it had gotten under my skin.

4

Midtown North occupied the old Eighteenth Precinct station house on West Fifty-fourth Street, and like the name said, it served a chunk of midtown Manhattan, including some famous tourist sites like Saint Patrick's Cathedral, Rockefeller Plaza, and Radio City Music Hall. I kept waiting for the day when I'd have to go over and work with one of the Rockettes, but it hadn't happened yet.

I headed toward my third-floor office, down a hall and around the corner from Terri's, and next door to Department Command. I made sketches for all the precincts, but Midtown North liked to claim they owned me. They'd given me the office six months ago, after I helped capture a guy the press had dubbed the Sketch Artist Killer. It was small, with one window that faced a brick wall, but at least I had one. It also had two chairs, a wooden one for me and a padded one that had taken me a month to get, but I'd insisted that witnesses and victims had to be comfortable. A week after I moved in I'd switched the cold fluorescent tubes to the warm daylight ones, not perfect but an improvement, and painted the walls a soft white unlike the rest of the station's dreary beige.

The AC was whirring but I'd brought the morning heat in with me, my shirt sticking to my chest. It was possible Con Ed had turned the power down, one of those intentional brownouts to prevent a total power failure. There were daily reports that the company couldn't handle the demand while every appliance store in the city was having sales on air conditioners.

I put a bottle of Poland Spring next to the witness chair, as I always did. While I waited I skimmed through the murder book, though I already knew about the case; Terri had been talking about it for days and it had been all over the press—the Hunter College kid, Ryan Kavanagh.

While I read I plucked at the small strand of black beads on my wrist. I never wore jewelry and it felt weird. But six months ago, when I got stuck on an important sketch, my *abuela* had dragged me over to her *botánica* on Lexington and 116th, and an *espiritista*, who worked out of the back room, got me unstuck. So when she told me to wear the beads for luck I figured it couldn't hurt, though I hadn't worn them since. After my dream, and the sketch I'd made of the falling man, I was feeling a little uneasy and thought, what the hell, and I'd put them back on.

A rookie led the witness into my office. Her name was Anna and she was about twenty, big blue eyes set in an oval face, full lips, and dark hair that tapped her shoulders.

"Nate Rodriguez." I smiled.

She sat forward in the chair, hesitant and uneasy.

I displayed my Ebony pencil. "You ever use one of these?" I had noted her art-student status and wanted to get her talking.

"No, they're too soft for me. You like them?"

"They're good for what I do," I said, and described a bit of my sketching process. I find that witnesses like to know what they're getting into, and in this case, with her art background, I thought she'd be particularly interested. "You're an art major, right?"

"Yes, painting."

"Sounds like fun." Every once in a while I thought about fine art versus forensic art, but I liked the idea that my art did something more than hang on a wall.

"I went to Hunter, too," I said. "Undergrad."

"Really?" Her eyes widened with skepticism. Maybe she figured sketch artists didn't have to go to college. "Did you study art?" she asked.

"That, and a lot of psych courses." I could have told her that I had a double major in art and psychology, which came in handy in my line of work, and about my police training and Quantico, but I didn't want to talk about me. "What sort of painting do you do?"

"Right now I'm doing a kind of insane realism, really detailed. I'll look at something, like a rock, and paint it really big, fill up an entire six-by-six-foot canvas, paint every nook and chip so that it becomes so real it's something else."

"Sounds interesting." It also sounded like she knew how to look at things, to study and memorize them. Drawing and painting from reality is a memory game. You look at something, take a mental picture, then attempt to get it down on paper or canvas.

We talked a bit more about painting, then I asked about the night her boyfriend was killed.

"We had dinner uptown, near Hunter, then went to the movies in midtown." She took a deep breath and let it out. "Like I told the other cops, I didn't see anything. I wish I had, but—"

I knew that sometimes people saw things and stored them away and didn't know it. Everyone did it, but visual people, artists, did it all the time for their work.

"I know it's no fun," I said. "But let's go back, okay?"

She nodded and I asked her to close her eyes and relax. Then I asked her if there had been a line to buy tickets at the theater.

"Yes, a long one."

"Can you see the other people?"

"No, I don't think so."

I thought a moment and had an idea. "Okay, try and see it like a painting, like something you're going to paint. You're on the ticket line and there are people around you. Look at their faces."

I watched her eyes flickering below closed lids. "Now you're going inside. Keep looking around at the people who are walking next to you, in front of you."

"I can see them, but no one stands out."

"Fine. Now you're in your seat. Any recognizable faces? Any of the people from the ticket line?"

"No."

"Okay, the movie is over, the lights come up, and you're walking out. Now you're in the lobby and—"

"Wait a minute. When we were walking out of the theater, I mean just after the lights came up, Ryan banged into some guy, or he banged into Ryan, and he went sort of ballistic, cursing and yelling. He was looking for a fight, so I tugged Ryan away. The whole thing only lasted a few seconds. I saw him again in the lobby, but I don't think he saw me; it was across the room."

"What sort of impression do you have of him?"

"Tall, but he was too far away."

"Okay, go back to when you saw him earlier, when he was just beside you, when he banged into Ryan. Look at him now, close up, like that rock you were painting, and tell me what you see."

Her orbicularis oculi tightened her eyelids to squints. "He had a square jaw with one of those, you know . . . a furrow in it, a cleft, like George Clooney or Cary Grant. And his face was very angular, superthin, like you could almost see the skull beneath it."

We went back and forth between specifics and generalities, his short spiky hair and dark heavy eyebrows. She was really

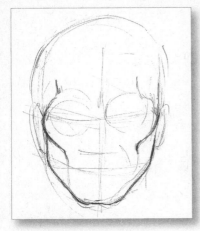

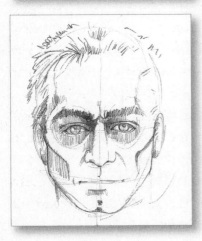

seeing him now—describing his big eyes—and I was starting to see him, too. Sometimes I feel as if I have actually slipped inside a witness's head, and that's when I make my best sketches.

We were in sync. She'd look at my drawing, tell me something, and I'd sketch it. It's why I believe in the pencil versus the computer. I've tried most of the programs, Identikit, FACES, but to me it was about the relationship, not the tools—and I can draw a nose faster than find one in a complicated made-to-order computer program.

"His nose was sort of thick," she said, "and his eyebrows came together at the center.

"And he had those lines around his mouth." She pointed out the nasolabial folds on her own face.

She described his lips, then went back to his eyes. "They were light-colored, but with really dark circles around them, like he hadn't slept."

After a while I turned my pad around so she could have a better look.

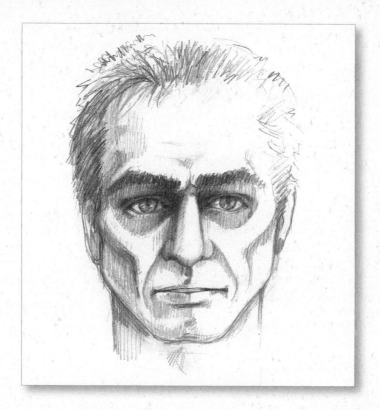

"Oh—wow—that's *him*! And I didn't think I'd seen *anyone*."

"The brain's a complicated little machine," I said. "There's the conscious part and the unconscious part. There's even a part just for recognizing faces called the fusiform gyrus, and another called the inferior temporal gyrus, which is used for objects. It's how you distinguish between your friends—so you don't mix them up or confuse them for a table."

She laughed, then looked back at the sketch. "You're really good."

I shrugged. It always embarrasses me when someone says that, but I told her she was good, too, which was true.

We spent a little more time on it. She told me where I should make little changes and alterations and when she was satisfied it looked like the guy from the movie theater, I thanked her and she left.

I took the sketch into the back hallway and sprayed it with fixative, really toxic stuff I never spray in my office. I use it so the sketches won't smudge, plus I like the idea that they will last. Maybe that part was just my ego. I use good-quality paper for the same reason, and cut it down to eight-and-a-half by eleven inches so it fits perfectly into case files.

I took another look at what I had done.

Usually when I do a sketch I feel a sense of completion. But this one felt like it was just the beginning.

5

Terri was down at Police Plaza, so I gave the sketch to O'Connell, the one guy on her task force who did not appear to resent me outright. Maybe he just knew my record—that one out of three of my sketches led to an arrest. Pretty good odds, though it was the two that failed that kept me up at night.

O'Connell was the oldest guy on Terri's team, early fifties, and about the same age my father would have been. He'd met him a couple of times, so maybe he felt a little protective and paternal toward me—or maybe I was projecting.

He reached for his thermos. I knew he laced his coffee with bourbon—I could smell it—though I didn't blame him. If I'd spent as many years in Homicide as he had I'd probably spend the rest of my life drying out at the Betty Ford Clinic. It was why I'd given up real police work the first time around—just too much ugliness that got to me.

He looked at the sketch, his puffing eyes evaluating it. "So, who is this?"

"Some guy who started a shoving contest with your vic, Kavanagh, inside the movie theater. The girlfriend described him."

"Really? She told me she didn't see anyone."

"Sometimes people have seen more than they remember." I held up my Ebony. "Power of the pencil."

"Nice work, Rocky."

He'd given me the nickname last time around. It was either Rocky or "kid," which I preferred, the former bringing to mind too many images of a punch-drunk Sylvester Stallone.

All the cops on Terri's task force had nicknames: O'Connell was Prince for some reason I didn't know, Perez was Pretzel, Dugan was Doogie, as in Howser. I called them by their actual names, though, because I didn't feel like I was quite in the club and allowed to get so chummy.

"Has anyone checked to see if this guy is in the book?"

"No. I just finished and you're the first to see it."

"Okay, I'll get it on the wire to the other precincts and see if they come up with anything." He said thanks, took the sketch, then a slug from his thermos.

On a mission. On a mission.

He jogs down the street, dodging and weaving, until he slams into the woman, who shouts, "Watch it, asshole!" and something comes apart inside his head, like a piece of glued-together pottery suddenly giving way. He feels the shards loosen and slide around as the woman, the street, the buildings, everything becomes a kaleidoscope of color and form, bringing with it a slew of painful memories, which he must concentrate to remember when all he wants to do is to forget.

The fragments expand, contract, then come together, and for a moment he feels whole again.

"On a mission," he says aloud, drawing confidence from the words. "On a mission."

The papers clutched in his hand are moist with perspiration. He concentrates on moving forward, holding on to reality, while he feels it seep through his fingers like blood.

The Princeton Club gave me the heebie-jeebies, all that dark wood and whispering, all those suits drinking their lunch, all of it still a surprise to me that Julio of East New York, aka Spanish Harlem, my best friend, *mi pana*, my stoner mate—Julio, who had spent two years at Spofford Correctional for young offenders—not only bought into all this shit but seemed to like it.

Nowadays Julio was a model citizen, the "Latino card," as he called himself, at a small but prestigious white-collar legal firm.

I spied him at a table, rail-thin physique in made-to-order pinstripes, curly hair cropped short—*No wetback locks for me, amigo*—the successful Anglo-Latino.

"Nato!" Julio stood up to embrace me. At least he wasn't embarrassed by me or the out-of-date sport jacket I'd thrown over my T-shirt and jeans.

"*¿Cómo estás?*"

I told him I was good, and asked about Jess and the baby.

"Beautiful, both of them."

Julio had married a blond associate partner at the law firm and they'd bought a brownstone up in the East Nineties, between Madison and Fifth, a once-beautiful neighborhood that had fallen on hard times in the sixties and seventies, revived in the eighties, and upscale ever since. I wondered if Julio had chosen to live there because it was only blocks from Spanish Harlem, though miles away in price tag and ambience, a sort of "fuck you" to his past.

I ordered a beer and a burger; Julio, broiled fish and a bottle of Perrier. He was a devout 12-stepper, who never missed a meeting.

He leaned forward, dark eyes twinkling, and I saw the old

Julio, the street kid. "Hey, I got me a brand-new Lexus, the one that parks itself."

"Pussy," I said.

"*¡Tan celoso!*"

"Me? Jealous? No way. I just prefer driving a car than having it drive *me*." I cuffed him on his pin-striped arm. "You getting rid of the Mercedes?"

"You want it?"

He was serious.

I was usually on guard not to compliment Julio on anything because the next day it often showed up. So far, an iPod, plus the best docking station, a BlackBerry which I never used, and an espresso machine that Terri had finally taken out of its box. Now that Julio had money, he wanted to buy everyone he loved anything they wanted.

"No, thanks," I said. "For me, a car in the city is too much trouble."

"Suppose I lend you one so you can come visit us in the Hamptons?"

The truth is, I loved my friend but I didn't love it out there—the cars, the houses, the money that just made me feel poor, and Terri despised it. A month ago we'd spent a weekend out there and Julio and Jess could not have been nicer, grilling lobsters and plying us with hundred-dollar bottles of wine, but it just made Terri uncomfortable, a dinner party the topper—lawyers, brokers, arbitrageurs, no one she felt she could talk to, self-conscious about her Daffy's and Century 21 markdowns and her Staten Island accent. I reminded her of Julio's humble origins but it didn't matter. Like me, she loved Julio and Jess, and loved playing with the baby, but no way I was getting her back to Long Island anytime soon.

Julio and I chatted about the Mets and the weather.

"Really sucks," he said. "It's much nicer at the beach, *pana*. You should come."

"You never quit, do you?"

"*Claro.*"

I smiled at my old friend. We were two tough kids playing at being grown up, though Julio was more successful at it. At least he dressed a lot better than I did.

"How's Terri?" he asked.

"She's good," I said, and asked again about his wife.

"The love of my life."

"Why she married you is still a mystery."

He called me *un tonto*, a fool, and I selected a few choice names for him and we slid into the street talk of our youth, laughing too loud until the suits at neighboring tables gave us looks, which only made us laugh louder.

"I don't want to get you kicked out of the club," I said.

"*Me?* I'm their resident Latino, remember? How's it gonna look if they throw me out?"

I asked how things were going at his job and Julio said never better.

"The law is a beautiful thing. I spent sixteen years breaking it, but now that I've moved from real estate to criminal, I'm upholding it."

"As long as you're making money, huh?"

"Don't be cynical, Nato. I do a monthly pro bono case and you know it."

"So what is it this month?"

"Could be a big one. You might even see my name in the papers."

"Yeah, the funny papers."

A guy was suddenly at our table, tall and wiry, perspiring in his striped polo shirt and jeans, the maître d' on his heels. "Sir—"

"I'm not staying," he said, a hand up in surrender, trying to catch his breath. "I'm just here to see this gentleman—and only for a minute."

Julio gave the maître d' a wink and a nod.

"Sorry. I stopped by your office and your secretary said you were at lunch. I remembered you were a Princeton man, put two and two together and, here I am."

"You didn't have to do that," said Julio, trying to smile, but a touch of anger narrowed his brows and tightened his mouth. "You could have left the papers with Allison."

"Oh, well, sure. It's just that, well, you said they were important."

Julio nodded, facial muscles easing. "It's fine." He looked from the guy to me. "Oh, Nate, this is Jerry, a client of mine."

The guy gave me a knuckle-crunching handshake, muscles around his jaw clenching and unclenching, right eye twitching.

"So," said Julio. "You going to give me those papers?"

"Oh, right." He laughed. He'd been holding them tight against his chest.

The maître d', hovering only a few feet away, leaned in. "Have you concluded your business, *sir*?"

"Jeez, it's like the army in here!" He saluted the maître d', who was not amused.

"It's better if I see you at the office," said Julio, offering up a sympathetic smile. "Okay?"

"Oh, sure, sure. I'll be there. You can count on that."

Julio watched the guy walk away, then turned to me. "It's not enough I've got to take clients' calls in the middle of the night, now I've got them delivering deposition papers at lunch."

"What's his story?"

"He's my pro bono case. Doesn't it figure? I mean, the freebie taking up more time than the paying customers?"

"He's certainly wound tight," I said, picturing his clenched jaw and twitching eye.

"Like a steel drum," said Julio.

A man with graying temples and a puffed-out chest stopped at the table and Julio introduced him as a senior partner from the firm, giving me a look that was easy to read: *No fooling around, bro, this is serious.*

The partner asked how we knew each other and I decided not to say from the ghetto or that we used to get high together and steal cars.

"We went to school together."

"Oh, so you're a Princeton man?"

The pars lateralis muscles lifting the guy's eyebrow were enough to tell me that he didn't believe it was possible that I'd gone to Princeton, which pissed me off because I could have gotten a scholarship just like Julio did. Some people read minds; I read faces.

"Junior high," I said.

"Ah," he said, as if that made a lot more sense. It tweaked the outsider status I sometimes felt, the Spanish-Jewish kid who wasn't sure where he fit in.

He turned to Julio. "I see you've got clients paying unexpected visits; best to discourage that at the get-go."

"I didn't encourage it," said Julio. "He just figured out where to find me. But you can be sure I *will* discourage it."

"Neat," said the man, looping his thumbs into his striped suspenders. "You know, you and the wife should come sailing with me and Candace one day. It would be really neat."

When the guy left I asked Julio about his *neat* new car and his *neat* fish and his *neat* Perrier, and in the middle of saying that the Princeton Club was really *neat*, Julio leaned across the table and growled a whisper that brought the old tough kid Julio back to life.

"Nato," he said, between his gritted teeth. "You say *neat* one more time and I promise to punch you in your *neat* little face." Then he sat back and grinned.

6

Guthrie's call was a shock.

"Just like that?" I said.

"Hey, it's not up to me."

"So where's it coming from?" The fan in Guthrie's office sounded as if it were inside the phone, half drowning out his words.

"All I know is that Rauder's office wants to close down the case."

"But it was Rauder who put me on the case in the first place. Why suddenly close it?"

"Hey, I don't know. All I know is it's over. So what? One less John Doe to waste our time."

"I wish I'd been told that before I went and spent my paycheck on supplies."

"Well, put in a requisition and I'm sure you'll get reimbursed."

"Which NYPD are you working for, Guthrie?" No way I was going to get paid for work I was not doing specifically for them.

"Sorry," said Guthrie. "But it's not up to me."

I hung up annoyed; asked to do something, then having it cut short without a decent explanation. Typical. The PD hated wasting time and money on unimportant cases, which translated as unimportant victims. But Guthrie was right. There was nothing I could do about it.

Spanish Harlem was just a few blocks north of the elegant Upper East Side but miles away in mood and lifestyle. The heat had brought everyone into the street: old ladies in housedresses gossiping on stoops; men squatting on inverted milk crates hunched over dominoes; kids with iPods or boom boxes blasting salsa music.

My grandmother had called and asked me to come up and I could tell from her voice that something was bothering her.

The subway's air-conditioning had been frigid and the wave of heat that hit me when I reached the street was like a soggy blanket. I was sweating after half a block.

I didn't like the idea of my *abuela* slogging around in the heat, so I hit the local *bodega* to pick up some basics—milk, juice, coffee, and a few Spanish items like beans and spices.

One less John Doe to waste our time.

I couldn't get Guthrie's words out of my head.

It just didn't make sense. Sure, cases were closed all the time, but this one had been newly reopened. So why close it again, and so soon?

I was still thinking about the Bronx John Doe when I ducked into the local *botánica*.

The place looked like a cross between an old-fashioned apothecary and Pee Wee's Fun House, jam-packed and colorful, shelves stocked with votive candles, beads in every color dangling from wires above a long desktop cluttered with trinkets, colored bottles, and musty boxes of potions. There were crosses and statuary everywhere.

I stared at a skull attached to a crucifix and for a moment I saw the Bronx John Doe's skull.

The proprietor, Elena Perez, brought me back to the moment. She flashed a bright smile made brighter by two gold-plated front teeth. She knew me by way of my *abuela*, who spent half her Social Security check in the store.

"*¡Buenos días,* Nato!"

She started her usual interrogation about my love life while I chose soaps and candles my *abuela* was always giving away to her clients free of charge. Elena suggested I wear cowrie shells and green beads, and that I see Maria Guerrero, the *santera* who had helped me with the sketch six months ago, but I wasn't in the mood to have gladiolas crushed onto my naked chest or raw egg dripped over my neck. I had been willing to go through it to catch a killer, but it seemed a little frivolous just to get laid. Plus, I had

Terri in my life. I chose not to tell that to Elena Perez, though, because she would want to know every detail.

There was new graffiti on the outside of my *abuela*'s tenement, the words BLOW ME and a badly drawn illustration beside it. I tried to rub it off with my shirtsleeve but it was enamel and I had no luck.

One time, when I caught a kid spraying FUCK on the stoop, I taped a Brillo pad to his hand and stood over him while he scrubbed it off. I didn't like the idea that my *abuela*—a churchgoing Catholic and devout Santerian—should have to see curse words every time she went in and out of her apartment building. I was always trying to get her to move, but I knew she never would. She'd been in the same apartment since she'd exchanged Puerto Rico for Manhattan more than fifty years ago, and she liked the neighborhood where she felt comfortable and enjoyed her status as a local celebrity with a steady stream of believers who consulted her about their past, future, and continual woes.

My *abuela* stood on tiptoes to plant kisses on my cheeks.

"*Oye, guapo,*" she said, holding my face.

To her, I was as handsome as any of her Latin soap stars.

She took the candles and soap I'd bought, and smiled, but it didn't last. I asked why she looked troubled and she turned it around and asked me the same thing. Sometimes we read each other too well.

The apartment was sweltering and I asked if there was something wrong with the air conditioner.

"*Es muy caro.*"

"It is *not* too expensive, *uela.*"

I paid her Con Edison bill so she wouldn't know if it was or was not expensive, but maybe that was the problem. She didn't want to run up a bill she knew her grandson was paying.

I went into the living room and switched it on.

The room was neat as a pin, walls dotted with crosses and pictures of saints along with a dozen framed drawings I'd made of my grandmother's visions over the years. Against one wall was a small table covered in a white cloth and draped with rosary beads—the *bóveda*, a shrine to the dead—above it a photo of my father that I knew well.

He was about my age in the picture, decked out in his NYPD uniform, the photo taken only a few months before he died. I wondered if he knew an hourglass had been turned over; that the countdown to his days on earth had begun. If he did, his Kodacolor eyes did not reveal it. According to my grandmother, by way of Oldumare, the creator and ruler of all creation, we all have a prescribed number of days on earth. But my father's had been cut short.

She came into the room and asked about Terri. I said things were fine, producing a smile on my *abuela*'s face. She was glad we were still together. When I'd brought Terri to meet her, she asked her if she had any Spanish blood and Terri had said no, but my grandmother was convinced she did—a sure sign that she liked her. The fact that I am half Jewish by way of my mother—which, according to Jewish law, makes me officially part of the tribe— holds no sway with my *abuela;* she considers me one hundred percent Spanish.

My grandmother's smile didn't last long and I asked again what was wrong.

She told me to bring my drawing pad and I followed her into the *cuartos de los santos.*

The room was changed every time I saw it, each time becoming more elaborate. At one time it had been her bedroom, but long ago she'd given it over to her personal mix of Catholicism and the Santerian gods, the orishas, makeshift shrines crowding the space: dolls and framed pictures of Jesus and saints; all manner of crosses, beaded and gilded; fake flowers; shelves filled with herbs, beans, and candy to feed the gods; strings of beads draped here and there; and candles, everywhere.

I knew that most of the stuff had been offerings or gifts. My grandmother rarely, if ever, took money from her clients. It an-

noyed the hell out of me but made her happy and I'd long ago given up trying to change her.

She lit candles, then took a moment to choose a strand of white beads dotted with coral, which she draped over my neck.

"I want you to draw for me a face, maybe fifty or sixty years old."

She started to describe it and I began to sketch. She knew the drill. We'd been doing this for years.

"*Su pelo está canoso,*" she said, touching her hair.

"White hair?"

"*Sí.* And the eyes are . . . *azules . . . un poco triste.*"

"Blue eyes? Sad eyes?"

"*Sí.* And the top, the, how you say, the eyelids, they are sloped. But above—"

"The eyebrows?"

"*Sí, sí.* The eyebrows come over the eyes a little and then go up." She was getting into it.

"The nose is straight, but at the bottom is . . . a little round. And the mouth is *una línea*."

"A line?"

"*Sí*, but with more on the bottom lip."

I turned the sketch around and she nodded enthusiastically. Then she gave me a few more directions and I went back to work. After a few minutes I showed it to her again.

She nodded, then sank into the chair and closed her eyes. A minute passed, then suddenly she gasped.

"*¿Qué pasa, uela?*"

"Another face," she said. "No, not a face . . . It is what is *detrás de*."

"*Behind* the face? You mean, like the bones?"

"*Sí, exactamente.*"

The John Doe's skull flashed in my mind.

"And you saw this before, in your vision?"

"No. I see it now." She sat forward clenching her crucifix. "It is *una señal*."

"A sign of what?"

She reached out and touched the beads around my neck. "When

I choose these beads I did not know why, now I know. These beads are for Obatala, the orisha for the bones. He is the—what is the word for someone who makes things of clay?"

"Sculptor?"

"*¡Sí!*" Her eyes lit up. "That is Obatala, the sculptor of all human form." She let go of the beads and her eyes met mine. "Obatala is trying to tell me something about this man. He needs to see you, Nato. He needs to tell you something *importante*."

"The man or Obatala?"

"The *hombre*, the man."

"Like what?"

"*No sé.*" She closed her eyes and sat back. "I see many *pruebas* for you, Nato."

"What kind of tests, *uela*?"

"Big ones, like rocks for you to climb over, but that is only *un simbolo*, a symbol." She opened her eyes and grasped my hand. "You must be brave, Nato. The orisha Eleggua has made a crooked path for you—and you must follow it to the end. But I will pray to make the path easier."

7

Three A.M.

Where's the goddamn remote?

He rummages through the bedsheets, balling them up, tossing them to the floor, the remote nowhere to be found; sags back, takes a breath and pats the military jacket he has fallen asleep in, and there it is, the remote, jammed into the pocket under his frayed name tag, O'REILLY, J.

He digs it out and aims it at the TV.

Click.

The ten best things about . . . Click. President Bush says . . . Click. Your singing is at a new low and that outfit, Simon says—Really nice, says Paula—Listen up, Dawg . . . Is he fucking kidding me? Click. And like I'm a survivor, not like those phonies dropped on some island. Click. Car bomb kills twenty in . . . Don't want to see that. Click. Late Night with Conan. Click. John Wayne in Alaska with Fabian from nineteen-when-the-fuck-ever and who the fuck is Fabian anyway? Click. Another oldie from who-the-fuck-knows-when but man, is she ever gorgeous, Liz . . . something, pretty dark angel I just want to fuck to death kissing that actor whose face got beat up in a car crash—not Dean the rebel without a cause who got killed but the other one, the other one, what's his name?

Think. Think. Clift. That's it! Mom told me about him—no, it was Jen who liked him, who liked the old stars, Jen . . . Oh, Jen, sorry, Jen, forgive me, Jen.

Her face appears and then it's his little girl's face, the two merging, morphing until they are one face, blond curls on fire, a screaming mask.

Oh, God . . .

Click.

Bond, Connery, not that blond sap Roger—whoever-the-fuck or the new guy with the scowl and . . . who cares except for the Bond girls.

Click.

Keebler elves. Chocolate chip. Oatmeal. Sixth birthday party, backyard, red, white, and blue balloons because of . . . which holiday . . . ? Not my birthday . . . Labor Day? No. Memorial Day? Damn, can't remember or . . . trying to forget. Ice-cream pops, Good Humor Chocolate Éclair with the thick hunk of chocolate in the middle.

Click.

Shopping channel. Fishing poles? Okay. Sure. Gimme two. Need a fishing pole like I needed the goddamn can opener. Scalp itching so much. Fucking infomercial freaks! Broke the opener on a can of Starkist, fucking vegetable oil all over the place, digging the fucking tuna out of the can slicing my thumb, blood everywhere, in the tuna; like I should kill those fucking Starkist bastards who are murdering porpoises and maybe those goddamn Green Peace freaks are right about that—kill the corporate bastards!—But what do they know, fucking A-holes, like they're so right, so high and mighty.

The night goes on. And on.

Finally the sun cracks through the darkness like a knife cutting through black satin.

Shower. Dress. Medicate. Go out.

Washington Square Park.

Where is he?

The guy ambles toward him, a hesitant smile.

"I didn't think you were going to make it, O'Reilly."

"How do you know my name?"

"You kidding? You don't remember? Plus, it's right there, on your jacket."

"Oh . . . right." He stares at the guy. He doesn't believe him. He never gave him his name, just his serial number, or did he say he was in a lovely tea garden? But the guy admits to knowing him. That confirms it. He's sure now. "My ankle is killing me."

"How come?"

"Broke it . . . a long time ago." He tries to remember how it happened, but can't. "My throat is so fucking dry, man. I got to get a bottle of water, but two bucks for water, for *water*!?"

"Yeah, it's robbery, but what can you do?"

"And so fucking hot."

"You could lose the old military jacket. That might help."

"No, it helps to . . . remind me."

"Of what?"

"Who I am." He stares, thinks: *But he already knew—and I know. This is the guy!*

"I get that," says the guy.

"It's a fact. I wouldn't lie."

"Why would you? I'm sure it's true."

"True? True?" He repeats the word robotically, mind stuttering into overdrive: *True. False. True. False.* "*A*, as in apple angry answer aardvark adverb adjective angular angles armpits adversaries articles ammunition amnesty amendment antidote ancestor asshole! Asshole, there's an *A* for you!"

"Jesus, I knew it! I wanted to talk about it last time but—"

He stops listening, head aching and so damn itchy it's driving him crazy, scratches at his scalp, flesh under his fingernails. "That's what you say."

"What?" says the guy.

"I swear I'm picking up 1010 WINS, the news, man, the news! What time is it? Day? Night?"

"Just look up."

He sees it: *the sun, the goddamn sun in the goddamn yellow sky. Man, I am so fucking losing it. How long can I stare at it, an hour, two? Maybe. No fucking maybes, man, burning my fucking eyes, but it doesn't matter, they're so fucked from no sleep.*

"Can't sleep," he says, and hears the voices in his head—*You're not supposed to sleep, you don't need to, you're a superman*—but thinks they are coming from the guy beside him. Staring at the sun, he says, "Here . . . it . . . comes!"

He staggers back.

"You okay?" the guy asks.

"What?"

"We need to talk about it, what happened."

He looks at the guy and remembers what he has come to do, and says, "I am in a lovely . . . tea garden."

"Jesus. Look, I can help you with all that. You'll be okay."

"O-kay?" The word cracked, then swallowed like a piece of glass.

"Yeah, I'll help you. What do you say?"

"False," he says, hoping that's the right answer, needles like ice and fire, poking at his brain, adrenaline pumping.

"Hey, man—hey! Shit! Cut it out! Stop!"

But nothing registers, not the pleas or screams or the face he thought he once knew now unrecognizable, his instincts long ago tweaked and reconfigured. He drags the man into the shadows while the noise and colors explode in his head. His fists, like a boxer on speed, pummel away, seizures grip his body, head shaking but no pain, just a tap-tap-tap on his skull as if someone, some *thing*, is knocking on the rear door to his cerebellum, a blinking dying neon sign in a back alley of his brain: *That action is not justified . . . that action is not justified.*

8

"Your mother called."

My apartment was freezing, air conditioner pumping full blast, Terri in shorts and a tee, hair pulled back in a ponytail. I told her she looked like a teenager and gave her a kiss. She told me I should keep my hands off little girls.

"I didn't know you were coming over."

"Isn't that okay?"

"More than okay," I said.

"I told your mother she could stay in my apartment when she's here."

"Really? That was nice of you."

"You don't sound very happy about it."

The thought of Terri and my mother chatting on the phone filled me with unexplainable angst. "I said it was nice."

Terri gave me a look—tilted head, squinty eyes.

"Well, she can't stay here," she said.

"Why not, it's all fixed up now," I said, though the thought of my mother staying in my apartment had never entered my mind.

"This building is scary, Rodriguez."

"You're not scared here, are you?"

"No, but I'm a cop."

It was true that my building was a little dicey. By day it was chock-full of businesses and sweatshops, but at night, deserted, and I was the only resident in the twelve-story industrial building. I had what's known as "Artist in Residence" status, which allowed me to live there as long as I used a portion of the space for my art business. I'd considered moving out after what had happened six months ago, had even looked around, but couldn't afford anything unless I moved to Brooklyn or Queens, and I didn't want to leave Manhattan.

"Why do you look so worried?" she asked.

"Me? I'm not worried."

"Bullshit, Rodriguez." Terri gave me another skeptical look. "What is it? You think meeting your mother is like I'm asking for your hand in marriage, or something?"

"It has nothing to do with you. It's just that . . . since my father died, it's been hard, that's all I'm saying."

Terri nodded. "I'm sorry if I pushed."

"It's fine. I just want to get through the visit."

"You think she's too smart for me?"

"Who? My mother?" It didn't look like I could get Terri to drop the subject. "No, she's nonjudgmental and easygoing, you'll see."

All true, so why did I feel so anxious about her visit? Maybe it was because we hadn't had a real conversation in twenty years. Sure, we bantered and acted normal, it wasn't like we'd had a fight or anything, just that things had gone off when my father died— something we had never discussed but was always there, between us. Ironic, you might say, my mother being a therapist and us not being able to talk about our feelings. Somewhere along the line we just forgot how, and then it had become too late.

I changed the subject. "My grandmother sent me home with

some *arroz con pollo*—that's chicken and rice to you, white girl—enough for three hungry men. She thinks you're too skinny."

"Clearly, she hasn't seen my ass."

"Your ass is perfect."

That produced a smile.

"By the way, your sketch was great, our first lead. I'm sending it out to every precinct, plus hard copies will be in cars and with patrol officers."

"Good," I said. "Oh, guess what; Guthrie canned me today."

"Really?" she said, exaggerating the word and I saw it, the lie, *leakage*, Ekman calls it, around her mouth, her lower lip sucked in right after she'd said "really."

"You know, don't you?"

"Jesus, how do you do that, Rodriguez? It's just not fair. I can never lie to you—though I wasn't."

"Just not telling me something, that it?"

"It was sort of a trade-off. Denton decided I needed you more than Guthrie did."

"And no one thought about asking me what I thought?"

"Don't pout, Rodriguez, it's unmanly." Terri forced a smile. "Look, I had nothing to do with it. It was all Denton's decision. You're not mad, are you?"

"It's just that I'm really into the sculpture, the reconstruction, you know. There's something about it, and I don't want to stop." I thought about what it was as I said it—the fact that I was sort of resurrecting the dead.

"So don't stop," she said.

"I'm not going to, but now it's on *my* dime."

"So when you're finished, you give it to Guthrie and you get brownie points. It's not exactly money in your pocket, but—" She stopped a moment. "Could you stop doing that?"

"What am I doing?"

"Chewing on your cuticles."

"Oh, sorry, old habit."

"Hold on."

Terri disappeared into the bathroom, came back with a small bottle that looked like clear nail polish, took hold of my right hand and started painting it on.

"What is this?"

"Something for thumb suckers and nail biters."

"This part of the Nate Rodriguez improvement plan?"

"It's just a start, baby." She laughed and finished painting my fingers. "Go ahead, give it a try."

I did. It tasted like peppery paint thinner. "It's gross."

"Exactly." Terri smiled, plopped onto the bed, and I joined her.

I picked up the remote and aimed it at the cable box. "You want to watch *24*?"

"Hmm . . . I was just thinking, now that it's cooled off in here you might go back to admiring my ass."

I was freezing.

Terri, the one who was always hot, had stolen the blanket and wrapped it under her body, so there was no way I could get it without waking her. I got up, turned the AC down, crawled back into bed, closed my eyes, but couldn't sleep. I tossed around for a few minutes but finally gave up.

I made my way in the dark over to the work area, the sketch I'd made of the falling man still on my worktable.

I stared at it, wondering if I was conflating things—the idea of my father's death with something I'd seen and buried in my mind without remembering.

I thought about my father falling, dying, but pushed it out of my head, and once I did that, any thoughts about adding to the drawing disappeared along with it.

I didn't want to go to bed thinking about my father's murder, so I turned to the facial reconstruction. I wanted to see what I could do with it and where it would take me and it wasn't just because I'd spent all that money on supplies. I felt as if I could bring this guy back to life, his face, at least, and wanted to try.

I'd hung the beads on a tack behind my sculpture supplies and they reminded me of what my *abuela* had said about tests and paths.

I was never sure how much stock to put in her visions and forecasts, but she'd proved herself more than once and it was hard to ignore what she said, though my rational brain always tried.

I skimmed through a couple of the forensic anthropology books, then my Quantico notes. After that, I rolled out some clay and went back to work.

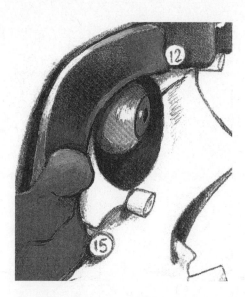

I spent a little time shaping and reshaping the clay around the doll's eyes but pretty soon my own eyes started to blur.

Rodriguez."

I opened my eyes and Terri was standing over me.

"Oh, you look good," she said.

"I must have fallen asleep."

"Careful or you'll start looking like that sculpture." She picked some clay off my face. "I have to get to work. Maybe your sketch will turn up something," she said, just as her cell phone started ringing.

9

There's some blood mixed with your vic's, two different types, which means we probably have your unsub's blood."

"That's good news," said Terri.

I held my breath beneath the mask.

Neither one of us had made it into the station. When Terri got the call she asked me to come along. Now I was wearing a paper bodysuit, staring at a face that looked like beef stew.

Another man killed in midtown, this one found in the bushes off Washington Square Park.

The vic's liver was in a scale, and there was something I didn't want to know about in a steel sink being hosed down by an assistant, beside it a small stand with a tray of test tube samples—urine, blood, and other liquids I couldn't identify.

Baumgarten was doing the autopsy. He was surprised to see me so soon again and I felt the same way. At least he wasn't eating a tuna sandwich with the victim's body laid out on a steel slab, naked, cut open.

"According to his driver's license, the vic was thirty-two years old," said Baumgarten. "Name is Peter Sandwell. The M.E. who had the body at Bellevue noted that the heart was beating when he was brought in. But he didn't last long, six minutes."

"Jesus," said Terri.

"He wouldn't have felt anything, if that's what's troubling you," said Baumgarten. "Blunt-force trauma to the back of the head means he was brain-dead long before he got to the hospital." He lifted the vic's head with a gloved hand.

The back looked pretty much like the front, a big mess.

"Smashed against a rock," said Baumgarten. "All sorts of debris back here." He eased the head back onto the slab gently and I liked him for it. "CSU took samples from the rocks and ground. I've got their report. It's a safe bet it will match whatever I take out of his skull."

"Right," said Terri, flat and cool, distancing herself, the way cops did, a necessity if you were going to make it working Homicide.

I was trying to do it too but not so successfully. I didn't have Terri's street creds, though I'd probably logged twice as many hours with witnesses and victims over the past seven and a half years, some of the cases just as bad and just as ugly as any a homicide cop ever got to see. Sitting with rape and assault victims day after day, I never got used to it, wasn't sure I ever wanted to. But right now, without a pencil in my hand, I couldn't distance myself from the work. A part of me wanted to pat the dead guy on the arm and tell him everything would be okay, while another part said a silent prayer to Oldumare and Obatala to watch over his *ori*, his soul.

"Looks like your unsub didn't care about leaving his DNA behind," said Baumgarten. "There could be flesh here that doesn't belong to your victim." He swabbed viscera onto glass specimen plates and into small sample packets.

"You thinking the unsub beat the guy to death with his bare fists?" I asked.

Baumgarten pointed to an area of the victim's cheek which he had just cleaned off. "You see those bruises? They're knuckle marks."

"The unsub wasn't wearing gloves?" asked Terri.

"There's no powder residue, no pieces of latex, which surely would have torn with so much force; no seam marks, either, which would have imprinted on the skin if he'd been wearing leather or suede gloves. So yes, I'd go with bare fists."

"Sounds personal," said Terri.

Baumgarten nodded. "There's a preliminary tox in the report and a fuller one to come."

"How long before DNA?" Terri asked.

"Could be a while," said Baumgarten. "There's lots of backup in the lab."

"Can't you speed it up?"

"You get me the authorization and I will."

"You're quite the stickler for authorization, eh, Baumgarten?" I said.

"I'm just doing my job," he said, giving me a serious look.

I slid into the passenger side of Terri's police-issued Dodge Charger and she turned the AC to high.

"God bless air-conditioning," she said.

"To hell with global warming, let's pump those chlorofluorocarbons into the stratosphere!"

"Don't start with me, Rodriguez, or you're in big trouble."

"Aren't I always?"

"No, but you will be." She looked away from traffic to give me a weary smile, then her facial muscles tightened. "Beaten to death. Jesus."

"Yeah, like you said, sounds personal." I thought a moment. "And Baumgarten said the perp wasn't wearing gloves, which is weird."

"Like he didn't care if he was caught, or—"

"He was so out of control he wasn't thinking."

"Right," said Terri. "You think it could be drug-related?"

"If it was drugs there'd be hacked-off limbs, tongue cut out, right?" She nodded. "And there were no witnesses?"

"Nada. Just the guy who found the body, who doesn't fit for it, no bruises or scratches on his hands, plus an alibi for the hours of death."

I opened the case report on Peter Sandwell and leafed through a few pages. "Thirty-two is pretty old for a student."

"What's your point?"

"No point." I scanned a page. "Says he was premed at NYU."

"And?"

"Just wondering if premed means anything."

"Like what?"

"I don't know."

"You seeing something here?"

"You mean like a sixth-sense sort of thing, like 'I see dead people'?"

"Did I say that?"

"No, but you thought it."

"I meant a connection to something I could be missing."

"Well, it's another white male college student. This one's older, but still, a coincidence."

Terri sighed.

No one liked the idea of a serial killer, but she had to be considering it. Every cop knew there was no such thing as coincidence.

"Sandwell is going to be Morelli's case," she said. "Denton is keeping our team exclusively on the Hunter vic."

"Unless it turns out that the two murders, Hunter and NYU, are related."

"Could you stop saying that?"

"I'm just stating the obvious."

"Are you intentionally trying to piss me off, Rodriguez? So far the computer geeks doing cross-checks between the two vics have found nothing that connects them."

"Except they were both students and both killed for no reason."

"But totally different MOs," said Terri. "Hunter vic stabbed and this one beaten."

"True," I said. "But two violent attacks, no theft involved, no drugs; it seems weird. And nothing has come up on the Hunter vic, and maybe this is a connection that could—"

"They are two *different* cases, Rodriguez. That's how it will be played until proved otherwise, got it?"

"Yes, ma'am."

Terri's eyes narrowed. "You see, this is when I'd tell you to shut the fuck up if we weren't involved."

"Fine, I'll shut up."

"Sorry," she said. "Autopsies put me in a bad mood."

"You, me, and the victims," I said. "So what do you want me to do now?"

"Go back to the Hunter case. That's why Denton gave you to me."

"I don't think I like the sound of that—Denton gave me to you."

"You're not going to start on me and Denton again, are you?"

"No, I swear. I just thought maybe I could help find the creep who mashed that poor guy's face to a pulp."

"Right now I'll have Perez, O'Connell, and Dugan follow through with the lab and the paper. Tomorrow, it all goes to Morelli."

"So use me today? I got a sketch out of the other vic, right? Maybe I can get one from someone connected to this case."

"Like who?"

I had been perusing the case file and was ready for her question. "How about the vic's roommates at NYU? Their statements don't say much, but they might have seen someone and not realized it."

"Fine." She sighed. "Go talk to the roommates. Then come back and tell me you found nothing that connects the cases."

10

The NYU dorm room was small, living room with a couch on one wall, bed up against the other, kitchenette with a half-sized fridge in an alcove, tiny separate bedroom with two beds and room for nothing else. Sandwell's was the bed in the living room.

His roommates were a study in contrasts, a crew cut who looked like a hayseed, and a greasy-haired guy with heavily tattooed arms.

I told them I was a forensic artist, which they found interesting, then compared ink with Tattoo Boy.

"Got mine when I was a teenager," I said, and showed him my inner arm. "Not exactly what I'd choose now. Yours is a lot cooler."

He displayed his arms proudly.

"Cool," I said. I really didn't want to spend the day on body art, but it was a way to get them talking. "So what can you tell me about Peter Sandwell?"

"He started out sharing with me in the other room," said Crew Cut, "but he talked in his sleep."

"Screamed is more like it," said Tattoo Boy.

"What do you mean?"

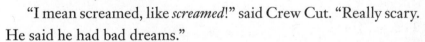

"I mean screamed, like *screamed*!" said Crew Cut. "Really scary. He said he had bad dreams."

"Did he say what about?"

Both roommates shrugged.

"So, you all premed, or just Sandwell?"

"All," said Crew Cut, "but me and Kevin here used to say Peter would be eighty by the time he was a doctor and have to treat himself for Alzheimer's." He laughed.

"Oh, that's cold, brother," I said. I wanted to tell him that one day real soon he'd be thirty and then forty and he'd be sorry for saying that, but it wasn't the time for a lecture.

"Was he on a scholarship?"

"I think so," said Tattoo Boy. "But I can't swear to anything 'cause I hardly knew the guy. I mean, it's summer school, and there's not a lot of time to hang out with classes all day long."

"I feel that. You guys must be working your asses off," I said. "So did he ever say what delayed him getting to college?"

"Nope," said Tattoo Boy.

"Never," said Crew Cut.

"So, like how about habits? Did he smoke, drink, whack off ten times a day?"

"Hey, if he was spanking the monkey," said Tattoo Boy, "I was not going to sit around and watch; you know what I'm saying?"

"Peter was a quiet dude," said Tattoo Boy, "except when he was tossing around and screaming in his sleep."

"Sort of antisocial," said Crew Cut. "But you know, underneath I think he was real angry. Like one time he went totally ballistic because I touched his stuff."

"What stuff is that?"

He indicated some open-shelved bins which now had NYPD crime scene tape across them. "So what happened?" I asked, riffling through T-shirts, underwear, and socks.

"I was just leaning against his stuff and he started screaming at me. I mean *really* screaming; half of it didn't even make sense, just crazy shit."

That hit a chord. "Did you really think he was crazy?"

"Sometimes," said Crew Cut. "Other times he was okay."

"What did he say when he wasn't making sense?"

"Fuck if I know," he said. "He'd just be mumbling under his breath."

"Are these his?" I indicated a stack of books and spiral notebooks beside the bed.

Crew Cut nodded.

I picked up an anatomy book, fanned the pages, and found a dog-eared photograph.

"Is this Sandwell?"

"Yeah," said Tattoo Boy, taking a look at it. "From a while ago, I'd guess. He looks a lot less ragged there. And I don't think I ever saw him smile."

He looked a lot better than he looked on the coroner's slab, that was for sure.

I turned the picture over. It said, "Me and Kathy."

"He ever mention someone named Kathy?"

"Nope," said Tattoo Boy.

"I'll be damned," said Crew Cut. "He had a girlfriend? The old dude was still getting a little, huh?"

"Guys," I said, looking from one to the other. "Life does not end at thirty."

"Oh, sorry, man," said Crew Cut. "I didn't mean you. You seem like a cool guy."

"And Peter didn't?"

"He was weird, is all."

I skimmed a notebook of Sandwell's, the first half filled with school notes in a careful, legible hand, then it was all numbers and letters, almost like a code, but I couldn't make sense of it. I tucked it under my arm. Then I stacked the books on top of the clothing bins and made a note to have someone pick them up and bring them to the station.

"He use any drugs?" I asked.

"I wouldn't know," said Tattoo Boy.

"Me either," said Crew Cut, hands up like he wanted no part of the question.

"Guys, relax. I don't care if you smoke the ganja, snort coke or drop acid. I'm just curious about Peter Sandwell." I didn't bother to tell them I'd done all three in my time. "I'm not a narc, " I said, and a picture of my father flew in like a fly through a side door of my brain and buzzed around.

"If Peter did drugs, he sure as shit wasn't sharing," said Tattoo Boy.

"Too bad, huh?" I gave them a knowing smile and they returned it. "So who did he hang with?"

"Not me," said Tattoo Boy. "He mostly hung out on the other side of the park, playing chess, when he wasn't in class."

"Either of you guys ever go over there to play?"

Crew Cut shook his head no and Tattoo Boy said, "No fucking way," as if I'd asked him if he ever had sex with a transvestite.

11

Every bench in Washington Square Park was filled—old people, nannies with kids, tourists, teens, every color of the ethnic rainbow represented. The large circular fountain area in the center was without water but I couldn't remember a time when it had worked. There were kids break-dancing in one part and a guy on a unicycle with a girl balanced on his shoulders in another. The edge of the circle was crowded with people, tourists taking pictures, a few people dancing along with the kids, but most were ignoring the show, talking to friends and doing their own thing.

Just outside the circle I spied an exchange: two white college-boy types handing a slightly older black guy a stack of bills, an obvious money-for-drugs exchange.

It brought me back.

Fourteen years old, a real tough guy, cigarette hanging out of my mouth, pack of Marlboros rolled into my shirtsleeve—Julio and I buying weed and pills right here in Washington Square Park, bringing it back to Julio's project apartment. If we'd had a brain cell working, we might have been worried about getting bad shit and ending up in the morgue, but we were usually drunk before we got stoned, so we never thought about it. Hell, we didn't think about anything.

The chess area was at the other end of the park, stone tables with checkerboard tops attached to the ground in a ring around the periphery of a rounded triangle, every seat taken, plus spectators standing. The group was a motley mix, white, black, Latino, old and young, but everyone looked serious, most players using a stopwatch to time their moves.

I opened my pad and started sketching, a way to seem unthreatening, just another Washington Square artist, doodling. But it gave me an opportunity to take in the scene and the various characters.

After a while I closed my pad, got out the photo I had of Sandwell, and started showing it around. Not everyone was cooperative. One guy I'd drawn, with the weathered face of a drunk, flicked his cigarette ashes onto the photo, then moved his knight and said, "Check," to his startled opponent. Other guys didn't even bother to look up. But a tough-looking black guy directed me toward the other side of the circle, to a white guy in his thirties, unshaven, wearing a military jacket way too hot for the day.

The military man was playing chess with a black kid who looked about thirteen. I was heading toward them when the kid said, "Checkmate," and the guy in the military jacket swiped his hand across the chess set and sent the pieces flying.

The kid stood up and yelled, "What the—!"

The guy didn't say anything, just got down on his hands and knees to collect the pieces. I decided to join him, a way to make contact that would seem offhand.

He gave me a look; brows knit tight, lips a taut line. But it was his knuckles, bruised and scraped, that got my attention.

I offered up the chessmen real slow, smiled, and noticed the frayed name tag above his pocket, O'REILLY, J.

His face was weathered, as if life had taken a toll, his eyes, sad.

He set the chess pieces onto the board and said he was sorry to the kid. Then he turned away and started walking, and I noticed a slight limp.

I caught up and showed him the photo of Sandwell.

He didn't acknowledge me, kept walking, but I stayed with him.

He was scratching his head in a fierce way, and grimacing.

"The guy's name is Peter Sandwell," I said. "I heard you sometimes played chess with him."

His face rattled off a slew of Ekman microexpressions—sad, mad, scared, involuntary asymmetrical tics—but he kept walking. There was something volatile about him, so I dropped back, though I kept an eye on him as I got my cell out to call the station.

The kid who'd been playing chess with him had followed.

"You know that guy?" I asked.

"Just from playing chess. That was like our third time, but never again. You see that shit he pulled?"

"He here a lot?"

"Off and on."

"That his name, O'Reilly, like it says on the jacket?"

"That's what he calls himself, Jimmy O'Reilly."

I wrote "Jimmy O'Reilly" on the edge of my sketch pad.

"Last time we played," the kid said, "I asked him about the jacket and he said he's had it since the war, since Desert Storm. Cool, huh?"

I told him I didn't think it was such a *cool* idea to hang around with O'Reilly and gave him my card.

"Forensic artist? What's that? Like the kind of sketch artist you see on TV sometimes?"

"Exactly," I said.

"That's cool."

I told him I might want him to come to the station and he said that was cool, too. Then I showed him the photo of Peter Sandwell. "Add like ten, twelve years," I said. "And make him a bit rattier-looking."

"Oh, yeah, I've seen him here a few times."

"You ever see him with O'Reilly?"

"Yeah, I think I did. But y'know, I mainly watch the moves, not the players. I've seen a lot of games here, played a lot, too. I bet you didn't know that Bobby Fischer started playing right here when he was twelve?"

"No, I didn't," I said, keeping an eye on O'Reilly, now several yards away.

"It's a fact," said the kid. "I'm going to be a champion, just like Bobby."

"I bet you will be," I said. I got his number and told him someone would be in touch.

O'Reilly bypassed the break-dancers and the crowd as he headed toward the arch at the park's Fifth Avenue entrance, and I hurried not to lose him.

At the edge of the park a tour bus pulled to the curb, blocking my view, tourists pouring out, aiming cameras at the arch, and when I got around to the other side, O'Reilly was gone.

12

The sun is melting on the New Jersey horizon like hot wax.

Around him, windows in the glass-and-steel buildings wink as if God is playing with a switch, details slipping in and out of focus, tops of skyscrapers so close he swears he can touch them, then disappearing.

He remembers the knife in his hand, the blood, the crowd dispersing, screams.

Only the *why* remains cloudy, a malfunction, like a transmission wire burning out, exactly what he has worried about for so long, finally confirmed. And the question of who will be next—which cannot be answered by true or false or A or B or none of the above or all of the above—terrifies him. He sees himself standing over his mother, dead on the kitchen floor, and trying to say he is sorry.

He should call her. She worries. But what would he say, here, now, when he has already decided, already answered the question that has been in his mind for days: to kill or be killed?

I keep telling you there's no gray area, you see, no shading, no right or wrong, I can't help myself, it's like zero to a hundred in a second and no turning back, and it's getting worse; you hear what I'm saying?

But they don't listen . . . when was that anyway, yesterday, a year ago, a decade, a lifetime?

No matter. This is what he has to do.

To kill or be killed?

He's got the answer. The only answer.

He blinks and it's just the city now, lights and smog and sky-scrapers undulating in the heat like go-go dancers.

"Beautiful, isn't it?"

He turns and sees the woman.

"What?"

"I said it's beautiful, the view, from up here. Hi, I'm Marjorie, from Kirkland, that's a little town just north of Seattle, and I can tell you there is nothing like this back there. But this heat, goodness, how can anyone stand—"

For a brief moment he sees her—red hair, freckles, open smile—and he feels so sad. "What time is it?" he asks, but does not hear the answer, shutting down again, all of it one long endless sleepless day, hours and minutes stretched out forever until now, this moment.

He turns and sees the orange fireball is not setting on the river but rising, closing in, about to explode. He looks again at the woman from outside of Seattle and she is no longer smiling, her face contorted, mouth stretched into an *O* and she is shouting something. He wants to tell her it's okay, that there's nothing to be afraid of, that he's not ever going to hurt anyone again as he grabs hold of the wire and hoists himself up, finds the opening and squeezes through, ignoring torn clothes, cuts, and bleeding fingers. He's free now and there will be no more pain, no more hurting, and that's what matters.

He balances a moment, arms out like a tightrope walker, sky-scrapers doing that lazy cootchie-coo, windows blinking like stars, all of it so damn beautiful.

He glances back at the redheaded woman and the crowd around her, all of them shouting and screaming as his mind converts them into a chorus of angels.

He unbuttons his shirt and lets it go; watches it ripple, flap, and sink like a wounded bird.

The angels are louder now, and he wants to tell them how sorry he is, that he didn't mean it, couldn't help it.

Then he takes a step, watches the concrete and glass slip away, and knows perfectly well that the singing angels are people, screaming, pointing at him.

He dips and whirls like a circus acrobat, windows blurring like waterfalls, and he feels so free and so perfectly unafraid.

13

I called the station, got O'Connell, and asked to speak to Terri. I wanted to tell her about my meeting with Sandwell's roommates and about O'Reilly. If he had attacked Sandwell and I'd just let him go it would be my responsibility if he did anything else. O'Connell told me where Terri was and that he was going there, too, and it opened a back door into my subconscious but I didn't stop to process it. I just shut my cell phone and headed out.

When I reached the perimeter there were police cars and vans ringing the area, a crowd like a thick clot of bees pulsating behind the rope, uniforms trying to control them; above the din a news chopper was circling.

I showed my temporary shield and they let me through. I looked for someone I knew and spotted Dugan, one of Terri's men, standing with a couple of cops from Homicide.

"Welcome to Ringling Brothers," he said.

He was right about that: It was a circus. They'd cordoned off Fifth Avenue, but a couple of news stations had gotten through and set up, reporters in makeup doing live broadcasts, harsh camera lights adding more heat to the drama. The streets were thick with uniforms and detectives, more cop cars and tech vans.

"Too bad you missed the main event," said Dugan. "Might have inspired you to draw a picture."

I didn't know if he was serious or ribbing me, but figured it was the latter. Last time out it had taken a long time for Terri's men to get used to having me around. I thought we'd gotten past it, that I wouldn't have to prove myself all over again, but maybe I was wrong.

One of the other homicide cops, a guy I recognized from the station, asked, "You draw the dead ones, too, Rodriguez?"

"Rocky draws 'em all," said Dugan, "and for *my* team." He slapped me on the back, suddenly my best friend, claiming ownership.

"Don't think the city has had one of these in a long time," said the other cop. He glanced up and I followed his gaze to the top of the art deco building.

"I remember reading that they used to find hundreds of dead birds down on the sidewalk," said Dugan. "Poor bastards would smack into the building on their way south, or was it on their way up north? You don't hear about that anymore. You think the birds are getting smarter?"

He looked at me, waiting for an answer, but I didn't have one. There was a nightmare image rising and falling in my brain.

"Who's in charge?" I asked.

"It's our jurisdiction," said Dugan, meaning Midtown North, "but half the NYPD has come out. Everyone wants to get a look, and you can't blame them, can you? Wish I had the popcorn and candy concession." He laughed and the homicide cops laughed with him.

"Hey, Rocky!"

It was O'Connell, red-faced and breathing hard; Perez beside him wearing his usual expression of disgust, nose wrinkled, lip curled up. Perez always seemed pissed off about something.

I addressed my question to O'Connell. "Russo here?"

He tilted his head toward a thick ring of cops just beyond us who were shielding the scene, and I headed toward it.

A uniform stopped me. Then I saw Terri and she waved me through.

There were maybe fifty cops in the circle, half of them on cell phones, a dozen techs on the ground, two up on the cab's crushed hood, a photographer on the trunk shooting pictures. The chopper was hovering dangerously close, blades whipping the air into a wild soufflé of wrinkled newspapers and bits of trash, blowing everyone's hair and rippling our clothes like we were in a hurricane. It felt like a movie set, totally unreal and staged.

"Jesus," I said.

"Yeah," said Terri.

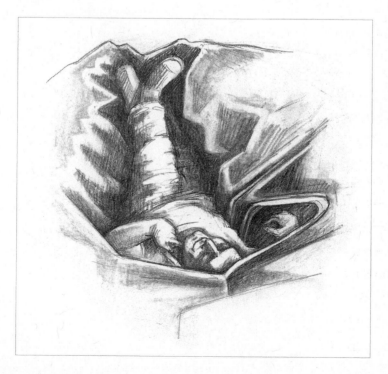

The man was wrapped in the taxicab's roof, the metal molded around him like rubber. I stared at the body, as the drawing I'd made of the falling man flashed in my mind's eye.

Terri left to confer with Morelli and I opened my pad. Obviously Dugan was right: I did draw them all. Though I wasn't sure why I wanted to right now.

But once I'd drawn him I knew: because I recognized him. I had sketched him before—with the Hunter College vic's girlfriend, Anna. It was the guy she'd described, the one who had started the fight with Ryan Kavanagh at the movie theater!

Terri came back, looked over my shoulder, then back at the scene. I wasn't sure she recognized him, but I never forget a face.

"A hundred and two floors," said Morelli. He shielded his eyes, looked up at the building, then down at the vic. "You'd think the body would be mush."

The M.E. had just come back from the body. "Inside, it is," he said. "You ever see the pictures of Princess Diana after the accident? Not a scratch on her face. She looked like Sleeping Beauty. But the impact sent her heart into her ribs so hard, it stopped cold."

"Lucky the cabby stepped out for a smoke, or we'd have had two dead stiffs," said Morelli.

The driver, a black man with a singsong Caribbean accent, was talking to a uniform and dragging on a cigarette as if his life depended on it—and apparently it had.

A guy with an acetylene torch was working his way through the metal taxicab top. Two guys from EMT eyed the guy with the torch, then turned to Morelli and Terri. "Okay to take the body when he's through?"

The M.E. nodded his approval, and Morelli and Terri did, too.

"I wonder how he got through the wire and out on the ledge?" she said.

"Witnesses said he squeezed through a six-, seven-inch opening," said Morelli. "Cut himself doing it, but I guess that doesn't matter when you're leaping off the top of the Empire State Building." He looked up, then down. "Guess he *really* wanted to die."

I imagined the body hurtling through the air, the moment of

impact, bones shattering, heart stopping, and hoped he had lost consciousness before he hit. I got one last look at his face, the odd smile on his lips, then the torch guy was finished and the EMT guys got a grip on the body, tugged it loose and zipped him into a bag.

14

It was a lock, the guy I'd drawn with Anna, and the jumper. And we had more than my drawings to prove it. The lab had made a match, too: blood work from the jumper that matched blood found on the victim, Ryan Kavanagh. He must have nicked himself when he stabbed the vic and left his DNA calling card.

We had a name as well: Wayne Beamer, thirty-five years old, with a psych discharge from the army sixteen years ago. Since then, he'd lived at home with his mother, in Queens, commuting to a job at an auto-repair shop on West Fifty-ninth Street in Manhattan.

So far no connection had been made between victim and per-petrator, no friends or family in common.

We put Beamer's prints through the NYPD's fingerprint database, but nothing came up. Then, AFIS, but the Automated

Fingerprint Identification System came back blank, too. He had no criminal record.

It looked open and shut. Murder. Suicide. And the word from the top was to get it finished, tie up the loose ends, fast.

Terri had her men working overtime: interviews with Beamer's boss, coworkers, and associates. She asked me to interview his mother. She knew what I did when I made sketches—got people to open up, to tell me what they knew and how they felt, and I was glad she trusted me to do it again.

I borrowed one of the new Chevy Impala RMPs from the police lot and headed over the Fifty-ninth Street Bridge, a route that took me out of Manhattan and into my past.

Twenty years ago, it was the preferred route when Julio and I would boost a car. We'd drive over the bridge, get stoned, look back at Manhattan and dream. It was usually pretty good till the drugs wore off and we had to ditch the car, hop a subway turnstile and leave our dreams behind.

I wondered what dreams Wayne Beamer had left behind as I drove through the Queens streets and found the house he'd shared with his mother for the past sixteen years.

There was a local news van parked across the street, the reporter asleep behind the wheel. Yesterday there must have been a dozen. The story had been reported by every TV news station and I'd caught a glimpse of Mrs. Beamer waving away reporters shoving microphones into her face, and wondered if she would talk to me now.

I parked halfway down the street so I wouldn't wake the reporter, and walked back.

The Beamer house was on a street that mixed private and

semidetached homes, in between a Pakistani deli and an empty lot which had become a dumping ground for old appliances. Most of the houses were aluminum-sided, the private ones with six-by-eight-foot patches of grass, most neglected and overgrown, but not the Beamers', which had bright red geraniums in window boxes and a small well-kept lawn.

It was hard to tell Mrs. Beamer's age. She had the parched complexion of a smoker confirmed by deeply etched whistle lines around her lips, her face puffy, eyes swollen.

"Please," she said after looking at my shield. "Must I go through it again? I have nothing more to say." Her facial muscles conspired to create a mask of heartbreak, muscles pinching brows and forehead, risorius muscles tugging her mouth down.

Our faces—controlled by an involuntary system of nerves and muscles—are like TV sets that subconsciously broadcast what we are feeling. Right now, Mrs. Beamer's face was tuned into a channel that played only sadness.

I took a chance and laid the sketch I'd made at the death scene onto a checkered table in the foyer.

I explained my job and how I'd come to draw it. I could have shown her the drawing I'd made earlier with the vic's girlfriend. But that was a portrait of a killer and this was the portrait of a victim, and I was pretty sure she'd prefer the latter.

"Oh my God," she said, her eyes filling with tears. "He looks as if he's sleeping."

"That's how he looked," I said.

"Thank you," she said softly, then looked past me and I saw that the TV reporter was heading our way.

"Oh, come in," she said. "Quickly."

She closed the door behind me and turned the lock.

"Go away," she shouted. Then she turned to me and sighed. "He'll eventually give up. Would you like some coffee?"

I followed her into a small tidy kitchen, light from a window dappling across the tablecloth, and watched her pour coffee, then tap a cigarette out of a pack. "I hope you don't mind. I was just about to stop when this . . ." She lit up and blew smoke toward the ceiling. "He really does look like he's sleeping," she said.

"Why do you think he looked so at peace?"

She glanced at me, then away, eyes tearing up again. "He was such a happy little boy."

I gave her a minute, then asked what she thought had happened; when Wayne stopped being that "happy little boy."

"It was the army," she said. "He wasn't the same after that. Post-traumatic stress disorder, they call it. He had nightmares and he'd wake up screaming."

It reminded me of Peter Sandwell—the guy beaten to death in the other case—and what his roommates had said about him—and I filed it away.

"Sometimes I'd go into his room and Wayne would be shaking and sweating and I'd just hold him like he was my little boy again." She stifled a sob by dragging on her cigarette.

"Sounds like you were a terrific mom."

The muscles around her lips managed a sad smile. "They said he was better, but . . ."

"Who?"

"The army psychiatrists. They had him on medication and he did seem better for a while. But they always came back, the nightmares, the shakes. Lately it was like something had snapped in him, like he was about to explode." She lifted her chin and light from the window washed away some of the lines and sadness from her face, and for a moment I saw that she had once been pretty. "He started having fights with his boss and coworkers and his boss said he threatened to kill him, but Wayne swore he didn't—or he didn't remember it." She sighed heavily, weary. "He worked in a garage, his latest job. There've been others . . . I didn't know what to do for him. Sixteen years since his discharge, *sixteen years*, and he never got better, only worse." She tapped the ash of her cigarette with nicotine-stained fingers.

"And the violent episodes, the anger, you say that was recent?"

"There'd been other times when Wayne got mad and sort of went off, you know, disappeared into his head as if . . . I don't know. But in the last year it had gotten a lot worse." She squashed her cigarette out. "You know, I wasn't surprised to hear about that boy, the college boy."

"You mean the young man Wayne killed?"

"Yes, but . . . that wasn't Wayne. Not the Wayne I know. Not Wayne before he went into the army. I never thought it was a good idea, the army, not for Wayne. He was a sensitive boy, you know. No good at school; college was out of the question. But he was good with his hands. I told him, 'Wayne, go to technical school, be an electrician, they make good money,' but he wanted to be a hero."

"And he saw combat?"

"Yes, but he never talked about it. When he was first discharged he went to see a therapist over in Jersey for treatment, for

mental problems, you know. But he wouldn't discuss that either."
She shook her head. "All I know is that he had a psychological
discharge and that they sent him to a psychiatrist who didn't do
him any good."

"So he wasn't injured physically?"

"No."

"And you talked to his doctor, his therapist?"

"Just one time. He said Wayne had seen some bad things and
it had affected his mind, but he wouldn't tell me what. He said he
and Wayne were *working* on the problem. I always figured Wayne
would tell me, but he never did." She lit another cigarette, took a
drag, and let the smoke out slowly. "It was the disease, that PTSD
that killed that boy, Detective, not my Wayne."

"I'm sure you're right," I said. "Was Wayne on any medication?"

"The police took the prescription vials, but I was the one
who filled them." She pulled herself out of the chair as if it was
an effort, rummaged through a draw of papers, came up with a
stack of prescriptions and spoke while she went through them.
"They had Wayne on the Prozac, then Zoloft, and then the Paxil.
He took that every day for a long time. But recently he switched
to . . ." She riffled through the scripts. "Here, Effexor. And there
was Klonopin and Ativan for when he got really anxious, but he
was taking another one called . . ." She stopped again to find it.
"BuSpar. Those were prescribed by some new doctor."

"So, Wayne was seeing this doctor?" I read the name:
"Rivkin?"

"I guess. Like I said, Wayne didn't tell me much."

I asked to keep the prescription and she shrugged.

"I hate to bring this up, but was your son taking any other
drugs, the nonprescription kind?"

She sighed. "Wayne had a little problem with drugs. I thought he'd stopped, but . . ." Her eyes filled with tears again.

"I'm sorry for your loss, Mrs. Beamer."

"Cioffi. Beamer was my married name. Call me Laure. I spell it with an e at the end, not an *i* or *ie*." She smiled, but it didn't last. "I did the best I could, but Wayne's father left when he was just a boy and it was hard, you know."

"Yes, I'm sure."

A picture flashed in my mind—my father, dead in the street—and I pushed it away with a question. "Can I see Wayne's room?"

"The other cops have been through it, but I don't see why not."

Single bed, narrow wooden dresser, couple of bookshelves, night table with three crossword books, no pictures on the walls, one of which was painted red.

"What's with the red wall?" I asked.

"One day Wayne just painted it. I think he'd been drawing on it first and maybe didn't like what he drew, so he just painted the 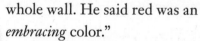 whole wall. He said red was an *embracing* color."

"Wayne liked to draw?"

"Oh, yes. Not so much lately, but he did."

She plucked a sketch pad off a shelf and handed it to me. I opened to the first page.

"This is really good," I said, studying the agitated, nervous line, and repetition.

"Wayne was good with his hands, like I said."

I flipped through a few pages, which were more of the same, though the imagery became slightly more bizarre.

Then the pictures started to deteriorate and were finally just a mess.

"Oh, I never saw these," she said. "Do you think his new medication made him scribble like that? Maybe they made him do what—you know—what he did to that boy." She sucked in a breath and shook her head.

I asked her if I could hold on to the sketch pad for a while and she nodded. She left me alone and I went through the drawers and opened the closet. I didn't know what I was looking for but I didn't find anything and after a while there was nowhere else to look.

I found Mrs. Beamer sitting at the kitchen table, a new cigarette burning between her fingers. "That's Wayne's work, too," she said, aiming her cigarette at a bucolic landscape painted in oil above the table. "He did it before he went into the army. It was the last real painting he did."

"It's nice," I said.

"Yes," she said softly, then looked down at the sketch I'd made of her son. "Is it okay if I keep this?"

I told her it was fine.

• • •

My cell phone rang just as Mrs. Beamer closed the door behind me, a detective from Investigations with information on O'Reilly. He gave me a last-known address and a telephone number in Hackensack, New Jersey.

I called and got O'Reilly's ex-wife.

"Is he in some sort of trouble?" she asked. "Because it wouldn't surprise me."

I said no. And she said, "Jimmy hasn't lived here in three years. It just got too crazy. *He* got too crazy.

I let her talk.

"Something really went off with him and I had to get him out; I couldn't trust him around me anymore, or our daughter. He'd become explosive, and it frightened me."

I pictured the guy in Washington Square, the frayed military jacket, his temper.

"He just wasn't himself after the army," she said. "He had nightmares and sweats and he was . . . I don't know how to describe it, but he was far away in his head, you know, disconnected, and he'd just go off."

"Do you think it was post-traumatic stress syndrome?"

"Why would I think that?"

"You said after the war he wasn't the same."

"What war? I said after the army."

"Oh, I just thought . . . You mean your husband wasn't in Desert Storm?"

"Desert Storm?" She snorted. "Jimmy never left Fort Dix, New Jersey. He was supposed to go, but he broke his ankle a few days before his platoon shipped out and ended up behind a desk for two years. I don't think they ever set it right, his ankle, because it left him with a slight limp. But that was the least of it."

I asked if he'd been seeing a psychiatrist and she said he had after his army stint, but not lately, that she knew of.

"We had a couple of good years, you know, when we were first married, then Jimmy went into the army because he thought they would pay for his schooling, we didn't have the money, but what a mistake that was! When he came back he was just . . . different. I put up with it for almost ten years, him going from job to job, the anger and depression, but it was finally too much."

I heard her sigh.

"Maybe it was always in him, but I didn't see any sign of it till after the army. You know, you might want to talk to his commander at Fort Dix. He called Jimmy a few times after he got out, to find out how he was and all, and they got together a couple of times for beers."

"Do you have a number where I can reach him?"

"I don't even have his name. It was a long time ago."

I made a note to find out.

"We met in high school, me and Jimmy. He was so much fun back then, life of the party, and really kind to everyone . . . but *that* Jimmy left me a long time ago."

It reminded me of what Mrs. Beamer had just said about her son.

"Last I knew he was living in some flophouse in Manhattan."

I asked if she had the address and it took her a minute to locate it.

"Hey, when you find him, remind him he's long overdue on his child support."

I called the station and got O'Connell. I told him about my visit with Mrs. Beamer and the address I had for O'Reilly. I asked that he meet me there in an hour.

15

There was no traffic on the bridge, very little as I cut crosstown, and I made it to Chelsea in a half hour.

The address O'Reilly's wife had given me was only a few blocks away from the Penn South Apartments, a sprawling brick complex that looked like an upscale housing project, but was, in fact, coveted Manhattan housing, and the place where I'd grown up. My parents had inherited the apartment from my mother's father—a pattern maker in the garment industry—after he and my grandmother retired to Boca Raton. I was about two when we moved in.

I pulled the Impala to the side of Eighth Avenue and Twenty-sixth and glanced up at the monolith I had called home for so many years.

I pictured my room, the walls plastered with posters of Che, Bob

Marley, Santana, and me in it, sulking most of the time. I could see my dad, too, decked out in his narc's costume: jeans, open-necked shirt, plenty of bling, his ever-ready smile.

If only he were here, I thought, the things I would tell him about the life I'd chosen and how it had worked out. Our last conversation, a screaming match, was already playing in my head, and there'd been no time to tell him I was sorry.

I hadn't been back here since I'd moved out and really didn't want to be here now, memories coming at me crosscut and fast. I pulled out and drove down Ninth Avenue, but the ghost of my father hitched a ride. Then I started thinking about my mother and the night my father died, and how after that she had disappeared, not physically but emotionally. But so had I, the two of us living in that apartment, doing time.

I wanted to talk about it now, to clear the air and get back to what we once had, but it seemed like too much history and I didn't know how or where to begin.

I pushed the thoughts out of my mind. I took in all the changes since I'd left the neighborhood: the bodegas and tenements replaced by spiffy new apartment buildings, trendy restaurants, gourmet food shops and gay bars, a complete face-lift except for the Alfred Court, a month-to-month rooming house just off the avenue. I'd never been inside, but the building brought back memories of my first case with Terri—a girl who lived there, murdered.

It was weird, how my life kept sliding back and forth over itself.

Inside, the lobby's black-and-white marble floors and ornate plaster ceiling alluded to a better time, though the marble was cracked and stained, the ceiling chipped and peeling, with missing chunks of plaster that revealed dangerously dangling wires.

There was a wide curving staircase and a guy at a desk in front of it straight out of central casting, somewhere between seventy and death, skin like sandpaper, cigarette drooping off his lower lip.

He looked up, rheumy-eyed and bored, then back to his racing form.

"James O'Reilly," I said. "He live here?"

"Haven't seen him in a couple of days," he said.

I slid my shield onto the racing form. "Let's go."

"Where?"

"To O'Reilly's room."

"You got a warrant?" he asked, as a man and woman entered the lobby.

The woman was in short-shorts and a bikini top and on closer inspection looked to be about sixteen though her heavy makeup made her appear older. She rubbed against me accidentally-on-purpose as she slapped a twenty onto the counter.

"How's it hangin', Pops?"

Pops's rheumy eyes ticked in my direction, but if she saw his warning she didn't care.

"Come *on*," she said, tapping her foot, eyeing the John at her side, guy in a seersucker suit rumpled by heat and his own nervous sweat.

"Give the lady her key," I said.

She tossed me a smile, wrapped her fingers—black nail polish, chipped—around the key, ushered the John in front of her, then glanced back. "I'll be free in an hour, honey," she whispered. "Maybe less."

I waited till the couple was out of earshot, then I asked Pops if he wanted me to call Vice. "Maybe bring you in for solicitation, while I'm at it."

"*Me?* You *kidding*?" He stabbed his cigarette out and made a production of searching through a desk drawer until he came up with another key. "I'm telling you, that crackpot O'Reilly isn't here."

"Fine," I said. "I just want to have a look around." I checked my watch. O'Connell would be here soon.

Pops pushed the key toward me. "O'Reilly's room is on six, top floor, 6-D, end of the hall."

I looped my hand under his arm and hoisted him up. "Sorry, but you're coming with me." I needed him to open the door because I didn't have the warrant to break it in.

The sixth-floor hallway had a faded rug dotted with trash, couple of sludge-filled coffee cups attracting flies, condom wrappers, stacks of old newspapers. And it was stifling, the air fetid and sour.

"You ever collect the garbage around here?"

"Not my job," said Pops.

At 6-D he knocked, then tried the key. The locked popped, but the door wouldn't budge. "Damn humidity," he said. "These doors are always sticking."

I had a bad feeling, so I told Pops to stand aside, leaned my weight against the door, and it gave way.

The smell hit us so hard, the old guy stumbled back.

16

The room was hot and dim, shade pulled down over the window, but there was no mistaking O'Reilly, service revolver in his hand, a puddle of dark viscous blood around his head.

I told Pops to go downstairs and call 911, tugged my collar over my nose and took a few steps closer.

I jerked the window shade up and light spilled into the room, dust motes dancing in slow motion, the scene illuminated in detail.

There was a crusty black-red blood above O'Reilly's ear where the bullet had entered, and another below, where it had exited—a really lousy shot. O'Reilly had died of blood loss and it might have

taken some time. I could see he'd been standing when he fired, the bullet lodged into the floor near the body. Then an image shot through my brain like the bullet through O'Reilly's.

Another falling man. This one hadn't jumped, but he'd surely fallen. I took a breath and looked past the body, suddenly riveted by what was above it.

No way it was blood splatter, not with a handprint and words. I stared at the bloody scribble, starting to feel dizzy. The room was hot and airless, the odor overwhelming, my stomach doing flip-flops. It had been only a day since O'Reilly died, but the heat had tripled the rate of decay, the body starting to ooze fluid.

I swallowed hard, found the mentholated ChapStick in my pocket and smeared it under my nose. It helped. A little. I looked at O'Reilly's face and felt guilt along with disgust. I should have

stayed on him, should have had him picked up immediately—
and would have, had Beamer not jumped off the Empire State
Building.

I looked at the wall again, the finger painting that O'Reilly had
made with his own blood while he was dying, and had a thought:
Maybe his bad shot had been intentional; maybe he had purposely
wounded himself so his death would be slow, so he could do this.
But my God, how fearless—how crazy—did you have to be to
shoot yourself in the head and know you would die slowly?

I tried to reconstruct the scene . . .

O'Reilly puts the gun to his head and pulls the trigger; bullet
enters above his ear, but on an angle; exits without going into his
brain; then he dips his fingers into his blood and paints the wall.

I studied the bloodred painting again.

They were definitely words:
Yes? No? True? Was it code, or
the scribbling of a madman?
And what was he trying to
say?

It looked like suicide, but I
knew that presumption could
be a mistake, that suicide was
easy to stage.

I tried to see the scene differently . . .

The perp enters; shoots
O'Reilly in the head, does a
lousy job but doesn't know it; leaves him there to die, never expecting he's going to get up and paint a message on the wall.

But if that was the case, wouldn't O'Reilly have spelled out his
killer's name?

I didn't know which scenario was right, murder or suicide, but Wayne Beamer was back in my mind, another man who had committed murder, then suicide.

I noted the gun in O'Reilly's hand, the way he held it by the barrel. Had he dropped it then picked it up—or had it been placed in his hand, clumsily?

The CS crew would be checking for gunshot residue on O'Reilly's hands and scalp to see if he fired the shot and would look for signs of another person's presence. If it was murder, they'd find trace. Any good coroner will tell you the same thing: Every time you interact with a body you leave something behind and take something with you.

I made a note of what O'Reilly had written on the wall, but there was no way I could duplicate it. It was too chaotic. I would need a photo.

"Jesus Christ!"

It was O'Connell.

"Is that O'Reilly?" he asked.

"Seems to be," I said.

There were sirens outside, and before O'Connell and I could say much more, there were footsteps on the stairs and then uniforms and techs from the Scientific Investigation Division crowding the scene.

17

We'd been in the small room next to Terri's office for close to an hour, a blinking overhead fluorescent driving me crazy.

"I never said they were the same. Clearly it's the work of two different people—Beamer's sketchbook pictures, O'Reilly's blood work on the wall—but there's plenty about them that's similar in the scribbling and the words."

I looked at Terri, then, in turn, O'Connell, Perez, and Dugan. I could see that none of them wanted to buy what I was selling: that both killers had been making insane-looking doodles that I thought looked pretty damn similar.

"I can see they were both scribbling, Rocky, but so what?" O'Connell took a sip from his thermos, then wiped his mouth with the back of his hand. "A million people make random doo-dles. Me, when I'm on the phone, I doodle up a storm. I'll show you sometime."

"Can't wait. Listen," I said. "I understand they *look* different because Beamer's are drawn in pencil and O'Reilly's was made with his blood, but you have to look past the style and see the content."

"*Content?*" Perez sneered. "It's just a bunch of squiggles and lines and half-words."

I tried not to take his dismissive tone personally. I knew he was in a nasty custody battle with his ex, fighting to see his kids, and felt for him, but I was starting to get pissed.

"How about pretending that someone, *anyone* other than *me*, is giving you guys the info, okay? That might help you see it."

"What's that supposed to mean?" said Perez.

He knew exactly what I meant, and so did the others, so I wasn't going to explain it. "Just look at the images, okay? They've both got the same words—yes, no, true—"

"Fine," said Dugan, finally looking up from his *Daily News*. "But explain to me why Beamer and O'Reilly—two guys who never met—would be making the same kind of drawing?"

"Well, that's sort of the big question, isn't it, Dugan? I mean, that's what we are here to find out."

Dugan shrugged. Like the others, he seemed content to stick with what they had: two perps, two vics; end of story. The lab had confirmed it was O'Reilly who had killed Sandwell, thanks to the bits of flesh he'd left on Sandwell's face during the beating. I was trying to take it a step further, tie the two perps together with Beamer's sketches and O'Reilly's blood painting, but no one wanted to go there. Like all cops, they wanted the crimes solved, the collars recorded, everything put to bed nice and neat, and here I was stripping the sheets to see what was under them.

To me, O'Reilly's death had answered the question of *who* killed Peter Sandwell, not *why*.

Terri had the initial CS and SID reports from O'Reilly's scene and was whacking them against her thigh as she paced. She hadn't said much and I wasn't sure what she thought. I knew she'd be happy to have the cases closed, too; they were murders that didn't need to be solved, the perps conveniently dead, with lab reports that tied them to the vics. But Terri was a good cop and she didn't like loose ends, and I knew that, too.

We'd been over the same material, what we knew and what we didn't know—that neither Beamer nor O'Reilly had any connection to each other, or to their victims. Everyone's prints had been run through AFIS, NCIC, even the DOJ, and nothing had come back.

Beamer and O'Reilly may have done the courts a favor by killing themselves, but it would have been better to have captured one of them alive so we could have asked a few questions. We had the killers but no explanations.

There were a lot of things I wanted to say, but I switched gears. "Was Peter Sandwell ever in the army?"

"His bio says no," said O'Connell.

I had been hoping for an easy answer, that Sandwell and O'Reilly, victim and perpetrator, might have served in the military together, something to connect them.

"Sandwell doesn't matter," said Perez. "He was the vic."

"You mean you don't care about the victims, Perez? I thought you were a cop."

"And I thought you were a sketch artist," he said.

"In case you forgot, I went through the academy," I said, "just like you. And I put in time at Quantico, *un*like you—"

"Why don't both of you just relax," said Terri.

I took a deep breath. I was annoyed with myself for losing it, for having to justify being there.

Dugan finally exchanged his newspaper for a case file. "O'Reilly's preliminary tox shows aspirin with codeine, Xanax, Klonopin, sounds like a Heath Ledger cocktail," he said. "All downers, which he countered with a little Dex."

"That combo alone could make you crazy," said O'Connell.

"But CS doesn't report any vials or scripts found at his flop house," said Dugan. "So there's no doctor's record. He must have been buying them on the street or online."

"Again, I don't see how any of this really matter since the perps and vics are dead," said Perez.

"Perez, you ever think about volunteering for victims' rights?" I said.

"Fuck you," he said.

"*Boys*," said Terri. "You're giving me a headache. And until we find out everything about these guys—perps *and* vics—to explain the murders, the media will keep saying we're lousy cops, so let's get some answers and put it to bed for good, okay?"

Perez let out a raspy sigh.

"Am I annoying you?" Terri glared at him.

"What? I'm not allowed to breathe?"

"On your own time," she said. "So, the cases look clean and simple, and hopefully they are. But no one wants this to come back and bite us in the ass, so let's make sure. For now, we feed the press what we want them to print—like Beamer being under a psychiatrist's care. When they get the news of O'Reilly, which will be any minute, we make sure to keep the incidents separate so no one infers there could be a connection between the two cases—and right now there are no facts to support that." Terri looked from Beamer's red sketch and the photo of O'Reilly's bloody wall at me, then away. "Media Relations is putting out a release that will say Beamer and O'Reilly were ex-soldiers with mental problems. Let the press chew on that for a while, get people mad at the shrinks and the military—and not at us." She held up a new file. "The results of a search on murder-suicides in the U.S. in the last six months. Two hits, one in Chicago, one in California. Neither murder had an apparent motive, like ours, but neither perp was a soldier, so in that way not like ours." She looked at each of the men and stopped at Dugan. "So here's what we're going to do. Dugan, you talk to O'Reilly's sister in Connecticut, just to be sure we aren't missing anything."

"You want me to go to fucking Connecticut?"

"You'll be in an air-conditioned car, for Christ's sake. What do you want, a driver?"

"That'd be nice," he said.

Terri didn't answer. She turned to O'Connell and Perez. "You two handle the paper."

"Could be a lot of paper," said Perez.

"That's why I'm asking *two* of you to handle it. Any more complaints?" She looked from Perez to Dugan, her features frozen, facial muscles tight. No one said a word.

"I want all lab updates, tox, anything and everything. Recheck bios and backgrounds, too. Make sure there is nothing in either vic's past that might have earmarked them for these attacks—clubs, affiliations, anything at all. I don't want these cases closed and have some reporter find out three weeks from now that Sandwell and O'Reilly were fifth cousins. You hear me? And share with Morelli. His team is backup."

Then she turned to me. "Rodriguez, get me verification on what the ex-wife said about O'Reilly—that he hadn't seen any combat. And go see the shrink that wrote those scripts for Beamer."

"Done," I said. "I have an appointment with him tomorrow."

Perez leaned toward me. "Your nose is looking a little brown, Rodriguez."

"That's because you keep trying to sit on my face, and I'm just not into that, so cut it out, okay, Perez?"

"Fuck you, Rodriguez—"

"I just told you, Perez, I'm not into that."

"Would you two just shut up?" said Terri. "We have a job to finish and I'm sick to death of this adolescent bullshit!"

I would have said, *It was him, not me*, but thought it might confirm her evaluation.

"When this is all finished you two can each have your own little fire truck and GI Joe and battle it out." She added a pinched smile and I felt like a ten-year-old getting chewed out by his teacher.

"Denton wants this closed, so let's get the information to him signed, sealed, and delivered with a neat little bow, okay?" She gave us each a look that said *I don't want an answer, just your cooperation.*

18

At least it's not a serial killer," said Terri.

I was eating a sandwich and watching TV; Terri, a salad, the plate balanced in her lap.

"That much we know."

"Are you being sarcastic, Rodriguez?"

"No, I was agreeing with you."

I glanced at the television, the news, a shot of the Empire State Building, a rehashing of Wayne Beamer's swan dive. Thanks to him, I had learned that thirty or so people had committed suicide by jumping off the building since its completion in 1931. One guy, who had leaped out of a sixty-ninth-floor window, hit the thirtieth floor and severed his leg, which had landed on the street much to the horror of lunchtime passersby; a year before, a man had jumped out the window of a vacant office on the sixty-sixth floor; recently, some daredevil freak had tried to parachute off the building but had been caught and was now being sued. Wayne Beamer held the distinction of getting past the guardrail on the Observation Deck.

"Let's say, for argument's sake, that both murders were crimes of convenience," said Terri. "That the two vics were just there when the guys went nuts."

"Possible," I said, momentarily putting aside my thoughts of the similarity I saw between O'Reilly's blood painting and Beamer's sketches.

"We could have chalked it up to two cases of post-traumatic stress disorder, but O'Reilly never saw any action, right?" She stopped, took a bite of her salad, and mulled the thought over while she chewed. "How did O'Reilly seem to you when you saw him in Washington Square?"

"Like I said, wound tight as a drum. I would have had him brought in if Beamer hadn't leaped and distracted me." I saw O'Reilly's face in my mind's eye. "He didn't say much, but his face registered plenty of emotions, just too fast for me to interpret."

"But you were asking him about Peter Sandwell, who he killed, so it's pretty likely that's what was going through his mind."

"Good point," I said. "I dug a little and got the name and number for his Fort Dix CO. Maybe I can get something from him."

"Okay, but we've got to close this out, or the feds will come in."

"You think so?"

"I know so."

"You can't just close it without answers."

"Who says? It's murder/suicide, neat and clean."

"The way the PD likes it."

"And you don't?"

"I just think there's something to Beamer's sketches and whatever O'Reilly was scribbling on the wall when he died, and I'd like to explore it."

"If we have the time."

"You don't want to know?"

"I don't have the luxury to explore every avenue, Rodriguez. My job is to get the cases closed. I'm already going a step further than necessary because I want to make sure when we close the cases, they *stay* closed."

I knew she was under a different kind of pressure than I was, that she had to answer to people higher up on the food chain, but I still spoke my mind. "I'm going to see Beamer's shrink tomorrow. Suppose he gives us something that opens the case up rather than closes it?"

Terri sighed.

"Hey, seeing the shrink was *your* order, not *mine*."

"Oh, bull, Rodriguez. You'd already made the appointment." She put her salad aside and studied me. "These cases have really gotten to you, haven't they?"

It was true.

A crooked path, my *abuela* had said; a path I needed to follow bravely. But it had nothing to do with bravery; it had to do with conviction, with finishing something I had started, with getting answers and honoring the dead. "I just want to know what happened; don't you?"

"Yes, but you've got to keep some distance if you're going to work Homicide, otherwise it'll kill you—and do me a favor. Stop fighting with Perez."

"He's fighting with *me*."

"You're both acting like babies, so just stop, it's driving me crazy."

"Tell him to stop."

"That's exactly what I mean. *Tell him. No, you tell him.* Jesus, boys are such idiots."

"That's why we need girls, to make us smarter."

"Ain't that the truth!" She went back to her salad. "I'm really nervous about your mom coming to town tomorrow."

"You deal with murderers all day but meeting my mother makes you nervous?"

"Meeting your mom is much scarier. After all, she created *you*." She smiled and touched my cheek. "You're going to shave, right?"

"For my mother?"

"For everyone, Rodriguez. Do the world a favor, and clean up your act."

"I thought you liked my act dirty."

"You never quit, do you?"

"Never. But you can relax about my mother, she's not scary."

"Easy for you to say."

Not at all, I thought.

"I left word with my doorman to let her in. I'll be at work. Can you meet her?"

"I'm doing a sketch at the Twenty-third. But I'm pretty sure my mother can navigate your one-room apartment."

"You think she'll like it?"

"Beats the cost of a hotel."

"That wasn't my question."

"She'll love it."

I had an image of my mother hanging out in Terri's Murray Hill apartment and wasn't sure I liked it at all.

"Dinner's at eight. Don't be late or I swear I will kill you, Rodriguez."

"You ever going to call me Nate?" I asked.

"Never," she said.

Terri nodded off halfway through *The Daily Show*, but I couldn't sleep. I kept thinking about my mother. Since the last time we'd been together, almost a year ago, I'd learned the truth about my father's death and wanted to tell her. But did I start with what I thought I knew twenty years ago, or what I knew now?

You know, Mom, I've been thinking about what happened to Dad twenty years ago and . . . I found out why Dad was up in Spanish Harlem that night and . . . I always thought I knew what happened, but . . .

My mind wouldn't quit, so I got out of bed and went over to my work area. I picked up one of my forensic books and read a couple of case studies, one about a dead man who had been accidentally preserved with mothballs, another where an entire body was reconstructed based on a piece of burned leg bone. It gave me confidence. If someone could create a body from a scrap of bone, I figured I could create a face with a skull.

I spent a few minutes going over the facial muscles in an anatomy book, then skimmed some of my old Quantico notes and got to work.

One of my Quantico teachers used to say that forensic art is a combination of science and intuition, so I let my instincts guide me as much as the rules. I worked for about an hour, then took a look at what I'd done.

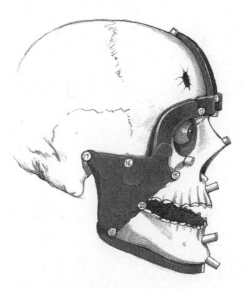

It wasn't much, but adding clay to the skull, getting a feel for the shape and structure of the John Doe's cheek and jaw, made me feel like I was starting to resurrect him.

I would have kept going but did not want to be tired or loopy when I saw Wayne Beamer's shrink in the morning or my mother at night.

I scraped the clay off my hands, but the face I was trying to create hovered in my mind.

It was sort of like what I was trying to do with Wayne Beamer and James O'Reilly—understand their lives so I could understand their deaths.

19

Richard R. Rivkin, doctor of psychiatry, had an office on Park Avenue, and a really nice waiting room—pastel-colored Oriental rug, comfy chairs, walls covered with framed posters from Lincoln Center's *Mostly Mozart* series.

I distracted myself with the prints, making mental notes of my favorites: an analytical Sol Lewitt, all pencil lines and written notes about how to create them; and a horizontal abstraction made of graceful interlocking forms by Susan Crile. Terri had been after me to get some art for the walls of my apartment or to make some, but I told her I did not want to live with my own work; I didn't consider it art and couldn't get my head around the idea of framing one of my sketches and putting it on the wall.

I folded myself into a chair and leafed through *People*—Paris Hilton out of prison, Lindsay Lohan back in rehab—but it was hard to sit still, my mind buzzing from the supersized Starbucks espresso I'd chugged to get me through a morning sketch.

The woman who came out of Rivkin's office was well dressed in that Upper East Side way, shades of beige, low-heeled pumps, pearls. We exchanged an awkward there-is-nothing-wrong-with-me look and a minute later Dr. Rivkin greeted me.

He was a small man, no more than five feet five, tailored gray suit, white-collared shirt and paisley tie, hair parted and perfectly in place.

I stuffed my T-shirt into the waistband of my jeans, a too-late attempt at grooming, and he showed me into his office, a variation of the waiting room—comfy chairs, antique desk, wall of books. He offered me the chair beside the window and started with a disclaimer.

"As I told you over the phone, Mr. Beamer was not my patient."

"But you did see him and prescribe drugs?"

Rivkin plucked a Blackberry off his desk and scrolled through it. "That was more than a month ago, and only one time. I don't really see how I can help."

"You just never know what piece of information could be helpful," I said and smiled. "So how did Wayne Beamer come to see you?"

"Through the army's psych services. Every now and then I see military men who are having problems."

"And they can afford you?"

"Well, they don't make up the major portion of my client list, if that's what you're asking. I was in the military right after college and they put me to work. I stayed on for a couple of years and they paid for med school. The army has been good to me, so I pay them back by seeing military personnel at prorated fees, what they can afford, some as little as twenty-five dollars a session."

"That's very generous."

"I see it as my duty." He glanced at his watch, ultra-thin and ultra-gold. It looked as if it cost my annual salary.

"I appreciate your time, so I'll make it quick, Doctor. Did you come up with a diagnosis for Wayne Beamer?"

"PTSD."

"Post-traumatic stress disorder?"

"That's right." Rivkin looked at me with interest for the first time. "Though, honestly, I think Mr. Beamer was just here to renew his meds. The army and the insurance companies won't keep paying for them if you're not under a doctor's care."

"And Wayne Beamer was not."

"Not that I know of—but I think he should have been. He was very worked up, very anxious."

"How so?"

"You realize this is confidential material, so I can only reveal generalities."

I nodded.

"He complained of sleeplessness and bad dreams, the most common symptoms of PTSD. I recommended that he see me a couple of times a week. He agreed, made the next appointment, but never showed up."

"And you didn't follow up with him?"

"I'm a psychiatrist, not a parole officer. It was *his* responsibility."

I understood Rivkin's reluctance to talk. Beamer had not really been his patient and he didn't need the blemish on his record, nor the possibility of a law suit.

"Of course," I said. "And this won't go beyond us. Did he tell you about his experiences in battle?"

"No, we never got to that. He talked only of his current problems—that he couldn't sleep and was anxious all the time. He also complained of—" Rivkin stopped to skim through some notes. "Fatigue, headaches, dizziness, and memory problems. I suggested he see an internist."

"Did you think there was a physical problem?"

"It was possible." Rivkin paused a moment. "I repeat, *possible*, that he was suffering from Gulf War syndrome."

"Which is?"

"A controversy. Some think it's a real thing, others do not. But there are an awful lot of soldiers who fought in the Gulf who suffer from the same symptoms." He turned to his bookcase, plucked out a binder, and skimmed through pages. "In 2004, a British inquiry concluded that thousands of U.K. and U.S. Gulf War veterans were made ill by their military service. The report claims that Gulf veterans are twice as likely to suffer illnesses than those deployed elsewhere, and they blame this on a combination of causes, like anthrax vaccine injections, use of pesticides to spray tents, exposure to nerve gas, inhaling uranium dust, and so on."

"Sounds pretty bad." I started to chew a cuticle, tasted the foul stuff Terri had been painting on my fingertips, and stopped.

"Very bad," said Rivkin, frowning. "There are reports of skin problems, shortness of breath, and a higher mortality rate from brain cancer and ALS; but again, there is evidence for and against this data."

"But you think it's true, that these symptoms are a result of Gulf War syndrome?"

"I think it's possible. Of course the arguments against it cite similar symptoms for Vietnam vets and soldiers who fought in the Second World War, but . . ." He plucked a magazine out of a stack on his desk, *The Journal of Toxicology*. "This came out just a couple of months ago." He opened to an article which he summarized. "Apparently a few days after the Gulf War ended in March of '91, soldiers were instructed to get rid of huge reserves of munitions and missiles in Khamisiyah, Iraq, which they detonated, and by doing so exposed more than a hundred thousand American troops to sarin and cyclosarin—nerve gas."

I'd heard of sarin because of the 1995 terrorist attack on the subway in Japan.

"Of the seven hundred thousand men and women in Iraq at the time, one in seven started to complain of the kind of ailments Wayne Beamer complained of—what was soon referred to as Gulf War syndrome. Interesting odds, wouldn't you say?"

He went on before I could agree.

"Until recently the Pentagon denied the exposure, and the Defense Department is still saying this particular data is an 'estimate' or 'guesstimate.' "

"Not something I'd like to hear if I was one of the unlucky one hundred thousand," I said.

"No," said Rivkin. "But it's still under debate and in the end the army may well be vindicated."

Interesting that the minute I agreed with the doctor, he backed down and gave the army's point of view. I guessed he wanted them to be innocent of any wrongdoing.

"No matter what," he said, "it was an accident."

"With deadly effects," I said.

Rivkin agreed with his eyes and the slightest nod of his head.

"So let me get this straight. You're saying that Wayne Beamer may have had Gulf War syndrome and not PTSD?"

"I'm suggesting that he had both, the former physical, the latter emotional."

"And you wrote him prescriptions for which?"

Rivkin sucked on his lower lip, a sign of nervousness, and I knew he was thinking about that law suit again.

"This is not going in any report, Doctor. Essentially this is an open-and-shut case. I just want to know what happened to Wayne Beamer, to make sense of it."

Rivkin pinched the bridge of his nose. "If Gulf War syndrome exists, and if in fact Mr. Beamer had it, I would not be the one to treat him, which is why I suggested he see an internist. I was just trying to deal with his anxiety and sleeplessness. I refilled a few prescriptions that he said he'd been taking for years and exchanged some older drugs for newer ones."

"But you didn't prescribe a stimulant?"

"Of course not. Why?"

"One showed up in his system."

"Well, he surely didn't get it from me." He sighed. "I'm afraid that drug and alcohol abuse often play a part in this disease, though speed can be a very dangerous drug. It overstimulates the brain and the central nervous system and impedes judgment. But I think he would have had to be taking quite a lot, considering that he was also on mood elevators and anti-anxiety drugs."

He sighed again. "I would have taken away the SSRI if I'd thought Mr. Beamer was suicidal—and if I'd thought he was dangerous to others—and I would have hospitalized him." He looked at me, his face a blend of sad and anxious, depressor anguli turning his mouth down, frontalis pars lateralis wrinkling his brow. "You understand I was simply refilling medications. They were not *my* prescriptions. He was not *my* patient."

"I understand," I said. "You were trying to give the man some peace."

"Yes," he said. "Exactly."

I unfolded a copy of the sketch I'd made of Beamer and showed it to him.

"What do you make of his smile?"

"Perhaps death came to him as release," he said. "He was obviously fighting some fierce demons."

"But he lost the fight," I said.

"Maybe he just took himself out of it," said Rivkin.

20

I called O'Reilly's CO, a retired lieutenant commander by the name of Kenneth Rathjay.

He said he didn't remember Jimmy O'Reilly and had nothing to say, but I told him I was coming to see him anyway.

I always like to see people's faces when I talk to them. As the great face-reading expert Paul Ekman says: "People lie with words, but faces tell the truth."

It was almost four, but I figured I had enough time to get to Hoboken and back in time for dinner.

I took the subway to Herald Square, transferred to the PATH train—the subway that runs under the Hudson River to New Jersey—and made it to Hoboken, Frank Sinatra's former water-front hometown, in under a half hour.

I hadn't been to Hoboken in a decade and the place had been transformed from working class to yuppie class, high-rise build-ings dotting the waterfront, new bars and restaurants everywhere I looked.

It seemed even muggier on this side of the river, if that was possible.

I followed Rathjay's directions, turned off the main drag and headed away from the river. Here, there were a few remaining delis and bodegas mixed in with modest homes, Rathjay's among them, tan, asbestos-sided, a metal gate.

Rathjay did not offer me a seat. We stood in his four-by-four foyer, a window fan blowing hot air at us.

"Don't know why you're bothering me with such old news," he said.

He had rough skin, a matching demeanor, and a good point. But I wanted to know why O'Reilly had beaten a man to death with his fists, then killed himself, and there weren't many people to ask.

I opened O'Reilly's case folder and showed Rathjay his picture.

"I don't remember him," he said. "You wasted your time coming here."

I reminded him of O'Reilly's broken ankle, and for a moment something slid across his face, then disappeared.

I'd brought a picture of O'Reilly's CS with me and showed him.

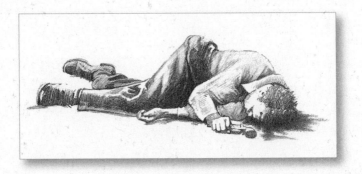

"If you're trying to scare me you're going to have to do better than that," he said. "You ever see a man blown to pieces, Detective, someone who just lost an arm or leg staggering about, looking for it?"

"No, and I'm not trying to scare you or have a pissing contest,

Lieutenant, but O'Reilly killed a man and I thought you could help." I put the pictures away. "I'm sorry I bothered you."

"Hold on," he said. "It's just that I had a lot of men serve under me and I can't remember them all." He rubbed a hand across his forehead.

"I'm not asking about all of them, just one; one you had drinks with."

"Did I?" Rathjay said it as if he really wanted an answer.

"That's what his ex-wife says. You called him and then had drinks."

"O'Reilly . . . Oh . . . yes . . . of course." He seemed to relax as soon as he remembered and motioned for me to follow him into the living room, where he sagged into an armchair, rubbed his forehead again, and frowned. "My memory isn't what it used to be."

"Do you have any dizziness or headaches?"

"Why?" he asked, the irritation and defensiveness back in his voice. "You a doctor?"

"No, it's just that a lot of soldiers have symptoms like that and—"

"You going to start on that Gulf War syndrome crap with me?"

"I just thought—"

"Well, you thought wrong. I'm fine. You get a little older you forget a few things, that's all."

"How old are you, Lieutenant?"

"Turned forty-eight yesterday."

"Happy Birthday," I said, realizing I'd judged him to be at least a decade older, but still too young to be losing his memory. "I'm sure you're fine."

He sucked in his gut. "I try to stay fit."

"So what can you tell me about James O'Reilly?"

"I'm not sure I remember anything," he said, shaking his head.

"Let's try something. Just close your eyes for a minute."

"Why?" he said, suspicious again.

"Just go with me on this, okay?" I explained my job to him. "I work with lots of people and get them to remember things they thought they'd forgotten—and I'm pretty good at it."

He closed his eyes.

"Can you picture the barracks at Fort Dix?"

"Sure, that's easy."

"Great. Hold that picture in your mind."

"Got it."

"Okay, you're in the barracks with your men, with O'Reilly. Now think of something specific, something physical, a picture on the wall, or—"

Rathjay's eyes were moving under his lids. "My sister sent me a quilt she made, all flowers, you know. I can see it plain as day. I put it on my bed and one of the men, not an enlisted man, a fellow officer, made a crack about it and later O'Reilly said that the guy was jealous and I thought it was a damn nice thing to say, you know."

He smiled, recalling the event, happy, I think, just to remember it.

"It was sometime after basic training—and I'd run my men pretty hard, for their own good, you understand, because they were going to need it when they went into combat—but by then I had a good relationship with them."

"Okay, stay with me, Lieutenant. You're in the barracks, your sister's quilt is on the bed, and O'Reilly made the comment about the officer being jealous."

"Okay . . ."

"Are you doing anything special?"

"We were playing cards. That was it, nothing special." He

smiled. "Me, O'Reilly, a few of the men, it had gotten to be a regular thing. I can see us playing cards and O'Reilly telling jokes. He was one of those life-of-the-party types, funny, good-natured."

"How'd he break his ankle?"

I watched Rathjay struggle to remember again, his eyes pressed tight.

"Oh, right, we were doing calisthenics and he tripped on something. Drill sergeant went ballistic, started screaming at him until he realized the poor guy couldn't even stand." He opened his eyes. "Weird thing was when we got back from the tour, O'Reilly didn't want to play cards anymore; he didn't want to do anything. Barely spoke to anyone. It was like *he* was the one who'd seen action and was the worse for it. It didn't make sense. He'd sat behind a desk while his platoon went off to fight and *he* was the one acting all fucked up." Rathjay rubbed his temple.

"You okay?"

"Just a headache," he said. "I kept asking O'Reilly what was wrong, but he wouldn't, or couldn't, say. Maybe it was because he felt bad that the rest of us had gone off and he stayed behind. One of the men didn't make it back."

"Do you know if he was seeing an army shrink?"

"I don't know. There's no hospital at Fort Dix. Used to be, Walson Army Hospital, but they closed it before we shipped out." He rubbed at his temple again. "I guess it's possible he could have been seeing someone off the base, some of the men did that to avoid the ribbing, you know. But if Jimmy was seeing a shrink it sure as hell wasn't doing him any good. He was depressed, and just sort of out of it. I worried he was taking drugs. I asked him, too, but he wouldn't say." Rathjay frowned. "After he was discharged I called his home to see how he was doing and he said okay and a couple of weeks later I was off duty and went to see him. But he wasn't okay. I went one more time but it wasn't much fun sitting across from a guy who wouldn't talk, so that was that." He sighed. "The army was my life, Detective. Twenty-eight years, you know. I never had time for much else. And they asked me to resign. The doc said I was fine, and I *am*."

"I'm sure you are."

"Sometimes I can remember, you saw that, right?"

"I did. You were sharp as a tack."

"I appreciate that, son." He pushed himself out of the chair. "I just need a couple of aspirin, that's all."

21

The PATH train's air-conditioning was good but I was sweating.

I was going to be late for dinner.

It was already eight-fifteen and I had only just passed the Fourteenth Street station. There were two more stops till Forty-second, and then I'd have to walk to Forty-sixth and over to Eighth Avenue.

I pictured Terri sitting at a table with my mother, a forced smile that concealed murderous thoughts: *Your son, oh, he's a dead man. Have some more wine, Mrs. Rodriguez.*

The train let me out in the middle of Times Square. It was crowded with tourists taking pictures and moving slowly. I elbowed past one group, shimmied through another, the air hot and thick.

By the time I got to the restaurant I was a mess. I took a deep breath, did my best to smooth my T-shirt, and went in.

The hostess who greeted me smiled and I blessed her for not mistaking me for a bum.

"Your party is waiting," she said. Something I already knew.

Orso is one of those chic theater district restaurants where you can eat at six to make an eight-o'clock curtain, but it's a lot cooler to eat at eight, when the out-of-towners are in a show and the place is left to New Yorkers and movie stars.

Tonight Alec Baldwin was holding court with the cast of *Saturday Night Live*, but I was too stressed to slow down and ogle them.

I saw my mother and Terri before they saw me, a half-empty carafe of red wine between them, each with a glass in hand, and they were laughing.

Were they laughing about me? Had I lost my mind, putting my girlfriend and my mother together? I'd never done that before. But then, there had never been a Terri before.

I took a deep breath.

My mother saw me and stood up to plant a kiss on my cheek. I caught a whiff of her perfume and it brought on scattered scenes from the movie of *My Life With Mom*—from drying my tears on the first day of kindergarten to cutting school, meetings with the principal, and finally that night when I couldn't dry her tears or she mine—two cops standing in our apartment telling us what happened—*two shots in the head; one in the heart*—all the air going out of the room; my life, and hers, changed forever.

"Oh, honey, you shouldn't have bothered to dress up," she said, giving me the once-over.

"Sorry," I said, smoothing my T-shirt again. "I was on a case and it got late. I wanted to stop home and change, but—" Why did I feel fourteen, and guilty of something—of everything? "Sorry," I said again. "If I'd gone home to change I would have been even later."

"Not possible," said Terri.

I gave her an I-couldn't-help-it shrug, and she gave me a smile that was closer to a sneer.

I told her she looked great and told my mother the same, both statements true.

My mother is fifty-six but looks forty, a total gym nut, and she looks like she's in better shape than me; tonight, wearing a stretchy top and black slacks with about eight Native American silver bracelets on one wrist and more or less the same on the other. It was sort of her trademark. She had been wearing them for as long as I could remember and I'd always liked them because they were a Captain-Hook-and-the-crocodile sort of thing—the bracelets broadcasting her arrival and giving me a chance to hide my stash.

My father used to say that when she rolled over in bed he would get up and get dressed before he realized it had been her bracelets and not the alarm clock, a story that always made my mother roll her eyes and correct him by pointing out she did not wear her bracelets to bed.

It made me smile to think of it.

"You need a haircut," she said.

My mother always thinks I need a haircut. I could shave my head and she'd say I needed a haircut. Maybe it was just her way of saying hello; saying something that we both understood didn't mean anything. She looked at me, then away, a habit she'd developed since my father had died. I recognized it because I did the same thing.

"Well, you look great," I said again.

She never seemed to age, her eyes bright and blue as ever, light brown hair streaked blond. No one ever figured us for mother and son; the only feature I had shared with her, my once long straight nose—broken twice in teenage brawls and once playing hardball—now had more in common with a prizefighter.

I smoothed my hair again and she reached for my hand.

"Oh, you've stopped biting your nails."

Clearly, I was getting the Judith Epstein Rodriguez assessment.

"I never bit my nails," I said.

"You know what I mean, the way you pick at your cuticles."

"Are these the sort of questions you ask your clients when you do therapy?"

The orbicularis oris muscles twitched at the corners of her mouth and she said she was sorry, but I felt sorrier for snapping.

"I painted his fingertips with that nail-biting stuff," said Terri.

"Really?" said my mom. "That's exactly what I did to stop him from sucking his thumb!"

"How old was he?" asked Terri.

"You don't have to answer that," I said to my mom.

"Twelve," she said.

"*Twelve?*" Terri hooted.

I ordered a Scotch, neat.

"Your mother was just telling me about Colorado," said Terri. "It sounds really nice."

"I like it much better than Virginia Beach," she said. "I'm glad I made the move. Nate, you should bring Terri for a visit sometime."

I gave my mother a look and said nothing, but Terri caught it, so I said, "Sure."

"And I mean it," said my mother.

"Thanks, Judy," said Terri.

"You're welcome anytime, sweetie," said my mother.

Judy? Sweetie? When had that happened?

It seemed like my mother approved of Terri, but asking me to bring her to Colorado was really her way of asking *me* to visit more often. Still, Terri must have scored some points, though I could see she was still nervous, pouring herself another glass of wine when she rarely drank more than a few sips.

"So what's the case that kept you so late?" my mother asked.

"Nate is working with me," said Terri, "in Homicide."

I was surprised Terri would talk about the case, though I guessed it was the wine talking.

"So what did you get from Beamer's shrink?" she continued.

My mother leaned in, interested.

"He said Beamer was either suffering from Gulf War syndrome, or PTSD, or both."

"Post-traumatic stress disorder," my mother said. "That puts him in the same boat as half of my practice."

"Really?" said Terri.

"My practice is right near Fort Carson," she said. "The number of returning soldiers with the disease is up something like twenty-five percent thanks to the war. Everyone thinks PTSD is a new thing, but it's been around for centuries. If you have a war, people are going to get screwed up—shell-shocked, battle fatigue, PTSD—whatever you want to call it. It's all the same thing."

"What about suicide?" asked Terri. "Is that part of it?"

"It can be. There were six at Fort Carson in the past year and that's only the ones that are known. I'm treating a soldier right now, twenty years old, three tours of combat, lost half his hearing in a car bombing, can't sleep or eat, and his superior officer calls him a coward and a fag because he doesn't believe that post-traumatic stress disorder is a real illness." She let out a deep sigh. "The soldiers come to me so their buddies and commanding officers won't know. Half the soldiers suffering with the disease don't seek *any* help because they're afraid of being belittled or ostracized. The army is trying to educate their personnel but they had better hurry. Someone suffering with PTSD is a time bomb that can go off at any time, and it doesn't take much. Anything can trigger the original trauma—a sound, a smell. A soldier comes home, a car backfires and he runs for cover. You know how many wives of soldiers suffering with PTSD wake up in the middle of the night with their husbands' hands around their throats? Too many."

"Jesus," said Terri.

"Yes." My mother kept going, on a roll, with two eager listeners, and I was happy she'd shifted her focus away from me. "I want to tell those wives to get the hell out of there but professionally I can't. Eventually they do leave because living with someone who has the disorder is hell. I'm sure you read about the Fort Bragg murders, four soldiers who killed their wives in a five-, six-week period. The army said they were all having marital problems before they were deployed and it was a coincidence." My mother's bracelets clinked and clanged as she spoke and it kept bringing me back to moments in my childhood, like Pavlov's dog or Proust's madeleines.

"Hell of a coincidence," said Terri.

"Of course they all self-medicate with alcohol and drugs to get relief, and it's the worst thing you can do."

"That's what our guys were doing," I said, and told her more about the Meth and Dexedrine in Beamer's and O'Reilly's tox screens.

"Very common," she said. "Something to escape with, but it totally screws with the prescribed meds. In the case of speed it counteracts the effects of the anti-anxiety drugs."

"So why take it?" Terri asked.

I could have answered the question from my own personal history, but decided to let my mother take it, which she did.

"Because it's a high," she said, "at least temporarily. And these guys are all so depressed, it gives them a break from that, for a while. You know, like you're blue so you have a drink and it's okay until you have the second and third, and then the booze wears off and you feel even worse than before. For those of us who know better, or are not predisposed to addiction, we stop, but with PTSD sufferers they often get caught in the cycle of addiction because their demons are too real and too terrifying."

I thought about my own demons, the ones I used to numb with booze and drugs. They would always be with me, but nowadays I faced them sober.

"These guys," my mother said, "they're explosive but emotionally shut down, so you can't talk to them. And the anger—" She waved a hand and her bracelets clanked. "You and I, our anger builds, you get annoyed, then angry, then angrier, right? But these guys go from A to Z in two seconds."

I was trying to make sense of it, Beamer's PTSD, wondering what it was that had finally set him off. "But why, after years of suffering from the condition, would someone *suddenly* explode?"

"No one really knows, though I'd say with most chronic PTSD sufferers it's not a matter of *will* they explode, but *when*? I guess with your guy it just took a long time."

"That might explain Beamer," said Terri. "He saw combat. But it doesn't explain O'Reilly, who didn't." She explained it for my mother, who listened attentively.

"If he exploded like that, then there had to be some trauma in his past," she said. "We now know that trauma actually changes your brain chemistry."

"I've read that happens with rape victims," said Terri. "But can someone have post-traumatic stress disorder without having had a serious trauma?"

"No. It has to be something traumatizing—though not necessarily combat." My mother raised the wineglass to her lips but didn't drink. "I could talk this over with Chris, if you'd like. He treats PTSD exclusively. I've learned most of what I know about the disease from him."

"Who's Chris?" I asked.

"Oh . . ." My mother took a long drink of her wine. "The psychologist who joined the practice a year ago. He's become . . . a friend." She arched a brow and twisted her lips, the asymmetry of her facial anatomy practically screaming: *I am lying.*

Do you think your mom liked me?" Terri slipped out of her blouse and tossed it to a chair—a first, she always hung things up. "And why the hell did you let me drink all that wine? She must think I'm a total drunk."

"I'm sure she doesn't think that."

"If you hadn't been late I wouldn't have had those two glasses of wine before you came. I could just kill you, Rodriguez."

"I'm sorry. And you did fine." I was still thinking about the PTSD and the soldiers who killed their wives.

"She invited me to visit, that was a good sign, wasn't it?"

I had never seen the tough Detective Russo so insecure. I ran my hand over her bare back. "Why do you care what my mother thinks?"

Terri stopped undressing and locked her eyes on me. "Oh, so you don't care what your mother thinks of me?"

"No."

"Oh, bull, I know all about mothers and sons. If the mother doesn't like you, you're toast, because she'll find a way to break it up."

"My mother does not interfere in my life. Right now I'm guessing she's just happy I have a girlfriend."

"Oh, so you mean it could have been any girl and she would have invited her to Colorado?"

"That's not what I meant." I sighed and gave her a hug. "My mother liked you."

"How can you be so sure?"

"Because she was all chatty and easy with you. I could just tell." The fact was that I hadn't seen my mother so relaxed and comfortable in years, which I attributed to Terri and told her so. "Hey, do you think my mother is involved with that shrink she mentioned, Chris?"

The thought of my mother with anyone but my father made me wince.

"Your mother's a really attractive woman, Rodriguez; why shouldn't she have a boyfriend?"

"A *boyfriend*? What is she, sixteen?"

"Oh, grow up. Do you really think your mother closed up shop at what, thirty?"

"She was thirty-five." Pictures of my dead father started mixing with ones of my mother and a faceless man named Chris. "And frankly, yeah, I thought maybe she had."

Terri tapped the top of my head and put on a baby voice. "I know it's wery wery hard for a little boy to imagine his mommy—"

"Don't say it."

"Relax," she said. "He's probably just a professional colleague, like, uh, you and me." She giggled.

"You're drunk."

"And whose fault is *that*?"

"I told you, I was in Hoboken with O'Reilly's army commander."

"Is the room spinning?"

"No, babe, that's just you." I knew she was drunk because normally she'd have wanted a full report on everything Rathjay had said.

Instead, she took two aspirin and got into bed.

But I wasn't ready for sleep.

The dinner, the cases, the shrink, the CO, all of it had me stirred up.

I went into the studio to work on the facial reconstruction. It had become my therapy, a way to keep my hands and my mind occupied.

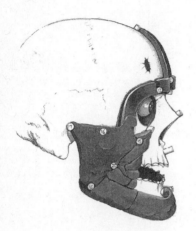

I picked up where I'd left off, moving into the jaw strip, adding larger pieces of clay to create what was called the "front triangle." I built it up around my tissue-depth markers, and did it quickly.

I checked my old notes and a couple of books to see where to go next, then made strips for the top of the head, careful to keep the clay even to approximate skin thickness while keeping in mind that my John Doe was on the heavy side.

I knew I'd be sorry in the morning, but I couldn't stop.

The whole time I worked I was thinking about Beamer and O'Reilly and post-traumatic stress disorder, soldiers who killed their wives, and my mother saying that if it wasn't combat that had traumatized O'Reilly, it was something just as bad.

22

R-E-S-P-E-C-T . . . "

The tune is playing in his head over and over, Aretha Franklin wailing as if the needle got stuck on an old turntable, the kind he used to have, but no more; now he's got nothing. "I Who Have Nothing" starts up, staccato, poignant, and Aretha dies, and he feels . . . how does he feel? He doesn't know. Can't locate the place in his heart where he is supposed to feel things. He touches the front of his head—yes, it's still there—rubs at the permanent *V* between his brows, then moves to his cheeks, the skin thick, without sensation, tries to remember what happened, but can't, rubs at his eyes, digs his fists into the sockets as if trying to get right inside his brain.

Question: There is a sinking ship and not enough room on the lifeboat and you must make a choice . . . a choice . . . a choice . . .

He knows the answer but it is coming from so far away it's like another lifetime, a test he once took and passed—or did he fail? He takes a long pull of whiskey, empties the bottle, and smashes it to the ground.

The answer is . . . the answer is . . . Throw him overboard!
Correct.

Question: How many . . .

No more questions!

Just one.

The answer is . . . Yes!

I haven't asked the question.

True! No, false!

Wrong test. Pay attention.

Yes? No? Yes? No? Yes? No?

You're not listening.

He puts his hands over his ears.

Stop doing that. Just listen.

I was only bringing the pizza—I never asked for this—I never—

Pain shifts from his head to chest to abdomen; hand inside his pants, he tries to arouse himself, to feel something, but it's no good; impossible.

Eyes closed, white rats racing around in metal cages, hurling themselves into walls, red eyes like lasers.

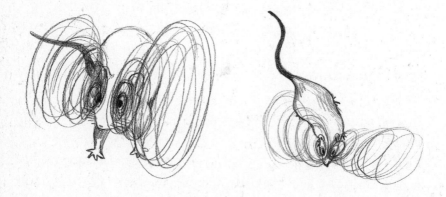

More music—"Losing My Religion"—coming from . . . where? A radio? TV? Brain waves? Microwaves? Tidal waves!

Hypothalamus . . . suprachiasmatic nucleus . . .

Voices: from the past, the present, the future?

It's okay. Don't think. Just act. Do it. Do it!

A squirrel skitters by. Then another.

Rats. White rats.

Do it! Do it! You still have the lightning-fast reflexes. You can't be touched. Go on. Kill Kill Kill.

One fast jab, the knife in, squirrel impaled on the tree. *Take that!*

The animal twitches, jerks, blood dripping down the trunk.

He turns and sees the crowd. *Who are they? The enemy—and why are they screaming?*

He screams back: "It's a rat! A fucking rat! It was going to attack me!"

Colors whirl in front of his eyes. Music pumping in his brain, he tugs the knife out of the tree and the rat drops to the ground.

And now he sees the crowd for what they are—rats, huge rats, red-eyed rats, their screams hideous rat shrieks, and one of them, the biggest rat of all, is trying to get the knife out of his hand and there is no way, no fucking way!

Kill Kill Kill.

The colors stop. The music fades.

He looks down at the ground, a man, curled up, twitching; and the knife in his hand, dripping red, and he feels . . . nothing, not scared or sad, nothing. But his scalp is itching so bad and his brain aches and there is that familiar popping sound and the slight *ping* of something electric and the smell of burned toast, and when he turns the knife on himself and plunges it into his chest he is not afraid to twist it and push it deeper until he feels it tear his heart to pieces.

23

I'm sorry," she said. "I can't see the face anymore."

We'd been working for about fifteen minutes, my office airless and oppressive, the air-conditioning for shit, but the witness was shivering. She tried to smile, her swollen lower lip not quite cooperating, hands shaking. I took a chance and laid mine over hers.

"It's okay," I said. "You're doing great. It will come back."

I was feeling pretty ragged myself after last night—the wine, the Scotch, my mother, Terri, staying up half the night working on a forensic sculpture that no one was paying me for.

I was doing double duty, working with Terri's task force and still making sketches. But I didn't want to give anything up. I loved my forensic artwork but had to admit I loved working Homicide, too. Making a sketch—when it worked—you got results in a half hour, instant gratification. Homicide took a little longer. But I liked following the clues and connecting the dots, though so far they were few and far between.

I turned to my bookcase, the shelf where I kept old yearbooks, eyeglass catalog, tattoo magazines, and the FBI Facial Identification Catalog, which I plucked out and handed to the witness. While she perused page after page of features—noses, eyes, eyebrows, lips—I chose a few pictures from my personal archive, faces I'd been collecting for years, all laminated and sealed under plastic. I've learned that some people do better when they have something tangible to look at, something that will jog their memory when they lose touch with what they have seen.

She went from one picture to the next, the fingers of her good hand—the one not in a sling—shaking as she moved from one to the other.

"There's something about this one," she said, selecting a picture and studying it. "I know. It's the scar! He had a scar, here." She tapped her forehead. "A whit-ish, curving scar, that went into his hairline."

It hit something in the back of my mind but I couldn't get at it.

She went from the scar to describing his wild hair and I started sketching it in.

"He was babbling half the time, nothing that made any sense," she said, her hands shaking again.

"Are you okay?"

She nodded, doing her best to be brave, and I admired her for that, though I knew she'd pay the price. You had to let it out sometime. Not that I subscribed to the spill-your-guts theory. I was president and lifetime member of the keep-it-all-in society.

"He kept touching his head—when he wasn't touching me, and—" She pulled in a deep breath. "It was like he was in pain, you know, wincing and—he was one of those crazies who should be locked away!"

"And that's what will happen. It's why you're here and why we're doing this. I know this is hard, but keep his face in your mind for just a little while longer. The more you can tell me, the easier it will be to catch him."

She nodded.

"Okay," I said, "he's babbling. Can you see his lips?"

She nodded again and described them.

Then I got her to move back to his eyes and the scar on his forehead, and we worked our way to the shape of his nose. She

was really seeing him now, describing one feature after another, even the rough texture of his skin, and I was seeing him, too.

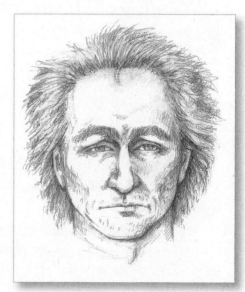

I wasn't sure how long we worked. I was lost in the sketch.

When I thought I'd gotten it all, I turned it around.

"Oh my God. That's him!" She took a deep breath and let it out slowly. "He doesn't look like much, does he, sort of sad, and not very strong? I remember thinking that, but my God, he *was* strong, maybe because he was so crazy, maybe he was on drugs. You know what he said when it was over? He said he was *sorry*."

There were tears in the corners of her eyes, the first since we'd started working, and I thought it was a good sign.

I looked over at the box of tissues I always kept beside the chair for witnesses and vics and was glad to see it was half full.

"I think my husband blames me," she said. "He told me I was stupid to be in Battery Park so late, but I'd just left my girlfriend and . . . how, how was I to know?"

"You didn't do anything wrong."

"Tell that to my husband."

"Look, here's the thing—men, we're kind of stupid. We try our best, but in the end we usually get it wrong. My guess is your husband feels guilty because he wasn't there to protect you. He's not mad at you. He's mad at himself. He'll get past it. Just give him a little time. And give yourself some, too. These sorts of things can bring you closer. It will be okay."

Her face relaxed, zygomatic major and minor muscles easing. Then the tears came full blast. She plucked a tissue out of the box, then another and another.

I turned back to my drawing so she wouldn't feel self-conscious. I added a bit more shading and when she stopped crying I told her again what a good job she'd done. Then I excused myself.

I found Schmid behind her desk and handed her the sketch.

"Nice job," she said. "I'll have copies ready to send out in the morning."

She thanked me, smiled, and asked if I was free for coffee. I told her I had a headache and a hangover—the truth—and would have to take a rain check.

• • •

Outside it felt like ninety, humidity you could slice. I was worn out and sad but it wasn't from the heat. Doing a sketch with a rape victim always took something out of me. Personally, I think men who rape and beat up women should have electrodes attached to their balls and brains, if they have any.

I thought about the guy who had attacked the woman and how she said he was crazy. Was crazy really an excuse? Wasn't everyone who committed a violent crime crazy? Defense lawyers seemed to think so, but juries didn't, and I wasn't so sure. It was a question of control, not just knowing the difference between right and wrong, wasn't it?

It brought Beamer and O'Reilly to mind, men who had committed violent crimes but must have felt remorse. Why else would they have killed themselves?

24

Witness number six, David Rappaport, and I quote: 'The guy was a complete lunatic, screaming about rats like he was in some sort of snake-pit insane-asylum movie.' "

Denton stopped reading from the witness statement and looked over the briefing room, eyes narrowed as he went from Morelli and his men to the detectives from the Central Park Division, finally to Terri and her task force and me.

I'd slipped into the meeting a few minutes late because of the sketch I'd been making. My head still ached and Denton's harangue wasn't doing it much good.

Denton exchanged the paper in his hand for another.

"Witness number ten, Maria Gonzalez: 'He stabbed the squirrel first, then the man who was trying to stop him. It was horrible. Horrible.' Witness number four, JoAnne Carson: 'I couldn't believe it, right there in Central Park, in the middle of the day, in broad daylight; my God, where were the police? I called 911. Aren't there supposed to be police in the park?' "

Denton smacked the pages onto a desk.

"I particularly like that part about where were the police.

Fourteen witnesses. *Fourteen*. And I can read most of what I just read from any one of New York's newspapers!"

The media had the story for the morning editions, thanks to some clever reporter checking the coroner's overnight log.

Denton turned to Bixby, commanding officer of the Central Park Division. "You want to tell me why there were no men in the Sheep Meadow?"

"Like I said, Chief, there'd been a mugging in Strawberry Fields and the chase took them into the Ramble and—"

"Everyone likes excuses when a man has been murdered in front of fourteen witnesses—and a couple hundred more who gathered around to watch both men die."

Bixby looked at his shoes.

One of his detectives said, "It all happened pretty fast, Chief. A couple of the witnesses say the guy was ranting one minute, next he's stuck a knife in the vic, then into himself."

"Yeah," said Denton, "that's what witnesses one through fourteen say in the *Post* and *News*."

"We're short on foot patrol," said Bixby. "As for mounted, they're basically there for traffic and wouldn't have been able to stop it if it went down as fast as reported."

"Thank you, Lieutenant, I'm sure that explanation will be a comfort to the widow of our vic, and it's good to know that our mounted police are basically worthless."

"That wasn't what I meant," said Bixby. "But the guy was one of those crazies, homeless, you know, and unpredictable, his whole life in a shopping cart, in and out of the bin and off his meds."

"Lieutenant, do you think I like standing up here and giving you shit? I'm just giving what I get, you understand? I've got to answer to higher-ups and you've got to answer to me. You want to keep making excuses, fine; I'll go to the mayor and say I'm real sorry about the incident in the park but don't worry because one of my best men assures me it was unpreventable, so what's your beef?" Denton snorted a sigh. "Hey, it's only the third murder-suicide in the city in the past two weeks, right? No big deal, nothing to get upset about. Mayor's going to like that, I know it, Bixby. He can use it when he holds the press conference to tell the good citizens of New York City that no, there is nothing in the city drinking water that is causing people to go ape-shit, which is what one of the tabloids is speculating, in case you missed it. And by the way, people, stop telling Media Relations to blame the army. I'm getting calls from their PR Department *and* the Pentagon—and some fucking colonel is coming to dress us down. I don't need this shit!"

He took a deep breath and looked at Morelli and Terri. "Do I dare fucking ask if there's been any progress?"

Morelli opened his mouth to speak and closed it.

But Terri picked up the ball. "First of all, we are not the only ones who are blaming the army," she said, very cool, very calm. "We can stop—and I will, Chief—but it's all over the media, and not just from us." Then she used my mother's statistics about returning shell-shocked soldiers and segued into the case. "We are investigating a link between the first two perpetrators, Beamer and O'Reilly, the fact that they were both suffering from post-traumatic stress syndrome." Then she brought up the suicides at Fort Carson and the murders at Fort Bragg and used the acronym PTSD about a dozen times. I knew it was essentially a smoke screen, but Denton was listening.

"Have you written this up?" he asked.

I figured he'd be regurgitating everything she said to the mayor and anyone else who was willing to listen.

"Yes. And I will get you full reports," she said.

"Very good," he said. "And make copies for the FBI, because they're coming in."

I caught the look on Terri's face, a swift microexpression, triangularis muscle tugging at her lips and chin, but she recovered quickly and neutralized her face.

There was a brief Q and A about what the feds were planning, Denton a bit evasive as he fielded the queries. Then the meeting broke up.

Denton asked Terri to stay and I hung with her team just a few feet away.

Dugan had buried his face in the *Daily News*, O'Connell hit his thermos, Perez, obviously nervous, made small talk, asking me about my Puerto Rican half like we were long-lost *hermanos*.

"Nice bullshit," I heard Denton say to Terri.

"It's the truth," she said.

"Yeah, sure," he said, "and the truth will set you free, huh? I'll use it with Hiz Honor, but I don't think the army is going to like it much."

"Maybe not," she said, "but both these guys were army, and they both cracked, and that's not bullshit."

She didn't bother to tell him that O'Reilly's crack-up didn't appear to have anything to do with the army.

"So what have you got on the new guy?"

"Still being checked out," she said.

"In other words, nada." Denton blew out a breath. "Sketch artist helping you any?" He looked in my direction.

"Yeah, in fact Rodriguez provided our first lead, the one to O'Reilly."

"Too bad you couldn't get to him before he killed himself."

"We were close," said Terri.

"Close never counts, Russo, you know that." He signaled me over. "Glad to hear you're contributing, Rodriguez."

"Doing what I can," I said.

"He's making a sculpture," she said. "But not for my team. I don't have exclusive rights on Rodriguez."

"Oh, no?" said Denton, a leer curling the corner of his lips.

"What do you call it?" Terri asked.

I could see she was using my work to distract Denton from her stalled cases.

"A sculptural reconstruction," I said.

"You know," said Terri, "one of those sculptures where you reconstruct a face from a dead man's skull. It's very cool."

"Oh, really. Which division you doing it for?" asked Denton.

I wasn't sure what to say. It was no longer NYPD business or NYPD-sanctioned. I wished Terri hadn't brought it up. "I'm just doing it to see if I can."

"But where'd you get the skull? You didn't kill anyone, did you, Rodriguez?" He gave me a look, something between a smile and a sneer.

"It's for Guthrie," said Terri, "up in the Bronx, a John Doe."

"Well, not anymore." I gave Terri a look. I didn't like her speaking for me.

"Guthrie's John Doe?" said Denton. "I didn't think that case was still active."

"It isn't," I said. "I'm doing it on my own time."

"Really?" Denton assessed me, one eye squinting. "Just don't send a bill to the NYPD."

"Wouldn't think of it," I said.

25

The naked body of a thirty-three-year-old black man, Floyd Billow, aka the Central Park Madman, as the press was calling him, was laid out on a stainless-steel slab, torso V-cut, flesh and muscle peeled back like one of those anatomical dioramas in a biology book, flesh gray-brown, organs waxy and purple.

This was getting to be a habit, me and Baumgarten spending our lunch hour together. Terri had sent me and Perez, the two of us now in matching paper suits.

Baumgarten was huddled over the body, plastic shield over his face to protect him from blood splatter, green gloves up to his elbows, apron from neck to knees.

"Take a look at this," he said, tapping the man's cheeks.

"Zit scars?" Perez asked.

"This wasn't caused by teenage acne." Baumgarten took hold of my gloved hand and poked my finger into Billow's cheek.

"It feels hard," I said.

"Yes. It's old scarring, years old, but I'm not sure what caused it."

"What about this?" I indicated another faint scar on his forehead and immediately thought about the rapist I had just sketched.

"It's not the same. I can check to see if it's superficial or goes deeper when I take off his skullcap." He moved down the body, flipped over a wedge of flesh that covered half the chest. "Look, it's here, too."

There were rippling scars similar to the ones on the cadaver's face.

Baumgarten poked at the tough flesh. "It's like leather."

"Do you think he was tortured?" I asked.

Baumgarten shook his head. "It doesn't look as if these scars were made with any sort of weapon, and they're not burns either. Maybe it's some kind of skin condition, but it's going to take some research." He continued to move down and lifted the man's penis, which was the size of a salami.

"Home of the whopper!" said Perez.

"Postmortem bloat," said Baumgarten.

"It should happen to me," said Perez.

"It will," said Baumgarten. "When you're dead." He aimed his scalpel at a small scar. "But look at this."

"Vasectomy?" I asked.

"Uh-huh."

"And he's got no balls," said Perez.

"Almost right," said Baumgarten. "They're here, but they're totally shrunken. I've seen this with men who have had their testes radiated for cancer."

"So he had cancer?" I asked.

Baumgarten aimed a scalpel at a chart lying on a nearby table. "Not according to the records from Bellevue where your perp had two stints, one as recent as six months ago. There's a complete medical in there if you want to check it out, but you can't take it, not yet."

"I know," I said. "Not until we get written permission."

"You copping an attitude with me, Rodriguez?"

"Me, never. I'm with you, Baumgarten; it's all about the paper."

"Comedian," said Baumgarten. He referred back to the medical report. "Your man here had what they note as 'possible scleroderma,' a rare skin disease."

"So that explains the scarring," said Perez.

"I don't think so. I can see why they confused it, but scleroderma is an autoimmune illness, and fatal. If it had progressed this far on the outside I'd see evidence of it on the inside because it goes into the organs and even the vascular system. I'm guessing Mr. Billow's physical problems were not the main concern of the doctors at Bellevue, so they probably never checked further."

"But what about the no balls?" asked Perez.

"I don't know yet," said Baumgarten. "I was just speculating about the radiation. There are any number of diseases that might have contributed to the shrinking of his testes."

"It's not a side effect of the vasectomy, is it?" I asked.

"You think any man in his right mind would get the operation if it was?"

Baumgarten made a good point.

"You ever read about the prison experiments in the sixties and seventies in, uh, I think it was Oregon? They got prisoners to *volunteer*"—Baumgarten made quotes in the air with his gloved fingers—"then they zapped their testicles with radiation for a couple of years. They were testing to see if they could figure out an easy male contraceptive, aka sterilization. That, plus, they wanted to see the effects of radiation on sexual function and the body in general."

"And they got away with this?"

Baumgarten nodded. "You know, I once heard a scientist say

that prisoners were the perfect lab rats—they're not going anywhere and no one gives a shit what you do to them."

"Real nice," I said.

"But Billow's prints went through the system," said Perez. "He had arrests for vagrancy and spent time in halfway houses and mental hospitals, but never prison."

"And those experiments were well before his time," said Baumgarten.

"What about his tox?" Perez asked.

"Haven't gotten it yet, but take a look at this." He pulled away muscle to expose a dark brownish-purple organ. "Cirrhosis of the liver. See the scarring there, that's fibrosis, the man was a drinker." He lifted the dead man's hand and I noticed his fingertips.

"Is that blood?"

"No, it's ink."

"Ink?"

"Yes, red ink, like from a pen, probably a permanent marker." *A marker. Red ink.*

"Where's his stuff?" I asked, my mind going into overdrive. "He had a full shopping cart, right?"

"It's in evidence," said Perez. "But there's nothing there you want to see, believe me."

26

When I saw who was on duty outside the evidence room I almost turned around, but it was too late.

Conchita Morales slapped her Spanish love comic onto the desk and gave me her hundred-watt-bright-red-lipstick smile.

"Oh, oh, oh, Rodreeeeguez."

"How's it going, Morales?" I said, as flat as possible.

"Why you never call me Conchita, *papi*?"

"Conchita," I said, and manufactured a smile.

She batted her lashes.

I was almost sorry Perez was not with me to take some of her heat, but he'd stayed behind to deal with Baumgarten's paperwork.

"I need to see the Central Park Madman's possessions."

"You can see anything you want, baby." Morales wiggled around in her seat and slid a form across her desk. "But first you got to fill this out, *papi*."

I hunched over the desk to fill out the form, Morales's perfume so strong I could hardly breathe.

"Nice perfume," I said. "Something you brewed yourself?"

Morales cackled. *"Eres tan chistoso, papi."*

Yeah, I was funny, all right. I handed her the form and she

made a show of tugging the key from her pocket as if she were doing a strip tease, then worked her ass out of the chair and stood up to unlock the door.

"Here you go, *guapo*." She handed me a pair of gloves. "Just remember, you gotta sign out anything you want to take, *papi*, so don't go putting things in your *pants*."

The evidence room was a mess: shelves crammed with cartons— old cases closer to the ceiling, dusty and cobwebbed; newer ones on lower shelves in bins marked with case numbers; some larger items tagged independently, like the shopping cart that was pushed against a rear wall, exactly what I was looking for, but empty.

I went through the lower bins looking for numbers that corresponded to the one on the cart. It took me a half hour of combing through ziplocked bags, bloodstained clothes, shoes, rusty knives, revolvers, an assortment of household items—iron, candlestick, rolling pin, all weapons that made me think of that board game, *Clue—Colonel Mustard in the dining room with the candlestick.* I finally found three large bins hidden on the bottom shelf, already relegated as unimportant, which the first bin confirmed: two pairs of shoes, brown and black, both scuffed and worn; three mismatched sneakers, Nike, Converse, Keds; a hooded sweatshirt, stained; a metal dish, three forks, a half dozen plastic spoons, a coffee mug caked with dirt, and a paper bag stuffed with packets of ketchup, mayonnaise, and grape jelly.

Bin number two contained an empty tissue box, a roll of toilet paper, an old transistor radio, and two blankets that set me itching. The third produced a broken gooseneck lamp, a thermos that rattled, two record albums—Jefferson Starship and REM—an assortment of threadbare sweaters, and a filthy gray woolen coat.

I had not found what I was absolutely certain would be there. Disappointed, I began putting the scattered contents away, when on a hunch I put a gloved hand into one of the coat's pockets and found a crumpled piece of paper. I flattened it on the evidence room's wooden floor.

The other pocket produced more of the same.

At first they looked like scribbles. Then I saw one was all numbers, the other had the word *true*, repeated over and over in red ink.

I knew that getting a requisition to take evidence would be a big deal but I didn't see how these would be missed, so I took off a glove, folded the pictures, and then did exactly what Morales had told me not to: I hid them in my pants.

27

I had them all laid out on the desk in my office—a new one from Billow's coat pocket, Beamer's sketch pad, and a picture of O'Reilly's blood-painted wall. Terri was sitting in the chair usually reserved for my witnesses, legs tucked under her.

"I keep coming back to why three men who didn't know one another would be making similar sketches," she said.

"Well, that's what I'd like to find out," I said.

"Maybe it's some sort of code," she said, "but I can't imagine our homeless perp working with code, can you?"

I looked from one picture to the other, my heart beating fast. There was something here; I felt it. "I don't know, but isn't it enough that all three perps made these weird drawings? I mean, it's something that connects them."

"But *how* does it connect them?"

Terri wasn't trying to be difficult, she was being a cop, asking the right questions, and I was frustrated by my failure to come up with answers. She stared at the images, the look on her face a complicated mix, excitement in her eyes, mouth pulling back with just the slightest touch of fear. I could see from her facial anatomy that she was resisting the idea of a connection even when she saw it, but then her facial muscles relaxed into a kind of acceptance. Our faces can't help but register emotions automatically—and truly.

I remembered what Silvan Tomkins, one of the pioneers of facial psychology, had said during a lecture, "The face is like a penis!"

The face, he explained, just reacts, our thoughts and emotions played out by muscles, tendons, and flesh that we cannot control. But I was pretty sure Terri wouldn't want to hear me say her face was like a penis.

"There's something else we need to discuss," she said.

"You found out I stole the drawings?"

"What?"

I tapped one of the crumpled sketches from Billow's pocket. "I took them from Evidence and didn't sign them out because I knew Morales was going to give me a hard time."

"More likely she'd want to give you a *hard-on*." Terri laughed. "No, who cares about that. It's about the G coming in."

"Like Denton said."

"It's the reason he chewed everyone out. I think he's embarrassed his men can't fix it and they had to send in the feds. I don't know what part they're going to play, if they're going to Bigfoot us on this or not. Could be they're just here to watch, to babysit."

"You know the G," I said. "They let the locals do the heavy lifting and they take the bows."

"You know, I don't really care if the G wants in or not, but

Denton said that my failure to produce on this case could cost me my task force."

"He's just jerking your chain, you know Denton."

"I think he'd really like to see me fail." She frowned. "But I can never tell, every conversation I have with that guy is like one big double entendre."

"Speaking of conversations, I would have preferred that you hadn't mentioned the sculptural reconstruction I'm working on."

"You mean to Denton, why?"

"Because it's no longer his business. The case was closed, remember? *You* won me in the raffle, not Guthrie."

"So what's the big deal if I mentioned it?"

"Because it's my business and I just wish you hadn't talked about it, that's all."

Terri sat back and folded her arms across her chest. "Do I need permission to talk about you?"

"Hey, you were the one who wanted to keep our personal lives out of work, remember?"

"I didn't think this was personal—or a secret."

"It's not a secret. Just something I'm doing on my own time, not the PD's, therefore *my* business."

"So what do you want me to do, ten Hail Marys?"

"For a start."

Terri sighed. "Okay, I won't talk about your shit ever again."

"Fine," I said.

There was an awkward moment, both of us quiet.

"Look, I'm just worried about Denton's plans for me, do you get that?"

"Yeah, I do."

"I'll tell you one thing: If Denton thinks he's putting me back in hot pants he's got another thing coming."

"You're getting way ahead of yourself. You're a good cop, and Denton knows it."

"You think a good cop never got screwed over, Rodriguez? I think he's just waiting for me to slip up again so he can hang me out to dry."

"So don't give him a reason. We're still on the case and we're going to get something. Trust me, okay?"

"I do. Why else would I be sitting in your hot as hell office looking at these three nut-job drawings that I wish to God you'd never put together?" She sighed. "So, you're going over to Bellevue, right?"

"Yeah, they're expecting me."

"And then?"

"Home. What about you?"

"I'm working late." She stood up to go. "Just don't let those Bellevue shrinks look inside your head, Rodriguez."

28

I could take the institutional green walls. I could even take the smell of feces and disinfectant. What I couldn't take were the bars on the windows. I kept thinking one of the burly-looking order-lies would slam a door, throw the lock, and there I'd be, hands curled around the bars, Nurse Ratchet coming to fetch me for a lobotomy.

Dr. Kaminetsky looked the part—graying temples, white lab coat, clipboard against his chest—but he seemed like a nice enough guy.

"This is a general in-patient floor," he said as I followed him down the hall. "Criminal offenders are one floor above." He aimed his clipboard toward the ceiling. "Don't worry. We've got double-locked doors and an alarm system."

I pictured Anthony Hopkins, face pressed against Plexiglas, taunting Jodie Foster.

"And Billow was up there?"

"No, he was on this floor. He hadn't committed a crime, not yet."

We came to a set of double doors, and the doctor used his card to open it.

"I thought the locked doors were upstairs?"

"The steel ones. We have precautions down here as well, though it's mainly to protect the patients. We don't want anyone to get lost. This floor houses patients who do not pose a threat." He stopped, hand on the door, and considered his statement. "Of course, in retrospect it appears as if Floyd Billow should have been on the floor above."

"Did he seem violent to you, crazy?" I asked.

"We don't much care for that word around here. It's not exactly a therapeutic term," he said, but smiled. "But no, Billow was agitated and anxious but did not appear to be dangerous." He pushed the doors open. "Here we are."

The day room, as Dr. Kaminetsky called it, was big and antiseptic-looking: white walls, cold fluorescent light, a TV hanging from the ceiling, Ping-Pong table, couple of card tables, easy chairs, a wall of windows hermetically sealed but no bars. The odor of Lysol was strong, but unable to mask the smell of baked fish and human anxiety.

There were a couple of guys playing Ping-Pong, one mumbling; a foursome at a card table, no one speaking; a dozen men in front of the TV, half of them asleep; another five or six milling around in hospital gowns and booties. All the attendants were black, and they stood guard while a nurse dispensed pills.

Kaminetsky must have caught my look because he said, "You get used to it."

I didn't think I would.

We crossed the room, doped eyes trailing us, and settled into a couple of seats in a corner.

I asked the doctor to tell me about Floyd Billow and he referred to his clipboard. "Arrested for vagrancy in May, but refused to go to a shelter."

"I read the arrest sheet. I meant your observations, and your diagnosis."

"Billow was a paranoid schizophrenic who seemed to hear voices. He would often carry on conversations with himself, ask questions and answer them."

I recalled that several witnesses to the Central Park attack had said that Billow was talking to himself.

"We'd stabilized him with medication and he seemed fine, so there was no reason to keep him here. You have to understand that it costs the taxpayers a lot of money, so we do our best to release patients as soon as possible. Don't get me wrong, we do not toss mentally incompetent people out into the street—"

"Forgive me if I sound naive, Doctor, but to send a paranoid schizophrenic back onto the street just seems, well . . ."

"Mr. Billow had been here for seven weeks. With medication he was lucid and even-tempered when he left." He sat up and looked at me, the area around his eyes tightening. "Detective, who do you think is paying for all *this*?" He swept a hand toward the scene behind us. "You, me, and every other citizen. And I can tell you this: If you stop people on the street and ask if they would like to donate a portion of their salary to house mental patients, they will say no. I volunteer a day and a half here every week. That's a day and half away from my practice—which *used* to be quite lucrative—now spent filling out insurance forms for HMOs so that I can get paid. So please, do not come here and judge me."

"I'm sorry," I said, and I was.

He waved away my apology. "You just voiced what everyone thinks: How dare we release all those nutcases into the streets. But no one wants to do anything about it. I'm sorry, too, Detective. I'm sorry about the state of the mental health care system and I'm damn sorry about Mr. Billow and what happened, believe me."

He shook his head and took a deep breath. "No one wants to be reminded of sickness and death. No one wants to see a person who has lost control. Mental illness isn't pretty, so we shut it away, out of sight. But then no one wants to pay for it. This is a state hospital and our funding gets cut every year."

I apologized again.

"No." He sighed. "I didn't mean to go off on you. It's just that you hit a sensitive spot."

His phrasing brought me back to Billow. "What about the scars on his body, his face, and chest?"

"I believe a diagnosis of—" He referred to his clipboard again. "Scleroderma."

"Which our chief medical examiner says is incorrect."

"Really? It was on his chart, which came to me from his last stay. The diagnosis was probably made some time ago, and never reexamined."

"Do you think he could have been tortured?"

The doctor took a moment to consider that. "It's possible, but Billow never said so."

"And did you know he was sterilized?"

"You mean his vasectomy."

"It appears he may have had more than that."

Kaminetsky arched his brows. He was about to say something when a Ping-Pong ball rolled between our feet. I looked up and a man in hospital gown and slippers was standing in front of us, mouth open, eyes droopy, hand extended.

I placed the ball in his palm and he turned away without a word.

The doctor watched the patient shuffle off. "Billow never talked about torture or sterilization, I can assure you. The fact is he didn't tell me much about his past and I'm not sure he could.

It was as if he'd forgotten it or blocked it out. Of course he had a severe drinking problem, which might have been the cause of his memory loss. On his correct medication he seemed like a gentle man beaten down by the world. The only thing he ever told me was that he had grown up poor, somewhere in New Jersey." The doctor flipped through several pages of Billow's history. "Here you go, New Hanover, New Jersey, but he never gave a street address."

"Any relatives?"

"Only thing he's written down here is 'Mother,' but no name or information about her. I can't tell you if she's alive or dead."

"Didn't the hospital try to speak to his next of kin?"

"I'm sure they did, but I guess they never reached her."

I made a note to look for anyone named Billow living in or around New Hanover, New Jersey, then I smoothed one of Billow's drawings onto the coffee table.

"Ah, Mr. Billow's *artwork*."

"So you know it?"

"He made drawings like that when he was delusional before we got his meds right. Once he was stabilized he stopped."

"I found this in the pocket of his coat, and there are more, maybe a dozen, so I guess he was off his meds."

"Clearly," said Kaminetsky.

"Can you tell me what it means, the word *true*?"

"I observed him making drawings like this many times, but I really don't know."

"Can you describe what he was like when he was drawing?"

The doctor closed his eyes for a moment. "My guess, he was reliving some traumatic experience. He would often shout out and wince in pain while he made them, but they were very automatic. I mean, his mind did not seem connected to the act. His hand seemed to move on its own. I asked him about them in our therapy sessions and he said they were—what did he call them?" The doctor scanned his notes. *"Diaries."*

"Of what?"

"He never said."

"Do you think it's significant that they're red?"

"Billow couldn't tell me. When I showed them to him he acted as if someone else had made them."

"Like a multiple-personality sort of thing?"

"No." The doctor glanced away, then back. "I'd say when he made them he was in a fugue state, you know, an entirely different time and place."

29

I'd been asleep when Terri came in around 1:00 A.M., the two of us too tired to exchange more than a missed kiss. I went back to sleep and she'd joined me. And then we'd overslept; Terri racing off to a meeting, me to make a sketch.

My sketch had gone okay, though the witness—an elderly man who'd seen a robbery from his window—was impatient and it took me a while to settle him into the process. By the time I'd finished I was late for the big meeting and had missed the "dressing-down" from the army colonel, a blessing, according to Terri.

"You know the type," she said, "silver crew cut, square jaw, puffed-up chest covered with more medals than 50 Cent has bling."

"Central Casting," said O'Connell.

We were in Terri's office, an eight-by-ten box with one window but a much better view than mine: couple of inches of Hudson River between two brick buildings; the walls painted a mossy gray. She told me she'd gotten the idea from watching Martha Stewart, who said green was a restful color, but if I ever repeated that to anyone she promised she would kill me. There were no personal items on her desk; no photos or knickknacks; mainly case files, open and recently closed, the open stack taller. Her computer was on, the screen saver a picture of cops and firemen from 9/11, above it, a framed citation from the mayor's office for her work on the Sketch Artist case.

"The colonel let us know that the army did not appreciate taking the heat for our *incompetence*," she said. "His word; not mine. The gist being that we—the country, that is—are at war, and by tainting the army we are being un-American, and we are to stop blaming the military."

"Guess he didn't like the press release," said Perez.

"Don't you fucking love it when they threaten your right to free speech but *you're* the un-American one," said O'Connell.

Dugan's head snapped out of his *Daily News*. "What are you, some fucking bleeding-heart liberal all of a sudden, Prince?"

"No, but I don't like someone telling me I'm not American enough." He took a slug from his thermos. "All my years on the force I've never seen any military interference and I don't like it. We have a job to do—just like they do."

The sudden military interest made me think they had something to hide. "Did the colonel offer anything on the two soldiers, on Beamer and O'Reilly?" I asked.

Terri shook her head. "Nothing we didn't already know. He said Beamer received an honorable discharge and the best possible treatment—which was interesting since no one said anything about him not getting good treatment."

"Colonel Sanders Fried Chicken Shit was not here to help the case," said Perez.

"No," said Terri. "As for O'Reilly, the colonel referred to his mental problems as 'civilian,' since the guy never saw combat."

"Convenient," I said.

"Very. And the G was there, too," she said, her lips pursing. "Telling jokes. Assholes."

"Guess you didn't think it was funny, eh, boss?" said O'Connell with a smirk.

"No."

He turned to me. "Rocky, you be the judge. Man comes into a bar, says to the bartender, 'Bartender, send that woman, I mean that *douche bag* down at the end of the bar, a drink on me.' The bartender looks at him, says, 'Sir, we don't talk like that in here.' Guy says, 'Oh, sorry, excuse me, but send her the drink anyway.'" O'Connell started laughing before he got to the punch line. "So, so, the bartender goes over to the woman and says, 'Guy over there wants to send you a drink, what'll it be?' Woman says, 'Make it vinegar and water.' "

"A riot," said Terri. "Don't you guys get it, what he was doing— trying to get all chummy with the *boys*—and I guess it worked."

"Oh, come on, boss," said O'Connell. "It was the only fun part of the morning."

"Well, comedy hour is over," she said.

"How many G men?" I asked, helping her change the subject.

"Two. The jokester, guy named Walter Peterson, and an older one, Matthew Barton, both built like linebackers."

"The G must grow 'em themselves," said O'Connell. "I'd say that Barton guy was close to seven feet."

"Steroids," said Terri. "Peterson had that stayed-too-long-at-the-gym look, practically bursting out of his gray suit."

"And they asked about you, Rodriguez," said Perez.

"Oh, yeah?" I said, trying to act cool. "Like what?"

"Like how come you was working with us. I said, 'How the hell should I know.' "

"Good to know I can always count on you, Perez."

"You think the G doesn't know about *you*, Perez?" Terri gave him a look, her brows raised. "Believe me, they know about *all* of us. It's their job. And there is nothing more they would like than setting us against one another so that you will give them the information they want. That's why Peterson is telling stupid jokes, so he seems like a regular guy. But these are no regular guys, you can count on that."

"So are they taking over, or what?" I asked.

Terri shrugged. "Official word is they're here in consulting-mode, babysitting assignment. And maybe that's the truth. We'll have to wait and see. Right now we have to give them case reports, autopsies, anything else they ask for, but you don't have to give them your opinions." She looked at each of us. "They want to know what's going on, they can find out for themselves."

"And they were real cozy with Colonel Sanders Fried Chicken Shit," said Perez.

"Yeah," said Terri. "A bit *too* friendly."

"But it figures the bureau is going to protect the military, right?" I said.

"Not always the case," said Terri, "but this time, yeah. I think you'd all better watch your step around those two."

We kicked that around a few minutes, then Perez and I brought them up-to-date on the Billow autopsy.

"That's a lot of weird shit," said O'Connell. "Tortured?"

"No proof of that," said Perez. "But maybe. We'll know more when the M.E. gets back to us." He filled the group in on our visit with Baumgarten and I let him take the stage.

After that Terri gave out assignments. The guys left but I hung around.

"I saw that smirk on your face, Rodriguez, when O'Connell told that stale joke."

"Sorry, all jokes make me laugh. I can't help it, I'm just a good audience."

"Oh, yeah? You know the one about the spic and the Jew?"

She made her point. "Got it," I said.

"The feds coming in and trying to get all buddy-buddy with my boys really pisses me off."

"*Your* boys?"

"Believe it. I worked hard to get them to respect me."

We were heading out of her office as Detective Schmid was coming down the hall.

"Hey, Rodriguez," she said. "We got him." The Sex Crimes cop dug into her pocket and came up with a copy of the sketch I'd made with the woman who'd been attacked in Battery Park. "Dead-on likeness," she said.

Terri looked over at the sketch in Schmid's hand.

"Really good job," said Schmid, tucking henna-red hair behind an ear and offering up a smile.

"Thanks," I said.

Terri sort of leaned in front of me, hand on hip, neck arched, head tilted. "So how are you, Schmid?"

"I'm good, Russo, real good." Schmid met Terri's look and returned the attitude.

I caught it, the little play they were enacting, Competition 101, and sort of enjoyed it, flattered.

"So who is he?" Terri tapped the sketch.

"Name's Tully," said Schmid. "Not the usual dirtbag; doesn't really fit the rapist profile, seems more scared than scary."

"Tell that to your vic," said Terri.

Schmid acknowledged that with a nod. "A real nut job, screaming and ranting, keeps saying that red ants are crawling into his eyes and nose."

"*Red* ants?" I asked. The word hit me like a caffeine rush.

"Yeah, like I said, a nut job. Now he keeps saying he's *sorry*. How do you like that? He'll probably plead insanity and get away with it, but—"

"Where is he?" I asked, cutting her off.

"In lockup."

"*Where?*"

"Relax, Rodriguez."

"Just tell me *where*."

"At the Rock, okay? Jeez."

"Can I have this?" I got a hand on the sketch.

"Hey, it's your sketch." Schmid gave me a look like I was crazed and at the moment, I felt like it.

"Sorry," I said. "Gotta go. But I'll buy you a drink to make up for it."

"Make that two drinks and we've got a deal," she said.

"Come on," I said to Terri.

"You're buying her a drink?" she said when we were outside.

"That's what you care about? It was just something to say. Didn't you hear what she said about this guy?" I smacked the sketch. "Red ants! The guy was ranting about red ants!"

"Yeah, I heard," said Terri. "But maybe you're getting ahead of yourself."

"I don't think so." It was all coming back to me, falling in place, at least I thought so. "Look, when I made the sketch with the vic she said the guy winced in pain and carried on like a crazy person. And he apologized to her at the end, said he was *sorry*, like Schmid just said this guy is doing. It's like Beamer and O'Reilly, killing, then feeling regret and killing themselves."

"But this guy hasn't killed himself."

"Not yet," I said.

30

Rikers was New York City's best-kept secret. The world's largest penal colony accommodating fifteen to twenty thousand local offenders, those awaiting trial who could not afford to post bail, others pending transfer to another criminal facility, all of them housed on an island in the East River in one of ten jails that made up the complex or on two former Staten Island ferries moored at the tip of the island, like floating cruise ships that aren't going anywhere.

Ask New Yorkers if they have ever seen Rikers and the answer is invariably no, though most have caught a glimpse of the place on their ride to LaGuardia Airport without knowing it.

Terri had called the Deputy Commissioner of Corrections to set up the visit, and rather than take a police car I hopped the subway, then the Q101, the bus that takes visitors to the island. It had just come over the Francis Buono Bridge—what everyone refers to as the Rikers Island Bridge, since that is its only destination.

I caught the familiar sign through the bus window.

Over the years I'd been to Rikers four times to make sketches and each time I always hoped it was my last. With its clinics and ball fields, chapels and tailor shops, gym, barbershop, grocery store, Laundromat, print shop and even a car wash, it felt like a lost city inhabited by tattooed thugs, a seething hive, Batman's dark Gotham.

The bus went through its checkpoints and so did I.

I was met by a guard named Jones, a large black man with sad eyes.

"Your man's in the infirmary," he said.

"Is he sick?"

"Yeah," said Jones, "in the head."

We headed over there, the sky low, gray-yellow clouds hovering. It had been the same in Manhattan but looked worse here, and felt even hotter.

"How long have you been working here?" I asked.

"Twelve years," he said, letting out a deep sigh. "I'm doing more time than the inmates."

He brought me over to the North Infirmary Common, two buildings, one a dorm for inmates with AIDS; the other, where Tully was being held, a three-story brick building with barred windows and a barbwire roof.

Inside it was bland, institutional, and reeking of disinfectant.

Jones passed me off to an orderly who led me to a nursing station.

"Tully, you said?" The psychiatrist, guy named Silvershein, was hunched over a Styrofoam container of grayish scrambled eggs and limp bacon. "Missed breakfast," he said. "Actually I missed breakfast and lunch, so technically this could be *brunch*, though I'm not seeing brunch on Rikers as a *New York Magazine* Best Bet." He pushed his eggs aside to scan a log. "Here he is—Tully, Matthew. I didn't connect the name to the patient. He was brought in right after I came on duty, took two interns to hold him down while I sedated him. He might still be out."

"I heard he said something about red ants."

"He said a lot of things, nothing that made much sense."

"Was he tripping?"

"You mean like on acid? It hasn't come up in his blood work, so I'd have to say no."

"Is he able to speak?"

The shrink shoved a couple of forkfuls of egg into his face and washed them down with black coffee. "C'mon," he said. "Let's find out."

In sleep, Matthew Tully looked innocent, though his hands were cuffed together, one ankle to the bedpost. I'd have recognized him even if I did not have the sketch with me, his face etched into my brain like all the others I had ever drawn. It was always a surprise to see when I'd created such a good likeness, but half the credit went to the witnesses who supplied the details. It was true, what the victim had said, that he didn't look very strong.

Silvershein plucked the chart out of a slot at the end of the bed. "His blood alcohol is high and there are traces of meth."

"Speed?"

"I'm guessing that's what had him flying—that and the booze. It can be a deadly mix." He flipped a page. "There's a history of alcohol and substance abuse." He plopped the chart back into the slot. "I'm heading over to the doctor's dorm for a quick nap, but the guard outside the door isn't going anywhere. Have him come in if Tully wakes up and you want to talk to him."

I said okay though I was pretty sure I could handle the situation; Tully was small and looked unthreatening. It was hard for me to imagine him ranting or attacking a woman and I wondered if I'd wasted my time chasing a dead end. I asked the shrink if Tully had made any sketches and he said no, then took off.

I settled into a stiff-backed wooden chair and looked Tully over—knuckles bruised, some scratches on his face, and high on his forehead the scar his victim had described.

For a while I just watched him sleep, his breathing even, then he started twitching.

"What—stop—please—don't—no—get away!" He thrashed about, cuffed hands banging around, his free leg kicking, the other one tugging against the cuff, which cut into his naked flesh.

After a few minutes his eyelids fluttered open and he looked at me.

"Name's Rodriguez," I said. "There's water there, beside the bed. Is there anything I can get you?"

He glanced over at the water, then down at his cuffed wrists, confused.

"What am I . . . doing here?"

"You don't know?"

He shook his head.

I held up my sketch of him. "This man attacked a woman in Battery Park and he looks an awful lot like you."

"That's . . . not me," he said, squinting.

"Sure looks like you," I said.

"You . . . don't . . . understand."

"Explain it to me while there's still time. Once the woman ID's you for sure, it's over."

"I can't . . . I don't . . . remember." His eyes started to blink and his body shook. "Stop!" he shouted, but not at me; he was looking at the ceiling, his cuffed hands trying to ward someone off.

"Is someone hurting you?"

He didn't answer but one of his cuffed hands started to make small looping gestures.

I went through my pencil case and found a red Conté pencil I rarely used, opened my pad and put it under his hand.

His fingers wrapped tightly around it. A moment later, with cuffs banging and clanking, face registering a dozen emotions—pain, anxiety, fear, anger—he was scribbling hard and fast, the Conté pencil wearing down.

After a while, he dropped the pencil, his body jerked, and the pad slipped to the floor.

"Are you okay? I'll call the doctor."

"No doctor! No! I don't want them to put me out again. I don't—" His eyes fluttered. "Sunday Monday Tuesday Wednesday Thursday . . . then . . . then *what*?"

"Friday," I said.

"Friday, right, *right*! Friday, franklin fasting farting farming folly frolic frumpy folksy fucking fuck fuck fuck—"

It was stream-of-consciousness babble, as if he had Tourette's syndrome.

"Funny funky, frothy filthy—"

"Matthew, what are you trying to say?"

"F-words. F-words F-"

"Why?"

He stared at me, mouth slightly open. I asked again but he didn't respond.

"What about the drawing?"

"What . . . drawing?"

"There, beside you, on the floor."

"Can't . . . see it."

I reached for the pad and when the blow came it was like a blast of white light followed by searing pain from the top of my head down to my jawbone. It took me a few seconds to realize that he had brought his metal handcuffs down onto my skull and now they were around my neck and he was tugging hard.

"Mother Nature mother humpers motherfuckers fuckers fuckers fuckers!"

The metal was digging hard into my neck and everything was blurring, floor and walls, the ceiling moving close then far, tilting. I tried to push his arms off, but couldn't. I heard myself yelling for him to let go but it seemed to come from far away.

31

I didn't hear the door open or see the guard, but the next thing I knew I was lying on the floor trying to catch my breath. Then I touched the back of my neck and my hand came away bright red and that was the last thing I saw until I woke up in a bed with Terri staring at me.

"Jesus, Rodriguez. You scared the shit out of me." She smoothed the hair off my forehead and I felt about ten years old.

"I guess that maniac knocked me out."

"Believe it."

"Where am I?"

"You're a guest of the Rock."

"Oh, great." I tried to push up from the bed but the room started to spin.

"Easy there, tiger." Terri put her hands on my chest and gently eased me down. "I can take you home after the doctor checks you out."

"You know, I can usually defend myself pretty well. It wasn't a fair fight."

"That's true. The other guy was in cuffs."

"Oh, that's a riot."

"Couldn't help myself," said Terri. "So what did you get from Tully other than a bump on the head?"

"Where's my sketch pad?"

Terri handed it to me and I found the page.

"It's like the others, the same kind of wild spirals and words." I pictured the other drawings, and that's when it hit me. "True, false, yes, no . . . It's a test!?" I pictured Tully hunched over the pad, his face screwed up in concentration. "Tully was taking a test. I think they were *all* taking tests!"

I thought about all the sketches; the words that didn't seem to make sense suddenly did. "They're answers to questions, you see what I mean?"

"Yeah, I guess, but what of it?"

I was trying to come up with an answer, my mind racing. "Okay, O'Reilly's blood painting had yes and no, true and false, all repeated and mixed up like he was answering questions. And Billow's little sketches, the ones I pulled out of his coat pockets, had numbers and words—*yes* and *no, true* and *false*." I stared at Tully's sketch. "But the big question is what sort of tests were they taking—and *why?*"

Two hours later I was back in a room with Tully. But this time they had him in a chair, wrists cuffed and attached to a bolt in the table, ankles to one in the floor, the guard close by. They'd given him a shot, some Valium to subdue him, hydrocodone for pain, and had added sodium pentothal to make him talk. He was awake, but his eyes were unfocused.

"Doc says to give him a minute," the guard said.

Terri and I waited and when Tully finally looked up at us, I asked in a calm voice why he had attacked me.

"I *did?*" he asked, his face screwed up with confusion.

"You *did*," I said.

"Its not . . . my fault."

"You'll have to do better than that," said Terri.

"It was . . . the devil."

"You're saying the devil made you do it?" Terri gave me a look, like *Oh, please.* "How?"

"He just . . . did." Tully's eyes were focused and awake now.

"So where did you meet the devil?"

"He found me."

"Where?" she asked.

"College."

"Was he a student?" Terri glanced at me and rolled her eyes. But I decided to take him seriously.

"Tell me about him?" I asked.

"It was for . . . the money."

"What do you mean?" I asked.

Tully started twitching and tugging at his cuffs.

The guard bolted forward. "Cut that shit out!" He slapped his hand down on the table and Tully flinched and quieted.

I told the guard to relax, and Tully the same thing. Then I asked him about the tests.

"College," he said again.

"You mean you took the tests in college?"

"No—I—no—"

"Just relax," I said softly. "You can talk to me. Tell me about college and the tests. It's okay."

"No no no no no no!" He started to bang his cuffs against the table and tried to kick out of his ankle cuffs, howling like an animal caught in a trap. Then the guard was on him and a minute later the doctor was in the room jabbing a needle into his arm and then he was quiet.

Most people would have been in la-la land from the amount of drugs I've been giving him. I can't believe he was violent again."

We were sitting with Dr. Silvershein outside Tully's room. "His body just isn't absorbing medication in a normal way. He's out now, but I can't say for how long."

"So questioning him some more won't be possible?" Terri asked.

"Not for a while," said Silvershein.

"I have a question for you," I said. "The scar on his forehead?"

"Yes, I saw that." The doctor tapped his fingers against his clipboard. "I have no proof because I haven't done the necessary tests but I'm guessing we might find that he had a childhood accident, a frontal brain injury."

"Why do you say that?" asked Terri.

"Because there have been studies of children who suffer frontal brain injuries, who later became wild and uncontrollable, sometimes violent."

"How much later?" she asked.

"Often years later. Studies show that for some reason it can take a long time for the violent behavior to manifest itself. That's the unknown part." He paused, looked at the ceiling, then back at us. "There have been very interesting studies done with violent prisoners that show they have some frontal brain irregularities, specifically in the hippocampus."

"Which is what?" I asked.

"It's the area referred to as the limbic structure. It straddles both hemispheres of your brain."

"So you're saying that children with this irregularity *become* criminals, or they *develop* the irregularity from committing the crimes?"

"Good question," said Silvershein. "We now know that the brain is affected by behavior and that it actually changes, physically, from trauma. But in this case, the prisoners seemed to have had their brain irregularities either from birth defects or from early trauma, and therefore they *became* violent. But here's the really interesting part. If that area of the brain is damaged or irregular, one may very well become psychotic and violent, like these prisoners, but it would be *uncontrollable* violence."

"Could you run that past me one more time," said Terri.

"Suppose you're a kid and you get a conk on the head which affects your frontal brain."

"Okay," she said.

"Years later, you're out of control, maybe even a criminal, a killer. But you would not be able to *plan* your murders. You'd be an *impulse* killer. You see, to be a cold, calculating criminal, that area of your brain must be intact."

"I get it," she said. "So clearly not all criminals have this irregularity."

"No, if they did they would not be able to plot out a crime."

It got me thinking about O'Reilly beating Peter Sandwell to death and Beamer stabbing that kid in front of the movie theater—violent acts that appeared to be unprovoked and out of control.

"Can you test to see if Tully has this abnormality?"

"I'll do an MRI and see if anything shows up." The doctor turned to me. "And it might not be a bad idea to get a picture of your noggin, too, Detective, just to make sure you haven't got a concussion. I don't think so, but . . ."

"Oh, I'm fine. I've got a hard head."

He shined his penlight into my eyes.

"I'll second that," said Terri.

"Okay, but take it easy. And if you feel dizzy," he said, "don't go to sleep. Get up—and call me."

32

Terri drove us back over the Rikers Bridge and I watched the buildings soften and blur as the hidden city slipped away.

When we got back to my apartment I was starving and Terri made me a ham-and-cheese sandwich, which was about as gourmet as she got.

"How'd you like Tully invoking the devil?" she said. "Crazy, huh?"

"Maybe," I said.

"You don't think he's crazy?"

"Oh, I do, and I have the bruises to prove it, but I think he was serious about that devil stuff." I took a few bites of my sandwich.

"Could be that he's building an insanity defense."

"You believe that?"

"No, not really," she said. "He was crazy. But the *devil*, come on." She nibbled a piece of cheese before she packed it up and tossed it back into the fridge.

"Well, suppose the devil is just a symbol; that he's not actually speaking about the devil per se."

"So, who then?"

"Well, it could be anyone really, some Svengali-type charac-ter—you know, like Charles Manson, someone who told him what to do."

Terri considered that, her lips pressed together. "Did O'Reilly ever say anything about the devil?"

"O'Reilly wasn't very talkative. And he was on a heavy cocktail of his own making, remember?"

"Which didn't stop him from killing Sandwell."

"No. And the same thing with Wayne Beamer." I thought a moment. "You heard what Silvershein said, that Tully's body wasn't absorbing meds. Maybe that was true of Beamer and O'Reilly, too."

"And what about the idea that something could be wrong with his brain? That was pretty interesting."

"Maybe that was true for all of them," I said. "Is it too late to check?"

"You mean look inside their heads?" she asked. "I'd have to get the necessary requisitions. And I can't imagine Wayne Beamer's mother agreeing to an exhumation, but I'll try."

"Tully said he met the devil at college, right? We should find out where he went."

"*You* should," she said. "I've got to get back to the station."

"I'll come, too. I have work I can do there."

"You're staying here and taking it easy. You heard the doctor."

"I'm fine."

"*Stay home.* That's an order. I don't want to see your face at the station, you hear me, Rodriguez?"

"Fine." I saluted. "I'll work on my sculpture."

"That's not resting." Terri looked at her watch. "I'll be home really late. Rest, okay?"

"Swear to God."

The minute she left I went over to my facial reconstruction. I looked at what I'd done and thought where I would go next.

I had completed the easy part. Up to this point it had been pretty much by the book. Now it got difficult.

I thought back to my Quantico class, the professor telling us that anyone could do the first part, but the second was based on intuition and feeling; that you needed to be an artist to pull it off, and that most of us would fail. But I had not. In fact, it was the second half that got me really excited and where I'd excelled. When the class had finished, the professor brought out a photo of the dead man and only my sculpture looked like him.

I scanned through my notes, reminding myself that the mouth and lips were determined by the teeth, but with my John Doe's smashed and broken, I had to take my measurements, using the ridge where the enamel met the root. Then I added what I guessed was the length of his teeth minus a fraction of an inch for the bite.

All the adding and subtracting got me thinking about the numbers in Billow's sketches and the idea that he was taking a test. It brought me back to cramming for exams in college with Dexedrine and caffeine to stay awake, mouth dry, mind in overdrive, and the crash that always followed. But what kind of test would make someone kill?

I worked more clay over the top of the skull, thinking about tests and torture and brain deformities, but none of it made any sense. Then I started on the mouth. I used a flat wooden tool to get the clay in place, then checked and re-checked the measurements.

When I started using my fingertips to smooth the lips, they seemed to know what to do without me telling them and I lost track of time.

I went back to the eyes, creating lower lids, first by putting strips of clay in place and molding them around the eyeballs.

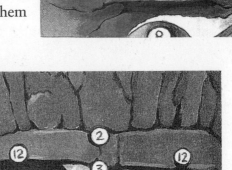

I got an odd sensation when I stepped back and looked at the eyes—as if they were staring back at me.

Who was this guy, and why was I so obsessed with recreating him?

I couldn't answer the question and I wanted to keep going but my head was starting to ache, my neck throb, and a large purplish bruise was blooming near my elbow.

It was nearly midnight. Terri would be back soon and I'd catch hell for working late, so I took a couple of Advil P.M. and fell into bed.

33

"How's your head?" Terri asked when I opened my eyes.

"Still attached, I think." It was pounding and the back of my neck felt like I had a noose wrapped around it.

"You look awful," she said, stroking the hair off my forehead. "Can I get you anything?"

"Hemlock?"

"That bad?"

"I'll be fine."

Terri stood up and tucked her mouse gun into her bag.

"You're leaving already?"

"It's after nine, Rodriguez. I've been sitting here waiting for you to wake up. I wanted to make sure you were alive before I headed out."

"After *nine*? Shit, I'm supposed to meet my mother at the Museum of Modern Art. I've got to get going." I pulled my aching body out of bed.

"Let me change that neck bandage. There's blood on it and you don't want to freak out your mom. Maybe you should wear a turtleneck."

"In August? In a heat wave? That's subtle."

Terri tugged the old bandage off and I tried not to yelp when she tore a patch of my hair out with it.

"You're no Florence Nightingale," I said, after the new bandage was in place.

"And you're not exactly up for the Purple Heart," she said. "Say good-bye to your mom for me—and tell her I really liked her, okay? You won't forget, will you?"

"Swear."

She kissed me and headed out.

I used my membership to get us into the museum, which always felt pretty cool, going in ahead of the crowd and tourists.

"You sure that was okay?" my mother asked.

"It's why I pay seventy-five bucks a year to be a member and I've only been here once this year, so they owe me."

My mother checked her bag and umbrella and I ducked into the men's room where I used paper towels to dry my face and rain-soaked hair. I had put on a sport shirt and I flipped the collar up to hide the bandage.

The first thing she said when I came out of the bathroom was "What did you do to your neck?"

"Nothing really, just cut myself."

"On the back of your neck?"

"I backed into . . . something."

"Into what?"

"A lamp." I ushered her up the staircase. "This weather is really something, isn't it?"

"Yes, I am going to appreciate Colorado when I get back."

"Why? Doesn't it rain there?"

"Yes, but we don't get this combination of heat and humidity. I always forget what a Manhattan summer is like."

"We've had some nice days," I said, starting to get defensive. I'd been bitching about the weather all week, and now I was defending it.

"I know—two days in June and about three in September. I used to live here, remember? Wait till you see the weather in Colorado."

"You can *see* the weather there?"

"I meant the scenery, but yes, smarty, you *can* see weather, you know—like snow on the mountains and blue sky." She gave me a look as if I was being difficult and I guess I was.

"Hey, look, one of my all-time favorite paintings." I used Picasso as a distraction.

"Really?" she asked. "How come?"

"Because it's just so ballsy. Picasso was way ahead of his time when he painted this. Look at what he's doing— breaking up the figures so they mesh right into the background, a really radical idea. And check out the two faces on the right, like African masks, which is what Picasso was referencing at the time."

"I love hearing you talk like this," she said. "It makes me feel as if I didn't waste my money on your college education."

It was a good safe subject, though a nagging voice inside kept urging me to bring up what I'd discovered about my father's death.

"Are you sure your neck is okay? That's a big bandage."

"It was all I had. It's nothing, really. Why are you suddenly so worried?"

"Don't you don't think I worry about you?"

"I'm a big boy."

"I know that. And I'm proud of you, of what you do. And your father would have been thrilled."

I felt one of those weird chills, and it threw me. She'd never said anything like that, not in the twenty years since he'd died.

"You know he was always proud of your talent, don't you?"

I looked at her, then away. I could see she wanted to have a conversation about my dad, and suddenly I didn't. I was a coward. I turned to another painting.

"Hey, check this out."

"It's a really emotional painting, isn't it?" she said.

"Yeah, all that crazy swirling paint, and hallucinogenic brushwork. Poor Vincent. Maybe he was too emotional. Dead at thirty-five by his own hand." It brought to mind some other young men, Beamer, O'Reilly, and Billow.

"Did you ever read the letters Vincent wrote to his brother, Theo?" she asked.

"Yeah, in art school; really sad stuff."

My mother closed her eyes and recited, "The burden grows too great at times."

"What Theo said when Vincent lay dying."

"He should have been in therapy," she said, sort of smiling and looking at me. I wondered if she meant *I* should be in therapy.

"But maybe if he'd been all mellowed out, the paintings wouldn't have been as good," I said.

"It's possible," she said. "But he might have been happier. There are whole schools of psychology about the artist as a tortured being in search of something to complete his or her damaged ego."

"You're not talking about *me*, are you?"

"No, you're not an artist."

I guess the look registered on my face at the same time she thought better of what she had said.

"I didn't it mean it like that. I meant you make art for your job. And best of all, you're not crazy, like van Gogh."

It was a good save but it still irked me, even though she was right: I was *not* an artist. And it was okay. I was doing what I wanted to do. But maybe it *wasn't* enough. Maybe that's why I was so damn committed to the work I'd signed on to do with Homicide. Maybe I needed to feel like I contributed more. Was I one of those tortured beings in search of something to complete myself? I was starting to sound like a Hallmark card.

"What you do is important," my mother said, as if reading my mind, though I knew she was actually reading my *face*, which is what we all do when we're paying attention.

"Yeah, I'm happy with it," I said, and we both got quiet.

The burden grows too great at times.

I kept thinking about Beamer, O'Reilly, Billow, and now Tully. Had the burden grown too great for them—and what was it, their particular burden?

"Why would someone not respond to sedatives?" I asked.

"What?"

"Sorry, I was thinking about a case."

"Oh. Well, I'm not a physician, but I can answer the question. The body is a complex machine and individuals react differently; one medication can react with another, cancel it out or become lethal. Which reminds me: Remember when we were talking about the Fort Bragg murders, the four men who murdered their wives? Well, I forgot to say that later it came out that three of the four men had been taking a drug called Lariam."

"Which is?"

"An antimalaria drug. The Pentagon and the Centers for Disease Control and Prevention sent a team to investigate. They determined that the murders could not have been related to side effects from Lariam, but I don't know. It surely raised more than one eyebrow in the medical community."

"You mean the drug could have caused them to commit murder?"

"I can't say, but it seemed like it. And think about how many times drugs are put on the market only to be recalled a year later. Look at thalidomide and Vioxx, wonder drugs, until they *weren't*."

I started thinking about the combination of speed and alcohol, a deadly combination, the doctor had called it. But was there another drug, something that could interfere with the absorption of a sedative, as in Tully's case?

"Are there any new drugs for treating PTSD?" I asked.

"New drugs come on the market all the time."

"Anything that would work against a sedative?"

"I'd have to check. I'm not a doctor, remember? Which reminds me; I saw your grandmother, terrific as always, but my God, have you seen her place lately?"

"I see it every week. You mean the *cuartos de los santos*, the house church she's set up in her bedroom?"

"Yes. It's really getting totally out of control. And clearly she has no problem prescribing for her clients, or whatever she calls them."

"She's prescribing candles and prayers and herbs. It's no big deal."

"Herbs are medicine, Nate."

"She's not doing anything wrong," I said, feeling defensive for my *abuela*.

"I just worry about her getting more and more into the occult."

"It's not the occult, it's Santeria. It's a religion."

My mother gave me a serious look. "*You're* not getting into it, are you?"

No way was I going to tell her that my *abuela* had gotten me to burn candles and to create an Eleggua shrine to protect my apartment because it would not make sense to my very rational, psychoanalytic mother. Hell, it didn't make sense to me.

"Me? No way."

"That's good," she said.

Another silence. My mother and I were pretty good when we were talking about her work or mine, but not good at much else. I considered bringing the conversation back to my father, but it seemed too late.

"By the way, Terri is terrific. What a smart, level-headed girl, and beautiful. I think she's good for you."

I wanted to ask her how she knew what was good for me, but I changed the subject to a group of Cézanne landscapes instead.

After that we walked through the museum not talking and I wasn't sure what she was thinking, but I finally got up the nerve and asked a question that was on my mind.

"So who is this Chris guy?"

My mother sucked her lower lip into her mouth, a sure sign of discomfort. "Oh. Well, I've been meaning to tell you about him for some time."

I felt my heart beat fast and wasn't sure why.

"I'm sorry I didn't mention him before. I think I was a little scared to, but we've been seeing each other, Chris and I, for, um, about seven months."

"Wow, that's a long time." Now I was glad I hadn't brought up my father. Terri was right: My mother—my *mother*—had a boy-friend!

"Yes, it is. Look, one of the reasons I came to New York was to tell you something." She cleared her throat. "Chris has asked me to marry him."

"Oh." I stared at the art on the walls.

"Are you okay with that?"

"Hey, it's not up to me."

We were both quiet again.

After a while she said, "You know, it's been a really long time since your father died."

"Uh-huh." It was the best I could come up with. It sounded petulant and immature, and I didn't like myself for it, but I was back in that place, back in the Penn South Apartments with Santana posters on the wall, a sulky teenager. I wanted to be happy for her but I kept thinking about my father, dead in the street. I wanted to tell her the truth; wanted to tell her how I'd blamed myself for twenty years, and what I'd discovered only a few months ago. I took a deep breath. "There's something I need to tell you."

She turned toward me and in that instant I saw it; I saw it in her eyes and the set of her mouth.

She knew what I was going to say; she had known it all along.

By the time she froze her facial anatomy it was too late.

A million thoughts were colliding in my brain, sending shock waves to my heart. I had never considered it from her side.

I cadged another look at her, then away, but it was still there, written on her face. She *knew*. She'd probably known from the beginning but could never say it. How does a mother tell her son that she knows he killed his father?

It made sense now; why we never talked about it; why we could make small talk, but not much else; and why we could not look each other in the eye.

"What?" she finally said, but I could see she was holding her breath.

"Nothing," I said. "Just that I'm happy for you."

She let out a breath and her lips twitched as if she was about to say something but had changed her mind at the last second.

We walked a bit, looked at paintings and didn't speak.

Finally she said, "Chris and I are getting married when I get back, and I thought . . . I hoped . . . you might walk me down the aisle."

"Oh—well—sure." The words stuttered out of me.

I felt as if the ghost of my father were beside me and I was the little boy who had always wanted to impress him until it was too late. I didn't know how I was supposed to feel. I wanted him to tell me it was okay, that I wouldn't be letting him down again.

A minute passed, then my mother said, "You'll at least come to the wedding, won't you?"

"If I can get off from work," I said, which sounded awful, and I knew it.

I left my mom at the museum and headed back to the station feeling bad.

The rain had stopped but it was even hotter than before, the air thick and dank.

I tried to imagine escorting my mother down the aisle, delivering her to a man not my father, but it was impossible.

Midtown North was just crosstown and west from the museum, not a long walk, but the heat was getting to me, so I stepped into a deli and bought a bottle of Poland Spring.

I was lost in thought when I bumped into a guy coming in as I walked out. I tried to step out of his way, he mine, but we kept moving in the same direction. Then we locked eyes. I recognized his face, though it took me a moment to place him.

"You're Julio's client, aren't you?"

"Mr. Sanchez? Yes, that's right."

The scene came back to me—the Princeton Club, delivering legal papers; and I saw now what I had seen on his face that day: tension in his jaw, a tic at the corner of his right eye.

"You have a good memory," he said. "Wish I could say the same."

"I never forget a face," I said. "It's just the nature of my work."

"Oh, really, what's that, your work, I mean?"

"Forensic artist—you know, sketch artist."

He shook a cigarette out of a crumpled pack, got it to his lips, but didn't light it. "How does that work?"

"I move features around on paper—nose, eyes, mouth—till I get them right."

"Oh. Maybe you could do that for me one day."

"Draw a face?"

"Yes. No." He shrugged, then smiled, that eye twitching.

"So how is your case going?"

"Good, real good. At least I think so, I hope so . . . because, well, I . . ."

"Hey, don't worry." I tapped him on the arm. "Julio's the best. He'll take care of you. "

"Oh. I hope so. I mean, I know that." He shifted his weight from one foot to the other. "I've got to get going." He tapped his backpack. "I've got to make these deliveries and don't want to be late for my meeting."

"With Julio?"

"Oh, uh, no. It's just my, uh, my support group." He looked away, as if embarrassed.

I wasn't so crass as to ask drink or drugs. I'd been there myself and had managed to quit without the help of a twelve-step program, but I sure as hell thought it was a good idea for anyone who needed it. With me it just took my father's death, years of punishing guilt, self-indulgence, and my best friend going to prison to set me straight.

I took him in: dark eyes, something sad in the way his inner brows pinched and tilted up. He seemed a little old for a messenger job, my age, possibly older, but maybe his life had been sidetracked by addiction, and I was no one to judge.

I watched him walk away, his gait quick but slightly askew, lurching a bit to the left, then right. Maybe he'd had a few drinks, though he hadn't appeared to be drunk.

Bumping into him brought it all back to me, my fucked-up

teen years and the way I was replaying them with my mother right now, particularly unappealing at my age.

I chugged the water, bought another, and thought about calling her to say I was sorry. But I couldn't decide if that would make it worse, so I didn't do anything.

34

When I got to the station I did my best to put my emotions in a box and set them aside.

Then I settled in behind my computer to do a little research on Matthew Tully. It was easy to pull his arrest sheets for vagrancy and his mental health records, but I had trouble finding a way to get at his personal history.

The NYPD's databases were great if you were looking for local criminals, and NCIC was great for tracking national crime, but Tully's name produced nothing.

I dialed a number on automatic, surprised it was still in my head.

"This is Hart."

When I heard her voice I almost hung up.

"Hello?"

"Hi, it's, uh, Nate Rodriguez."

It was a few seconds before she said, "You must be kidding."

"How are you, Karen?"

"What do you want?"

I should have expected that.

Karen Hart was a lawyer who worked in the legal department at bureau headquarters in Virginia. We'd literally bumped into each other the first week of my forensic course at Quantico; I had my head in a book and she was running.

I pictured her in Spandex, blond hair pulled back, beads of sweat on her forehead, the image morphing into her sweat-soaked skin next to mine in bed only a few days later and every night after that for almost a month.

She called me shortly after I left Virginia to say she was due vacation time and wanted to spend it with me. I told her I was busy but would get back to her. I did. Six weeks later. She told me I was an asshole and hung up. I thought about calling her back to apologize. I wanted to explain that I was . . . what? Not ready? Scared of commitment? Liked my freedom? All true. When I finally called two months later, she said it was too late.

"I need some information."

"Seven years, and not a word from you. Jesus, Rodriguez, you were always a ballsy guy, and I don't mean that in a good way." She sighed. "Is this official?"

"No, not really."

She hesitated, then said, "What is it?"

I asked her if she could find out which college Matthew Tully had attended and she called me an asshole but said she'd call me back.

I waited by the phone wondering why I'd been such a jerk with Karen Hart. Bad timing was the best excuse I could come up with. I'd met her long before I learned the truth about my father and was still so racked with guilt that I couldn't reach out to anyone.

The phone's ring startled me. It hadn't taken Hart long, but that shouldn't have surprised me. The bureau has a way of finding information fast, even faster these days, with the Patriot Act opening up everything from library withdrawals to Internet perusals.

"Burlington County College," she said.

"In Vermont?"

"No. It's in Pemberton, New Jersey."

"Which is where?"

"For Christ's sake, Rodriguez, go do a Mapquest or something."

"Sorry. Do you have his transcript there?"

"Anything else? A kidney, perhaps?" She sighed again. "It says here that Burlington is connected to Drexel University for degree programs, which is what Tully did. And he obviously hit the books. Transcript shows he was a biology major and aced most of his classes."

"What about after college?"

"Hmm . . . There are a few arrests for vagrancy."

"Yes, I have that. Anything else?"

"Some hospital records for drug and alcohol abuse."

Just like Billow, I thought.

"Anything in there about post-traumatic stress disorder?"

"No."

I wondered what had happened to make a promising student like Tully lose his way. "Do you have his background, family info, anything like that?"

"What am I, the fucking public library?" She sighed for the third time. "Father David, electrician; mother formerly Flora Getz, homemaker, also worked at the local cleaners' as a seamstress. Blue-collar family. No other kids. Both parents deceased. Not very interesting."

"So why would the FBI keep a dossier on him?"

"Who knows? Could be the vagrancy charges. Anything else?"

I thought a moment. "Do you happen to know a couple of agents named Matthew Barton and Walter Peterson?"

"No, but I don't know every agent. Why?"

"Well, they're here, in New York, looking over my shoulder."

"They're looking over a sketch artist's shoulder?"

"I'm working a homicide at the moment."

"Oh, right. I heard you've been doing that."

That shouldn't have surprised me either; that the bureau knew what I was up to.

"Can't you look them up, or something?"

"Are you trying to get me fired?"

"I just thought you could give me a little background, you know, a heads-up on these guys."

I listened to her fingers typing on a keyboard. A few seconds later she said, "There's nothing on them."

"What do you mean, *nothing*?"

"Well, I just did a general scan, field agents, DEA, U.S. marshals, Immigration, and their names didn't come up."

"Are you saying they're *not* agents?"

"No, I'm not saying that." She paused. "They could be Special Op or Homeland Security, and not listed. But I'm not *saying* anything, you got that?"

"Sure, but why would the bureau send Special Op or Homeland Security to watch over an NYPD homicide case?"

"You tell me, Rodriguez." She cleared her throat. "Look, I've got to go."

I thanked her and told her I appreciated her help.

"Yeah, sure," she said. Then she asked, "You seeing anyone?"

I told her I was.

"Brave girl," she said, and hung up.

I sat back and stared at the wall. So who were Barton and Peterson? G-men for sure—no one impersonated a fed, not these days. But if they weren't regular field agents, what were they? And why were they here?

I went online, Googled their names and the bureau, but there was nothing. I thought about calling one of my old teachers at Quantico, then decided it was a bad idea. I didn't want to look that interested. But my paranoia went up a notch and it made me think I was right about a connection between the perps. The case had to be bigger than we thought if we were attracting this kind of attention.

I went back to the computer and found the website for Burlington County College. It didn't seem like the kind of place to drive a student insane. I scanned the faculty list but wasn't sure what I was looking for. I called Karen again and asked her to see if any of Tully's teachers were still at the school.

"This must be a red-letter day," she said. "Two calls from the great Nate Rodriguez in one day—and after only seven years."

I told her again I was sorry and she mumbled "Asshole" under her breath and said she could not send me the transcript, but read off the professors' names and I wrote them down quickly. I thanked her and she asked me not to call her again.

35

Special Op?" said Terri, eyebrows raised.

"I don't know that for sure," I said. "But according to a friend at Quantico, Barton and Peterson are not your everyday field agents."

"You have *friends* at Quantico?" said Perez, eyes narrowed in my direction.

"Rodriguez has friends *everywhere*," said Terri.

"Yeah, I'm this year's poster boy for Unicef."

The squad was gathered in the small conference room next to Terri's office, the one with the blinking fluorescent light.

"So why are they here?" said O'Connell, reaching for his thermos.

I could see he was nervous. Perez, too, the levator palpebræ muscles widening his eyes; Dugan's face was pretty much a carbon copy. They'd all had their share of bureau run-ins, never fun.

"Hey, Special Op, field agent, FBI, CIA, or the fucking YMC, they're here for one reason," said Terri. "To watch our moves."

"Or to protect their ass—or someone else's ass," I said. "And my guess would be the military."

Terri leaned across her desk and looked at each of us. "Just tuck this information into the back of your minds. Knowledge is power, remember? So watch your step and your mouth around these guys. All you know is they are two field agents out of the Manhattan bureau, never let on you know differently. They want to be covert, let them be." She paused to make sure she had our attention, and she did. Then she continued.

"I agree they're here for some sort of damage control, not to do any of us damage, so don't give them a reason. The bureau may not be what it once was but these are paranoid times and I don't want any of my men in unnecessary trouble. Whatever their game is, we'll eventually find out—and if we don't, fuck it and fuck them!" She took a deep breath. "We still have our job to do and that's all any of you has to think about."

Then she turned to me and asked about Tully to bring the subject back to the case.

I told everyone what I'd learned and asked if we could get Tully's IRS forms and W2s to see where he'd worked after college.

"Only if you can come up with Reasonable Cause," Terri said.

"He attacked a woman, isn't that enough?"

"You ever hear of civil liberties or right to privacy?" she asked.

"Yeah, but I figured the current administration got rid of them."

O'Connell laughed and it broke the ice. Dugan went back to the *Daily News*, and Perez sneered; business as usual.

"I've got Tully's medical update," said Terri. "MRI confirms he has some damage to his brain." She explained what the doctor at Bellevue had told us about prefrontal brain injury and violent behavior. "It probably explains his outbursts."

"Did the doc say how the damage occurred?" O'Connell asked.

"No, but he said it was old."

"Can we see if Beamer or O'Reilly had anything similar?" I asked.

"Beamer's in the ground; remember?" said Perez.

"Thanks for reminding me," I said.

Terri gave us each a look and we shut up.

"I've requested an exhumation," she said, "but like I thought, his mother is fighting it. She'll eventually lose, but she's hired a lawyer, so it will take time."

I scrolled through the portrait gallery in my head and pictured Beamer, the sketch I'd made of him on top of the taxi, his face miraculously unscathed, and could not remember if there was a scar on his forehead.

Terri got out O'Reilly's autopsy report. "There's no reported injury or scarring on O'Reilly's skull, but the M.E. notes some irregularities in the brain, possibly attributable to drugs and alcohol."

O'Connell had gotten the full toxicology report on Billow, and handed out copies. "Note the point-oh-eight blood alcohol. And look at the tranqs and pain meds, which are plenty."

Terri scanned the report. "So what's modafinil?"

O'Connell shook his head.

"Hold on," she said, skimming through the other case reports. "It's here, too, the same drug, modafinil, in O'Reilly's tox."

I looked through Beamer's. "But not here, in Beamer's tox."

"Maybe someone in SID can tell us what the drug is." She got the phone to her ear.

"I see . . . When was that? Uh-huh." She jotted a note. "And it's used for . . . I see. So it's . . . What was that? . . . Got it." She hung up and filled us in. "Science Investigation Unit says modafinil is a sleep-disorder drug commonly marketed as . . ." She glanced at her notes. "Provigil."

I pictured admen sitting around dreaming up drug names, fabricated words that evoked associations to feelings, like Ambien for ambience and Lunesta, which somehow sounded lunar and dreamlike. But Provigil sounded to me like the opposite of sleep, conjuring images of soldiers on duty or sentry patrol.

"Is it something new?" Dugan asked.

Terri regarded her notes again. "Food and drug approved it in 1998 to treat sleep disorders associated with Alzheimer's and Parkinson's."

"So it's not on the market as a sleep aid?" I asked.

"Just the opposite," she said. "It keeps you awake."

Something about that hit a note in the back of my mind.

"Apparently Provigil is the black-market drug du jour on college campuses these days," she said.

College, tests, numbers, letters, true or false.

"So where would Tully and O'Reilly get it?" I asked. "Neither one was in college."

"According to SID, it's a script drug, but only for the diseases I mentioned." She looked back at the case notes. "I don't see anywhere that either of these men had Alzheimer's or Parkinson's."

"Billow was living on the street, so where'd he get it?" asked O'Connell. "Street sale?"

"And doesn't it make more sense that someone as crazy as Tully would rather sleep off his demons than stay awake and deal with them?" I said. "And that goes for O'Reilly, too." Another thought came into my mind. "This Provigil is supposedly hot with students, right? But the only students we have in this equation are not perps, they're vics."

"You suggesting the vics could have been selling it?" asked Perez.

"Or using. We should check *their* tox screens, too."

Terri was back on the phone relaying answers to questions as she got them. "The vic, Sandwell . . ." She gave a thumbs-up.

"Traces of modafinil in his tox. And what about Ryan Kavanagh . . . Yeah, I'm holding." A moment later she gave us a thumbs-down. "No for Kavanagh."

Again, no consistency; Sandwell, the overage NYU vic, was using the drug, but the Hunter vic was not.

Terri was still on the phone. "You said the drug has been around awhile, right? Uh-huh . . . Got it." She hung up and turned back to us. "FDA approved Provigil for Alzheimer's and Parkinson's but long-term side effects are not known. It's never been approved as a stay-awake drug even though it's making its way into the general population, popular with long-haul truckers and airline pilots."

"Makes me feel real good about getting on a plane," said O'Connell.

"Where are *you* going, Prince, fucking Bermuda?"

"What's your problem, Doogie?"

"Sorry, it's that fucking blinking light. It's driving me nuts!"

"Stop reading the newspaper and your eyes might stop hurting," said Terri.

A lot more than the light was driving me nuts—the fact that half the killers were taking the drug and half the vics, too. It just didn't add up.

36

The medical supplies are on his back, weighing him down but he needs them for the mission, has to get there, get through this heat and this dust. He pictures his buddy, Ron, injured, bleeding, depending on him, and he will not let him down, not let anyone, or anything, stop him.

Day, night; it's all the same to him.

He pops a pill and moves stealthily. He knows the enemy is out there, waiting, hiding, like the tanks, which idle and look deserted, but he knows better.

He hunches closer to the ground, heat coming off the sand in palpable waves, humidity like he never felt before, not in the desert, the sand strange, almost rocklike, feet burning inside his boots.

But he will not quit. He has his orders.

He keeps going, unafraid, the world around him quiet except for the sound of distant thunder, gray-black clouds erupting on the horizon, moving closer and closer until he is *in* it, the sound and the heat and the blast, the earth shattering, exploding inside his head.

The red fades to gray, the dust settles.

Horns beeping, people shouting, tires screeching, sirens, announcements, billboards blinking garish neon, all of it in supersharp hyperfocus, and he sees it is not sand but sidewalk, and the tanks are taxis and buses, and he thinks he will start screaming along with the sirens.

He stops on the corner, leans against a mailbox, shirt soaked with sweat, swipes a hand across his brow and takes a deep breath of air so thick with moisture it's like sucking on a sponge.

A few minutes to collect himself, to get his bearings, to take another pill.

Then he tugs the package out of his backpack, notes the address, heads up the street and sees the numbers, three, four feet tall, chrome and glittering.

He pushes through the door and stops at the desk.

"Hi," he says. "I've got a package for . . ."

He shows it to the guy at the desk, who directs him to the delivery entrance, outside and halfway down the block.

A blast of hot air hits him in the face and triggers something— *a mission, someone hurt or dying or . . . something*—but he can't get at it, can't remember what it was.

He plucks his damp shirt away from his chest, flaps the fabric back and forth to dry it, impossible in this humidity.

A horn blares and he ducks, the guy from the desk suddenly outside, beside him.

"Hey, fella, you okay?"

"Me? Oh . . . sure," he says, the world around him spinning, then slowing.

"It's just there," says the guy, pointing toward the delivery entrance.

"Got it," he says, tapping his backpack. "Everything's under control."

37

My eyes were burning, too much staring at computer screens, but I couldn't quit, couldn't tear myself away from this case. It was like making a bad sketch; you tell yourself it will get better if you just keep going. And sometimes it does.

I Googled Peter Sandwell. The only thing that came up was a newspaper article about his high school's wrestling team. I noted the name of the school, got the number, and called.

It took the guidance counselor a few minutes to find his transcript.

"Here he is, fifteen years ago, oh my, what a long time that's been," she said, in a chipper Dana Carvey "Church Lady" voice. "I started just after that, so I don't remember this young man. But let's see. Ah, he had very good grades. Isn't that nice—and his SATs were impressive, particularly his math score, seven-eighty, almost perfect. I'm not really a fan of the SATs, of any testing, for that matter. I mean, really what can it prove, it just doesn't—"

"What else?"

"Um . . . Let's see, he was captain of the wrestling team. Now that's good, something colleges look for, you know, the extracurricular activities, very important, even more so today; I mean, if

you haven't built a schoolhouse in Africa, I can tell you it's not easy
to get into the Ivy Leagues—"

"And his college?"

"Thomas Edison State College, a local school. He got a full
scholarship. Isn't that nice? We're not a wealthy community, so a
lot of our students go to state schools and—"

I stopped her again, asking if the school kept track of its students, and she said they tried. But there was nothing else on Peter
Sandwell. I thanked her and hung up.

I spread all the men's bios across my desk.

On Sandwell's I wrote, "Thomas Edison State College."

On Tully's, "Burlington State College, Pemberton, New Jersey."

I looked at O'Reilly's bio and circled "Fort Dix" without really
thinking about it.

I went from one file to another, but nothing came to me. And
yet I believed it was all here, in the lives of these perps and vics. I
just couldn't find it.

Burlington State College and Thomas Edison State College
were both state schools. But did that matter? I'd first thought Burlington State was in Burlington, Vermont, but had not asked about
Thomas Edison State College. I assumed it was in Ohio, Thomas
Edison's birthplace, but when I went to the school's website I was
wrong again. It was in New Jersey.

That's when I started to feel it, the slight pulsing of adrenaline.

Two schools in New Jersey.

I scrolled through the Edison College website and noticed a
subject area titled "Military/Government Affairs"; under it the
phrase "Special Ties to the Military," with a map that showed the
college was practically next door to McGuire Air Force Base.

I Googled the base. It was in Burlington County.

The same county as Burlington State College, which was in the town of Pemberton, three miles from Fort Dix, and adjacent to McGuire Air Force Base.

My adrenaline was pumping faster. Finally, a link between O'Reilly, Sandwell, and Tully, a geographic one.

Then I checked dates. Sandwell's and Tully's college years overlapped three out of four years. And when I looked at O'Reilly's service record at Fort Dix, it was the same years, too. All three men had been neighbors for at least two years.

I knew it didn't prove anything but proximity, but it was something.

That left Beamer and Billow.

When I saw that Floyd Billow's bio listed his birthplace as Hanover, New Jersey, I couldn't type fast enough, and then I saw the map: Hanover, Pemberton, Fort Dix, and MacGuire, side by side, only minutes apart.

Now I had Billow, Tully, O'Reilly, and Sandwell in the same area at the same time, all close enough to have met.

But Beamer lived in Queens, had never lived in New Jersey, nor gone to school there or done any military service in the state.

I reached for the phone and punched in the number.

"Mrs. Beamer?"

"Cioffi."

"Yes, of course. Sorry, this is Detective Rodriguez."

"I am *not* going to allow anyone to dig up my son, Detective. It's a waste of time to try and persuade me because—"

"That's not why I'm calling. I just need to ask you something. Did Wayne do any of his military training at McGuire Air Force Base or at Fort Dix?"

"No."

"You're absolutely sure about that?"

"Oh, yes."

I thanked her, feeling deflated, and was about to hang up when she stopped me.

"Wayne never did any training at those places, but the psychiatrist he saw, the one right after his discharge, he was right near there."

"Where?"

"Near Fort Dix."

"You're sure about that?" I said, my adrenaline pumping again.

"Yes. There was only the one time when I went with Wayne, but I remember seeing Fort Dix. We passed right by it and the doctor's office was only a couple of minutes away."

"Do you think you could find it again?"

"Oh, no. It was sixteen years ago, and like I said, it was only the one time."

"You wouldn't happen to have that doctor's name or telephone number?"

"I'm afraid not."

"How about an old bill or—"

"Wayne stopped seeing that doctor after a year, and frankly, I was glad. I think he did Wayne more harm than good."

"Do you think you could describe the doctor or his office?"

"I don't know, maybe, but . . ."

"Mrs. Cioffi, do me a favor. Close your eyes and try to picture yourself in the office, the feel of the chairs, the color of the walls, any posters or—"

"The walls . . . were painted red. I remember asking about that and the doctor saying that red was a very *embracing* color."

Now I remembered she had told me the same thing in her son's bedroom when I'd asked about the one wall Wayne had painted red.

I knew that somewhere buried in her subconscious was an impression of the doctor, so I led her through some relaxation exercises, got her to breathe deeply, and asked a few of my usual questions. It wasn't the same over the phone—I couldn't see her face and judge her emotions—but it was something. I got her to focus on the color of his hair and she said it was dark. From there we moved down his face. "I'd say he was about forty," she said. "With glasses, I think, yes, wire-framed glasses, but . . . I can't think of anything else."

We tried a bit more—more breathing, more associations, but without my props and pictures to stimulate her visual memory, she couldn't see it.

"You said you drove there, so let's try that," I said. "You're in the car with your son. Look at the windshield, the light playing across it, then turn and look at your son."

"Yes," she said, "I can see him."

"Good. Now, try and remember how you felt. You were concerned, but hopeful, right? Thinking, maybe this doctor can help him."

"Yes, exactly. I remember saying to Wayne, 'Maybe this doctor will be the one.' " There was a pause and I had a feeling she was back in that car, looking into the past.

"I remember the office. There were several doctors there."

"Like a clinic?"

"Yes, that's it."

"Let's go back a moment. You're walking up to the building. What do you see?"

"It's ordinary . . . red brick . . ."

"Are there any signs, a name you can see?"

"No. In fact, I remember thinking that it was odd, that there were no signs to say what the place was. I never would have found it by myself, but Wayne had been going there for a little while, so he knew how to find it."

"What about inside? At reception, say, a stack of doctor's cards or—"

"I don't remember seeing any, and I know I never had a card. Really, it was such a long time ago, Detective. Is this important?"

"I'm trying to get all the information I can for this case, Mrs. Cioffi."

"What *case*?" she said, and I heard her voice move from the past to the present.

"It's for the investigation, to try and find out what really happened to your son."

"I don't think that will ever happen, Detective. And I am not going to help the police dig up my son!"

"I understand, and that's not what I meant."

She sighed into the phone. "I'd like to help you, but I don't remember anything else."

I tried to get her back to the memory, but I'd lost her. She couldn't go back there now, or didn't want to.

I hung up and rewrote my list.

Beamer sees shrink at clinic near Ft. Dix.

O'Reilly at Ft. Dix, sees shrink near Ft. Dix, possibly same as above. (Check local clinics.)

Tully at Burlington State College, Pemberton, N.J.—3 miles from Ft. Dix.

Billow, born Hanover, N.J., in Burlington County.

Sandwell at Thomas Edison State College, near McGuire A.F. Base, Burlington County.

Then I went back to the Web. I searched for mental hospitals in the area, but all the clinics seemed to be local medical services, the physical kind, not mental. After a few minutes I got frustrated, so I called Terri, told her what I'd learned, and she connected me to the NYPD Research Department.

Manuel Torres, acting head of RSD, acted like he was not one bit happy to help me. I didn't have the time but I played my ethnic card, the old *granfalloon*, as Kurt Vonnegut would call it, the idea that, if you share something with another human being, say, both Democrats or Jews or WASPs, or in this case, Spanish, you must agree on everything else.

So I made a joke, in Spanish. Then I talked about the Puerto Rican Day Parade and how great it was, even though I'd never been. Then I asked where his *gente*, his people, were from, and he asked about mine and I told him about my *abuela*, and just like that we were best buds, *amigos*.

Thank you, Kurt Vonnegut.

He took down all my information about the towns and places and got back to me with a list of hospitals, clinics, doctors, dentists, and local psychiatrists.

It took me twenty-five minutes to call all the shrinks and leave messages on their machines; not one actually picked up the phone.

Then I sat back and started to chew a cuticle. It had been days since Terri had painted them and I picked until the skin around my thumb started to bleed. I just couldn't sit still. I started calling the hospitals and asking them about shrinks who had worked there in the early nineties, but I didn't really get anywhere until I called Virtua Memorial in Burlington County and the receptionist put me through to Personnel and a really nice woman named Sally Owen suggested I call her friend.

"She works at Buttonwood Hospital, over in Pemberton," she said. "In Mental Health Services. If anyone can help you find a psychiatrist in this neck of the woods, Carolina can."

38

Carolina Escobar turned out to have a soft cozy way of speaking that made me think right away she'd make a good shrink, and I said so.

"Oh, no, I'm just an administrator," she said.

I asked about her name and she said her parents were from Venezuela and I told her about my dad being Puerto Rican and there I was, into the Spanish bonding thing again. She asked where I lived and said her favorite Argentinean steakhouse was only a few blocks from my New York apartment. By then we were fast friends.

"I've been at Buttonwood Health Services for almost a decade," she said. "I guess that's why I sound like a therapist. You hang around therapists and mental health workers for twenty years and you end up sounding like one."

"I thought you said a decade?"

"I did. But I was at the Lucas Lab and Research Center before that for almost ten years."

"What's that?"

"Mainly a research facility, like the name says."

"And what do they research?"

"Nothing, not anymore. It was closed in ninety-seven."

"But you were there for ten years?"

"Yes."

I did the math: ten years at her present job, ten years at the last put her at the Lucas Lab in 1987. "So you were there in ninety-one?"

"That's right. I stayed there till the facility closed."

"Why did it close?"

"I'm not certain. I think it was because several of the top doctors and scientists left for other labs."

I asked a few questions and found out that most of the doctors were biologists and chemists, but she couldn't tell me what they actually did.

"I've been at Buttonwood for so long, it's all beginning to blur. It's a good thing I'm retiring in less than six months, and it's a good thing they're both affiliated with the government."

"Why is that?"

"Because of my pension. The government will accept the ten years at Lucas and the ten I'm about to finish up at Buttonwood."

She asked me why I was asking all these questions and I decided to tell her the truth.

She said she'd try to think about the doctors at the Lucas Lab and would get back to me.

My cell rang before I closed it.

"Oh, it's you," I said.

"Well, that's a warm welcome," said Terri.

"Sorry, I had the phone to my ear and was expecting someone else."

I told her where my string of calls had taken me and she said to keep notes and write everything up. I couldn't tell if she was happy I was connecting the dots, or not. Then my call-waiting beeped and it was Carolina Escobar, so I didn't get to ask.

"That was fast," I said.

"Well, the minute we hung up I pulled up the news stories on your cases and one of the names just jumped out at me."

"Which one?"

"Peter Sandwell. I'm pretty sure I knew him—if it's the same Peter Sandwell."

I did my best to describe Sandwell, his coloring and build, taking into consideration what he might have looked like sixteen or seventeen years ago.

"That sounds like him. He was just part-time, a very sweet young man. He worked for one of the doctors at the lab, a Dr. Gambel, who I knew quite well. Ah, see, I can remember something," she said. "Many of the doctors hired their own assistants, college students mostly, occasionally even high school students who were interested in science, and I know Peter was because he talked to me several times about becoming a doctor one day."

And clearly he was trying to do just that a lot later—premed at NYU at thirty-two.

Carolina Escobar took a deep breath. "My God, to think he was murdered."

"Is there anything else you can remember about him?"

"Just that he seemed depressed toward the end, when the lab was closing, but I guess that was because he was going to lose his job."

"And what about Dr. Gambel?"

"Oh, he quit before the lab closed."

"To go to another lab?"

"No, I'm pretty sure he was retiring. I remember now that he said he was moving back to New York, but he didn't say anything about a job there."

"You said something about Buttonwood and the Lucas Lab being affiliated with the government. How did you mean?"

"Just that they were both government-subsidized, which is why

I'll get my full pension—if I can last another five months here."
She laughed. "The Lucas Lab was fully subsidized, either part of
DARPA or reported to DARPA. I'm not sure which.

"What's DARPA?"

"That's the Defense Advanced Research Projects Agency. It's
a science agency—biology, technology, inventions, like that. Did
you know that the Internet was originally called the Darpanet?
That's because someone at DARPA designed the first mouse and
needed something to attach it to, so they invented the Internet.
Isn't that something?"

"I'll say. So was it DARPA that closed the lab?"

"I don't know."

I asked what Gambel did.

"He was a research doctor, mainly, a scientist."

I made a note of it, got the spelling of the doctor's name,
thanked her and called Information. There were two Jonathan
Gambels in New York City, only one listed, and I tried it.

"Is Dr. Gambel in?" I asked.

"I'm sorry, *who*?"

"Jonathan Gambel."

"Well, there *is* a Jonathan here but he's my sixteen-year-old
son, and though I hope and pray he might one day turn out to be
a doctor, right now he's a professional slacker!"

Another time I might have laughed, but I just asked her if she
knew a doctor with the same name, a relative, perhaps, and she
said no.

I called Terri back and asked her to get the unlisted number,
and she did. It was a 212 exchange, Manhattan. She asked that I
keep her posted, and I promised I would. I still couldn't read her
but didn't take the time to ask because I wanted to keep going and
see where the path would lead me.

A man answered on the sixth ring.

"Dr. Gambel?"

There was a long pause before he said, "Yes?"

I told him who I was, and that I was a cop. I didn't see any reason not to. Then I asked about Peter Sandwell.

He sucked in a labored breath. "Sorry . . ." He hesitated. "I never heard of him."

"I realize it was quite a while ago. You may have forgotten, but he was your assistant at the Lucas Lab, in Pemberton."

"Oh . . ." Another labored breath. "Well, I had quite a few assistants, but . . . I think you're mistaken. Is he in . . . some sort of trouble?"

"Dr. Gambel, I just spoke with a Carolina Escobar, who worked at the lab. You remember Ms. Escobar, don't you?"

"Oh . . . yes . . . of course. A . . . lovely . . . woman."

I wasn't sure if it was his breathing that slowed him down, or nerves.

"How . . . is she?" he asked.

"She's fine and *she* says Peter Sandwell was your assistant."

"Really? I must have . . . forgotten. It . . . was a long time ago." He wheezed and started to cough.

"Are you okay?"

"Asthma," he said.

I gave him a minute to catch his breath. "Did you know that Peter Sandwell is dead; that he was murdered?"

"Uh . . . yes . . . I . . . read . . . about . . . it," he said, taking short breaths in between words. "A . . . tragedy."

"But a minute ago you asked if he was in *trouble*. Why would you ask that if you *knew* he was murdered?"

"Oh . . . I—I didn't realize who you were . . . talking about . . . at first."

His breathing sounded worse and he asked me to hold on.

I wasn't sure if it was a ploy, a delaying tactic, but a minute later he was back. "Sorry, I just needed my inhaler. Steroids, the modern miracle."

He sounded better, so I pressed on. "Did you ever see Peter Sandwell after the lab closed?"

"A few times, yes, but I didn't know the man who killed him."

"Did you say you *didn't* know James O'Reilly?"

"That's right."

"Why would you say that?"

"What do you mean?"

"I mean, it was an odd thing to say, Doctor. I didn't ask if you *did* know him."

He didn't answer and I listened to him breathe, some of the labor back.

"Dr. Gambel, are you there?"

"Yes . . . I'm here."

I took a chance, a bluff. "It's funny that you mentioned O'Reilly, because Carolina Escobar said he was your patient."

"James O'Reilly? Oh, no, she's quite wrong." He took another deep breath. "I didn't see patients. I'm a clinical biologist, Detective, not . . . a therapist. I believe Mr. O'Reilly was seeing a therapist at the clinic, not me. Ms. Escobar is mistaken."

"So now you're saying you *did* know him, is that correct?"

"It was all so long ago, but . . . I guess I did." He forced a laugh, began to sputter and cough.

I didn't let it stop me. "And I take it you know that James O'Reilly is dead, too, don't you, Doctor?"

He paused, then said, "Yes," and the word had a different tone, soft and resigned.

I waited, listening to the doctor's labored breathing, holding myself in check, my own breath coming faster from the adrenaline rush.

"I'm not a well man, Detective." He paused. "Can you meet me?"

"What?" I hadn't expected that. "Yes, of course."

"It would be easier to discuss what I have to say in person, and I have some papers that might be of interest to you."

I asked him where he lived and he said the Upper West Side but didn't want to meet in his apartment. I told him Midtown North was not far away, but he didn't want to meet there either, so I told him I'd meet him anywhere, and he chose the Time Warner Center, at Columbus Circle.

"Under the Botero sculpture," he said. "Do you know it?"

"I can be there in fifteen minutes," I said, pacing, the phone to my ear.

"No," he said. "I need a little time to get things in order. Can you give me an hour?"

I said okay, though I didn't know how I was going to calm myself down for an hour after talking to a man who not only knew one of our vics, but knew the man who had killed him.

"How will I know you?" I asked.

"What do you look like, Detective?"

I told him I was tall and dark; that I'd be wearing faded jeans and a white T-shirt.

"In an hour," he said. "Under the Botero. *I'll* find *you*."

39

The music is blasting inside his head, drums and electric guitar, that song, Ron's favorite, stuck on repeat, "Lawyers, Guns and Money," playing over and under the explosions and screams, the two fused long ago and far away, building, building and—*kapow!*—like a shot of Benzedrine right into the brain!

He bolts up, sweat-soaked, pillow damp, smelling of fear, an emotion he cannot understand. Pain, yes, but fear, no.

A dream, that's all it was, a bad dream. I'm okay.

The room comes into focus—flocked wallpaper, peeling; chipped wood molding; blinking numbers on the digital alarm: 2:36 . . . 37 . . . 38 . . . 39 . . . 40 . . .

Was he really asleep? *Asleep?* But he never sleeps. Or maybe he's still sleeping.

The screams are still in his head—or is it the guitar?

He shakes a pill out of a vial, swallows it, lights a cigarette, and stares at the swirling blue smoke; his life breaking apart, drifting away.

But no, he's got a chance. He's got help, the support group, and he's going to make it. If only the noise would stop, the static and explosions, like there are loose wires in his brain, electric sparks threatening to short-circuit.

Another pill: emotion in digestible form.

Some hero.

He lies in bed watching digital numbers erase time.

Finally he gets up, showers, dresses, combs his hair, gathers the papers and puts them into his backpack.

He crosses the street, telling himself he is fine, then a taxi hits a manhole cover, a bus backfires, a siren blares, and his throat constricts, dry eyes burn, and it's a battlefield—mines and tanks, the enemy everywhere.

The dust clears, a man in uniform approaches; his brain computing: *How do I play this?*

He stands up, pats the dirt from his pants, and smiles.

"You okay?" the cop asks.

The world around him spins, then slows, positive to negative, the enemy's eyes blue, then blood-red, and he says, "I am fine, sir," very carefully, very slowly. "I tripped, that's all. But I will be fine, more than fine, superfine."

"You sure?" The cop stares at him, suspicious.

"Yes, I'm fine," he says, then turns away and with the enemy's red eyes burning holes in his back he waits until he is able to cross the battlefield—bombs exploding, smoke everywhere—to fish more pills from his pocket.

The meds travel on saliva and blood to arteries and veins, make their way into his brain and he is calm again. He knows he can make it to his destination, tell his story simply and plainly, and then everything will be okay.

40

The Time Warner Center is an anomaly for
New York, not just a corporate headquarters
but a large upscale mall in midtown Manhattan, a mix of food shops and bakeries, clothing, shoes, and bookstores, and some of the
city's most expensive restaurants. It's like a
city within the city, like Rikers, but the food
and people look a lot better.

When I got there it was jammed, overheated New Yorkers
seeking refuge in the air-conditioned atrium, and me dodging
baby strollers and tour groups, teens with iPods that apparently
made them blind as well as deaf, businessmen screaming into
Mr. Spock–like Bluetooth gadgets—everyone plugged into some
device or another—the world of the future here and now, loud and
in your face. And all of it adding to my angst.

I had been standing under the oversized Botero sculpture for
twenty minutes, pacing, wired.

Gambel was late. I'd given him the hour he'd asked for and it
had stretched into an hour and a half.

My eyes locked on every man who came in: a fifty-something

man in khakis, a silver-haired guy in a three-piece suit, a fat man in a tank top, a skinny one in sweats, none of them giving me a second glance.

I called Gambel again but there was no answer. He's on his way, I told myself.

But then another ten minutes passed and I started to worry.

Had I been duped?

I thought it through: I call Gambel out of nowhere, announce who I am, tell him I am investigating a case where he knew both victim and perpetrator, then give him enough time to make a getaway. Yeah, duped, and a dope.

But he'd sounded sincere. Yeah, like every criminal I'd ever known, all practiced liars.

But was Gambel a criminal? I had no idea. Was I creating conspiracies where none existed? I didn't really know anything about the man other than the fact that Peter Sandwell had been his assistant sixteen years ago and O'Reilly had seen a therapist at the clinic where he worked.

I started pacing again, peered into store windows, one eye always on the entrance.

Another ten minutes came and went. I called Gambel. I let the phone ring a dozen times.

Then I called Terri. I explained that I'd reached Gambel and was supposed to meet him but he'd stood me up.

"Why didn't you call me?"

"I'm calling you now."

I asked if she could get a reverse operator for Gambel's address and she wanted to know why I thought he was so important.

"Because Peter Sandwell was Gambel's assistant way back when—and because Gambel seemed to know James O'Reilly. How's that for important?"

I paced back and forth under the Botero sculpture waiting for her to get back to me. It couldn't have been more than a few minutes but it seemed like an hour.

"I have an address for Gambel, but you are not flying solo on this, Rodriguez. Perez is on Fifty-seventh Street. I'll have him meet you."

"No, I need to talk to Gambel alone. I need him to trust me. I can't go in there with Perez."

"You're not doing this alone." She paused. "Okay, *I'll* meet you. Corner of Eighty-first and Riverside."

"What's the address?"

"On the *corner*," she repeated. "In twenty minutes."

41

There was no shade on Riverside and Eighty-first. One way the sun was in my face, the other, on my neck. I felt as if I was being roasted on a spit and Terri's twenty minutes had already stretched into thirty by the time I spotted her car.

She pulled the Charger beside a hydrant and got out.

"I'm melting," I said.

"Poor baby," she said.

"Let's go." I couldn't stand still.

"Jesus, Rodriguez, relax."

"I can't. This guy could be gone by now."

She handed me the Post-it on which she'd written the address and we headed down the street.

"You could have given me this on the phone so I didn't have to bake on the corner. You didn't trust me to wait for you, that it?"

She answered me with a look that said: *You got that right.*

"There it is," I said, matching the address on the Post-it with the numbers on the brownstone.

We headed up the stairs. The front door intercom had six names, "J. Gambel" was on two. He didn't answer the buzzer.

I tried him on my cell again, let it ring for a full minute, then hung up.

"Maybe you *did* scare him off," said Terri. She pressed a couple of other buzzers.

A moment later there were two overlapping voices.

"Either one of you the super?" she asked.

A woman's voice said, "Who wants to know?"

"The police," said Terri.

"Under the stairs," she said.

"I am not the super," said the woman peering through the gated door on street level. "I am the owner. My name is Sherree Elks, that's with two *e*'s, the Sherree part, not the Elks part." Her voice was high and reedy and she enunciated every word as if taking a class in diction. "Elks is my stage name. I was born Sherry, with a *y*, Sherry Eczwizniski, dreadful name, don't you think? May I see some identification, please?"

Terri produced her badge.

"What about you, handsome?" She eyed me through the gate.

I started to get my temporary shield out, but Terri said, "He's with me."

"Lucky you," she said, and opened the gate.

Sherree Elks was around seventy-five, a tall, skeletal woman, possibly beautiful at one time, in a dragon-lady sort of way, now looking as if someone had leached the last drop of moisture out of her; a face made of angles, skin like onion paper, hair dyed strawberry, and fully made up—lipstick to match her hair, false eyelashes two inches long.

I told her we were looking for Dr. Gambel.

"We-ll," she said, drawing out the word, "you have come to the right place. He is on two."

"He isn't answering his bell," said Terri.

"Then he must be out."

"Look," I said. "I spoke to him a couple of hours ago and he was home. Did you happen to see if he went out?"

"I do not spy on my tenants, officer."

"Of course not. I just thought you might have seen him leave, as your windows are on street level."

"I was busy rehearsing my lines." She gave me a look and I could see she was waiting for me to ask—*What lines?*—but I did not.

"We really need to see Dr. Gambel," said Terri. "Now."

"Well, I cannot help you with that."

"Suppose I insist that you open his door," said Terri.

Sherree Elks's mouth tightened, strawberry lipstick snaking into whistle lines. "I would consider that a breach of Dr. Gambel's privacy and I know how these things work. You need a warrant. I watch my share of *Law and Order*."

"Fine," said Terri, "I'll call for a warrant."

"Hold on." I offered up my best smile, the one that works on both of my grandmothers, the combination nice Jewish boy and Latin lover. "So," I said, "what are you rehearsing for?"

Sherree's face lit up and she took off. "I am playing Violet in *Suddenly Last Summer.* Last year I was the mother, Amanda, in *The Glass Menagerie.* Of course I am *way* too young for that part, but I wore a gray wig. Our theater company has been doing Tennessee Williams for years; before *Menagerie* it was *Milk Train*, and what a part that was, Flora Goforth, don't you just *love* that name, not Tennessee's most successful play, I'm afraid, a late one, nineteen-sixty-something, before your time." She laid one of her bony hands on my arm, blood-red talons tapping my flesh. "The movie version was called *Boom*, I think, or something silly like that, an absolute fiasco, Richard Burton as a young poet and Elizabeth Taylor as a dying old woman when she looked the picture of health. But our production was superb, the crème de la crème. The *Village Voice* called my performance *stirring*."

"I'll bet you got an Obie nomination," I said, referring to the off-Broadway version of the Tonys.

"I did *not*. Though many people in the theater world thought I was robbed."

"I'm sure you were," I said.

Terri was tapping her foot and I gave her a look. Working Sherree Elks for a few minutes was a lot faster than getting a warrant.

"So," I said, "tell me about Dr. Gambel?"

"A lovely man. He helped me go over my lines." She leaned in close, the smell of gardenia-like perfume suffocating. "I think he has a bit of a *thing* for me," she whispered.

"And when was this, when he helped you with the lines?" Terri asked.

Sherree answered Terri while looking at me. "Earlier today. He was coming back with coffee. He's retired, you know, lovely man, terrible asthma, though. It was so hot in my apartment, the air conditioner, just isn't doing what it should, so I was sitting on the steps and I asked Dr. Gambel if he wouldn't mind playing the part of Dr. Sugar, and he did. Did you ever see the movie, from the seventies, with Montgomery Clift as the doctor and Elizabeth Taylor again, this time as a mental patient?"

"No," I said. "I'll have to rent it."

"Do that," she said, "and when you do, picture me in the part played by Katharine Hepburn."

"I can't wait," I said. "And I'll bet you were a lot better than Kate."

Her face practically cracked from her smile.

"Listen, Sherree. It's real important we get into Dr. Gambel's apartment. He'll never know. It will be just between us."

"Oh, I don't know, perhaps it is best if you do get that warrant. I don't want to get in trouble with Dr. Gambel."

Terri looked almost pleased that I'd failed to win Sherree over with my charm. "I'm calling it in right now," she said, reaching for her cell.

I knew she was bullshitting. There was no way we would get a warrant. So I went to Plan B.

"Sherree," I said. "Hold that pose!"

Sherree Elks froze as I slipped off my backpack, got out my pad and pencil, and started whipping off a sketch.

"Man, have you got it all," I said. "The bones, the features."

Sherree lifted her head and posed like she was Helen of Troy.

Terri had stopped tapping her foot, but her lips were a knot of impatience.

"Just two more minutes," I said.

"Let him finish," said Sherree.

Two minutes later I tore the sketch out of my pad and handed it over. It was a good likeness, though I'd given her the drawing equivalent of a face-lift.

"Oh, my, you have really captured me," said Sherree, studying the portrait. "I'll just go get those keys to Dr. Gambel's apartment."

"See," I said when Sherree was out of earshot.

"Yeah, but that was fifteen minutes of my *life*," said Terri. "This had better be worth it, Rodriguez."

Sherree Elks was back in less than a minute.

We followed her inside and up the stairs.

She knocked gently on the door. "Dr. Gambel?" she whispered. "It's Sherree; are you in, dear?"

I leaned past her and rapped on the door so hard it shook, my impatience finally getting the better of me. When there was no answer I told Sherree Elks to use the key.

42

Terri asked Sherree Elks to wait outside Gambel's apartment, but she followed us in, now fluttering around his body like a hummingbird.

"Oh my God, oh my God, is he breathing? Dr. Gambel, Dr. Gambel. Oh my God. Maybe it's just the heat. Why isn't the air conditioner on? It must be a hundred in here, oh my God, oh my God."

Terri took her gently by the arms and got her into a chair facing away from the body.

I slipped on gloves and checked for a pulse in Gambel's neck, my hands shaking, and it was not just because the man was dead. I recognized his face.

It was the man I had drawn from my *abuela*'s vision! But how was that possible?

There are some things that we cannot understand, Nato. Some things we cannot explain.

I stared at Gambel's face. There was no mistake. It was the same man. And it sent shivers through my body.

"He's dead," I said.

"I can see that," said Terri.

"Oh—my—God," said Sherree Elks.

There was an inhaler on the floor at Gambel's feet, but I didn't touch it.

"Now what?" Terri asked.

I knew what we had to do.

"Take Ms. Elks downstairs," I said. "Then come right back up."

Severe asthma attack. Possibly caused by the heat."

The M.E. was speaking to Barton and Peterson, who had arrived just minutes after Terri and I finished searching the apartment.

"You sure?" asked Barton.

"No," said the M.E., "but it's my best guess without opening him up and taking a look at his lungs." A techie had bagged the inhaler and the M.E. held it up in front of Barton. "Beta-agonist inhaler with salmeterol and formoteral. Great drugs in the short term, but use them too much and you run the risk of weakening your lungs, opening them up to all sorts of infection and inflammation." He squinted at it through the plastic bag. "Looks like this is the last of six refills. Your vic here has probably been overusing the stuff for way too long."

A tech team was vacuuming the rug, the noise setting my nerves on edge.

Barton leaned in close to the M.E. and whispered something I couldn't hear.

After that, they zipped Gambel into a bag and I watched Peterson take Terri by the arm and lead her into the hallway.

I had already gone through it with Barton—*Why was I here? Did I know who Gambel was? What had he said to me?*—though I had a feeling he knew the answers. I told him that I'd discovered Peter Sandwell had worked for Gambel and wanted to see if he could tell me anything that might illuminate the case. Barton finished up with the M.E. and came back to me.

"So Gambel was dead when you arrived?"

"Yes," I said. "I already told you that."

"I still don't understand why he wanted to meet you." He looked down on me, a fairly new experience, as I topped six feet. Barton was a pituitary case if there ever was one.

"He didn't," I said. "*I* wanted to meet *him*."

Barton had completely neutralized his large square face.

I remembered reading that the FBI was now teaching Paul Ekman's face-reading technique as part of their core program. Barton had probably watched Ekman's videotapes and practiced—and he was good. I couldn't read him at all.

The techies finished vacuuming, opened the machine, dumped the contents into a bag, and slapped an FBI sticker on it.

I was starting to get the picture.

I tried to remember what I'd said to Terri on the phone. Had I mentioned Gambel's papers? What if they'd been listening to our calls? It would account for their quick arrival on the scene. Though not quick enough. Terri and I had been able to make a search of Gambel's drawers and closets, but found no papers, no photos, nothing. It was as if his entire personal history was missing.

Had the feds already been here? Was this all just a part of their ruse?

They could be Special Op or Homeland Security. Karen Hart's words were playing in the back of my mind.

Barton inched forward until I was backed up against the wall. "Tell me again why you wanted to speak with Gambel?"

"Because Sandwell, one of the vics, had worked as an assistant to Gambel a long time ago, like an intern or something. And I thought perhaps Gambel could shed some light on him, on Sandwell."

"Why would you think that?"

"Because I'm a cop."

"Really?" said Barton, a hint of a sneer on his lips. He looked at me for a long moment. Then he said, "What did you think of the 9/11 attack on America?"

"What?" I wasn't sure I'd heard him correctly.

"It's a simple question."

"It was a terrible tragedy," I said.

"I understand you were there, at Ground Zero, that day."

"I was nearby, at Police Plaza, when it happened."

"Really? Because *I* heard you were down at the Trade Center."

"Well, yeah, I was, later. I went with some firemen."

"*Oh?* Why was that?"

"Because I wanted to help. But I don't see what this has to do with Dr. Gambel."

Barton didn't respond. He was using a well-known police technique: Intimidate the suspect, then go quiet and wait for him to fill the silence. So I stopped talking.

A minute passed.

"You spend a lot of time in the outer boroughs, don't you, Rodriguez?"

"What do you mean?"

"Just that it's odd—you working in Manhattan, and being in Queens and the Bronx all the time."

If I was right, he was letting me know they were following me.

"I work for all the precincts," I said. "Sometimes I even go out of state to do a sketch."

"Really?" said Barton, though I was sure he knew that. Then he said, "Like New Jersey?"

"I haven't made a sketch in New Jersey for some time."

"Oh?" He let that hang there. Then he said, "You know you just can't trust the word of a man with a failing memory."

O'Reilly's CO, Rathjay, was that who he meant? But I wasn't going to play the game of answering his nonquestions, which were simply meant to intimidate.

Barton looked at me for another long minute, and we had a staring contest. But I could neutralize my face even better than he could.

"So tell me about your phone conversation with Gambel."

"I told you. It lasted less than two minutes. I explained to Gambel that I was a cop and wanted to ask him a few questions about Peter Sandwell."

"And he invited you over?"

"Yes."

"And that was it?"

"Yes."

"So you never got to speak to Gambel in person?"

"No."

Another long pause. "You realize there will be a problem if I find out otherwise, so you're absolutely sure about your answer?"

I said, "Yes," and saw something in Barton's face relax, the muscles in his cheeks and jaw easing slightly, enough to tell me that this was his main concern: that I hadn't actually gotten to speak to Gambel.

"He was dead when I got here," I repeated, and did not have to freeze my features the way he did because I was speaking the truth and knew my face would not betray me.

Barton and Peterson had dismissed me and Terri.

"The G are such—" Terri stopped speaking when we caught sight of Peterson under the steps, talking with Sherree Elks.

"Next year," said Sherree, "we are doing *Night of the Iguana*. I will play Maxine, that's the part Bette Davis made famous on Broadway and Ava Gardner in the movie. Personally, I think I would be better as Hannah, the Deborah Kerr role. She has the best line; she says, 'Nothing human disgusts me.' "

Sherree had recovered well, her bony hands fluttering around Peterson's face like moths.

At the moment he looked as if *everything* human disgusted him.

I glanced up at the second-floor brownstone window and caught a glimpse of Barton parting the curtains. When he saw me looking at him he let them fall back into place.

"Who the hell *are* these guys?" I whispered to Terri as we slid into her Charger.

43

Have you asked Denton?"

"About Barton and Peterson? Yeah. He told me to do my job and mind my business," said Terri.

"And this isn't *your* business?"

"Apparently not."

"Well, whatever it was Gambel wanted to tell me they sure as hell didn't want me to find out. Do you think they killed him?"

"The feds?" Terri turned away from the traffic long enough to give me a look, brows raised. "I don't know what their game is, Rodriguez, but don't go off on conspiracy theories."

"You don't think it's possible?"

"Anything is possible, but no."

"But things were just starting to line up and I think Gambel might have been able to tell me why."

"*If* he was telling you the truth."

"Why would he lie?"

"Because you called and intimidated him; how about that?"

She had a point, though I wasn't sure I had forced him to say anything.

"There's still Tully," I said.

"Meaning what?"

"I can talk to him again; see if he knows anything about Gambel or the lab."

"You ready for another bump on the head?"

"I'll wear a helmet and keep a guard in the room. What about you?"

"What about me?"

"How are you going to handle the cases now?"

Terri stared through the windshield but I could see the muscles under her skin moving ever so slightly as she thought it through. "I don't know. But I don't like them shutting me down and bigfooting my case. I don't need a cold case, *several* cold cases, on my record." She whipped the car around Columbus Circle and hit the brakes when a cab cut in front of her. "The way those guys waved me out of that crime scene like I was some *girl* really pissed me off."

"They didn't exactly treat *me* with respect," I said. "And Barton asked me what I was doing at Ground Zero."

"Why?"

"Intimidation, I'd guess, which was starting to work. And he all but came out and said they'd been following me."

"That's just their style, to make you think they know all your dirty little secrets." Terri chewed her lower lip, and I wondered what Peterson had said to her—what dirty little secrets of hers he implied he knew.

She gunned the engine and cut the Charger down Fifty-fourth Street.

"Sad, isn't it?" she said. "All the competition and shit between us and them, the G and the PD. Why can't we all be one big happy family?"

"Yeah, like the Sopranos?"

Terri laughed. "Honestly? I'd play ball with them if they'd play ball with me."

"Dream on," I said.

They had moved Matthew Tully off Rikers and into Saint Vincent's Hospital in Greenwich Village, which was a lot easier to get to and a lot less scary. Lucky for him, he had developed some sort of bronchial infection and they did not want it to spread and infect the entire island population. It got me thinking about Gambel's sudden death from asthma. True, the guy had sounded short of breath when I spoke to him; but dead, just a couple of hours later? My crap detector wasn't buying it.

A nurse gave me a mask and I went into Tully's room.

He didn't look as if he'd be able to tell me anything. Maybe it was the infection or maybe it was the meds the doctors were feeding him. He looked bloated and doped, sitting up in bed, head forward on his chest, wrists and ankles cuffed, but he didn't look like he needed any restraints.

They'd posted a uniform and he offered me his seat but I told him to stay and dragged another chair in from the hall.

"Matthew," I said, "how's it going?"

He struggled to focus. He didn't look like he could remember his mother's name.

"He been like this for long?" I asked the uniform.

"Yeah, pretty much out of it," he said. "But he talks like a banshee in his sleep."

I turned back to Tully. "I've got a few questions; you with me?"

His eyes found me, but he didn't respond.

"Do you remember Burlington County College in Pemberton, New Jersey? Does that sound familiar?"

Nothing.

"You went to school there, to college, remember?"

Still nothing.

"How about the Lucas Lab?"

He blinked, but it could have been a reflex. I needed something to jolt his memory. I thought again about the sketch I'd made and what the woman he'd attacked had said about him.

He kept touching his head . . . It was like he was in pain.

I got up and asked the guard if he'd stand right beside me. Then I reached forward and pressed my hand hard against Tully's forehead.

He reared back as if punched, hands to his forehead, cuffs banging against his face. He looked like a scared dog and it gave me an idea.

"Matthew," I said. "*Listen* to me. You *must* do this. It's an *order*. We're going to start the test now."

But he didn't respond. Maybe he was too far gone, too drugged. His eyes were hooded and flat again, mouth slack.

"Try calling him number six," said the uniform.

"What?"

"He keeps calling out 'Number six' in his sleep, asking himself questions and answering them. It doesn't make sense but . . ."

"Number Six," I said.

Tully's eyes snapped into focus. "Yes, sir."

What was this?

"Number Six, we are going to start a test."

The depressor glabellae muscles tightened Tully's brow with concentration and before I could say anything, it was stuttering out of him.

"A B A C A D B B C A A D E E A B C C A A B D C C A B E A A A C—"

His thumb was twitching at his side as if he were clicking a remote control.

"B D A B C C D D E A A B B E E B—"

"Number Six," I said. "Test over."

Tully stopped short.

I thought for a moment. "What was my last question, Number Six?"

Tully focused on a point past my head, a dead stare at nothing in particular, and answered in a robotic tone.

"If—train—X—is—traveling—at—twenty—miles—an—hour—and—train—Y—is—traveling—at—sixteen—and—both—trains—started—at—two—o'clock—p.m.—from—a distance—of—one—hundred—miles—apart—at—what—time—will—they—reach—their—destination? A—eight p.m. B—six p.m.—C—seven p.m.—"

"And the preceding question?"

"Which—of—the—following—presidents—was—assassi-nated? A—Grant. B—Lincoln. C—Kennedy. D—all of the above. E—none of the above."

"And the first?"

"Hawaii—was—ratified—as—part—of—the—United—States—in—what—year? A—nineteen fifty-nine. B—nineteen—"

The questions made no sense.

"Who taught you this?" I asked.

Tully was still reciting answers to the questions about Hawaii.

"Number Six, where did you learn this?"

He stopped talking and his features froze.

"Number Six, step forward."

Tully lunged forward, cuffs rattling as he attempted to get out of bed, and I stood back.

"Stop!" I shouted. "Number Six, at ease."

Tully sagged back into the bed.

"Hey, Number Six," said the uniform. "How about barkin' like a dog?"

Tully started to howl.

"That's not funny," I said, and the uniform bit his lip.

"Number Six, *stop* barking," I said, and he did.

What the hell was this?

Tully had not been in the army. He had no military record at all. But if he had not been in the army, where had he learned this?

It took me a few seconds to come up with an answer: the Lucas Lab. I didn't know if I was right, but it was the only thing I could think of and it set my nerve ends tingling.

"Number Six, where did you learn this?"

Tully's facial muscles tensed, but he stared straight ahead, said nothing.

"Number Six, what is your mother's full name?"

"Flora Getz Tully."

"And where did you go to college, Number Six?"

"Burlington State College, Pemberton, New Jersey."

"And where are you now, Number Six?"

He hesitated a moment.

"I—am—in—a lovely—tea—garden."

"What?"

Tully looked around the room, but his pupils remained fixed; he was not really seeing anything.

"*Where* are you, Number Six?"

"I—am—in—a—lovely—tea—garden."

I asked again and got the same response.

"Number Six—"

"A—lovely—tea—garden—a—lovely—tea—garden—a— lovely—tea—garden—a—lovely—"

"Number Six, there is *no* tea garden. You are in a hospital."

"I—am—in—a—lovely—tea—garden," he said, then leaned forward and with the back of his cuffed hands gently touched the scar on his forehead. When I moved closer, I could see he was crying.

Terri closed her office door behind me before I could tell her anything.

"It's official," she said. "FBI all the way. No more NYPD involvement. We're out."

"And that's it?"

"That's it."

"Where's it coming from?"

"The top. From Denton, via the bureau, and who knows where else—the army, the fucking White House? For all I know it could be the former KGB, since we don't know who the hell Barton and Peterson are actually working for."

"Now who's going all conspiracy theory?"

Terri sighed.

"Is there a verdict on Gambel's death?"

"I have no idea."

"Can't you requisition the autopsy papers, or something?"

"Gambel's body is *gone*, Rodriguez, shipped to another morgue, Quantico's, I'm guessing. It's a federal case, didn't you hear me? The only ones who are doing any requisitioning are the G. They want all of our files, everything." She started pacing.

"Do you think they know about Tully?" I asked.

"Not from my lips, but they seem to know everything else and I'm guessing they know about Tully, too."

"So now what?"

"Now? Nothing."

"So what do you want me to do?"

"If you're not working on a sketch, go home."

"Just dump everything we have on the case?"

"I just told you, Rodriguez; it's over."

It wasn't like Terri to back down so easily.

"Are they threatening you?"

"Look, a wrong move could cost me my job—and Denton let me know that loud and clear." She blinked a few times, her features going angry and sad all at once.

I tried to put my arm around her but she pushed me away.

"Don't," she said.

"Why not?"

"Because you're going to make me cry, for Christ's sake, and that's the last thing I need to do." She took a deep breath. "Just go make a sketch or go home, and don't push this, okay? It won't be good for me—and it won't be good for you, either."

"Look, I can—"

"No, you *can't*. Whatever it is you think you can do I don't want to hear it, not now. Just go home."

44

I had no sketch scheduled, so I did what she said, I headed home.

But I was pissed; pissed at the feds, and pissed at Terri. I didn't like her telling me what to do; I didn't like her telling me there was nothing I could say that would make her feel better. Wasn't she the one who was always telling me to open up and talk?

It felt like the case was coming between us; that working together had been a mistake.

I decided to walk. I needed to burn off some steam and the city felt like a sauna, so it seemed right. Halfway home I was sorry. The heat was worse than ever, humidity like the rain forest. The newspapers were full of stories about old people dying in stifling apartments, Con Ed straining to keep up with demand, and failing. They'd already cut power and the city felt like it was melting, with predictions of more heat and record-breaking temperatures to come. I needed to get away, away from the cases, away from New York.

I decided to call Julio and take him up on his East Hampton offer. I got my cell phone out and saw I had four messages, all from Lieutenant Rogers, one of Guthrie's men up in the Bronx. I had promised to make a sketch with a witness, and had totally forgotten; a first for me. It was too late now, so I just called and left an apology. I said I'd do the sketch at his convenience. I felt like a fuckup and I was right. The cases had taken over my life. But I still didn't want to walk away.

Maybe I was just trying to get the respect that I could never get as a sketch artist. Hell, I was tops in my field, had helped crack one of the biggest homicide cases of the past year, and still some of the detectives treated me like a second-class citizen.

But I knew that wasn't really it. I just wanted to know what had happened to Beamer and O'Reilly, Billow and Tully, and now, Gambel. Being disrespected by other cops I could live with; being shut out of a case that was just coming together, unacceptable.

My mother used to say I was just like my father: stubborn. And she was right. The more people said no to me, the more I pushed back.

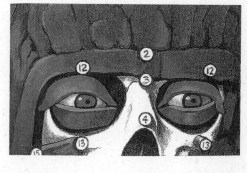

When I got home I went right to work on the facial reconstruction. Maybe I could redeem myself with Guthrie if it turned out to be something that he could use toward an arrest, which would be a good thing for both of us.

The clay was cracking in a few places, so I got some water and smoothed over the fissures and that was all it took to get me back into it.

I rolled out clay and cut strips, added the upper eyelids, and for the moment I forgot about the FBI.

It doesn't always feel good to make art, but it sure as hell distracts you, and right now that was exactly what I needed. Making a sketch with a witness was one thing, but this was different—there

was no one telling me what to do. I was alone with the work. As I measured and molded, rolled out clay and added it to the face, I could feel it taking on more and more life.

I'd covered most of the skull except for the nose. There was a simple formula for figuring out its length and width based on the skull size and nasal opening. I measured the distance from the subnasale to the pronasale, then created a loop of clay, attached it to the nasal cavity, and started to shape it.

I stood back, looked at one side, then another, once again trying to make sense of who this guy was and why I was so determined to finish. My stubborn streak was part of it, sure, I didn't like to admit failure and I didn't like to quit, but there was something else, something waiting to be revealed—a face that would tell me something that I needed to know. I started thinking about what my *abuela* had said about following a path, and it kept me going.

I let the sculpture direct me; tell me where to fill out the clay and where to cut away. I was seeing and feeling him through the touch of my fingers, imagining the flesh and muscle under my hands. I covered every inch with small bits of clay, occasionally smoothing the surface with my fingertips, pressing sandpaper into it to create skinlike texture, and with each new thing I did, it took on more life.

There was no way to know what his eyebrows would have been like, but I trusted my intuition as I used the pointed edge of my wooden tool to incise them.

I stopped and looked at what I'd done. I didn't know why but it felt right, like this was the guy, like he was looking at me and waiting to tell me something.

I touched the fleshlike clay and stared into the plastic eyes that seemed surprisingly lifelike.

After a while I rubbed the clay off my hands and started to make a list of what I would need for the final touches: a lighter-toned face makeup, a brown eyebrow pencil, and something for the hair. I wasn't sure about the length or how much, but decided I'd go to New York Costume on lower Broadway, buy a cheap wig, and cut it up till I got something that felt right for the face.

I took another look at the reconstruction, but a different face came into my mind, Matthew Tully's.

I called Saint Vincent's to see how he was doing.

The receptionist asked if I was family and I told her I was a cop.

"He's no longer here," she said. "He's been moved."

"*What?* Where?"

"I'm sorry," she said, "but I don't have that information."

I asked to speak with the doctor in charge.

"Yes, what is it?" The doctor sounded as if I'd woken him up.

I asked about Tully and he told me he'd been moved to a research facility.

"Which one—and why?"

"I don't know," he said. "It wasn't up to me."

"Who was it up to?"

"Look, you'll have to get that information elsewhere. I don't have it."

I called Schmid in Sex Crimes and asked if she'd authorized Tully's move.

It was the first she'd heard of it and she wasn't happy. I asked her to connect me to Homicide, and I got O'Connell.

"Has to be the G," he said. "Who else could it be?"

"But how would they know about Tully?"

"You kidding?" he said. "Just let it be, Rocky."

How had they found Tully, a rape suspect, not yet connected to the other cases?

My paranoia ratcheted up another notch, and I thought about Barton implying they'd been watching me. I washed up, feeling like there were cameras on me, like I was in that reality show *Big Brother*, and I wanted out.

At the door I got an odd, queasy feeling, turned back and got my gun. I couldn't say why but felt better when I slipped it into my pocket.

Downstairs, the lobby was deserted, the dim light an invitation to crime. I'd mentioned this more than once to the realty company that owned and operated the building, and they told me if I didn't like it I should move out. It didn't faze them that I was a cop, which said something about the power of the NYPD versus the power of New York City real estate moguls.

The sun had set but it was still hot and muggy, a light drizzle starting up. I'd only taken a few steps out the door when I saw him.

45

The guy was something out of a Raymond Chandler novel, trench coat and hat, just standing there, across the street. When he saw me he started walking away, slowly, and no one but tourists walk slowly in New York—and my block is not exactly a tourist attraction.

I started down the street and we kept pace, but when I crossed over to his side he picked up speed and turned the corner.

When I got there he was gone. I looked north and south, hand on the gun in my pocket, glad I'd brought it with me, but he was nowhere.

The street was dark, not much open but a bodega and a bar. I peeked into both, but didn't see him.

I walked a couple of blocks north to my neighborhood coffee shop, telling myself to chill out, but couldn't. It seemed to confirm that the feds had someone tailing me.

Inside, the coffee shop was half empty, two booths with teens who were complaining loudly about missing their bus to Jersey, another with a guy who looked as if he'd scratched together just enough change for his cup of coffee.

I opted for the counter, ordered a burger and fries, and thought about the FBI usurping the case. It wasn't like Terri to give up so easily. Denton must have leaned on her hard.

I ate my burger, chatting with the counterman about baseball and the heat wave, and it passed the time, though it didn't do much for my mood.

Back outside, I looked for the guy in the trench coat but the street was empty, mist rising off the sidewalks.

Terri was working late and I didn't feel like being alone, so I stopped for a nightcap. Two guys with matching gray ponytails were at the bar, one in leather pants that seemed deadly in this weather. There was a good-looking woman in her forties, dark hair, tank top, paint-splattered jeans that made me think she was an artist, sitting at the end. I slipped onto the barstool beside her, ordered a Brooklyn lager, and she gave me a smile.

"You think this heat will ever end?" she asked.

"Yeah, sure," I said, "when the polar icecaps melt and Manhattan is underwater it should get *really* cool."

"Whoa!" she said, and turned away.

Oh, I was a charmer, no doubt about that.

"Sorry," I said, but too late.

I drank my beer staring at the TV over the bar, a *Seinfeld* episode I knew, where Elaine is moving into the apartment above Jerry's and he's not happy about it. It got me thinking about the way Terri had pretty much moved into my space, something we'd never discussed that just sort of happened. Lately the combination of working together during the day and being home together at night got me wondering if it was too much togetherness. But here she was working late and I missed her.

Clearly, there was no way I was ever going to be happy.

I ordered another beer, watched the rest of *Seinfeld* and stayed for the news. The arty woman and the guys with gray ponytails were laughing and it was getting on my nerves, so I decided to call it a night.

I headed back to my apartment, the air heavy, street lamps infusing the mist with acid-yellow light.

My lobby was empty, but the back door that led to the stairwell, ajar. I peeked in and shouted hello; no one answered. The new superintendent, who lived in the basement, was forever leaving the door open no matter how many times I told him it was dangerous. He didn't know what had happened to the last super, and I wasn't the one to tell him. I slammed the door shut and took the elevator.

My *abuela* has always said that I am *intuitivo*, that I feel things before other people do, and I had a bad feeling before I got to my floor.

46

It took me a few seconds to process it: *lock and door handle pried off, door open.*

Holy shit!

I knew the rule: Don't go in. Wait for the police. But I *was* police.

I took a few steps in, heart pounding against my rib cage, pivoted around the sofa, time slowing down and expanding all at once; a few more steps, gun out in front of me, another pivot around the half-wall that defined the bedroom.

The mattress was slit down the center, stuffing bulging out like intestines, my TV and CD player missing.

Shit!

I had only one closet, filled mainly with Terri's clothes, all dumped on the floor, torn and ripped.

I sidestepped my way into the kitchen—cabinets open, plates, cups, saucers on the floor, broken.

In the bathroom the medicine cabinet was open, too, contents all over the floor.

I went through the place three times till I was sure there was no one there. Then I let out a breath and called it in.

This was the fourth break-in I'd had in my seven years of living in Hell's Kitchen, two of them in the first year I'd lived here. Then the neighborhood improved and it wasn't until six months ago that it had happened again—or so I thought. It had never been proved, the only thing taken one of my sketches. Now I was starting to think I was pushing my luck. Three strikes and you're out, and here I was going on number four.

I crossed back over the mess in the living room, exchanging fear for anger: all my new furniture ruined, my stuff trashed.

That's when I saw it—or what was left of it—the sculptural reconstruction facedown on the floor, clay mashed, skull cracked, armature bent out of shape.

I didn't like having my place filled with uniforms and detectives, most of them standing around smoking cigarettes and making small talk. But when a narc called me over to ask what I kept in my mattress that was so important the perps had to slit it open, I lost it.

"My fucking kilo of cocaine, what else! Sure, I slit the damn thing open every day, take my stash out, and stitch it back up!" I shouted this about an inch from his face.

He reached his arms out to push me back and I almost punched him, but Terri stepped between us.

She tugged me away and told me to relax. She was trying to act all cool, not let on that the woman's clothes at the bottom of my closet were *hers*.

The cops weren't taking the break-in seriously—the unanimous opinion, junkies; the only exception to that opinion, mine—but I couldn't say what I really thought: that it had something to do with Gambel's death, because I had no proof other than my paranoia.

Finally, the cops cleared out.

The minute they did, Terri made a beeline for the closet. She held up a blouse with a sleeve hanging off. "Damn it, I just bought this—and this—" She plucked a torn dress out of the heap. "Shit!"

"I'll buy you a new one," I said.

"I can buy it myself, Rodriguez! That's not the point." She started picking through the rest, tossing torn and ripped clothes across the room, which wasn't helping any, but it was her first chance to react emotionally and she was entitled to it.

She stopped rustling through the clothes and stood up. "Fuck it! Let's just get out of here."

"I'm not letting whoever did this run me out of my apartment," I said.

"Run you out? Who are you, Wyatt Earp?" She gave me a look. "Well, I'm sure as shit not staying here. This is what—the third break-in you've had?"

I nodded. I didn't want to say it was the fourth.

"And you want to hang around and wait for the next one, that it?"

"I'm just not leaving."

I wasn't sure why I wanted to stay. Maybe it was symbolic to me; that we'd been pushed out of the case and I didn't want to be pushed out of my apartment, too.

"Come on, Rodriguez, there's nowhere to sleep."

"I'll use my old sleeping bag."

"Don't be stupid. Let's go to my place."

"And what if they come back?"

"For *what*?" She did a quick three-sixty assessment of the damage.

She was right. There was nothing left. They'd taken everything, including my toaster oven, clock radio, espresso maker, and an electric teapot.

"And if they *do* come back, you shouldn't be here," she said.

"I have my gun."

"So now you're going to shoot someone?"

"Only if I have to." I took in the mess, the unnecessary destruction. "I think someone is trying to send me a message."

"Junkies?"

"I don't think it was junkies."

"Who, then?"

"Barton told me if he found out I was holding back on him there'd be a problem. Maybe this is his way of sending me a message."

"That's just fed talk. This isn't their style."

"You mean they don't try to take out dictators with hired assassins or topple governments by arming rebels or lock up political prisoners without any cause or torture prisoners on U.S. army bases or bug private citizens?"

"You're getting carried away."

"That tends to happen when someone breaks into my place and destroys all my stuff."

"Look, sure, the feds do big stuff like bump off dictators, but no offense, honey, you're not exactly big stuff. Sorry, you're big where it counts." She tacked on a grin, but I was way past sexy innuendoes and smiles.

"You didn't see the way Barton looked at me when we were at Gambel's apartment—and you didn't hear the threat in his voice."

"You're one man, Rodriguez, a cop who makes sketches for a living. Why would they come after you?"

"Because I've been talking to people like Wayne Beamer's psychiatrist, a one-time army shrink—and to O'Reilly's commanding officer, and now to Gambel, who turned up dead."

"But Gambel didn't tell you anything."

"Barton doesn't know that. And the fact is Gambel *was* going to tell me something—and give me some papers."

"Which we didn't find."

"Maybe because someone got there first—and took them."

"If the feds had gotten there first they'd have been there when we arrived."

She had a point but I wasn't satisfied. Gambel's death was just too convenient.

"And how did they find out about Tully, who, in case you didn't know, is missing."

"Tully's gone?"

"Yeah, someone moved him out of Saint Vincent's, but the doctor won't tell me who—or where he is."

I watched Terri take it in, eyebrows drawn together, lips puckering and unpuckering. "Still . . ."

"Hey, I speak to Tully, he's *gone*. I speak to Gambel, he's *dead*. If you don't think I'm making those G men uncomfortable, then I'd say you are on that long river called d' Nile, baby."

"Gambel died of an asthma attack."

"Supposedly."

"So you think this break-in is to scare you off?" She looked around the apartment and came to rest on the smashed sculptural reconstruction. "And what would be the point of destroying that?"

"I don't know."

Terri came over and touched my hand. "That's exactly what

I'm saying, Rodriguez, you don't know. Look, you're upset, it's natural, anyone would be, but I think you've let the cases get to you personally because you're—"

"What, just a sketch artist, and inexperienced, is that what you were going to say?"

"No, you're damn good at homicide. I was going to say because you're letting your imagination get the better of you." She let go of my hand. "But maybe you *should* just go back to making sketches."

"It was *you* who wanted me on this case, remember?"

"No, it was Denton."

"Oh, so you didn't want me?" I felt the heat coming off me, the anger.

"Can we just stop this? Come home with me and we can deal with the mess tomorrow."

"No, I'm staying."

"Fine." She plucked a blouse out of the pile on the floor. Then she threw it back down. "Stay here and play the macho asshole if that's what you want, but I'm going home."

I called three different locksmiths from the Yellow Pages, every one advertising twenty-four-hour service, and not one of them responded to my call.

I slammed the phone down, grabbed a tool off my worktable and started scraping clay off the floor so hard, I was taking up the wood beneath it.

I was furious at Terri for what she'd said about not wanting me on the case, and furious at myself for pushing her to say it. Maybe I *was* being paranoid, but reading faces was my strong suit and Barton's face had told me that he meant business.

But why the hell had they destroyed the sculpture? Was it simply malicious?

I didn't know what to think but it was a moot point. The sculpture was ruined and I hadn't taken a single picture of it. I wouldn't be able to show it to Guthrie—or to anyone else.

I picked the doll's eyes out of the clay, plunked them onto my worktable, and dumped the rest of the clay into the trash.

I didn't want to look at it anymore so I went into the bedroom and exchanged the ruined mattress for my sleeping bag. I crawled in even though I was wide awake, questions buzzing in my head like gnats.

How had Gambel really died? Where had they taken Tully? And how the hell did they know I'd be out tonight?

I sat up and saw him in my mind: the guy in the trench coat standing across the street. *Of course.* Now I was certain he'd been watching me. Did he give someone a signal that I was going out? Had he watched me go into the coffee shop and into the bar?

I got up. I went into the living room and dragged the ruined couch until it was wedged up against the front door. Then I found my gun and got back into the sleeping bag. I kept the light on because I didn't want to be in the dark and I was pretty sure I wasn't going to be getting much sleep.

47

My nerves felt scrambled and raw when I finally extracted myself from the sleeping bag, my body stiff, head aching. I must have slept, because I remembered a dream where I kept falling, over and over.

I took a long shower and let the hot water beat on my face until I felt awake enough to deal with the mess in my apartment.

I swept up the broken dishes and put the furniture back in place. I called Crate & Barrel and asked how much it would cost to recover the slashed couch, but it was almost as much as buying a new one, so I did. I couldn't afford it but didn't want to live with something that would remind me of another break-in. My mattress was a goner, so I ordered a new one. The whole time my mind was racing about Tully and Gambel, and I couldn't let it go.

I called Buttonwood Health Services and asked for Carolina Escobar.

The receptionist said she wasn't in. I asked when she'd be back, and she said never.

"What do you mean, *never*?"

"She's left, you know; quit."

I asked to speak to a supervisor and the woman who got on said, "May I help you?" in a tone that did not sound like she wanted to help me at all.

I told her I was a cop and asked what happened to Carolina Escobar.

"Nothing *happened* to her," she said. "She left."

"Left for where?"

"I have no idea."

I didn't buy it. I got off the phone, went to the online White Pages, and found Carolina Escobar's home number.

An answering machine picked up. I started to leave a message when I was interrupted by the real thing.

"I can't talk right now," she said.

"I called the lab and they said you'd left."

"That's right."

"Why?"

"I decided to retire early."

"And lose your pension?"

"I, um, didn't lose . . . all of it."

"No one quits their job with only five months left until *full* benefits. *No te creo*."

"I'm sorry if you don't believe me," she said.

I did not need to see her face to know she was lying. "Who got to you?"

"No one *got* to me, Detective. But I have to go now."

"Look, if this is my fault, I'm sorry, and I'll try to fix it, I promise. Just answer one question for me?"

She didn't say anything but I could hear her breathing.

"Did Gambel work with other doctors? Was he part of a group or did he work alone?"

"I can't remember."

"You remember just fine. Please. I know someone has gotten to you, Ms. Escobar. Don't you want to fight back?"

"Abraham Brillstein and Victor Mantooth," she said, and hung up.

48

I called Terri and told her I needed to speak to her, but she said she didn't want to meet at the station.

A half hour later she was waiting for me at the Fifty-ninth Street entrance to Central Park. She didn't smile when she saw me, just looked over her shoulder as if checking to see if there was anyone behind her.

We headed into the park, a few people on the path, but it was quieter than usual.

"Are you still mad at me for last night?" I asked.

"You're letting the cases get to you on a personal level and that's not good, Rodriguez. You can't work Homicide if you get personally involved."

I wasn't sure if she was talking about the cases or about us, so I let it go. I tried

to put my arm around her but she moved away. "Someone could be watching."

"Who?"

"I don't know, but I keep feeling as if I'm being followed. Maybe I'm being paranoid, but . . ."

I didn't think so. I told her about the guy in the trench coat. Then I told her about Carolina Escobar. "Tully is missing, Gambel is dead, and now Escobar has been fired. Every time I speak to someone who can give me something about this case they're told to shut up, they disappear, or they die."

"I still say you're getting carried away."

"Yeah, then how come you keep looking over your shoulder and are too afraid to talk to me about your own case at your own station house?"

"Because the case is no longer ours, can't you get that?"

"Yeah, I get it and I'll stop checking it out; soon, I promise. But how about getting me Gambel's phone records? I want to see if he talked to anyone between the time I spoke to him and when he died."

"Jesus, Rodriguez, are you deaf? I just told you, it's no longer our case, it's over!"

"I heard you. I just want to tie up a few loose ends for myself, that's all."

"Fine, go talk to Williams in Records. He deals with the private data brokers for the PD. But leave me out of it!"

She walked on ahead of me, her arms folded across her chest. I followed her off the path toward the carousel, the happy sound of organ music coming at me, the exact opposite of what I was feeling. For a moment neither of us spoke. We watched the painted ponies go up and down, kids hanging on, laughing and scared, two teenagers making out.

Then Terri said, "Look, I tried to finish up my cases and I was told to stay out or I'd be in trouble. The bureau has threatened to use my old Tip Line fuckup against me and I know Denton won't support me when the chips are down."

"They can't do anything with that, it's years old, and you've done plenty since then to prove you're a terrific cop."

"Are you really that naive, Rodriguez? They can do anything they want; they can make anything appear bigger and badder."

Of course she was right.

"I'm not going to help you if you insist on pursuing this case. I can't afford it. Maybe you can, but I can't."

It was true. I did not have to play the sort of games Terri had to, to get where I was. I was a free agent and she was not. "Okay, but—"

"No buts. Stop asking me to jeopardize my career to satisfy your curiosity, because I won't do it. There is no case here, no one to arrest—perps, vics, they're all dead. Denton has told me to bury it, and that's exactly what I'm going to do. If the G wants to muck around with it, that's their business."

"Am I the only one who wants to know what happened?"

"Why can't you just let it go?"

"I'd like to, I really would, but innocent men have died, Terri, innocent men who killed other innocent men. Someone has to care."

"Oh, please, can the sentimentality, Rodriguez."

"I'm not being sentimental," I said, though I was not entirely sure which of my emotions was guiding me. "I've run away from a lot of things in my life, but I won't run away from this just because someone is trying to intimidate me."

"Oh, so this is some sort of bullshit way to make up for the fact that you let your father die; that it?"

"That was a low blow," I said.

Terri looked sorry, sucking her lower lip, but she didn't say it.

"I'd just like some answers, is that so bad?"

"And what about *me*?"

"I'll keep you out of it."

"That's impossible, you're working for me."

"And what if there are more of these guys out there, Terri, more guys like Beamer and O'Reilly and Billow and Tully, time bombs about to explode; what then?"

"It's not my problem."

"I can't believe you're saying that. You don't mean it."

"I do," she said, but her face betrayed her, a tic at the corner of her eyes, the slightest quiver around her mouth. She did care, but she was scared of losing her job. "And there's nothing more to talk about unless you say you'll drop it."

"I will," I said, "after I get Gambel's phone records and find out why Carolina Escobar was fired."

Terri's face went from anger to disappointment. "You realize you're making a choice, Rodriguez."

"No, I'm just—"

"Yes, that's exactly what you're doing, so let's be clear about it." She stared at me, eyes fixed on mine. When I didn't say anything, she turned her back on me.

"Terri, come on—" I tried to stop her, my hand on her arm, but she shook me off. I stood there and watched her walk away.

I went back to the station but avoided passing her office. Our fight was still in my head and my insides were in a knot. I knew I had pushed her to say some of the things she'd said, but I still didn't like them, particularly the stuff about my father. A part of me wanted to barge into her office and hug her, but another part wouldn't budge. I didn't want to get her in trouble, but I wanted answers.

I called Williams about Gambel's telephone records.

"Piece of cake," he said. "Everyone uses private data brokers these days, not just the police—insurance companies, lawyers, even private citizens. And hey, it's a lot easier than waiting for a warrant, though some people do see it as an invasion of privacy."

I would have agreed if I wasn't the one requesting the information.

It took him ten minutes to get me what I wanted.

"Two outgoing calls and three incoming on the last day," he said, and gave me the numbers.

One of the incoming was mine, but there were two calls after that, one outgoing and then one incoming.

"Whoever Gambel called, they called him back," said Williams. "It's the same number."

"Do you have a name to go with the number?" I asked.

"Mantooth," he said. "Victor Mantooth."

49

It was one of the names given to me by Carolina Escobar, one of the men who had worked with Gambel: Victor Mantooth.

I made the call. I had to.

"Dr. Mantooth? I wonder if you have time to see me?"

"Who is this?"

I said I was calling for a consultation, that I'd seen other therapists, but my post-traumatic stress disorder had not gotten any better.

"I'm sorry to hear that," he said. "But my psychiatric practice is very limited. I only see a few clients."

"You helped a friend of mine way back when," I said, and took a chance. "Wayne Beamer."

He paused. "I'm afraid you're mistaken. I don't know anyone by that name. But . . . if you're local, I can try to squeeze you in."

Clearly, Wayne Beamer's name had opened the doctor's door.

When I told him I would be right over, he did not object.

• • •

The brownstone was in Murray Hill, not far from Terri's apartment. Three stories, nothing special, Mantooth's office on the ground floor, the waiting room small: two chairs, no magazines to pass the time. But the doctor did not keep me waiting.

He ushered me into an office crowded with books that spilled onto a large wooden desk, an easy chair, even the couch.

"Sorry," he said, as he plucked books off the chair and offered it to me.

He was tall and thin, about sixty, with red-rimmed eyes behind wire-frame glasses, which he kept adjusting higher on his nose with long spidery fingers topped with nails that were just slightly too long. "Tell me again who it was who gave you my name?" he asked as he settled in behind his desk.

"Wayne Beamer."

He tapped his chin with one of those long fingers. "Sorry, I still can't remember him."

I looked for signs of lying, features that ticked, muscles in opposition and asymmetry, but his hands kept fluttering about his face, distracting me.

"It would have been fifteen, sixteen years ago," I said.

"Sorry, but the name doesn't ring a bell. He was your friend?" He rippled his fingers along his lips.

"Yes, we were in the same outfit, in the army."

"And you stayed in touch with him after the service?"

"Yes. He had a hard time."

"And he said I helped him?" He adjusted his glasses, on, off, then on again.

"Yes."

"I just can't remember him. Must be old age." He smiled a Cheshire cat grin, wide and false, not a hint of eye muscles tightening. "So, um, how is he doing?"

"Not too well. In fact, I'd say really bad. He jumped off the Empire State Building."

"How . . . awful."

I studied his face: eyes blinking, those fingers tap, tap, tapping on his lips.

"The story got a lot of attention. I'm surprised you didn't see it on the news or—"

"I don't watch television," he said too quickly, "I'm afraid I usually have my nose in a book. Was your friend in treatment?"

"Yes, like I said, with *you*."

"Oh, but that was such a long time ago." He caught himself. "I mean, if I ever saw him. I wish I could remember. Did you know he was suicidal?"

"All I know is he was in a bad way, and he said it had something to do with what had happened to him years ago."

Mantooth constructed a look of compassion—brows knit, lower lip out. "Combat is a terrible thing."

"Yes, but he was referring to something that happened *after* that."

"You mean personal problems."

"I think it had something to do with his treatment."

Mantooth sat back and drummed his long nails along the edge of the desk. "Really? Like what?"

"I don't know, but maybe you do, as you treated him back then."

"I wish I could help, but . . ." He shook his head. "I just don't know what to tell you. Could be he was having hallucinations, which isn't uncommon to PTSD—as I'm sure you know." He stared at me over the top of his glasses. "You're not thinking about ending it all, are you, Mr. Rodriguez?"

"Me? No."

"Well, that's good. I'm sure the death of your friend has been on your mind, weighing you down, the guilt of his death and all, thoughts that you should have done more to help him; am I right?"

I nodded solemnly.

"It wasn't your fault. We can't help people who don't want to be helped." He sat forward and laid one of his spidery hands on mine and I fought a chill. "Now tell me about *you*."

I told him I'd been in Desert Storm and had come back with PTSD; that I couldn't sleep and forgot things; and that I had trouble controlling my temper.

"I see." His fingers were tapping at his lip again. "Are you taking any medication?"

I remembered the most common drugs used to treat the disease and mentioned a few.

"Well, there are new drugs coming out every day and I'm sure we can find something to help you." He gave me another phony smile. "I don't see many patients. I'm what the kids call a slacker, not that I'd let *my* kids call me that." He wrapped his hand around a plexi box frame on his desk and turned it toward me. It was a family photo: Mantooth looking a lot younger, a woman I took to be his wife, and three boys, none of them smiling.

"Nice-looking family," I said. "I envy you."

He stared at the photo and I saw the first genuine emotion shape his face, brows and mouth tugged down with sadness.

"Your kids are grown?" I asked.

"What? Oh. Yes. Grown . . . gone." He put the photo down, rearranged his face into a mask of calm, and asked, "Do you have a family?"

"No, no one," I said. "I couldn't handle one, not with, you know, the PTSD."

"So there's been no one to talk to about your friend?"

"No one at all."

"What a shame," he said, and added an artificial frown. "But I'm sure I can help you. Why don't you just give me your home address and phone number? Do you have a card?"

Clearly, my NYPD sketch artist card would not be a good idea, so I just wrote the information down and handed it to him.

"Oh, you live just crosstown," he said.

"That's right."

"Alone?"

"Yes."

He tugged a desk drawer open and came up with a vial of pills. "These should help you get started. They're a mild sedative, very soothing, very safe. Why don't you take one now, just to take the edge off your anxiety."

I unscrewed the cap and shook a small yellow pill into my hand. "What is it?"

"Just something to help you relax."

I asked if he had any water and he went to get it. When he came back I acted as if I still had the pill in my hand and pretended to wash it down.

"That's going to help," he said. "And take one tonight about an hour before bed. It will help you sleep. In fact, take two. They're really very mild."

I thanked him and he showed me out, a spidery hand on my shoulder.

But I didn't go home.

• • •

I waited two doors down under a deli awning, a perfect view of Mantooth's front door, but I was hidden in the shadows. I wasn't sure what I was waiting for, but then a guy showed up. He rang Mantooth's bell, shifting his weight nervously from one foot to the other. A minute later Mantooth opened the door, ushered him in quickly, looked up and down the street, then shut the door.

I went into the deli, bought a can of soda, came back outside and stood under the awning again. I sipped the Coke and checked my watch every couple of minutes. The guy came out of Mantooth's brownstone in twenty. He turned and headed in my direction. I took a couple of steps back and just as he passed in front of me, dropped the empty Coke can. It clattered on the sidewalk. He turned toward the sound and I got a good look at him. Then he kept going. He had a piece of paper in his hand with some writing on it and I couldn't help but wonder if it was my address.

I had the yellow pills in my pocket and decided to bring them to the small lab that operated out of the basement of the station. It was too hot to walk, so I hailed a cab.

But the car that stopped for me was not a taxi.

50

I was wedged between Barton and Peterson, who did their best to fill the seat and make me as uncomfortable as possible. I asked where they were taking me but got no response, so I knocked on the glass that separated the front and back seats.

"Hey, driver," I said. "Take me to the Stage Deli. I'm dying for a pastrami on rye."

He didn't turn around, and neither Barton nor Peterson seemed to think it was funny.

"What, no jokes today, Peterson?"

He didn't react. Neither of them did.

"What the fuck is this?"

The two of them just sat there, stone-faced, silent.

They drove me around for half an hour, first crosstown, then down through Tribeca, the triangle below Canal, a cool-cat neighborhood, then farther downtown past Ground Zero, where the car took a sharp right toward the river. It was a business neighborhood densely populated by day, quiet now, just a few people on the street heading toward restaurants and clubs. I thought about calling out to them when the car stopped in front of a building construction site, but the windows were shut, doors locked. Barton and Peterson waited till the street was clear before they ushered me out, one on either side of me, each gripping an arm.

Inside the building, everything was in mid-construction, half the walls indicated only by metal studs, others with unpainted Sheetrock, everywhere gaping holes with electric wires and cables snaking out across floors and ceilings.

Barton and Peterson took me into a back hallway; rough concrete, unlit. I thought they were going to beat the crap out of me but they just marched me up a staircase.

I stopped asking what the fuck they were doing and switched to a jokey, forced banter—"How about those Mets crapping out like that; this weather really sucks, doesn't it?"—but it was total bullshit, more for my benefit than theirs; I was scared.

On the fourth or fifth floor we stopped at a landing. Peterson pushed open a heavy door, the light suddenly blinding.

They ushered me into the middle of a large room with several smaller ones branching off it, fluorescent lights overhead casting everything in a harsh blue-white glare.

"So, what is this, gentlemen, the bureau's new HQ or Auschwitz West?"

"Why don't you shut the fuck up?" said Peterson, his first words since I'd been abducted.

They led me into one of the smaller rooms. It had a new metal desk, the same blinding overhead light, two chairs, and a wall lined with a mirror that I knew was two-way.

I was sweating, my mouth dry. Here it comes, I thought. I tried to brace myself for the first punch.

"Sit," said Barton.

I did.

He gave me a pencil and a sheet of paper and told me to write

down everything I had done, and everywhere I had gone, in the
past two days.

Then they left and said they'd be back in five minutes.

It was almost an hour before Peterson poked his head in, saw
that I hadn't written anything on the paper, scowled, and dropped
a file onto the desk.

"See you in ten minutes," he said.

The file had my name on it and one other word: *Confidential.*

It was so obvious I almost laughed. I knew they were watching
me through the mirror, waiting for me to go through the file, but
no way that was going to happen.

I kept telling myself they couldn't do anything to me, but I
knew that wasn't true. Six months ago, the FBI had put me through
the wringer and it hadn't been pretty. And this time I wasn't even
sure if Barton and Peterson were FBI. If they weren't, I had no
idea what they were capable of.

Still, I felt like playing with them. I picked up my confidential
file, stood in front of the mirror, hesitated as if I was about to open
it, then dropped it back onto the table.

I could practically smell them fuming behind the mirrored glass.

Then I picked up the pencil and started drawing. I knew they
intended to let me sweat another hour, but I thought they'd be

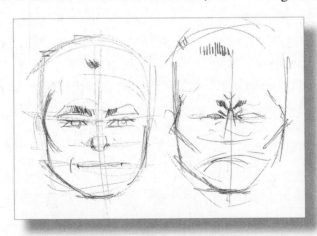

interested to see what I was doing, and it was my way to pass the time without losing my mind.

Ten, fifteen, twenty minutes passed. They were really playing with me, but I was playing, too. I kept my left arm over the top of the paper so they couldn't see what I was doing.

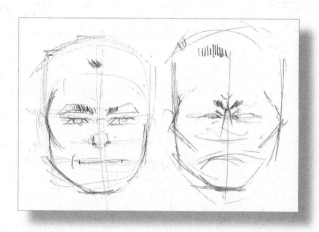

I was just adding a humorous addition to the faces when they came back into the room.

I made a dramatic gesture of flipping the paper over. I figured they'd want to see it as much as I wanted to see my confidential file.

Barton stood over me using his size for intimidation, but at least he blocked out the glaring light. Finally, he said, "You know you're impeding a federal investigation."

"How?" I said. I wasn't trying to be a smart-ass; I really wanted to hear what he had to say.

Peterson leaned in from the other side. "I'd hate to see you selling your sketches on the boardwalk at Coney Island."

"Could be worse," I said. "I could be wearing a gray suit day after day and violating citizens' rights."

"Funny guy, aren't you?" he said, the corners of his lips twitching with anger. He wasn't as good at neutralizing his face as his partner. He went and stood behind me, which was disconcerting, and intentional.

Barton pulled a chair over, sat across from me, plucked a packet of Juicy Fruit out of his pocket, unwrapped two sticks and folded them into his mouth. He chewed for about three minutes without speaking. Then he said, "I told you there would be a problem if you didn't tell me the truth."

"But I did."

He looked straight at me, chewing his gum, cool and unruffled. "You were asked to stop looking into this case, but you just won't stop."

"I'm just trying to be a good cop."

From behind me, Peterson snorted a laugh. "You're a fucking sketch artist."

"Check my record, Peterson. I went through the academy, even spent some time at Quantico." I lifted the confidential file off the table and offered it up. "Didn't you read this?"

Barton plucked it from my hand and laid it gently back onto the table between us without speaking.

"I don't get it," I said. "Beamer and O'Reilly were ruled suicides, right? So how can I be interfering in two suicides—two closed cases?"

"Because they're equivocal cases," said Peterson.

Barton lifted his head and gave Peterson a look that said *Be quiet*.

"Equivocal, which means they're still open to interpretation. I know the terminology," I said. "So what are they, closed or equivocal?"

"It doesn't matter," said Barton, very calm.

"It does to me. But my task force is off the case, or didn't you hear?"

For the first time Barton allowed his face to show me what he felt, what Ekman calls the "unilateral contempt face"—a sneering mouth, raised lip, one eyebrow tugged down. From there it went to contained anger—mouth set tight, eyes open and glaring. He leaned across the table. "Do you think I am playing some sort of game with you?"

Oh, how I wanted to say *yes*, but I saw the genuine anger building in his face and thought better of it. "No. There are six men dead, and I do not think that's a game."

Peterson moved from behind to in front of me. "You're still playing the stupid, drugged-out teenager who got his father killed, aren't you, Rodriguez."

I couldn't control the involuntary flinch, but I kept quiet.

Then Barton leaned even closer, his soured Juicy Fruit breath in my face. "You realize it took about a minute to get *that* piece of information."

"Less than a minute," said Peterson.

Barton opened my confidential file and started to read. "Nathan Rodriguez, mother Judith Epstein, formerly of Forest Hills, Queens; mother, Rose, lives in Boca Raton, Florida. Judith Epstein married to Juan Rodriguez, of San Juan, Puerto Rico in—" He stopped and looked up. "You consider yourself a Jew or a Puerto Rican?"

"Buddhist," I said. "No, I take that back; Santerian."

"Oh, of course," said Barton. "Like your sweet grandmother up in Spanish Harlem. Dangerous neighborhood. I'd hate to see anything happen to her."

"That's a cheap shot, Barton, even for you."

He just stared at me. "Where was I before I was worried about your granny?"

"Detailing my parents' marriage, really interesting stuff," I said, getting more mad than scared, doing my best to stay calm though I could feel the adrenaline itching under my skin.

"Well, then you might find this more interesting." He ran his blunt-nailed thumb along a page. "You and Julio Sanchez buying drugs from Willie Pedriera, former guest of the state at Green Haven Correctional; now dead, like your father, leaving your mother a widow at a very young age, though I see here she is now having *relations* with a coworker in Colorado." He looked up and I caught the slightest hint of a smile.

That was it. I bolted up, knocking my chair back. "You think you can scare me with my teenage history or the fact that you're *spying* on my mother? What next, Barton, a black hood over my head, electric prods on my genitals? Where'd you get your training, Guantánamo?"

"Real funny," said Peterson.

"Not funny at all," I said.

But Barton kept his cool. He just looked at me, his face a mask. "You see, Rodriguez, we've got everything we need in here—the accounts of you buying and selling drugs; your arrest at fourteen; how your best pal, Julio Sanchez, did two years in Spofford—"

Peterson leaned in and plucked a page from the file.

"Your NYPD record, which details the six months you spent as a shitty street cop and the way you couldn't cut it. We've got it all, see: what you eat and where, when you sleep, and oh, this *is* interesting . . ." He grinned. "*Who* you're sleeping *with*." He let that hang there for a minute. "And you can tell your little girlfriend that her Tip Line fiasco is just for starters, you reading me, *amigo*? And while you're telling her that, tell her there's a glass ceiling in the NYPD for little girls who sleep with their bosses and coworkers, not to mention a not very nice name that goes along with it."

My arm reeled back so fast I would have popped Peterson in

his smug little face if Barton hadn't grabbed me. Peterson went on, his face inches from mine.

"We've got it all," he said, "from boosting cars at twelve years old to sending your old man up to East Harlem to die a year and a half later."

I felt like I was drowning, could see my father dead in the street and my mother sobbing and those two cops in my parents' apartment delivering the bad news.

Peterson came in so close the blackheads on his nose were in sharp focus. "So listen up, *amigo*, because we can make it very bad for you—but even worse for Terri Russo." He backed up and shook his head, disgust on his face.

Then Barton let go of my arms and I sagged into my chair.

They had me. It was one thing if I wanted to end up doing portraits on a boardwalk, but taking Terri down with me was something else. She was right; we were tied together.

"What do you want?" I said.

Barton opened a notepad and clicked a ballpoint pen. "First, where were you earlier today?"

"When?"

"When we picked you up."

"I thought you knew everything about me?"

Barton didn't say anything, some anger building behind his features, and again it hit me: They really didn't know where I'd been. The G, who knew everything, or thought they did, had lost their tail on me. So they didn't know about Mantooth.

"I was on my way into the station," I said.

"By way of Murray Hill?"

I tried my best to look sheepish. "I was picking up some stuff from Russo's apartment. It's in Murray Hill, but you already know that."

Barton nodded, and I could see it in the way his mouth relaxed: He believed me.

Then he asked, "I want to know what you got from Gambel."

So we were back to that. "Is that what this is all about?"

I could see from his face that it was.

"You could have saved us all a lot of time and energy and asked that right away because I got *nothing* from Gambel, *nada*. He was dead when I got there, I told you that, and it's the God's-honest truth." I painted on an innocent wide-eyed look. Barton and Peterson exchanged a brief raising of eyebrows, the slightest tilt of heads, looks that said: *Maybe he's telling the truth.*

"I had one phone call with the guy that lasted less than two minutes. I was going to meet him but when I got to his place he was *dead*. I told you that before and I wasn't lying."

I looked from one to the other to see if they were buying my story. "And listen, I want to be perfectly honest with you guys." I whispered this so they had to lean in close. "Russo and I, we're over." I hoped I was lying, but I wasn't sure. Still, I wanted to protect her, to keep her out of this. "Look, I had a good time with her and I'd rather not see her hurt. She's a good cop. And for the record, she told me I was officially off the case and to go back to sketching." That much was true, so I didn't have to construct a face to cover a lie.

There were still traces of skepticism in their eyes, but they'd done their best to scare the hell out of me and they knew it. They wanted to believe that I was now telling them the truth.

"Look, I promise to stay out of your way. Just don't trash my apartment again."

"What?" Peterson's boyish face twisted with confusion.

"Oh, come on, guys, you can quit the act now."

"We did *not* trash your apartment," Barton said, coolly. "We don't do things that way. This is the way we do things, face-to-face, man-to-man."

That almost made me laugh but I knew it wouldn't go over well.

"Okay," I said. I no longer cared. If they wanted to play it that way, fine. But I had one more thing to ask. "Who are you guys?"

"What's that supposed to mean?" said Peterson.

"There's no record of either of you in the bureau."

I thought I saw the crack of a smile appear on Barton's thin lips. "Let's just say we're your shadow, okay, Rodriguez?" Then he pushed away from the table and stood up. "Any more questions?"

"Yeah; can I go now?"

He nodded.

"Oh, I almost forgot." I flipped over the piece of paper. "This is for you two, suitable for framing."

"Hey," said Peterson, as I headed toward the door. "I don't have a fucking mustache."

I didn't wait around to hear Barton say, "Neither do I."

• • •

They had kept me up past midnight, the sky a muddy gray-black over Lower Manhattan. There had been more rain, the streets wet, thick mist blurring edges and giving the city the look of an old black-and-white photograph. I was pretty worked up and walked a few blocks to burn off my angst. I headed over to Hudson Street, which was quiet, just a couple of people out, taxis trolling for fares.

I'd only walked a couple of blocks when I got the feeling I was being followed. I looked around but didn't see anyone. Maybe Barton and Peterson had decided to keep the tail on me, or maybe I was being paranoid, but I didn't think so. I walked another block and when I knew for sure I was being followed—my antenna practically vibrating—it was too late.

The blow came from behind and knocked me to the ground, and the guy was on me so fast I couldn't see him, though I heard him and smelled him. Everything was happening in triple time: the city spinning, buildings tilted, arms and fists, snatches of a silhouetted face in blurry close-up, time and space colliding like jump-cuts, and one of us, or both of us, cursing, then another voice shouting and the guy was off me and running and someone was picking me up, asking, "Hey, you all right?" and I saw the blur of my attacker disappearing down the street while another man took off after him and I tried to catch my breath.

"Jesus Christ, Rodriguez!"

It was Barton.

A minute later Peterson came back, huffing. "I lost him," he said.

"Good thing for you we were heading this way," said Barton, cool as ever.

My heart was beating fast. I was trying to hold on to the series of images my retina had snapped off during the fight, but everything was blurring. I tapped at my body to make sure I was all there and saw that my palm was bleeding and my jeans were torn at the knee where I'd fallen.

"You just keep inviting trouble, don't you?" said Peterson.

"What's that supposed to mean?" I tried to make out his expression but it wasn't possible in the dim street lamp.

"Go home," said Barton.

I flagged down one of those trolling taxis and sagged into the back. Barton and Peterson showing up at exactly the right moment seemed too convenient.

Did I owe them my life or were they the ones trying to do me damage?

51

I couldn't go home; not after the break-in and my lock still broken, Barton and Peterson abducting me, being attacked and looking over my shoulder awaiting the next blow. Who was it who said that paranoia doesn't mean the whole world really isn't out to get you?

I had the cab drop me at Midtown North.

My floor at the station was pretty quiet, most of the offices closed, distant phones ringing, someone typing, a muted conversation somewhere down the hall.

I closed my office door and turned on the air conditioner. It sputtered a few times, then whined to let me know it was alive, semi-cool air wafting in through a filter that begged to be changed.

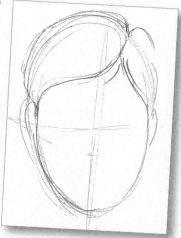

My body was aching and exhausted, but my mind was wide awake with faces—Barton's, Peterson's, and Mantooth's, in particular. But when I tried to picture the guy who had come out of Mantooth's brownstone, the image began to dissolve and break apart. I sharpened a pencil and got to work. I didn't want to lose the face before I found out who he was.

I started the way I would with any witness, asking myself about the general shape of his face and his hair. I put myself back under that deli awning. I heard the Coke can hit the sidewalk. I saw the guy turn toward me and held on to the memory, working as fast as I could to get it down.

It was coming back to me in a rush now, the boyishly handsome face, sun in his pale, vacant eyes, the square cut of his jaw, even the dimple in his chin.

But what I remembered most was that he was smiling for no apparent reason, a grin that bordered on something malevolent, and when that came back to me I slipped inside the memory and the sketch drew itself.

I sat back and looked at what I'd done, and that's when it hit me; that I had seen him again, in bits and pieces, blurred and close up, fists coming at me on the street just before Barton and Peterson had come to my rescue. The man who I had seen coming out of Mantooth's building and the man who had attacked me were one and the same.

52

The stuttering of the air conditioner was the first thing I heard; sunlight cutting in through my office window causing me to squint.

I'd fallen asleep at my desk.

I lifted my head slowly and with difficulty. There was paper stuck to the side of my face. I peeled it away and saw it was the sketch I'd made last night, a bit smudged and crumpled, but it was nothing compared to the way I felt, head splitting, body like I'd gone a few rounds with Muhammad Ali.

It was a few minutes before 6:00 A.M., not too many people in yet, and I made it down the hall and into the men's room without anyone seeing me.

My reflection in the mirror said it all: dark circles under my eyes, a purple bruise on my jaw, three days' growth of beard, hair sticking up in all the wrong places, charcoal across my cheek.

I washed my face, wet my hair and ran my fingers through it. Then I used my finger and soap to brush my teeth. It wasn't much; I could pass for human but was cutting it close.

I got a cup of black coffee from the vending machine in the hall outside my office. The consensus at the station was that it was chemically colored water with liquid caffeine added, but it would have to do.

Back in my office I looked at the sketch and thought about Victor Mantooth. It was only a matter of time till Barton and Peterson found him. And then what? Would he disappear or die mysteriously? Clearly Mantooth was dangerous—he'd sent that smiling psychopath to rough me up and maybe more—but how did he fit into all this?

I needed to know more.

I found some aspirin in my desk and washed them down with the coffee. It was worse than expected and I had expected it to be very, very bad. It burned my throat and left an acrid metallic aftertaste on my tongue.

I turned on my computer, laid my fingers onto the keys, and was about to type in "Victor Mantooth" when the other name Carolina Escobar had told me came into my mind: Abraham Brillstein.

I checked the online White Pages. It listed two A. Brillsteins in Manhattan, one in Minneapolis, and one in Cleveland. The first two turned out to be Amy and Arlene. The one in Cleveland, a veterinarian named Arthur; in Minneapolis, Ariel.

I went from the White Pages to Google, typed in "Brillstein" and "Mantooth"—and bingo!—there they were, a team. I scanned the links and clicked on a Newark *Star-Ledger* article from 1991.

NEW JERSEY SCIENTISTS PROVE FEARLESS

The Lucas Lab, a combination mental health and research facility, has just been awarded a research grant from the Defense Advanced Research Projects Agency (DARPA) to further their studies, though the exact amount of the grant was not disclosed.

Scientists at the lab in Pemberton, New Jersey, have taken recent developments in isolating the "fear gene" a step further. U.S. researchers had already reported on a gene called stathmin, located in the amygdala portion of the brain, an area that is believed to control both our learned and innate fears.

Now, three scientists at the Lucas Lab have bred rats without the gene. In a study that compared brain-altered rats with a control group, rodents were exposed to a loud noise, then set loose in an open space. The normal rats hovered in the corners, terrified, while the biologically engineered rats moved easily into the center of the space, seemingly unafraid.

I tried to take it in, pictured a strain of fearless rats invading my office, and that got *my* own fear gene going.

Victor Mantooth, psychiatrist and neuroscientist, Abraham Brillstein, biogeneticist, and Jonathan Gambel, biologist, used several methods in their work, including electromagnetic stimulation and an intracranial operation, which they are now trying out on monkeys.

When asked if the procedures would ever be safe for humans, Dr. Mantooth laughed. "Monkeys," he said, "are a lot easier to deal with than humans."

I pictured Mantooth in his Murray Hill office, his spidery fingers and Cheshire cat grin. My head was spinning with images but I forced myself to stay calm, to concentrate, to keep reading.

Dr. Gambel explained that transcranial magnetic stimulation, or TMS, was a noninvasive process already being used with stroke patients to stimulate movement. He described the procedure, where a magnetic coil is attached to the head to send magnetic and electric impulses into the brain, as simple. "Some volunteers," he said, "complain of a loud tapping sensation on the skull, as if someone were knocking on their brain, but so far that's the worst complaint."

Dr. Gambel pointed out that this "knocking" was simply the scalp muscles contracting. Other volunteers, he said, complained of a severely itchy scalp. Both conditions, according to the doctor, were temporary, though the long-term side effects of TMS are unknown, as are the effects of intracranial disruption.

The ethical question of whether or not it would be a good thing to create a species of human beings with no fear was put to the doctors. All three said the prospect of altering the human fear gene was a long way off.

The long-term effects are unknown.

I tried to replay what I knew and what I'd seen: scars on foreheads and drugs in bloodstreams, Tully's rapid-fire answers to imaginary questions, words and letters scribbled in notepads and painted on walls with blood; men who had killed, then killed themselves; loners whose promising lives had disintegrated; all men who had spent time at or near the Lucas Lab.

I thought about fearless rats, fearless monkeys, and fearless men. Wayne Beamer, who had leaped off the Empire State Building; James O'Reilly, who had put a bullet in his head; Floyd Billow, who screamed of rats while twisting a hunting knife into his own heart.

I had no proof but I knew it, I just knew that they had done it—had gone from rats to monkeys to men.

That's what Gambel was going to tell me. That's what Barton and Peterson were so intent on keeping a secret.

And who could blame them? The idea of genetically altered rats and monkeys was one thing, but genetically altered men, fearless men, ones who had short-circuited and gone into the street to kill would be very big, very bad news for the government who had funded the project.

I scanned the article again and saw it, the name of the agency that Carolina Escobar had mentioned: DARPA.

I typed in the acronym and the official website popped up.

My adrenaline was pumping, eyes skittering across pages, up and down columns, picking up generalities.

Apparently, DARPA was the main research and development organization for the DoD, the Department of Defense. It funded so many different kinds of technologies it would take me days to go through them, a week to read the mission statement.

But one thing was clear: DARPA was a cutting-edge science agency that produced, among other things, bionics, memory chips, and video games to train soldiers how to fight and kill. A game called Ambush! caught my eye. It was currently being used by eight hundred cadets at West Point, dozens of army bases around the U.S. and Europe, and by soldiers in Iraq and Afghanistan. I couldn't see why a soldier in the midst of a real war would want to play a cyberversion in his downtime, but maybe I was wrong.

I scrolled and clicked, checked out programs like Biodynotics, which explained how DARPA scientists were producing biological appendages far exceeding anything H. G. Wells or Isaac Asimov ever dreamed of: artificial limbs that could practically think; the Deep Bleeder Acoustic Coagulation program sounded like something out of a Wes Craven horror film but was in fact a synthetic system to stop soldiers from bleeding to death on the battlefield; Intestinal Fortitude focused on developing a vaccine to fight diarrhea and creating "fiber-biotics," which, if I understood correctly, somehow turned what they referred to as "nontraditional food stuffs" into instant energy for soldiers.

The DARPA programs read like sci-fi novels.

There was the Z-Man project, which sounded like something straight out of Marvel Comics, an adhesive that turned soldiers into Spiderman by giving them the ability to scale walls.

Less entertaining, though just as riveting, were discussions of Biological Warfare Defense, which broke down into the self-explanatory Protecting Human Assets and Biology to Enhance Military Systems. Both sounded scary.

But it was the Peak Soldier Performance program that stopped me cold. Its aim: to maintain peak physical and cognitive performance in the battlefield. There were subcategories like "tolerance to extreme climates by means of thermoregulation," and "combating muscle fatigue by exploring biochemical etiology," discussions of urban warfare concepts and new and novel ways to "tag, track, and locate targets"—all sorts of programs directed at creating a new and better "warfighter."

There was HURT, the Heterogeneous Urban Reconnaissance, Surveillance, and Target Acquisition team; RAID, the Real-time Adversarial Intelligence and Decision-making program, discourses on biology and neuroscience, and a lengthy discussion of new accelerated ways of teaching and learning and testing, which made me think of Tully spewing rote answers to unasked questions, and O'Reilly's, Beamer's, and Billow's wild scribblings of words like *yes* and *no*, *true* and *false*.

I read descriptions of a new class of drugs called ampakines, which pretty much did away with sleep, and again I was thinking about O'Reilly and Tully with Provigil in their veins and wondered how long they'd been awake, and if that was why they had exploded.

If DARPA scientists made good on their word, the United States was well on its way to having an army of supermen and superwomen, and Brave New World was upon us.

The long-term effects are unknown.

I pictured Tully attacking a woman in the park and telling her he was sorry; of James O'Reilly beating Peter Sandwell to death with his bare fists, then shooting himself in the head; of Wayne Beamer stabbing the Hunter College student in front of the movie theater, then diving off the Empire State Building. Were they all superwarfighters run amok; men whose wiring had gone bad, who had killed without fear or constraint, who had exploded, then imploded?

My natural ampakines must have been kicking in, if there was such a thing, because I was wide awake, my mind spinning.

I tried to collect my thoughts, sat back and glanced at the sketch I'd made last night, and that's when I remembered.

It took less than twenty seconds to sketch it in—the scar.

Jesus Christ! Mantooth was still at it! He'd cut into another brain and rewired it.

I wanted Mantooth so bad I could taste it. But I wanted to find this guy even more; to get some answers and help him before he exploded.

I got my service revolver out of the bottom desk drawer and slipped it into my pocket.

53

I caught a taxi in front of the station.

A block from Mantooth's brownstone I got out. I didn't imagine he would just let me in, so I went back to the deli and stood under the awning. I tried to think it through while I stared at his front door.

It finally dawned on me that I should not be doing this alone. I pressed the autodial for Terri's number, then stopped. I hadn't spoken to her since we'd fought and didn't think she'd be happy to hear from me. And I didn't want her, or anyone else, telling me to quit. Not now.

The owner of the deli, a Korean guy, kept peering out at me. I must have looked like a vagrant with my disheveled clothes and beat-up face. But I wasn't feeling any pain. There was too much adrenaline in my bloodstream.

I had just made the decision to call for backup when Mantooth's front door opened. He came out rolling a suitcase and I just went into action, dashed across the street dodging cars and taxis and didn't stop till I was right in his face.

"Going somewhere?" I said.

The shock registered in his arched brows and open mouth.

I had the gun in my pocket and I jammed it into his side until I had him backed up against his front door.

"Inside," I said, "unless you want to scream for help. I'm sure the police would be real happy to come to your aid."

My hand was shaking but he couldn't see that and I kept my face as hard and neutral as possible.

He reached into his pocket, but I grabbed his hand.

"The key," he said.

I knocked his hand away and got it myself. His passport was in there, too.

"Planning a long trip, huh?" I unlocked the door, led him inside, then pushed him into a chair.

"What are you doing here?" he said, his voice going high and strident. "You're crazy."

"Something you're an expert on, aren't you, Mantooth—insanity, fear, cutting into people's brains."

His spidery hands were shaking at his sides.

"I'm going to call the police now." I took the cell out of my pocket. "But I have a few questions I'd really like to have answered before they get here."

His red-rimmed eyes were darting in all directions.

"Is the FBI on to you or are you cooperating with them?"

"What are you talking about?" His face went from confusion to fear. It was clear he didn't know that they were looking for him.

Then I got the crumpled sketch out of my pocket and held it in front of his face. "What did you do to him?"

He tried to keep the emotion off his face, but his lower lip was trembling.

"I know all about you and your little experiments at the Lucas Lab. Gambel was going to tell me all about them and give me some proof, but he made the mistake of calling you first."

"You're insane."

"No, I don't think so. You see, I *know* that Gambel called you right after he talked to me because I have the phone records. He told you he was tired of keeping the secret—that it was eating him up inside—that he'd made up his mind to come clean. You argued, but he wouldn't listen. You begged him not to talk, maybe you even threatened him, but he wouldn't budge. So you went to his apartment, killed him, and took the papers, the proof of what you had done at the lab. Where are they, Mantooth?"

"I have no idea what you're talking about," he said, trying hard to maintain his cool, but his jaw muscles were rippling under the skin, giving him away.

"What'd you do, hold a pillow over Gambel's face? He wasn't a strong man, and his asthma was bad. It couldn't have been very difficult to kill him. But the FBI has Gambel's body and they're going to find out exactly what happened to him. Maybe they already have. By now, no question they have his phone records, too. You're finished, Mantooth."

He looked me in the eye, the Cheshire cat grin playing across his lips. "Actually, I would say it is *you* who is finished."

I sensed the shadow at the back of my head too late.

It was Mantooth's boy, the guy in my sketch, with a gun to my head. He reached around and took mine.

"Very good," said Mantooth. Then he came up close to my face and said, "Gambel was indeed a weak man, weak of spirit and weak of body. It took one steroid shot to bring him to his knees. After that, well . . . I couldn't let him take me down with him, could I?" He shrugged. "Lance, keep a close eye on Mr. Rodriguez."

"That's right," I said. "You watch me, Lance, while you let the doctor who fucked up your brain get away."

"Shut up," said Mantooth. "Lance, this man is here to hurt us, to hurt *you*."

"No way, Lance. Hey, I didn't appreciate the tumble we took last night, but hell, that's blood under the bridge. I forgive you. It's not your fault. The doctor here did a little redesign of your brain and you can't quite control yourself; I know that, and I understand."

"You are wasting your breath," said Mantooth. "Lance takes his orders from me, not you." He waved a hand at Lance, and said, "This man is the enemy. He has killed your buddies on the battlefield, and now he is here to kill *you*."

Lance pressed the gun harder against my skull.

"Look around, Lance, this is *no* battlefield. It's a brownstone in New York City and I am *not* the enemy. I didn't kill your buddies. I'm here to help you. This is no battlefield, and it is no lovely tea garden, either."

I felt the gun tic against my head, Lance's hand vibrating slightly. I'd made a connection. At least I hoped so. Otherwise, I was dead.

"What'd he do, Lance, get you to wear one of those magnetic tiaras, the kind where he can zap your brain? And that was just for starters, wasn't it? Before he started slicing and dicing."

The vibrating of the gun against my head was stronger now. I was either getting him to see the truth or he was losing it, ready to explode.

"Lance, bring him over here," said Mantooth.

Lance pushed me toward a chair and stood in front of me.

I looked up and saw it again, the scar at the top of his forehead.

"He messed with your brain, Lance, I *know* that, and I'm sorry, *really* sorry. You have nightmares, right, and your head is itchy all the time and you can't sleep no matter what, and you feel brave but you're not sure why."

I had his eye now and saw the microexpression of anger that flashed across his face followed by sadness and confusion, the gun shaking in his hand. It was one of those small mouse guns that Terri favored, but I knew a well-placed shot into my head would do the trick.

"It's hopeless," said Mantooth. "You can't get through."

"I know what he *did* to you, Lance. You tell him that you're in pain and he says it's normal, that it will go away, but it *never* does, does it, no matter how many pills he gives you. He stole your life and—"

"That's enough," said Mantooth. "This man is here to arrest you, Lance, to lock you up and put you in a cage like an animal."

"That's not true," I said. "Think back, Lance. There was a time when you felt differently, when you could think for yourself and sleep. And there was someone in your life, a woman, maybe, who you cared about, and who cared for you, a time before you came to see Dr. Mantooth, before all the pain and the nightmares and—"

Mantooth tore off a swath of tape and slapped it across my mouth.

I knew what was about to happen, that Mantooth would have Lance shoot me, then he'd turn around and kill Lance. He'd make it look like Lance had killed me, then committed suicide, just like all of the other men.

Lance took a step toward me and placed the gun against my skull. He was staring down at me, so I put everything into my eyes and the muscles of my face, all my thoughts and emotions, trying to communicate through a look like I never had before.

I watched him cock the pistol and I braced myself. Then I heard the popping sound as the mouse gun fired.

54

I saw the red dot, half the size of a dime, just above Mantooth's right eyebrow. A few seconds later blood trickled out of it.

Then Lance put the gun against his own forehead and pulled the trigger.

I saw the tiny bullet fly out the back of his head and hit the wall.

And then I saw something I have never seen before. He fired the gun again. And this time, I swear, he was smiling. He teetered

a moment, then started to fall. He fell in gradations like a stop-action film, and I saw it again: the falling man in my dream.

Lance hit the floor with a thud, but he was still breathing, blood pulsing from the two shots he'd fired into his own head, more bubbling out of his mouth.

I cradled his head; he smiled again, then closed his eyes.

Mantooth was standing over us.

"Am I . . . hit?" he asked, eyes open wide, stunned. There was a thin line of scarlet inching its way down his cheek.

I had no idea how much damage the mouse gun had done, but blood was snaking its way toward his jaw.

"Skin like . . . leather," he said, his eyes blinking. "True . . . body . . . armor."

I tore the tape off my mouth. "Take it easy," I said.

Mantooth stumbled forward, his hands gripping my shoulders. The blood reached his chin and started to drip off, small droplets hitting the floor and splattering. The tiny bullet must have lodged itself inside his head, and the idea that this mad scientist might have suffered a blow to his prefrontal brain was not lost on me.

He took in a soupy, clogged breath. "There are . . . always . . . casualties."

I took off my shirt and tied it around his head. His skin had gone chalk-white, a thin film slipping over his eyes. Then his body jerked, his eyes flickered, and he slipped from my arms. Again I saw the falling man from my nightmare.

My white shirt had soaked through. It looked like a vermilion bandanna tied across Mantooth's forehead. He looked up at me, lids still flickering, risorius muscles around his mouth causing his lips to quiver. There were a million questions buzzing in my head but it was too late; he was gone.

I checked for a pulse in his neck but couldn't find one.

I got my gun from the floor and then my cell to make the call, but I knew what I had to do first. I had to find Gambel's papers.

I looked at Mantooth on the floor next to Lance—Frankenstein and his creature. It was a sad tableau, but I didn't have time to be sad.

I unzipped Mantooth's suitcase, pushing aside underwear,

shirts, toiletries, and below I found the plexi-framed family photo which had been on his desk. But there were no papers.

It was a three-story brownstone. The papers could be hidden anywhere.

I started in his office, pushed papers around on his desk, tugged open drawers, swiped books from shelves, but I was just making a mess.

I stopped, took a deep breath, and tried to think it through.

Mantooth was planning a getaway, so he would take them—unless he had destroyed them.

But destroy the history of his experiments, his life's work? It would be like an artist destroying his paintings, and I couldn't imagine that.

They're on him, I thought; *they have to be*.

I started with his jacket, then his pants, all his pockets, but came up empty. I looked from Mantooth to Lance, then started to pat Lance down, too. I dug my hand inside his shirt and pants, but there were no papers on him, either.

I just couldn't figure it.

I sat back on my heels and did a slow inventory of the room—there was nowhere to hide them. I glanced back at the suitcase and that's when it registered, the weight of the family photo.

I pushed clothes around again, got a grip on the plexi box, flipped it over, saw the piece of cardboard that had been taped over the back, and tore it off. Gambel's notebook was inside.

I opened to the first page.

The Fearless Experiment
October 1991
Day 1

Subjects separated into categories, decisions of
treatment and experimental options considered:
chemical, intracranial electromagnetic stimulation,
intercranial surgery.

Subjects:
#1 Malcolm Smith
#2 Ronald Myer
#3 James O'Reilly
#4 Wayne Beamer
#5 Jerzy Leslaw
#6 Matthew Tully
#7 Floyd Billow
#8 Peter Sandwell
#9 Joseph Caldwell

(*Note: Doctors will verbally refer to patients by number only.)

AIMS
Eliminate sleep but maintain peak performance
Increase learning capacity
Reduce or eliminate fear

I flipped a few pages, my heart beating fast.

Peter Sandwell (now #8) asst. to JG, young, excellent
health, anxious to volunteer for study. Started him

on 20 mg a day of amphetamine and modafinil with addition of ampakines to maintain peak performance. After 3 days of no sleep subject is still alert, bright, can learn at high rate and tests well above average.

Subject has already shown slight dependency on drugs. Reevaluate after one week.

I skipped ahead and stopped at a diagram Gambel had made of the brain.

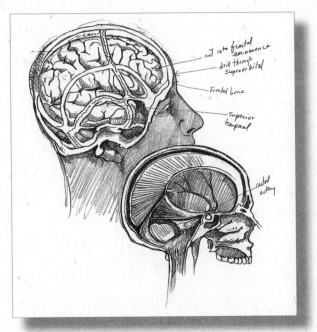

Then I read what he had written below it.

Billow (#7) recuperating well after intercranial surgery. Cogent and responds well to stimuli. Like a lab rat, he exhibits no fear when provoked. Have presented subject with extreme duress—piercing noise, frightening imagery—but there is no fear response recorded.

Subject experiences pain but does not react. So far no
visible side effects except for occasional fits of anger
easily controlled with benzodiazepines.

I was flipping pages quickly now, reading bits and pieces of
information.

Have effectively controlled and maneuvered subject's
arm (Beamer, #4) by electromagnetic stimulation from
as far away as fifteen feet. After several hours arm
moved as if by itself, though spasmodically.

Ampakines and TMS has #5 and #9 both responding
well to testing and scoring high above average after
two weeks of no sleep. Subjects complain of dry mouth,
itchy scalp, hallucinations (always described as "red"—
possibly due to CX717, which appears to affect color
vision). Administer 10 cc Valium along with prednisone
for itching. More TMS for prefrontal cortex stimulation
has reduced spasms but increased anger.

O'Reilly (#3) has experienced two panic attacks
and shows signs of occasional violence (attributable to
earlier substance abuse?). Controllable with additional
Prozac, Klonopin, and Tricyclic drugs.

I closed the notebook. I'd read enough for now.

I called Baumgarten and asked him to come to the scene. Then
I called Terri and told her to bring a couple of her men and a CS
team.

"What the hell is going on, Rodriguez?" she asked.

"You want to be the detective who broke the case?" I said.
"Then get here. Fast."

55

Barton and Peterson arrived after Terri and O'Connell and the CS crew, who were already at work, along with a dozen more cops and uniforms, techies dusting and bagging and crawling around like ants at a picnic.

The bureau boys looked mad as hell, but there wasn't much they could do to control the scene; it was too far gone.

I knew I didn't look good standing there in a bloodstained T-shirt and jeans, my shirt wrapped around Mantooth's head, soaked through with blood.

I told Barton what I'd told the cops: that Mantooth had called and I'd come to see him. I said Mantooth thought I knew something about Gambel, but I didn't know what.

"So what do you know about this guy, Mantooth?" Barton asked, his eyes squinting and blinking, the neutral mask he usually wore cracking, a sure sign that he was nervous, and I knew why: He'd been assigned to keep this under wraps and had failed.

"Nothing," I said. "What do *you* know about him?"

He answered with a question. "Did he say anything about Gambel?"

It was still all about containment; trying to find out what I knew. But it was too late and I was pretty sure he knew it.

"All he asked," I said, "in his dying breath, was if Gambel had given me some papers." I looked at Barton and scratched my head. "Do you know what he was talking about?"

I needed to keep up the charade just a little bit longer. I didn't know if he was buying my idiot act, but I kept it up. I said I'd heard the shots outside the door and burst in to find the two men on the floor; that Lance was already a goner but I had tried to save Mantooth. I told him that Mantooth said the other guy had shot him, then shot himself.

Baumgarten, who was crouched over Lance's body, looked up. "Right now it appears as if that's the way it happened." He glanced from me to Barton to Terri, unsure of who was running the show.

"There's obvious GSR on this one," he said, swabbing Lance's face. "Plenty of powder burns. I'd say he put the gun right up against his forehead—and more than once."

"Is that *possible*?" asked Barton.

"Not unheard of," said Baumgarten. "Particularly with a mouse gun. Weird, though. It takes some kind of fool bravery."

I knew all about that *fool* bravery, but wasn't going to say.

"Your two vics have the same body temp," said Baumgarten. "They died at about the same time. But I'll do more tests back at the morgue."

"Hold on," said Barton, exchanging a look with Peterson. "We're taking the bodies."

"Oh, no, you're not," said Baumgarten, whipping off his mask. "Not till I get authorization and release papers from all parties involved."

"I'm a federal agent," said Barton.

"I don't care if you're J. Edgar Hoover," said Baumgarten. "First on the scene has possession of the bodies."

"I'll take full responsibility," said Barton.

"You can take me to the prom for all I care," said Baumgarten. "Those bodies are under my care until I get the proper authorization to let them go."

I wondered about the terminology "under my care" when it came to dead bodies, but I knew Baumgarten wouldn't let them out of his sight until he had the proper paperwork in triplicate, or until Barton knocked him unconscious.

"Best I can do is hold off on the autopsies," he said, "but I've got to follow procedure. Sorry, but it will be my ass, not yours, that will be hung out to dry. You bring me the proper authorization and the bodies are all yours. Till then, I'll keep 'em on ice."

The EMT team was zipping Mantooth and Lance into body bags, and the CS team was packing up, so I figured it was a good time for me to leave, too.

"I'll send you copies of Rodriguez's statement and all the paperwork," Terri said to Barton.

"Gee, that's swell of you, Russo," said Barton. Then he turned to me. "Just remember our conversation, Rodriguez."

He turned to Peterson, nodded, and they marched off.

Outside, I asked Terri to wait while I conferred with the EMT driver to make sure the bodies got to the city morgue and nowhere else. Then I got into her car.

It was awkward between us, neither one of us knowing quite how to act.

"What conversation was that?" she finally asked.

"With Barton? It was nothing."

"I can see you're lying, Rodriguez."

She could still read me better than anyone.

"It was the usual bureau bullshit, you know—'You'll never work in this town again' sort of crap."

I could see the skepticism in her eyes.

"You look awful," she said. "Someone punch you in the jaw?"

"Just follow the EMT van," I said. "I'll explain everything later."

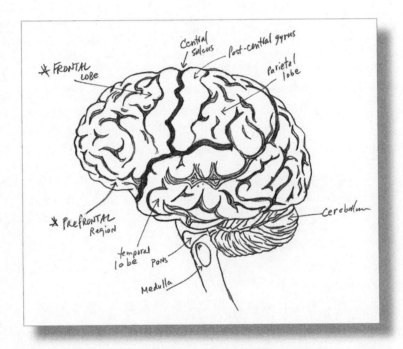

56

Intercranial surgery: catheter inserted between orbitofrontal cortex and limbic system. Subject seems to have no memory of operation after one week. Decision making somewhat restricted. Difficulty judging and/or moderating emotional reactions but testing excellent. Data learned at high speed and under extreme conditions.

"This is like science fiction," said Terri.

We were at the morgue, reading from Gambel's notebooks, which I had stashed in Lance's underpants. I had counted on Baumgarten being the stickler I knew he was and he did not disappoint me. I'd asked him for a minute of privacy with the cadaver and for once he did not ask for written authorization. He knew something was up and did not want to be implicated.

Terri flipped pages and we read the notebook together.

Note:

Surgically altered prefrontal cortex makes it difficult for subjects to show restraint. Subjects #3, #6, and #9, heavily sedated and now appear normal. Long-term medication may be necessary to control certain subjects.

Note:

Activities which require planning appear impossible for all surgical subjects with prefrontal "damage" while simple reacting is unaltered. Rapid learning by rote very successful with all subjects.

Plan B:

More surgery for subjects 4, 7, 8. Cauterize strathmin to totally remove "fear gene." Postpone surgery on subjects 1, 2, 3, 5, 6, and 9 until signs of psychotic behavior are under control.

"Jesus," said Terri. "What possessed them?"

"I guess they got so lost in their work they forgot they were men," I said. "Forgot their subjects were men, too."

Terri flipped another page.

Note:
Have tried several masking techniques with subjects
and "tea garden" appears to have worked well.

"That explains it," I said, thinking back to Tully. "They found
some way to brainwash the men. When I asked Tully where he was
he said he was in a tea garden."

"It's like that movie," Terri said. "You know the one, where the
soldiers are brainwashed and forced to commit murder."

"*The Manchurian Candidate*," I said, and felt a chill as I read
another passage.

Fear Experiment #28:
Hypnotized Subject #7 (Billow) two weeks after 2nd
amygdale surgery; described in detail battlefield
strewn with dead bodies and live mines; asked him
to enter and retrieve battle plans; placed folded
map in center of room "battlefield." Subject entered,
ducking and covering ears as if bullets and bombs
were exploding, but did not exhibit any fear. Subject
successfully retrieved map.

Fear Experiment #29:
Hypnotized subject #3 (O'Reilly), described same
scene. He was told that his best friend (played by
Dr. AB) was wounded in "battlefield."

#3 entered "battlefield." Once there he was told by
Dr. AB that the enemy (played by subject #2, Myer) was
approaching. #2 was asked to approach #3 from rear as
quietly as possible.

#3 rescued "best friend" (Dr. AB), then attacked
"enemy" (#2).

#3 had to be put in restraints and tranquilized.

#2 suffered four broken ribs, broken nose, minor contusions, slight concussion, and was hospitalized here for six days before releasing.

"I don't fucking believe this," said Terri. "They were playing war games, but for real."

Subject #4 (Beamer) showed me notebook of his "drawings." Says they happen "automatically" in times of stress.

Have noticed that other subjects all have this "scribble" side effect.

Other odd side effects: free-associative verbalization after testing (i.e., repetitive words with same letter).

"Sound familiar?" I asked.
Terri nodded.

Subjects #9 (Caldwell) and #3 (O'Reilly) back in the "real world" over two years now.

#9 appears to be functioning well despite depression and anxiety. Have prescribed more medication.

#3 complains of depression, irritability, trouble concentrating and hypervigilance. Says his wife is going to leave him.

Dr. VM prescribed antidepressants. Probably better that subject live alone, like #9.

"He's writing about a man whose life is disintegrating," said Terri. "And he's happy because it's easier for them if the subject 'lives alone.' "

"I think he was also afraid of what O'Reilly might do to his wife," I said, "like those soldiers at Fort Bragg."

"I'm starting to feel sick," she said.

Subject #4 (Beamer) fifth anniversary in "real world." Complains he never sleeps. Says mother wants to talk with us about his depression. Dr. VM discouraged. Took him off modafinil though it appears to have lasting effect in preventing sleep. Subject reports no sleep for two-three weeks at a time, then intermittent naps. Increased SSRI antidepressants plus 10 mg Ativan and 10 mg Xanax. Test scores remain high and constant.

Subject #1 (Smith) seventh anniversary. 2nd surgery now one month old. Usual complaints, itchy scalp and "tapping." Has been exhibiting behavioral disorders, lying, does not cooperate or obey rules, fights with others. Positron emission tomography (PET) shows lower levels of metabolic activities in frontal brain. Surgery may have caused too much damage to impulse-control limbic center. Consider removing #1 from study. (Call state mental facility to take subject.)

"Jesus Christ, this is too horrible," said Terri. "They fuck up a man's brain, then toss him into a state mental facility."

"Remember that stuff about damage to the prefrontal brain and violence? Looks like the doctors proved it."

Terri shook her head. "Isn't there some sort of government watchdog for this kind of research—this kind of *torture?*"

"From my Internet searches it appears there are institutional review boards called IRBs, but they're primarily based in universities and teaching hospitals, and overloaded. And the FDA only inspects about one percent of *all* clinical trials."

"Not very good odds that they'll catch the bad guys."

"No. And nowadays, it's the same people, who are volunteering over and over again for experiments. It's called 'guinea-pigging.'"

"Who would do that to themselves?"

"People who need the money, Terri. Poor people." I imagined these "volunteers" strapped into beds, IVs in their arms, ingesting all forms of potentially poisonous drugs—and all for money. "It's ironic, isn't it? I mean, you've got a poor person, who can't afford health insurance, volunteering to test a drug that he or she will not be able to afford when it's FDA-approved."

"Wonderful country," Terri.

"But now I hear there's a website that's devoted to watching and documenting research abuse."

"About time. Too bad it didn't exist for these guys."

"Really too bad," I said.

"Are they all dead, the scientists who took part in this butchery?" Terri asked. "I'd love to petition the court to perform brain surgery on *them*."

"Gambel is, and now Mantooth. I looked up Brillstein; he died a few years ago."

"Too bad," she said, and turned to the last pages of notes.

I can no longer do this. In the name of science is no longer justification. When I look into the subjects' eyes I see what we have done, the pain we have caused, the damage to these men, their relatives and countless others. I discussed terminating the experiments with AB and VM but they did not agree. They have, like me until now, lost all perspective, and worse, their humanity.

But I have put an end to the project. I have contacted DARPA, which is now cutting all funding and possibly closing the lab. They have asked that all information remain confidential for fear of lawsuits, and I have complied. I am a coward. But at least I have put a stop to something that never should have begun.

I am keeping this documentation for scientists to read and heed in the future. It is, I am afraid, what constitutes my life's work. I have told AB and VM of its existence and have let them know I will make it public if they pursue this work.

It was signed, "Jonathan Gambel."

57

We have to make this public," said Terri, gripping Gambel's notebook. "It's our only protection."

"I agree, but first we have to find these other guys, the subjects. We only know five of them."

Terri and I hadn't stopped to talk about ourselves and what had happened between us. Right now it didn't seem important. I figured we'd talk about it, deal with it at some point, but that was for later.

I made a quick pit stop—home to change my clothes—then we went to the station and ran the names we didn't know through NCIC and VICAP. The only one who came up was Malcolm Smith, a guy who was serving a life sentence for murder at a supermax facility, Pelican Bay, in California.

Terri called the prison and spoke to the warden.

Smith, who was now thirty-six, had killed a man with his bare hands when he was twenty-three. He was considered dangerous and volatile. He'd assaulted guards and several inmates over his twelve-year internment.

We found his military stats, two tours of duty in the Gulf, discharged with PTSD, and he saw an unnamed therapist when he was back at a desk job at Fort Dix. A year later he killed a man.

"He should be in a mental facility," said Terri, "not a prison."

"We'll make sure of that later," I said. "For now he's locked up, which is not a bad thing."

There was no Ronald Myers in the criminal system, and it took us over an hour to figure out that there were no records of his existence because he had killed himself in 1996.

That left Joseph Caldwell and Jerzy Leslaw.

We did a search on Caldwell, and had to do a lot of eliminating—it was a common name—but finally found one who had been at McGuire Air Force Base between 1991 and 1994. After that we picked up two addresses in Cincinnati, three different ones in Minneapolis, and his last known address in Marion, Illinois. The guy had become a drifter. But the Illinois address was four years old and there was nothing after that. Not a trace.

"Maybe he's dead, too," said Terri. But there was no record of his death to be found.

We gave up on him for the time being and switched to Leslaw. He had no criminal record, but his military stats showed he too had served in the Gulf, discharged in 1992, with no other information.

The DMV provided an address from a four-year-old expired Pittsburgh license and a phone number. I dialed it right away.

"You must be looking for my son," the man said. "I haven't spoken to him in over three years. He's been a problem since he was in the army, sixteen years ago. He had that post-traumatic business and never got over it. And no one helped him, not the military, not the government. What's the point? I mean, your boy volunteers for service, fights for his country, and then the country turns her back on him. Damn shame."

"It is," I said.

"He lived with me until I remarried, but the new wife wouldn't put up with his moping and outbursts, and who could blame her. He was always starting trouble, always fighting. It's what broke up me and his mother."

"Where did he go?" I asked.

"Back to live with his mother, my ex, but she died a year ago. I think it was Jerzy who killed her. I don't mean that literally. I mean the pressure of it all."

"I'm sorry," I said.

"Everyone's sorry, but who's doing anything to help our young men and women?" He sighed. "He called me for money but I couldn't afford to lend him any."

I asked if he had a current address for his son and he said no.

After that Terri and I searched through more databases, IRS, credit cards, hospitals and morgues, but came up empty.

"It's like he disappeared," she said.

"There are plenty of people living in SROs with no income and no tax records," I said.

We didn't know where to go from there.

"How about the FBI?" I said, only half joking.

"My guess," she said, "they're still stinging from fucking up the case and are now going into distancing mode."

"They're lucky the papers are reporting Mantooth and Lance as just another murder-suicide. So far their screwup is safe."

"Until we release the notebook," she said.

"And you can bet they're looking for it as we speak. You think they're still watching us?" I asked.

"Believe it," she said.

"We'd better find Caldwell and Leslaw before they kill someone or throw themselves off a building," I said.

"And then we hand the notebook over to the media."

"Right," I said.

Terri's cell phone rang. "It's Denton," she said, looking at the number. "I've got to take it."

She went into the hallway, leaving me with too many scenarios about why he was calling.

After a minute she was back, her mouth tight and worried.

"The bureau called him."

"Barton?" I asked.

"No, some big shot from Quantico. They want all the case files on what went down at Mantooth's place and they made it clear it's their investigation, not ours. Denton says they specifically mentioned me—and *you*."

"Like how?"

"Like we are not to be within twenty feet of the case. And Denton says I'm to keep an eye on you."

"Fine," I said, "you can watch me day and night."

It was the first time since we'd been together that I dared say anything like that, but my timing was off.

"This is serious, Rodriguez. Who knows what those guys can do to me—to *us*."

"Look, we've got big-time insurance now, Gambel's notebook, remember? We make that public and the feds will be so busy making excuses they'll forget all about you and me. Listen, if we don't find Caldwell and Leslaw by tomorrow we give the book to the press, okay? And if we do find them, it's the final feather in your cap."

"Did you have to say *final*?"

"Don't worry."

"Yeah, right," she said. "How'd you get to be so brave, Rodriguez?"

"Just stubborn and stupid."

"Not stupid," she said. "Look, what I said about your father . . . I'm sorry."

"No, you were right. I think his death does drive me. But now it's more than that. It's like, I can't let all these guys down, you know what I mean?" I saw them in my mind's eye—Beamer, O'Reilly, Tully, Billow, and now Lance, men who committed heinous acts beyond their control; men who had been manipulated and destroyed; lost men, fallen men.

"I think I do," she said. "Look, I'll get the task force on Leslaw and Caldwell. Nobody has to know why."

"Good," I said. Then I asked, "Do you think we have five minutes to get a drink?"

"I don't think that's a good idea, not right now."

I saw her point. It was better if everyone thought we were still broken up, and maybe we were. I wasn't sure.

"I'll get the guys on these missing men," she said. "But you have to go home. Whatever turns up by tomorrow, turns up. If not, we have the notebook for the press, agreed?" She put out her hand.

I tugged her gently toward me and kissed her. She didn't resist.

Then I stepped back, let go, and started to walk away. Halfway down the hall I turned back and Terri offered me the first smile I'd seen in a long time.

58

It was still hot but the sky had darkened with clouds that threatened rain and maybe relief.

I wasn't quite ready to go home and still wanted a drink, so I called Julio as I headed crosstown.

"Mr. Sanchez's office." His secretary sounded very official until I told her it was me.

"Oh, hi, Nate. *¿Qué pasa?*" She giggled.

Julio's secretary always thought it was cool to try out her three Spanish phrases on me. According to Julio's wife, Jess, Allison had some huge crush on me.

"I'm fine, Allison. How about you?"

"Me? Oh, I'm doing okay."

"The boss in?"

"Sorry, he's with a client."

"Just tell him I called and wanted to buy him a ginger ale."

Allison giggled again. "Will do. But I'm leaving in a few minutes, so maybe you should try his cell in about fifteen, okay? He'll be finished by then, at least he should be. He was supposed to be finished a half hour ago."

"Client chewing his ear?"

"You got it," she said.

I told her I'd call Julio in a while, thanked her, and hung up.

I was already on the East Side, so I just kept walking. The air had gotten heavy and electric, the way it does when it's about to storm, but it felt better than the heat.

It wasn't impatience that made me call back five minutes later, just a weird feeling I couldn't place. But Allison was gone. A machine picked up and I didn't bother to leave a message.

I walked five or six more blocks thinking and praying we would be able to find those missing guys. Then I tried Julio's cell, which went directly to voice mail, and I hung up. A minute later I hit redial. It went to voice mail again, and I couldn't say why but it made me uncomfortable. I told myself I was being crazy, but couldn't shake a bad feeling, *algo malo*, my *abuela* would call it.

I tried Julio's cell one more time and when the message came on I left one asking that he call me. Then I tried another number.

His wife answered on the second ring.

"Nate, how are you?"

"Fine, Jess, listen—"

"God, I feel like we haven't seen you in ages. When are you coming over? And you've got to see Sam, he changes every day."

"I know. I'm a lousy godfather. I'm sorry. How is he?"

"He's just great."

"Look, I was trying to reach Julio and—"

"Oh, he must still be at the office. He promised he'd leave early. You know how we're both usually there till midnight—well, not me, not anymore, not since Sam. I'm getting my priorities in order. I keep telling Julio he's going to miss his son growing up but—Nate, maybe you can talk to him."

"Yeah, I will, Jess, I promise. Like I said, I was just trying to call him. I'm on the East Side and wanted to see if we could grab a drink, but—"

"Did you try his cell?"

"Yes, but he isn't picking up."

"Really? He's got the new iPhone and I swear he's more attached to that thing than he is to me." She laughed. "So how's Terri?"

"Fine, great. Listen, Jess—"

"You know, you guys should come out to the Hamptons—"

"Yeah, we will. So, what do you think is keeping Julio?"

"Oh, I *know* what's keeping him, or rather *who*—an impossible client, Julio's charity case, his pro bono client."

His pro bono client. I pictured the guy. "I think I met him, tall, high-strung—"

"I'll say. He's ex-army, very screwed up; sad, really. No one would work with him except your bighearted friend Julio. Of course it could become a landmark case, a class-action suit against the U.S. Army, so—"

The chill worked its way up my back like an electric shock. "What's his name?" I asked, trying hard to sound casual.

"Leslaw," she said, "Jerzy Leslaw, though he goes by Jerry. Is something wrong, Nate?"

I managed to say, "No." I did not want to alarm her. "Nothing at all."

59

I called Terri and got her machine, too. I told her I had located Leslaw, but wasn't sure how to handle it. I was afraid that sirens and uniforms could set Leslaw off and frankly, I had no idea what was really going on. For all I knew, Julio and Leslaw could be having a convivial drink.

But I didn't think so.

I was about ten blocks from Julio's office. I tried to hail a cab but couldn't get one, so I just kept walking, picking up a little speed.

My cell rang and I practically jumped.

"You found him? *How? Where?* What's going on?" It was Terri. There were sirens in the background and lots of street traffic.

"Where are you?" I asked.

"At a crime scene in the jewelry district, a diamond merchant shot."

"Sorry," I said, then explained the situation and gave her Julio's address. "I have no idea if there's any trouble and Julio is smart and tough, but I'm heading over. Can you meet me there with some backup?"

"I can't leave, but I'll send a team, stat."

"No cavalry. You know how these guys are, supersensitive to noise and authority. I don't want to spook him and set him off."

"Right," she said.

"How soon can you break away?" I asked.

"As soon as I can, and I'll bring a few men."

"Right," I said. "But tell them to take it easy. And no sirens."

The sky had gone almost black, distant thunder and lightning, the air so still it was like someone had turned off a switch and was just waiting to turn it back on. I headed toward Julio's law firm, four floors of a brownstone on Forty-first between and Park and Lex. I was walking fast, telling myself to calm down, that nothing had happened, that Julio was smart and could handle the situation.

I had only gone two blocks when there was a bolt of lightning followed by a clap of thunder so loud I thought it was an explosion, and then the rain came. More lightning streaked between sky-scrapers, and in seconds the rain was heavy and hard. People were running for cover, ducking into stores and under awnings; curbs filling up, rivulets that became streams in a matter of minutes, sidewalks disappearing. I was soaked, hair in my eyes, feet slosh-ing, plus a sharp pain in my knee from last night's fall. I stopped to give it a moment's rest and that's when I felt it, the same feeling I'd had for days: that I was being followed.

But by who? The feds? Here? Now?

I looked one way, then the other, people everywhere rushing to get out of the downpour. Then I looked across the street and saw him, the Chandler character, just standing there, on the corner.

The rain had made visibility difficult, but it was him, the same guy from the other night. But I didn't have time to think about him, not now. If the feds had kept their tail on me, so be it. Right now, I had to get to Julio's office.

I took the next streets at a run, rain soaking through my clothes, weighing me down but not stopping me.

Twice I looked back but didn't see him, the guy in the trench. Maybe I'd lost him. Maybe he'd given up.

I didn't stop to catch my breath until I got there. Then I stood across the street from Julio's office and watched the rain coming off the brownstone like waterfalls.

I couldn't be sure if Julio and Leslaw were still in the building, but lights were on in the third-floor windows.

I got out my cell and called.

This time someone answered, but it wasn't Julio.

"Where's Julio?" I asked, trying to stay calm.

"He can't talk right now."

"Is this Jerry, Jerry Leslaw?"

He didn't answer, but I could hear him breathing.

"Jerry, listen, this is Julio's friend, Nate; you know, we met a couple of times, at the Princeton Club and then the other day, remember?" I was trying to make a human connection. It had worked for me before, with Lance. "Listen, I really need to talk to Julio."

Leslaw was still there, but not talking, and I knew it had to be bad. So I took another tack.

"Jerry, listen to me; we've got a serious situation here, on the battlefield. A pal of ours, of *yours*, your *best* pal, he's down and we've got to get to him. You're the only one who can save him— your best friend."

"What? What?" His voice went breathy, frantic. "Not Ron? It can't be Ron!"

I tried to run the list through my head, closed my eyes and saw it, *Ronald Myer.* "Yeah," I said, "it's him, Myer, Ron Myer. And he's hurt, Jerry, real bad. You got to help. You got to let me in. I've got to get ammo and bandages. Ask Julio to help you. Have him buzz me in, okay?"

A moment later the buzzer sounded and the lock popped open, and I was in. I stopped and took a deep breath. "Listen," I said into my cell. "I'm coming up. I need your help."

The stairwell to Julio's third-floor office looked ominous.

I took the first step slowly, the cell to my ear. "Jerry, are you still there?"

"Yeah," he said, "I'm here." The tenor of his voice had changed, the frenetic tone now cool, too cool.

"I'm coming up," I said, "to get bandages for Ron."

"Ron Myer is dead," he said, and hung up.

60

I headed up the staircase, my gun shaking in my hand. It sounded like Leslaw had snapped. I had to keep going.

It will not be finished until you have traveled the whole path. Be brave, Nato.

My *abuela*'s words were in my head and they helped calm me. A very crooked path had led me here, to Leslaw, and to my friend.

I reached the third floor, holding my breath, took a few steps into the dark reception area, and saw a light.

I bolted across the room, pushed the door open, and pivoted in.

There was a young woman at a desk. She looked like a kid, probably just an intern. She was terrified and I didn't blame her, but I got my hand over her mouth before she could scream.

"I'm not here to hurt you," I whispered. "I'm the police. There's an incident down the hall. You need to get out of here. I'm going to take my hand away but you can't make a sound."

She nodded, eyes wide with fear, but she was quiet.

"Go down the stairs as quietly as possible," I whispered. "There will be other cops here soon and you need to let them in. Can you do that?"

She nodded again.

"Tell them I'm here, on the third floor," I whispered, "and send them up."

I watched her tiptoe into the hallway and down the stairs. Then I made my way toward Julio's office.

61

I was trying to think what I'd say to calm Leslaw. He knew Ron Myer was dead and I had lied to him. I hoped I hadn't totally blown my credibility.

I saw light under Julio's door, swung it open, gun out in front of me, dropped to a crouch, and froze.

Leslaw had Julio in front of him, arm locked around his chest, a bayonet blade across his throat.

My first thought was Julio; I needed to keep him calm.

"*Todo va a salir bien,*" I said.

"Yes," said Julio, quietly, measuring his words. "It will be okay. Jerry, here, he's just upset, that's all, but we're going to work it out, right, Jerry?"

There was no way I could chance a shot; Leslaw was wearing Julio like a body shield.

"Jerry," I said, "let Julio go."

"No, I can't do that, man, they're not going to do that to me, not going to take me."

"Jerry, listen," I said, as calmly as I could, trying to think of what to say and how to say it. "No one is going to hurt you, no one.

Julio is going to help you; remember, the class action suit? He's the only one who can do it."

The bayonet was trembling in Leslaw's hand.

"O'Reilly is dead," I said. "Beamer is dead. Billow is dead. Sandwell is dead. Your friend, Ron Myer, is dead. They are *all* dead, Jerry. It's up to you to tell the story, *their* story and *yours*. It's all up to you, Jerry."

"The story . . ." His eyes met mine, haunted and sad. "The mission, yes, that's it . . . to tell the story but . . . I can't remember. I thought I could but . . . the tanks came and the mines and then . . ."

"Julio knows your story, Jerry. *He* can tell it. He can help you. He'll tell the story and make people understand what happened. He's your lawyer, Jerry, that's why you went to him, remember: to tell your story."

"'Lawyers . . . Guns . . . and Money.' " He mumbled the song in a half-whisper, then looked at me, the muscles tugging his lips into an odd smile. "They killed Zevon, Ron's favorite, you know that, right?"

"Okay," I said, playing along. "But you're safe now. They're gone. And Julio will help you."

He pulled Julio closer, the bayonet against his throat. A thin line of red appeared, running down into Julio's white collar.

"Julio!"

"I'm okay," Julio said.

"Jerry, you've got to listen; you've got to stay with me. I know it's hard, but you can do it."

"Can't . . ." he said. "Too hard." Then he looked past me and started reciting the way Tully had. "First president of the U.S. was, was George—George—George—"

"Washington," I said.

"Washington, right; then Adams, Jefferson, Madison, Monroe—James, not Marilyn—Marilyn with the tits and ass and sad eyes and maybe they did that to her, the fucking FBI and CIA—"

His hand holding the bayonet started to tremor again, badly. I was losing him.

"Jerry, listen to me—"

"Killed her because she was fucking JFK, so they blew his head off, then Bobby's, and Martin Luther King and Billie Jean King and Nat King Cole and blue-eyed soul—"

There was a clap of thunder, the windows lit up by lightning. Leslaw jerked and crouched, as if ducking a bomb, taking Julio down with him, and I had a thought.

"Listen to me, Jerry; Ron Myer is dead. But your other friend, Julio, he's right there with you, and he's been hit, he's bleeding. Look at him. He's wounded, maybe dying. You're his only chance, Jerry. You got to get your buddy out of there, *now*! You've got to get Julio off the battlefield!"

Leslaw's eyes were darting in every direction.

Lightning exploded in the window again and he spun around, Julio moving with him.

"Now, Jerry, now, while there's still time!"

Leslaw crouched low to the floor, bayonet out in front of him, arm around Julio's waist, dragging him as he moved forward.

Julio started to struggle and I knew that was a mistake.

"Go with it, Julio. Let him *save* you."

Julio went limp and Leslaw tightened his grip, slashing the bayonet into the air at an invisible enemy. Thunder clapped and he ducked again, still inching forward.

"You're almost there, Jerry, you're a hero, saving your friend. Keep going. They can't touch you."

There were footsteps on the staircase. Then Terri and her

men burst into the room flanked by more detectives, weapons drawn.

I knew it looked bad, Leslaw dragging Julio, the blood on Julio's neck.

I saw the guns aimed and called out to try and stop it as the shots were fired.

62

One time you mentioned a meeting," I said, "a support group."

I was exhausted and achy. I'd slept in the hospital waiting room so I'd be there when Leslaw woke up.

Now I was sitting beside his hospital bed. His arm was in a sling. He'd taken a bullet to the shoulder which had knocked him down but given me enough time to stop the cops from killing him.

Now he was on antipsychotic drugs and enough tranquilizers to subdue an elephant. According to the attending shrink, there were new drugs, even surgical possibilities, but no guarantee that he would ever be right again.

"I have to have their names, Jerry. It's important."

"No. I can't do that. It's not right."

"Listen to me, Jerry. These guys are time bombs; you know that better than I do."

"No way, man. It's like AA, you know, I just can't divulge that information." His jaw tightened with determination. "But none of these guys were at the Lucas Lab with me, I'll tell you that much."

"Who are they, soldiers with PTSD?"

"Some," he said. "And a few who think they had stuff done to them, like what was done to me, at other labs, or in the army. But don't ask me about them because I can't tell you, I made a promise."

"They'll be okay, taken care of, I'll make sure of that, but we need to find them to get them help."

Leslaw took a deep breath and his eyes went moist. "These guys all have regular jobs, some of them families. They're trying to make a go of it. I'm not going to take that away from them."

"But so were *you*, Jerry, trying to make a go of it, remember? And look what happened."

"No," he said, "you don't understand. I *can't*. Haven't you ever given your word?"

"Yeah, I have, but if it meant a life, I'd break it; I'd have to."

"Not me," he said, and turned away.

"Look." I was unable to keep the threat out of my voice. "The doctors can give you truth serum and make you talk, if they have to."

Leslaw turned back to me and laughed without a bit of humor. "I've been programmed, man, remember? Anyone asks me about Lucas or something I don't want to tell them, my mind goes to that lovely tea garden, remember? So, go ahead, shoot me up with whatever you got. Tell the docs to give it their best shot. But I'm telling you, it's a waste of time."

"Jerry, please, you don't want anyone else to get hurt, do you?"

"No, but I'm not going to give you those names. Those guys have gone through hell and I won't let some doctor get them and turn them into Thorazine zombies. Forget it," he said. Then he turned away and stopped talking.

• • •

The next day Leslaw's story headlined every newspaper.

Human Lab Rats!—Guinea Pigs Are Us!—the media as sensitive as ever.

It was all anyone could talk about and that seemed like a good thing.

The military kept mum, but DARPA issued a statement saying that the agency had closed the Lucas Lab long ago "at the first sign of any unsanctioned practices," which they claimed were never proved, and added that they had never gone public with the story to "protect the patients' First Amendment rights to privacy." A savvy PR move.

DARPA was granting interviews and stories to spread the good word about their mission and past achievements. I learned that the agency had been inspired by the Soviet space race and the launching of Sputnik, the first unmanned Russian space mission fifty years ago, which had caught the U.S. by surprise. DARPA was formed so that would never happen again.

There were several editorials and op-ed pieces, one about the military's "black budget," which essentially meant there was no public knowledge of how much money they had or could spend; another about the problem of scientists not getting funded unless their inventions could be used for defense.

Terri got her fifteen minutes of fame as the lead cop on the case and I got about five, as one of the cops who helped solve the case along with the rest of the task force, which received its second commendation from the mayor.

Publishers were vying for Jerry Leslaw's story and he promised to donate half the profits to soldiers with PTSD, which seemed like a decent thing to do and made me think he was softening, so I visited him a second time. I asked again about the men in his support group, but he wouldn't budge. I knew that another task force was being formed to ferret out the men and told him so, but he said they had already disbanded and it was going to be really hard to find them, and he was glad.

I showed him crime scene photos of Beamer and O'Reilly and of their victims and tried to make him feel guilty. "There will be more violent deaths like these, Jerry. Do you want them on your conscience?" But it didn't work.

He said they were entitled to a life and wouldn't give up their names no matter what I said.

That's when I thought I might volunteer for the new task force; the idea that there were more guys out there ready to explode terrified me.

There were lots of stories about ethics and who was to blame, but the one I found the most interesting came from Matt Lauer, an interview with a DARPA scientist on the *Today Show*.

"I can't condone what those other scientists did," he said, a nice-looking man with glasses, graying temples and a kindly, paternal quality, hand-picked by the agency, I had no doubt.

"So what about human experimentation?" Matt asked.

"Well," he said, calm as could be, "there are volunteers for things like testing endurance or muscle fatigue or body temperature or sleep habits, but if you mean putting implants into people or giving them electric shock, *no*. And there are very strict rules governing volunteers."

He went on to cite various statutes, most of them recent, and how much of what had become law in the U.S. was a result of the Nuremberg trials and the atrocities Nazi doctors had carried out on their very much living, nonvolunteer, human subjects.

"Of course you know the phrase 'All's fair in love and war,'" he said. "Well, we are at war, Matt, our American way of life threatened. As a scientist working for defense I feel that it is my duty to make *our* soldiers bigger and stronger than the enemy's."

"Even if it costs lives?" asked Lauer.

"War costs lives," he said. "A lot of lives. Here's a question for you, Matt." He gave Lauer an earnest look. "Is it worth sacrificing a few lives in the lab if it will save thousands on the battlefield?" He held up his hand before Lauer could answer. "Suppose they wanted to test poison gas on a handful of prisoners. Sounds terrible, I know. But suppose these men have committed violent, heinous crimes, and by testing the poison on them scientists could come up with an antidote that would save millions of law-abiding people in the event of a biological attack on an American city; and suppose, just suppose—go along with me here, Matt—that the attack was going to take place in *your* hometown. What would you say then?"

"Well, that's a heck of a question," said Lauer. "But I'm not sure it's ethically okay to kill in the name of the greater good. It seems like an awfully slippery slope."

The scientist was good; he even had me going there for a while. But Lauer was right: Who gets to decide who is bad enough that it's okay to cut into people's brains or shower them with poison gas?

The media wouldn't quit and I was glad to see it. Science agencies were busy making all sorts of assurances that there was no such testing or experimention going on in *their* labs and the *Times* ran a piece that said Congress was going to be looking over the shoulder of DoD, which didn't seem like a bad idea, though I wasn't sure it was true.

· · ·

I made about a dozen calls till I reached someone high enough on the food chain to get Carolina Escobar reinstated. She had laid her job at the Buttonwood Health Clinic on the line for me and I was determined to get it back for her. A threat that I would give the story to the ever-hungry press if she was not rehired and did not receive her full benefits at the end of her five months did the trick. She called me soon after to thank me, but it was the least I could do. I was becoming quite the little crusader, and it felt good.

I still hadn't done anything with Gambel's notebook and wasn't sure what I would do until Terri told me that the FBI was still making bad noises in her direction. Then I accidentally-on-purpose left it open on my desk when a reporter came to interview me, and excused myself to hit the men's room. When I came back the reporter was practically drooling. I agreed to give him the notebook if he got the story on page one and included the bureau's mishandling of the case, and he did both.

After that Terri didn't hear anything from Barton and Peterson, and when I called Karen Hart, my ex-girlfriend at the FBI, to thank her for her help, she told me that Peterson had been fired and Barton transferred to a two-man office in Hutchinson, Kansas, recently named one of the most boring towns in the U.S., which made me smile.

Still, the papers wouldn't quit, nor the news shows, but after a couple of days I went back to my life of making forensic sketches, my scrapes and bruises fading. Terri and I were seeing each other, but taking it slow. She hadn't moved back in with me, and frankly I was thinking about looking for a new apartment.

I had plenty of sketches to make for plenty of precincts, but the thing that kept haunting me was that damn sculptural reconstruction which had been destroyed.

I didn't think that Guthrie, up in the Bronx, cared one bit

about the John Doe who had been shot, then burned beyond rec-
ognition, but I still did. I was curious to know why the case had
been shut down, and who the guy was that I had come so close to
re-creating.

I considered remaking it, but when I looked at the mangled
armature and broken skull I knew it was hopeless. I was about to
throw out the fake blue eyeballs, still on my worktable, when I got
the idea.

63

Estaba esperándote," my *abuela* said.

"Why were you expecting me, *uela*?" I kissed her cheek. I hadn't called and it was not our usual Thursday-night dinner.

"Because your *camino* is not over."

"Really?" I said. "I thought my path had just ended."

She shook her head and beckoned me to follow.

In the living room, under the photograph of my father, the *bóveda* was set up with a new white tablecloth and goblets filled with water. I knew she had been asking things of her ancestors. I looked at the photo and felt a chill, not the bad kind, just something under my skin, as if my father's spirit had slipped inside me.

"Soon," she said, "soon your crooked path will be over, Nato, and it will make sense."

"Can't you make sense of it now?" I said.

"No," she said. "*Paciencia.*"

It was hard to have patience at this point.

She turned suddenly and gripped my wrist. "That *hombre*, Nato, the one from my vision, the one you make the picture of?"

"*Sí, uela*, what about him?" She was referring to my sketch of Gambel.

"*¿Está muerto?*"

"Yes, he *is* dead. But how did you know?"

"The *egun*," she said. "The dead. Iku came to me just now with that face."

Iku: the grim reaper of Santeria. As a boy my *abuela* would tell me that she would never let a client know when she had seen the quasi-deity of death in a reading; she never wanted to frighten them. Instead, she scared the hell out of me.

I followed her into the *cuartos de los santos* and was about to tell her why I had come, but she beat me to it.

"You need to find another face," she said. "One you have lost."

"You know, *uela*, sometimes I think you're a witch."

She waved a finger at me. "Do not call me *una bruja*, Nato. I never practice *billongo*."

"*¡Perdón!* I'm only kidding, *uela*, you know that."

"Do not kid about such things."

I said I was sorry again, and she tapped my cheek, something between an affectionate pat and a slap.

"I will ask Eleggua to open the path," she said, and went over to the shrine, a big rock with cowrie shells for eyes, mouth, ears, and a slightly carved nose.

"He is the messenger, but not always to be trusted," she

said. "Today, I will ask him not to be jokey with us. We must do the *ebbo*."

"A sacrifice?"

"Just something to feed the orishas." She opened a bag of shredded coconut and sprinkled it over the rock shrine. "The Eleggua's favorite," she said. *"Quiero que esté contento."*

"Yeah," I said, "I want him to be happy, too."

She moved from one shrine to another, one with crutches and cowrie shells and a bead-encrusted knife; tore open a bag of dried beans and spilled them onto the shells. Then she unscrewed a bottle of rum and dripped it onto the beaded knife.

"This is for Oggun, the orisha of all human effort," she said. "He will help."

I respected my grandmother's rituals, and tried to be patient, though it wasn't easy; I was anxious to get started.

"Nato, *¿Qué color ves?*"

"What color do I see?"

"Sí. Cierra los ojos."

I did what she asked: I closed my eyes. "I see green and black," I said.

She smiled. "The colors of Oggun. He is ready to help you."

I sharpened a pencil and we began.

"You have seen this face, Nato. Think about it now, the size and shape, the feel of it under your fingertips."

I felt a rush, something between excitement and anxiety; I had not told her about making the face out of clay. Now I just listened, her words working on me. I had made so many sketches with my *abuela*, she knew what to ask and how to get me started. She asked about the man's age and weight and it started to come back to me. It was just what I would do with a witness, except *I* was the witness.

Think about the *ojos*," she said. "*La forma* and the *color*."

The fake eyes I'd used flashed in my mind, and how I created sagging eyelids of clay over and around them.

"See it in your mind, Nato."

Then my *abuela* sat back and hummed a song she had sung to me as a boy, "Spanish Lullaby" by Marty Robbins, about a father and his baby son. She sang it in Spanish and it brought my father back to me, and I kept drawing until I too sat back, and there it was, the face of the burned John Doe that I had molded out of clay, now captured on paper.

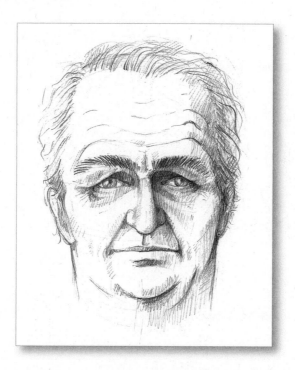

My *abuela* turned the sketch around. "There is something this man needs to tell you, Nato, something *importante*."

"He's dead, *uela*. He can't tell me anything."

She reached out and touched my hand. "Nato," she said. "The dead can tell us many things if we are ready to listen." Then she draped a string of green and black beads over my head. "Oggun helped you before, now you must take him with you."

I asked if it was okay if I wore the beads under my shirt and she smiled and said yes. Then she said, "You are coming to the end of the path, Nato. Soon it will be clear."

64

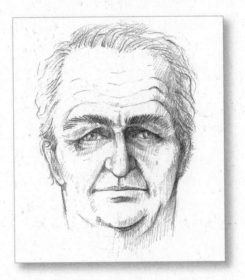

Guthrie looked at the sketch, too many emotions on his face for me to read, but none of them good.

"What's the matter?"

"How did you do this?" he asked.

I didn't think he was asking about Oggun and Eleggua and shredded coconut, so I asked what he meant.

"I mean, who described him to you?"

"No one," I said. "I made the sketch based on the reconstruction I'd originally made from the skull."

"I told you that case was *closed*."

"Yeah, but I'd already started the reconstruction, so I just kept going. It was on *my* time and *my* dime, if that's what's worrying you."

"Who says I'm worried?"

He didn't have to say it; his face was saying it for him.

"Do you know the guy?" I asked.

"No," he said and tried to smile but it was a fake. He slid open his top desk drawer and took out a crumpled pack of cigarettes. "Been trying to quit," he said, shaking one out and lighting up. He gave the sketch a sideways glance, then closed the pad. "I'm afraid you wasted your time, Rodriguez." Gray smoke twirled out of his nostrils and he waved it away. He used the tips of his fingers to push the pad closer to me, as if he didn't want to touch it.

It was still raining, the sky dull pewter, puddles everywhere. I stashed the sketch pad under my shirt and headed toward the subway. Clearly something about the sketch had gotten to Guthrie, but he wasn't going to tell me what it was.

Then I thought of someone who might be able to help.

Chief of Operations Mickey Rauder ushered me into his office, arm on my shoulder in that paternal way he had that made everyone like him. "Been meaning to call and say congrats on the fine job you did with Russo."

"Thanks," I said. "But I'm here about that case you assigned me, too, the one for Guthrie in the Bronx."

"Oh, the guy who was burned and shot. How'd that work out?"

"You don't know?"

"Know what?" Rauder's features pulled toward the center of his face.

"I thought *you* were the one who closed the case."

"Not me," said Rauder. He squeezed his bulk into the chair behind his desk.

"Maybe I misunderstood Guthrie," I said. "But anyway, I made the sculpture from the skull, just like you asked. It got ruined, but . . . well, that's a long story. Just take a look at this." I laid the sketch on his desk.

"Well, I'll be damned." Rauder's mouth fell open and his hound-dog eyes widened. "That's Joe Vallie."

"Who?"

"Ol' blue-eyed Joe," he said, and those blue doll's eyes were in my mind again.

"Vallie was a cop," he said. "A narc, same division as your father. He started earlier but they overlapped a few years. Same years I was there." He plucked a framed photo off his wall, blurry and gray.

"Here we go. It's a bad picture. You can't really see him here— second from the end, with the cap. And he was a lot younger when this picture was taken." Rauder looked from the photo to my drawing. "But I saw him a few years back, and that's him all right, in your sketch, no question."

The guy beside him looked familiar, too, but it was the man on the other end of the group that was vying for my attention—and my emotion.

"I never saw this picture of my dad," I said, feeling my mouth go dry.

"It was taken at one of those retreats. Our CO at the time, Lieutenant Corrigan, God rest his soul, good man, thought we should all hang out and be family, but that never happened. Nature of the beast, the narc life—all day long with hoods and dope dealers, you just don't want to spend your time off with your fellow narcs after that, you know what I mean?"

I stared at the photo of my father, feeling a mix of emotions: sadness, pride, guilt.

"That's me right in front of your old man. I was young but not looking so good, was I?" He smiled, but it quickly turned into a frown. "Those two on the end, with the hats . . ." Rauder shook his head, replaced the photo, and I watched his face go through a series of expressions—doubt, caution, maybe a little fear—as if he was deciding about whether or not he was going to tell me something.

"Here's the thing," he finally said. "IAD had Vallie under investigation; kickbacks from drug dealers, they said, and maybe worse—there was talk of drug trafficking. IAD never got to the bottom of it because Vallie quit and took the information with him. He denied it, of course, said he was quitting because his *integrity* was called into question. But hell, if he was innocent why not hang around and be exonerated, right? That's what I'd do. He ended up with some shitty night-watchman job in the Bronx is what I heard, though I didn't keep up with him. No one did. The man became a pariah. The only one who wanted to pursue the case was your dad. He didn't think it looked good for the division to leave a case hanging like that, and he was right."

"So my father was investigating it, the case against Joe Vallie?"

"Not officially. Corrigan didn't want him to, told him it was just a stain on the department and to let it go, but he wouldn't."

It was obvious where I got it, my stubborn zeal to follow through and make things right.

Rauder tapped my sketch. "You mind if I hold on to this?"

"Nobody else wants it."

"Oh, I wouldn't be so sure about that," said Rauder. "And do me a favor. Don't talk about this, not to anyone."

"Sure," I said. Then I remembered. "I already showed it to Guthrie."

"Oh?" Rauder tapped his fingers against his lips. "What did he say?"

"That he didn't recognize the guy."

Rauder was quiet a moment, his face screwed up in thought. "That's okay," he said. "But no one else has seen it, right?"

"No, no one."

"Keep it that way." His facial muscles were working overtime, wrinkling his brow. "And come see me first thing in the morning."

I called Terri and told her about the sketch, about Guthrie's reaction, about Rauder's, and everything else. Then I asked her to come over. I didn't want to be alone, and I didn't want just anyone, I wanted Terri. I missed her. I missed the smell of patchouli when she was close and its lingering aftermath on my pillows; I missed the way she folded the bathroom towels in thirds and how she insisted we use a top sheet; I missed her makeup in my medicine cabinet and the traces of her black mascara messing up my sink; I even missed her criticism and that crap she had painted on my cuticles.

And I told her.

She said she wanted to come over but was at a crime scene—some big-shot executive stabbed to death in his midtown office—and would be there most of the night.

"I really want to see you, too," she whispered and there was something in her voice, something I couldn't place.

"Anything wrong?" I asked.

"You mean other than a stiff on the floor and a roomful of cops and techies?" She laughed, then paused. "We need to have some quiet time to talk, just you and me."

"Sounds serious."

She paused again and said, "We'll talk about it when I see you."

I didn't like the sound of that, and it added to my anxiety. The meeting with Rauder had stirred me up, not to mention my *abuela* saying my path was not yet over.

I spent half the night cleaning up things that didn't need cleaning and by the time I got myself to Rauder's office in the morning I looked like shit.

But Rauder looked even worse; dark circles under his bloodshot eyes, mouth pinched tight with worry.

"I'm going to have to trust you," he said. "Can I do that?"

"Of course," I said.

"Juan Rodriguez's son," he said, more to himself than to me, shaking his head as he settled into the chair behind his desk. He laced his fingers together and leaned forward, his eyes on mine.

"Okay. We already knew the Bronx John Doe was a murder for hire, right? No surprise there. The surprise came from you—that the vic was Joe Vallie. I got to say that really knocked the wind out of my sails." He picked up a pen and started rapping it against the edge of his desk. "I'm telling you this because you're already involved and I figure you're the best man for the job, unaffiliated as you are."

"The job?"

He put a hand up and I let him go on, his facial muscles vacillating between doubt and determination. "Here's the thing. I spoke to a couple of guys in narcotics and they gave me names of snitches they're using these days and I spoke to a few—and you know how that works, one snitch leads to another. But that doesn't matter." He waved a hand. "What matters is I got to someone who said he knew what happened to Vallie—and when I asked him to tell me he describes the crime scene like he was there—only he swears he wasn't—says he knows the guy who contracted the guy who whacked Vallie—says that guy told him the killer bragged about not stealing the vic's watch." Rauder took a much-needed breath. "So I look at the murder book and I see that the vic was wearing a fancy Rolex and it came back to me, the watch."

I remembered it, too, and nodded as Rauder went on.

"So the snitch says that he doesn't have any names—that everything was done by disposable cell phones—but he tells me the shooter is a local guy and not all that expensive, so I ask, just out of curiosity, what it costs to have someone killed nowadays, and he says 'It depends.' I say, 'On what?' He says how difficult the contract is, an easy kill—and he says Vallie was easy 'cause he lived alone and in a shit hole—goes anywhere from fifteen hundred to a few grand, with a few hundred for the fixer."

"Not much for a life," I said.

"No," said Rauder. "Snitch says he can get me to the guy, the one who hooks up the shooter's contracts, who will get me to the other guy. So I get that number, buy one of those disposable cell phones, and start calling. I call the first guy and he gives me another number. He tells me to call and say that 'Victoria and Albert need to talk,' and to leave my number. I get a call back in fifteen minutes. The shooter. I tell him I'm looking to buy information. He asks, information about *who*? I say, Joe Vallie. He gets real quiet a minute, then says that'll cost me a grand and he wants it up front. I say, what guarantee have I got that he's going to tell me anything once I give him the money? He says, none, but that no one ever complained and that he's got *integrity*. Then he tells me to get in touch with his runner, a guy named Ervin, who is going to pick up my cash, and I did." Rauder sat back in his chair and took another deep breath.

"And that's why I need your help." He looked into my eyes. "I want *you* to deliver the money to Ervin. No way I can do that, and I don't want to involve anyone in narcotics or any other department. You see my point?"

I nodded. I didn't say anything. And I waited.

Rauder opened his desk drawer, got out an envelope, and handed it to me. "That's cash," he said, "so don't lose it."

"I guess you figured I'd say yes."

"I just figured you'd want to know about the guy whose face you sketched, that's all."

I followed Rauder's instructions. I took a cab to Battery Park and waited outside the ticket booth for the Statue of Liberty. The weather was still spotty with dark clouds that threatened more rain, but it did not deter the tourists, plenty of them going in and coming out, smiling and excited. I could see the statue in the river, a blurry gray ghost, and didn't think she looked all that inviting to sightseers or to immigrants.

Rauder told me that Ervin would approach, hold out a cigarette and ask for a light; that I should say, "How are Victoria and Albert?" and he'd say, "They're fine and send you their best."

I couldn't stand still. I paced back and forth, checked out everyone with a cigarette. I felt as if I could use a smoke myself, but not the tobacco kind.

Then a wasted-looking guy with stringy dreadlocks sidled up to me and we did the routine. I felt like I was in a low-rent spy movie. I gave him the money, watched him walk away, and when he went into the subway, I followed.

65

I waited on the end of the platform until Ervin got on the train. Then I did, too. I kept plenty of people between us and every couple of seconds I cadged a peek at him through the crowd. He had an old Discman plugged into his ears, his eyes closed, slowly bopping to the music, and I was pretty sure he was stoned. When he switched trains I hid behind a man who gave me a look when he stopped short and I plowed into him, but Ervin was oblivious.

He got off at 161st Street, the Yankee Stadium stop, a place that always brought me back to the smell of peanuts and popcorn and beer on my father's breath, and the way he cheered and always, always talked about Roberto Clemente, the first Puerto Rican major league ballplayer and how he'd died in a plane crash en route to Nicaragua to deliver food and supplies to earthquake victims, and how he had made his people proud.

I had my father, the brave cop, in my mind as I followed Ervin.

I watched the errand boy shuffle down a crummy-looking street, then disappear into a tenement. I waited a minute, then followed and wrote down the address.

. . .

I spoke to the shooter" were Mickey Rauder's first words when I got back to his office. "He said the Vallie hit came by way of a snitch we used back in my time, a kid named Gringo, Spanish kid, well, he *was* a kid—we're talking twenty years ago. I'm surprised to hear he's still alive, let alone in the game. It only took me a few calls to get to him, to Gringo."

The muscles in Rauder's forehead tightened and he was doing a lot of lip sucking like he was again debating whether or not he should keep talking, but he did. "The little punk was scared shitless. But here's the thing: He said the guy who ordered Vallie's hit had contacted him again and he'd hooked him up with the same shooter."

"You mean recently?"

Rauder nodded. "This is bad business, Rodriguez, very bad. There are some pieces to this that, well, that I didn't see before." Rauder's orbicularis muscles twisted his mouth. "I've been thinking about this for hours and I just don't know what I'm going to do about it. Not sure what I'm going to do with you either."

"What does that mean?"

"It means I got you into something I had a bad feeling about and now I don't know what the hell to do about it."

That's when I told him I had followed Ervin, and gave him the address.

"You're sort of a cowboy, aren't you?" he said, annoyed, but a smile teased his lips. "I shouldn't be surprised, knowing your dad."

Then he got serious again.

"I can't do this without backup. But I can't have this out there, not yet, maybe not ever. You understand?"

I nodded. I thought I did.

"Okay," he said, a resigned look on his face. "If we're going to do this, let's go."

• • •

Rauder and I left Police Plaza and walked six blocks without speaking. We ended up in an Irish pub, sat at the bar, and ordered beers.

"Your father was killed while he was off duty," he said.

I wasn't expecting that and it threw me.

"Official ruling was that he got himself mixed up in some drug exchange; that he was in the wrong place at the wrong time." Rauder took a sip of his beer, then put the bottle down and looked at me. "How old were you when he died?"

"Do we have to talk about this?" I asked.

"Yeah," he said. "We do."

I didn't know what Mickey Rauder knew about me, or my teenage drug problem, but I couldn't think straight, my emotions rising like high tide. "I was almost fourteen," I said.

"I'm sorry," he said.

"Me, too," I said.

We were both quiet a moment, then he said, "I'm pretty sure now I know what happened to your dad."

I braced myself because I thought he was going to say he knew it was my fault.

"He was following up on Vallie's case even though Corrigan didn't want him to. Like I said, IAD had let it go once Vallie quit, but your dad said if the division didn't police itself, who would? We were standing at our lockers when he said it and I can picture that moment like it was yesterday." Rauder closed his eyes. "His locker was open and there were a bunch of your drawings taped inside the door. He turned to me and told me he'd gotten a lead about Vallie; that he was going to meet someone and asked me if I'd go with him as backup."

Rauder paused and sucked in his lower lip. "I didn't want to be with druggie scumbags for the rest of my life, you know, and there was an opening in Investigations—a stepping-stone to an administrative job—and for that I needed Corrigan's recommendation. So I said no." He paused again. "And that was the night your father got killed. So you see, I owe him."

"Are you saying it was your fault?"

"I'm saying I'm pretty sure your father got killed because he was looking into the shit Vallie was into—and I'm saying I should've been there. I know it's too late to fix it, but now I've got another chance to set it straight."

"And that's why you brought me along?"

"I figured you had a right to be part of this more than anyone," he said. "You believe in fate, Rodriguez?"

I thought about my *abuela*'s orishas and what she had taught me, their names suddenly in my head. Ochosi, the patron of those seeking justice, and Eleggua, opening paths and doorways. Maybe everything had been leading me here, to this moment. "Yes," I said. "I do."

"Damn funny thing, isn't it? There I am sitting in my office thinking about a million and one things, and out of the blue—twenty years later—Juan Rodriguez's son brings me a drawing of a dead man and it turns out to be freakin' Joe Vallie! I swear to God when I saw that I got a chill like never before in my life. But then I realized it was all coming around, you know, that I had a second chance to make it right, to make it up to your old man, and to you."

I wanted to tell him that he didn't owe me anything, but the plan had already been made and he was right; I wanted to be part of it, because it was my second chance, too.

We sat and talked it through for a few minutes.

Rauder had set it up, the trap. He'd paid the snitch, Gringo, to make an anonymous call, to say that he had information about Joe Vallie's murder.

"And Gringo says he took the bait," Rauder said. "Damn it, the bastard took the fuckin' bait." He rubbed a hand over his face and it smudged his features. "I had hoped to God I was wrong, but it doesn't look it." Rauder looked at me, his face a mix of sad and mad, eyebrows up, lips taut. "He told Gringo where he wanted to meet, but he won't be meeting Gringo. He'll be meeting *me*. I'm risking my job doing this. But it's the right thing to do, the only thing."

A picture of my father came into my mind, and I knew what I needed to do, too. "No," I said. "I'll go. I can do this. I want to."

Rauder shook his head.

"You just told me that my father was killed because someone wanted to keep him quiet. Now, maybe we have that someone. You have to let me do this. You said it before, I'm unaffiliated. I can do this, and you can't. You can't risk your career and your pension just because you said no to my father twenty years ago."

I kept up the argument until Rauder agreed.

Then he filled me in on everything he knew and what he suspected. He told me he'd protect me if it didn't go well and I smiled because if it didn't go well there was no way in the world he would be able to protect me.

66

According to Rauder, Tito's had been around forever, a place he'd go to meet snitches and dope dealers twenty years ago.

There were yellow lights over the bar, smaller ones with little shades at the booths in the back that cast everything in a cold acidic tinge. There was an old Motown song, "Tracks of My Tears," Smokey Robinson & the Miracles, playing, and it sounded like a dirge.

The bar was standing room only, guys you wouldn't want to meet on a dark street. A few of them eyed me and probably made me as a cop but didn't seem to care.

I took a table in the back restaurant part just like Rauder had told me. It was far enough that anyone who came in wouldn't see me, but I would see them.

A waitress, sad and worn-looking, asked me what I wanted. I ordered a beer and she brought me a bottle of Bud. I drank it, watching the front door, trying to tamp down my adrenaline while Smokey Robinson went on about his fake smile and his tears. I felt ready to jump right out of my skin. Then the front door opened and I saw him. The hat didn't do anything to disguise his face.

I watched him work his way down the bar, no doubt looking

for Gringo. When he got to the end he took a few steps into the restaurant and saw me. For a minute I thought he was going to do an about-face so I stood up fast, and our eyes met.

"Well, well," he said, affecting ennui. "What are you doing here, Rodriguez?"

I wanted to ask him the same thing but I already knew, so I just said, "Looking for someone?"

"Tito's is my old stomping ground," he said, and manufactured a smile. "Every once in a while I stop in."

"Sure you do," I said. "Let me buy you a drink." I waited a half-second beat, then said, "Thanks for meeting me, *Gringo*."

The smile smeared off his face like cheap lipstick.

"Why don't you have a seat," I said.

"I don't think so." Denton stood there, eyes locked on mine, upper lip curled in just the hint of a sneer.

"I made a sculpture of the Bronx John Doe."

"So I heard," he said. "I also heard it got all smashed up. Boo-hoo."

That's when it hit me. I'd blamed the break-in on the FBI, but

I'd been wrong. It had been Denton. The grin on his face confirmed it.

I unfolded the sketch of Vallie and laid it on the table. "I showed this to Guthrie."

"You think I care about Guthrie?" Denton slapped his hand onto the sketch and crumpled it into a ball.

"It's a copy," I said.

"So you made a drawing, so what?"

"Of Joe Vallie, your ex-partner, who was killed."

His lips tightened into a mean thin line. "You plan this little escapade all by yourself, Rodriguez?"

"That's right."

"So what do you want?"

"I thought for starters you could pay me the way you were paying Joe Vallie."

Denton suddenly grabbed my shirt with both hands and tugged me toward him. "Now you listen to me, you little shit, this game is over—just like you. You're dead."

I knocked his hands off me and shoved him back. "No, *you* listen. You don't scare me. I know all about you and Vallie running a little drug business on the side. IAD tapped Vallie and you convinced him to quit. What did you tell him—that if you stayed on the job you could take care of him? And you did, for a while. Then you got this big job and you started thinking that Joe Vallie was a liability, right, an albatross, your weak link—the one guy who could drag you down and ruin you."

"I don't have to listen to this." Denton turned to go but I got a grip on his arm.

"You can't just walk away because, you see, I've got names. I've got Ervin and Marco and Gringo, who all put you in touch with the shooter who killed Vallie."

Denton laughed. "You think anyone gives a shit about a wash-out like Joe Vallie or a few low-life snitches? No one is going to believe them, Rodriguez—and no one is going to believe *you*." He came in so close I could smell his cologne and the cigar on his breath. "Vallie thought he could put the squeeze on me, and look what happened to him."

"Cheaper to have him killed than keep paying him, that it, Chief?"

Denton straightened up and smoothed his jacket. "You'd better watch your step, Rodriguez. You never know who's out there look-ing to do you harm."

"Is that a threat?"

"Hey, it's a dangerous town, *amigo*, that's all I'm saying. You never know who is following you with bad intentions."

I pictured the Chandler character and I knew then that Denton had put him on me.

"Just remember what happened to your *papi*. He thought he was smart, like you, but that junkie punk, Willie Pedriera, he took him out with three little shots." He aimed his hand at me like a gun. "Pop, pop, pop."

I stared at him as it came together, my father chasing down Denton's and Joe Vallie's drug connection: Willie Pedriera—the same dealer who had serviced the neighborhood kids, the guy who Julio and I bought our drugs from. All those years I thought I'd known the truth; all those years I'd blamed myself because I thought my father had gone after Pedriera to stop him from sell-ing drugs to me. But my father hadn't gone after Pedriera; Pe-driera had come after him. On Denton's orders.

"Your old man died in the street like an animal," said Denton. "And it looks like you want to join him—"

My heart was racing, blood pumping in my ears so hard I could barely hear him. I threw the punch before he saw it coming and then he was on the floor, dirt on his Armani suit, blood coming out of his nose.

He stood up swatting the dust off his pants. "Oh, Rodriguez," he said, very calm, very slow, "you . . . are . . . so . . . dead."

Arrogance twisted his lips into a smile, and I let him have the last word. I let him walk out of Tito's.

Then I went into the men's room to check the wire taped to my chest. I leaned down and said, "You get all that, Rauder?"

By the time I saw Rauder again he'd already raided the address on 162nd Street in the Bronx, arrested the shooter and made a deal: a get-out-of-jail-free card in exchange for information and testimony.

The shooter admitted he'd gotten the contract to do Joe Vallie. He said he'd never met Denton, but Gringo had bragged about the big-deal client he was bringing to him and told him who it was. He said Denton had contacted him again, recently, to have me killed. He admitted to stalking me to learn my routine. All he'd been waiting for was a final wire transfer to his island account and I'd have been a dead man.

67

I expected a huge scandal, Perry Denton's public humiliation, a trial and conviction, but I would have to wait a little longer for that.

The way it went was Rauder sat Denton down and told him what he had—the snitches, the shooter, the island account, my testimony, and the tape from Tito's. He suggested a quiet resignation or everything would go to IAD and the media.

He told me Denton did not go down easy.

As a cop Denton knew the evidence was circumstantial: A good lawyer could have the tape deemed inadmissible; the word of a snitch and a convicted felon wouldn't mean much; and my testimony was far from impartial. But it was a hell of a lot of circumstantial evidence to make go away. And the trial, Rauder pointed out, would be Court TV's next big hit. Manhattan's Chief of Department on trial for murder and corruption would be big news. Rauder was giving him a break; maybe he didn't want the NYPD to suffer through a scandal.

I watched the news conference on television, Denton looking a little less shiny than usual, faking a smile when he announced his plans for retirement to "be with my family and pursue other interests."

I taped the conference and played it in slow motion the way Ekman had taught us to do at Quantico. In slow-mo, Denton's face betrayed his fury—upper lip curling away every few seconds to expose his teeth like a snarling dog. But then the weirdest thing happened. I blinked and saw him falling.

Maybe it was symbolic, the big man falling from grace, but I swear I saw it.

I sat back and thought about all the falling men who had led me here, to Denton.

You are coming to the end of the path, Nato. Soon it will be clear.

My logical mind fought against everything my *abuela* had been preaching to me most of my life, but I couldn't deny that she had seen Gambel's face before I had—or that she had helped me find Joe Vallie's face when I'd lost it.

I had put the string of beads on the shelf above my worktable, draped them over a candle my *abuela* had given me months ago, and set them both in front of a photograph of my father.

Was he the falling man? The one who had been trying to get my attention and set me on the path? I thought I'd figured out his death on that last case with Terri, but I'd been wrong.

Now that I knew the truth, maybe he would stop falling; maybe now his *ori*, his soul, would finally rest.

Terri called me minutes after the conference. I had not prepared her.

"Jesus Christ! I can't believe it! Did you hear? What do you make of it?"

"More than meets the eye," I said, knowing one day I'd tell her everything. "And I can't say I'm sorry to see him go."

"No kidding," she said. "I'm thrilled. That fucker was out to get me. And, you know, I think Mickey Rauder is going to make a hell of a good chief." Then she said we needed to talk and she was coming right over.

68

I showered and shaved and splashed on some of the cologne Terri had bought for me. I put on a clean white shirt because my *abuela* always said that white brings good luck.

I met her at the door and for once I couldn't read her expression. It was an odd blend, brow furrowed with worry, her sweet mouth almost smiling.

"You look pretty," I said.

"So do you," she said. "Someone die, or something?" She looked me up and down.

"I cleaned up for you."

"And you did good," she said, and smiled again. "I never told you what a great job you did."

I shrugged, but I liked hearing it.

"Don't be modest, Rodriguez. You did. You hung in there, and I appreciate it."

"At least we got the bad guys," I said.

"Yeah, but I'm still worried about the guy we never found, Caldwell. I alerted the DOJ and the Illinois State Police. Maybe they'll find him. Or maybe he's dead."

"The Department of Justice will find him if he's ever committed a crime," I said.

"*If,*" said Terri, and it set my mind worrying, thinking about the other men, the nameless ones in Jerry Leslaw's support group; the ones who were out there somewhere, ticking.

"I'll keep on it," she said, then took a deep breath, her facial muscles suddenly taut.

"What is it?" I asked.

"Give me a second." She took another deep breath. "Okay, I'm not going to sugarcoat this and I'm prepared to deal with it by myself, so don't feel obligated."

"What are you talking about?"

"I'm pregnant."

I felt my legs go a little weak and something inside me tightened.

"Jesus, Rodriguez, if you could see the look on your face."

"Are you sure?" I asked.

"About your face or being pregnant, because I'm three weeks late and two home pregnancy tests say I am."

"Wow."

"Is that all you have to say?"

"Just give me a minute."

Terri looked at her watch. "Go. Either you're in or you're out, Rodriguez."

I'd never imagined being a father and the idea was pretty terrifying.

"I still have half a minute, don't I?"

"Don't kid about this," she said. "I need to know where you stand."

"Well, I'm standing."

"Barely," she said.

"I guess I'm in."

"You *guess?*"

"It was just a figure of speech. I'm in."

"I hoped you'd be happy," she said, her mouth turning down.

"I *am* happy." I tugged her toward me and wrapped my arms around her while I tried to get my mind around the news: me, a father.

I looked over at my *abuela*'s beads hanging over my father's photo and felt my emotions rising and falling.

Terri looked up at me. "I don't want you to do this out of some bullshit obligation, Rodriguez. I've taken care of myself for a long time and I can take care of a baby, too."

"No, it's great," I said. "Really, it is. It's just that I feel like *I'm* still a baby."

"Oh, that's for sure," she said, and patted my cheek. "You and every other Y chromosome. But don't worry, I can take care of *two* babies."

Terri and I flew to Colorado for my mother's wedding, my *abuela* just across the aisle. She made us both wear green and yellow beads for the orisha Orunla, who had power over human destiny. She told Terri she had made a sacrifice to Ocuboro, who had power over life and death, so she needn't worry about the plane crashing, which made us both nervous. She spent the entire flight staring at the small TV in front of her, working the remote like she was a kid with a Nintendo.

Terri and I were tired of talking about the case and about Denton, but I wasn't quite ready to talk about babies or diapers or where we would live or, God forbid, if we would get married. We watched a movie and I ate four packages of Smokehouse Almonds

washed down with several Cokes and a beer, and my hands were
shaking.

I suggested we use the bathroom and join the mile-high club
and Terri said I was a complete idiot. Then she laid her head onto
my shoulder and said, "I need to hear you say it."

"Say what?"

"That you love me, you asshole." She whacked my chest again.

"Oh, that."

"Jesus, it's like asking you for a kidney, Rodriguez."

"I'd lend you a kidney any day," I said.

"Yeah," she said, "sooner than you'd say the *L* word."

"Doesn't that refer to lesbians?" I said.

Terri hit me again.

The wedding ceremony was small: me and Terri; my *abuela*; my
mother's husband-to-be, Chris; and his two grown sons by way of
a first marriage, one a lawyer in San Francisco who had read about
me and was impressed. I had to admit that made me like the guy.
The other one was a painter in New York, and doing okay, with a
gallery I'd heard of, which made me just the tiniest bit jealous. My
mother hadn't told me that Chris was a widower and I wondered if
loss had played a part in their getting together.

It took me a while to relax, though the champagne helped. Everyone took turns toasting the happy couple, including me, and Terri
said I did okay, though I was still feeling awkward and not quite
myself.

At one point my *abuela* leaned across the table and asked when I
was going to marry Terri, and I got all flustered and Terri laughed
and kissed my grandmother.

Then Chris stood up and made a toast.

"To the most wonderful thing—I mean, *person*—I mean, *woman*—" He stuttered and laughed, and it made me like him. "Oh, hell," he said. "Here's to you, Judy. Thank you for coming into my life."

His eyes were shining when he said it, and so were my mom's.

"I love you," he added, and I thought maybe he could teach me how to say it so easily.

The reception was at a ranch, some friend of Chris's, and picture-postcard beautiful with snow-covered mountains everywhere you looked, a relief after the New York summer; the air crisp and clean.

Soon after we got there my mother asked me to take a walk.

The sun was setting across the mountains and I said it was just about the prettiest place I'd ever seen, and my mother said she hoped I would visit often.

Then we were quiet and I could tell she wanted to say something, but I spoke first.

"You're not still mad at me because I acted like a jerk when you told me you were getting married, are you?"

"No," she said. "I understand that your mother getting married takes some getting used to. I shouldn't have sprung it on you."

"I'm happy for you," I said.

She smiled but her zygomatic major muscles were tugging her smile toward anxiety.

"I need to say something and I'm going to say it really fast because it's difficult, so don't interrupt me," she said. "I know what happened. I know why your father went up to Spanish Harlem that night. But I don't blame you for what happened. I never did."

I started to speak but she stopped me. "I was the adult. You were a kid. I should have been there for you, but I was thirty-five and my husband had just died. I was scared and sad and confused and I was not a good mother."

"You were fine, it's okay."

"No, it's *not* okay. I should have helped you."

"I wouldn't let you," I said. "You did the best you could and that's all any of us can do. You were coping with your grief and . . . so was I."

She stood back and assessed me. "When did you get so grown up?"

"About ten minutes ago," I said. "Look, there's something important you need to know about that night. It wasn't my fault."

"I understand that, Nate. And it's okay. I don't blame you for what happened to Dad."

"No, I mean it *really* wasn't my fault. I thought it was for a long time, but it turns out that Dad was up in Spanish Harlem because he was investigating a crooked cop." I stopped for a moment and thought about Denton, the crooked cop, and the crooked path it had taken to find him. "That's why Dad got killed." I explained it the best I could, and my mother listened.

"I spent twenty years feeling guilty for something that wasn't my fault, and so did you," I said. "The facts don't change the past, but it can be different now, we can be different."

My mother touched my cheek and her bracelets clinked and clanged and it brought me back to being a kid and how much I'd always loved the sound.

"I have wonderful memories of your father and I know you do, too," she said. "Now we can talk about them."

I smiled, too choked up to say anything.

"And if I haven't said it before, I'm crazy about Terri."

"That's good," I said, "because I am, too.

My mother took my hand. "Come on," she said. "I'm missing my own wedding."

• • •

When we got back to the party it was in full swing. There was a Mexican tune playing and Terri was dancing with my grandmother. It was quite a sight. My *abuela* in a pink dress with big purple flowers and enough jewelry to sink a ship; Terri in pale blue, hair up, simple gold hoops in her ears and a smile that made me love her. When the song ended and the band switched to a slow tune, my *abuela* marched Terri over, practically shoved her into my arms, and we both laughed.

"Did you tell your grandmother?" Terri whispered.

"Tell her what?"

"About the baby."

"Of course not."

"Well, she just gave my stomach a pat and said I was going to have many *bonita* babies!"

"The woman's a witch, what can I say?" I looked over and my *abuela* was smiling at me.

I pulled Terri close and whirled her around the dance floor.

When the music stopped, she said, "You're a really terrible dancer, you know that, Rodriguez."

"It's a fact," I said, "but I'm going to be a hell of a good father."

APPENDIX

Although this book is a work of fiction, many actual programs, articles, and experiments were used for research. The following information is publicly available.

DARPA: The Defense Advanced Research Projects Agency is the central research and development organization of the Department of Defense (DoD), with an annual budget of about $2 billion. Some specific programs referred to in this novel are currently being sponsored by DARPA.

- Peak Soldier Performance
- Preventing Sleep Deprivation
- Biological Warfare Defense
- Accelerated Learning
- Biodynotics
- Deep Bleeder Acoustic Coagulation
- Intestinal Fortitude
- Z-Man

For more information see the DARPA online website, http://www.darpa.mil/.

Human Experimentation

There is a long and nasty tradition of human experimentation in this country. These are but a few examples:

- The testing of mustard gas on soldiers.
- The Tuskegee Syphilis Study (which used 200 black men as human guinea pigs).
- Organ transplants, injecting of live cancer cells, effects of chemicals, drugs, and exposure to radiation on "volunteer" prisoners.
- LSD experiments on both prisoners and soldiers.
- The spreading of *Bacillus globigii* bacteria over San Francisco and Oahu, Hawaii, and the releasing of mosquitoes infected with yellow fever over Savannah, Georgia.

For further reading and more specific information I recommend:

- Goliszek, Andrew, *In the Name of Science*, St. Martin's Press.
- Moreno, Jonathan, Ph.D., *Undue Risk*, Routledge edition in arrangement with W. H. Freeman and Company; *Mind Wars*, Dana Press; *Is There an Ethicist in the House*, Indiana University Press.

The "Fear Gene"

Researchers at the Howard Hughes Medical Institute at Columbia University reported their discovery of the human "fear gene" in 2002. Since then, researchers at Columbia, Harvard, and Rutgers universities have continued studies and experiments in fear and anxiety. A sampling of "fear gene" articles include:

- "Researchers Discover Gene That Controls Ability to Learn Fear," *Howard Hughes Medical Institute of Columbia University*, December 13, 2002, http://www.hhmi.org/news/kandel3.html
- Cromie, William J., "Researchers Find Gene for Fear," *Harvard News Office*, December 1, 2005, p. 5

- Britt, Robert Boy, "Fear Factor Gene Discovered," *LiveScience*, November 17, 2005, http://www.livescience.com/health/051117_fear_factor.html
- Alexander, Brian, "Sports Authorities Fear Gene Doping Not Far Off," *MSNBC*, February 26, 2006, http://www.msnbc.msn.com/id/10628586/
- Carey, Benedict, "Study Pinpoints Gene Controlling Fear," *The New York Times*, November 18, 2005
- Carey, Benedict, "Brain Injury Said to Affect Moral Choices," *The New York Times*, March 22, 2007, p. A22

Post-Traumatic Stress Disorder, Gulf War Syndrome, the Fort Bragg Murders

There are numerous articles about the physical and emotional aftereffects of war. The articles below offer insight and alarm.

PTSD

- Frosch, Dan, "Fighting the Terror of Battles That Rage in Soldiers' Heads," *The New York Times*, May 13, 2007
- Stannard, Matthew B., "The War Within," *San Francisco Chronicle*, January 29, 2006, p. A1
- Priest, Dana, and Anne Hull, "The War Inside," *Washington Post*, June 17, 2002
- Frosch, Dan, "3 Buddies Home From Iraq Are Charged With Murdering a 4th," *The New York Times*, January 12, 2008
- Sontag, Deborah, and Lisette Alvaraz, "Across America, Deady Echoes of Foreign Battles," *The New York Times*, January 13, 2008
- Sontag, Deborah, and Lisette Alvaraz, "Combat Trauma Takes the Witness Stand," *The New York Times*, January 27, 2008

GULF WAR SYNDROME

- Urbina, Ian, "Troops' Exposure to Nerve Gas Could Have Caused Brain Damage, Scientists Say," *The New York Times*, May 17, 2007, p. A20

FORT BRAGG MURDERS

- Starr, Barbara, "4 Wives Slain in 6 Weeks at Fort Bragg," CBS News, July 26, 2002, http://www.cbsnews.com/stories/2002/07/31/national/main517033.shtml
- "Fort Bragg Killings Raise Alarm About Stress," CNN Washington Bureau, http://archives.cnn.com/2002/US/07/26/army.wives/
- Ricks, Thomas E., "Slaying of 4 Soldiers Wives Stun Ft. Bragg," *Washington Post*, July 27, 2002, p. A3
- "Army to Press Medical Inquiry at Fort Bragg," *The New York Times*, August 24, 2002, p. A8

CIRCARE: (Citizens for Responsible Care and Resarch) http://www.circare.org/

Mission Statement: CIRCARE is a human rights organization dedicated to the protection of human subjects in research and medical treatment.

CIRCARE's mission is to raise the ethical and professional level of human subject research and medical treatment to a level that is compatible with the principles stated in the National Human Research Protection Act (NHRPA). Support for the enactment of the NHRPA is one of the most important missions of CIRCARE advocacy.

CIRCARE is particularly concerned with the protection of vulnerable subjects, i.e., the mentally incapacitated, children, seniors, the homeless, and the poor.

A more comprehensive list of books, articles, and related information can be found on my website: www.jonathansantlofer.com.

ACKNOWLEDGMENTS

My thanks to Suzanne Gluck, David Highfill, Gabe Robinson, Janice Deaner, Betty Lew, Danielle Bartlett, and everyone at William Morrow/HarperCollins; Carly Cross; my daughter Doria; and especially my wife, Joy.